LEGEND *of the* FIVE RINGS

The realm of Rokugan is a land of samurai, courtiers, and mystics, dragons, magic, and divine beings – a world where honor is stronger than steel.

The Seven Great Clans have defended and served the Emperor of the Emerald Empire for a thousand years, in battle and at the imperial court. While conflict and political intrigue divide the clans, the true threat awaits in the darkness of the Shadowlands, behind the vast Kaiu Wall. There, in the twisted wastelands, an evil corruption endlessly seeks the downfall of the empire.

The rules of Rokugani society are strict. Uphold your honor, lest you lose everything in pursuit of glory.

BY THE SAME AUTHOR

DOPPELGANGER
Warrior
Witch
Dancing the Warrior

LEGEND OF THE FIVE RINGS
The Eternal Knot

THE MEMOIRS OF LADY TRENT
A Natural History of Dragons
The Tropic of Serpents
Voyage of the Basilisk
In the Labyrinth of Drakes
Within the Sanctuary of Wings
Turning Darkness into Light

ONYX COURT
Midnight Never Come
In Ashes Lie
A Star Shall Fall
With Fate Conspire
Deeds of Men

ROOK AND ROSE
The Mask of Mirrors
(as M A Carrick, with Alyc Helms)

VAREKAI
Cold-Forged Flame
Lightning in the Blood

WILDERS
Lies and Prophecy
Chains and Memory

SHORT STORY COLLECTIONS
Maps to Nowhere
Ars Historica
The Nine Lands
Down a Street That Wasn't There

Born to the Blade
(with Michael R Underwood, Malka Older, & Cassandra Khaw)
Driftwood

The NIGHT PARADE *of* 100 DEMONS

MARIE BRENNAN

First published by Aconyte Books in 2021

ISBN 978 1 83908 040 1

Ebook ISBN 978 1 83908 041 8

Cover art by Nathan Elmer

Rokugan map by Francesca Baerald

Distributed in North America by Simon & Schuster Inc, New York, USA

Printed in the United States of America

9 8 7 6 5 4 3 2 1

ACONYTE BOOKS

An imprint of Asmodee Entertainment Ltd

Mercury House, Shipstones Business Centre

North Gate, Nottingham NG7 7FN, UK

aconytebooks.com // twitter.com/aconytebooks

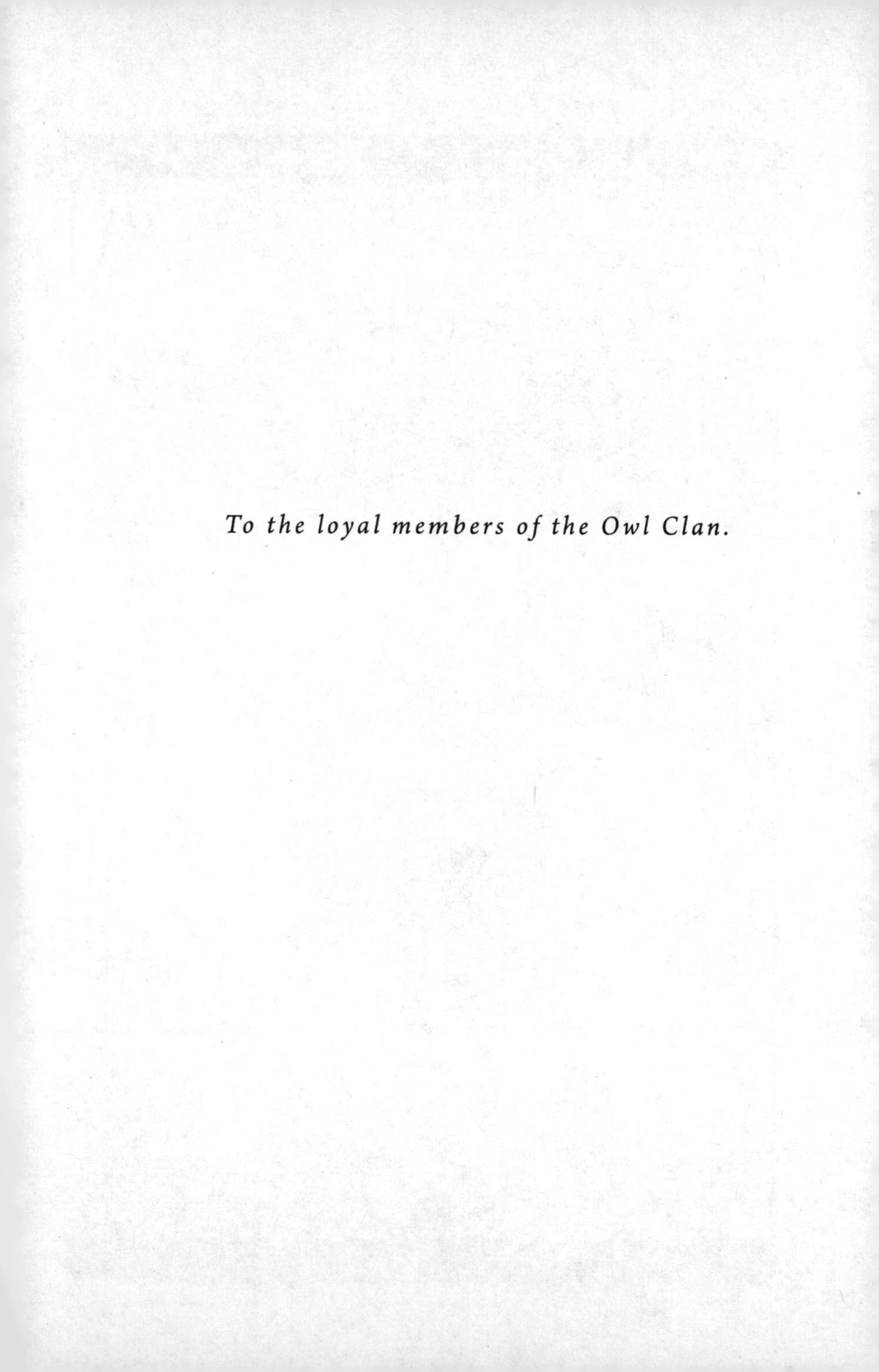

To the loyal members of the Owl Clan.

Dragon Lands
Phoenix Lands
Rokugan

CHAPTER ONE

The road to Seibo Mura was steep, and barely deserved the name. Every half-mile or so, Ryōtora's pony heaved a great sigh, as if to remind her rider that she was working *extremely* hard and surely deserved a rest. After he patted her on the neck, she would saunter inconspicuously in the direction of the nearest edible greenery, until he clicked his tongue and tugged at the reins, nudging her back on course.

At least she was more talkative than the two ashigaru escorting him. One trudged along in front, the other behind, and even after five days on the road, Ryōtora had difficulty telling them apart. One was named Ishi and the other Tarō, but they had the same square jaws, the same thinning hair, the same look of being weathered by sun and wind and snow until they were as hard as the stone around them. He'd made one attempt to engage them in conversation the first morning they set out, but the sheer stiff awkwardness of his own pleasantries made him want to crawl into the nearest gully and hide. Before long, he gave up.

He never found it easy to talk to peasants. Not on a normal day, and even less so now, on his way to Seibo Mura.

His way *back* to Seibo Mura.

The pony's sighs abated as she devoted all her attention to picking her way down a rocky decline that looked more like a runoff than a road. Ishi – unless it was Tarō – leapt from one footing to the next as nimbly as a goat, keeping clear in case the pony should suddenly fall. That image made Ryōtora shudder, and at the next opportunity he reined her in and dismounted. Tarō – unless it was Ishi – took the reins, and Ryōtora followed the pony and two peasants on foot, swallowing an undignified curse when a stone turned under his foot and wrenched his ankle.

At the bottom of the slope, one ashigaru held the reins while Ryōtora remounted. The other said, "Would my lord like to press onward, or find a campsite for the night?"

Ryōtora was no delicate lowland flower. His duties took him through the hinterlands of the Dragon Clan's provinces, from one peasant village to the next. But for the last two days there had been no villages at all, and so they'd had to sleep rough. Even at the height of summer, that wasn't a comfortable option – especially when the clouds above the higher peaks told Ryōtora a storm was building there.

"Press on," he said at last, hoping he wouldn't regret it. "We should be able to make Seibo Mura by nightfall."

If the road had been in anything like good repair, they would have. But it was poorly enough maintained that Ryōtora mistook a level stretch of ground for the real path, and didn't realize his error until they'd spent precious daylight traveling in the wrong direction. And as they retraced their steps, the storm caught them.

He hunched his shoulders beneath his straw cloak, trying not to read an omen into this ill luck. But everything about this journey felt cursed, and had from the start. *If only I hadn't been in Heibeisu when the message came…*

He wiped water from the tip of his nose and tried to banish such thoughts. This was his duty, and Regret was one of the Three Sins. If it was the will of the Fortunes that he return to Seibo Mura, then so be it.

The clouds and the high wall of the mountains meant the light faded fast, and the moon was too close to new to be in the sky. Ryōtora would have given up on reaching the village and just made camp, but no suitable location offered itself. He dismounted again to lead the pony, letting her set the pace as she carefully chose her footing in the increasing gloom, and tried to be grateful that at least the chill of the rain was easing the throb in his twisted ankle. If they didn't find shelter soon, they would have no choice but to stop where they were, and at least wait for the rain to pass.

At last the ground leveled out. And not too far away, Ryōtora thought he saw lights glimmering.

Spirit lights? he wondered. Such things liked to lead travelers astray – or over cliffs. But he felt like they had reached a valley floor, and these had the warm glow of true flame.

Without warning, one of his ashigaru shucked his pack and readied his spear with a speed that made the pony sidle. A moment later a voice came from the trees: "Stop! Name yourself!"

Ryōtora swallowed the rapid beating of his pulse. With his thoughts on spirits, and the tale he'd heard in Heibeisu… but the voice was young, and heavily laden with the thick accent of the north. Though it did its best, it didn't quite succeed at sounding fierce. *A sentry,* he realized. *And a determined one, to be out in this weather.*

He raised his chin, showing his face as best as he could in

the murk. "I am Agasha no Isao Ryōtora, sent from Heibeisu in response to your message. These two ashigaru accompanying me are Ishi and Tarō." He silently promised the Fortunes that he would learn to tell them apart.

His words produced a brief silence. Then a rustling, followed by a thump as the sentry dropped out of a nearby hemlock. Ryōtora couldn't see much, but now that the voice wasn't raised in strident challenge, it sounded female. "Just you?"

"And two ashigaru," Ryōtora said – though how much use they would be, he couldn't guess. It depended on what was happening in Seibo Mura.

She stood quietly for a moment. When she spoke again, she sounded discouraged. "I'll take you to Ogano's house."

"You don't need to stay here and keep watch?"

"No," she said, her tone going flatter still. "I was looking out for you, not the monsters."

Even in the dark and the rain, Ryōtora could see the damage.

The light cast from a few houses picked out the silhouette of a burned building, jagged timbers still pointing accusations at the sky. Ryōtora's guide, muttering a brief warning, led him around the edge of a pit torn into the ground. Rough-hewn beams propped up the roof of another house whose side wall had been ripped away.

She brought him to what he suspected was the largest house in the village. It spilled light from the edges of the shuttered windows along the raised veranda, as if the owner didn't care about saving lamp oil for the winter. As if he didn't expect to still be here when that season came.

When Ryōtora's guide knocked at the door, no one opened

it. Through the steady patter of the rain, though, he thought he could make out a sudden flutter of voices inside. His guide knocked again, and after a moment a nervous-sounding man shouted, "Who is it?"

"Rin," the girl said. "With a samurai from down south."

The voice got closer, but the door still didn't open. "How do I know it's really you?"

"Because the moon ain't full," the girl said, in a tone that barely avoided appending *you idiot* to the answer.

That seemed to be persuasion enough to unbar the door, but it only opened a crack. Although the figure that appeared in it was an unreadable silhouette, Ryōtora felt a suspicious gaze weighing him. "What's your name? And who sent you?"

Ryōtora repeated his introduction, adding, "I was sent by the governor of Heibeisu."

"You could be lying," the man said. "I know the stories. Women asking to come in from the snow. Babies crying in the fields. All tricks, to make us let our guard down."

Yōkai. Many people went their whole lives without ever meeting such a creature outside of the tales told around the hearth at night. But if the reports out of Seibo Mura were to be believed, this man's caution was justified.

"I am going to pray to the kami," Ryōtora said. "If they answer me, it will take the form of…" What should he choose? What would this man not interpret as a sign that he was a yōkai?

Casting his gaze around, Ryōtora made out a broken pick lying on the ground, the sort of thing a miner would use in his work – or in his defense. "The haft of this pick will be made whole."

He knelt and linked his hands into the sacred shape of a mudra, murmuring a prayer in a low voice. That done, he laid his palms on the broken pieces and brought them into alignment, then plucked a few strands of hair from his head and wound them around the haft. The earth kami within the wood remembered being a whole stick, and remembered growing from the tree; it wasn't difficult to convince it to grow together once more.

When he lifted the heavy pick, the girl made a muffled sound of surprise. While Ryōtora had introduced himself as an Agasha, not all who bore that name were shugenja, especially not in the vassal families. Plus, it was entirely possible these people had never seen even so minor a wonder before.

But the man, when he spoke, didn't sound impressed. "I suppose you'd better come in."

A rural house like this one didn't have a finer entrance for honored guests. Ryōtora murmured a formulaic apology for intruding as he stepped across into the earthen-floored working area. To his left rose a stretch of wooden planks, with a cheery fire burning in the sunken firepit – that was the source of most of the light. But the sliding panels that gave access to the rest of the house were closed, and Ryōtora saw no one else.

That seemed unlikely. The headman of the village – which this certainly must be – would have at least a few servants working for him, not to mention family.

As Ryōtora wiped rain from his eyes, he saw that his guide was a girl of no more than fourteen, her hair braided behind one ear, with a short sling coiled in her hand. The man could have been anywhere between thirty and sixty, and possibly cousin to Ishi and Tarō. "Just one of you?" the man said. Ogano, according to Rin and the records in Heibeisu. The headman of Seibo Mura. The records had said nothing about him being so rude.

"And two ashigaru," Ryōtora said, nodding at Ishi and Tarō.

"Ashigaru are like a quarter of a bushi. A half at best. And a bushi was no use to us last time."

The disturbances in Seibo Mura had begun over a month before. A panicked messenger had come to Heibeisu, babbling of monsters and spirits tearing the village apart, and the governor sent a magistrate to look into it – a bushi, Mirumoto Norifusa. But the chaos lasted only three nights; by the time Norifusa arrived, it was all over. He'd searched the area and found no sign of anything untoward. So he'd returned to Heibeisu, writing it up as a tragic incident. Random, and unexplained.

A month later, it happened again.

Ryōtora said, "I assure you, headman, that I will do my best to–"

"To what? To bring our dead back to life? To restore the houses the monsters have destroyed, the mine shaft they collapsed? If you can work miracles on that scale, shugenja, I'll be the first to bow my head to your feet."

Nothing about Ogano hinted at the possibility of bowing. Elsewhere in the Empire, his hostile insolence toward his social superior might well have earned him a beating. He should have immediately offered to hang up the samurai's cloak, brought him a towel to wipe himself dry with, escorted him to a seat by the fire. Not accused Ryōtora of uselessness while he dripped onto the packed earth of the working area.

Even in the dark, though, Ryōtora had seen enough to understand that the peasants of Seibo Mura had suffered horrors. They were used to long winters, harsh snows, avalanches and rockfalls and the hazards of a life based around mining… but these "monsters," whether they were yōkai or something else, were a different matter.

"I will do my best," Ryōtora repeated. "If the pattern so far holds, you have nothing to fear until the next full moon – but I won't trust that it will. Beginning tomorrow, I would like to speak to every inhabitant of this village in turn, however old or young, to learn what I can of what's been happening. And I will see about creating defenses, so that if the problem *does* recur, you will be more prepared for it."

Ogano scowled. "Defenses. Well, that's more than the other one offered."

From behind one of the screens came a new voice. "I *assume* you mean that bushi from before."

It slid aside to reveal another man, this one far too well-dressed to be any resident of Seibo Mura, in a kimono embroidered around its hem with a motif of climbing vines. Behind him crouched all the people Ryōtora would have expected to see in a household like this one: a woman who was probably Ogano's wife, four children, and an older man and woman he guessed were servants. The man who'd spoken made a reassuring gesture and then slid the door shut behind himself, as if thin paper and wood could grant any protection if trouble should arise.

"Asako Sekken," the man said, bowing. "From Sheltered Plains City – my mother is the steward of the Kanjirō Library there. And you are?"

He would have heard Ryōtora introduce himself outside, but to bypass the formalities would be rude. And the elegance of his bow… his manners were as courtly as if they stood in the home of a daimyō rather than a village headman. What was a member of the Phoenix Clan doing here?

Ryōtora gave his name for the third time, almost stumbling over it. Everything about Asako Sekken might have been purposefully crafted to throw him off balance. A samurai from an influential family, rather than a mere vassal; a refined scion of the court, rather than an itinerant shugenja; an outsider in a village suffering from troubles no outsider should know about.

And with his pointed chin, his arched eyebrows, his bony hands and wrists that made a graceful dance of every gesture... he reminded Ryōtora far too much of Hokumei.

"It is a pleasure to meet you, Sir Ryōtora," the Asako said with another bow. "I'm afraid I arrived last night and took the room that should be yours. But four and a half mats should be enough for us both – I promise, I don't sprawl. Or we could lay our futons in that room instead." He gestured at the larger chamber behind him, where Ogano's family and servants still hid.

Ryōtora gathered his scattered wits. "Forgive me, Lord Asako, but what brings you to this village?"

"Why, the same as you, I imagine. Whatever has been going on in this place."

"So the Phoenix know about these events?"

It came out too sharp. But Sekken merely smiled and said, "One of us does, at least."

His words weren't very reassuring. The Dragon and the Phoenix were on cordial enough terms, and often found common ground in their shared interest in spiritual matters. Like any close neighbors, though, they sometimes squabbled over those same points of shared interest – particularly when the Dragon granted free rein to something the Phoenix deemed heretical. Or when the Isawa decided that, as the greatest shugenja family in the Empire, they were the only ones who could be trusted to handle some issue properly.

He's not an Isawa. Which meant Sekken was not, in fact, *quite* the worst possible Phoenix to have shown up in Seibo Mura.

Before Ryōtora could say anything else, Sekken turned to Ogano. "I think we've established that he's not some kind of malevolent shapechanger, yes? In which case, we should let your family out of hiding. Come on!" That last was directed to the people in the room behind him – Sekken had opened the door again without waiting for Ogano to reply.

That's more than the other one offered. Ogano hadn't been talking about Mirumoto Norifusa, but his unexpected and unwanted Phoenix guest.

The women and children crawled out onto the wooden floor of the main living area and bowed low, touching their heads to the polished boards. Given Seibo Mura's isolated location, it was entirely possible they'd never seen two samurai at once before.

For a while the situation took on something more like the bustle of a normal household. The elderly woman went outside to see to Ryōtora's pony, while the wife brought Ryōtora a towel and then hastily prodded up the hearth in the earthen-floored workspace to cook something for her new guest. The oldest son helped her; the youngest child, fat-cheeked and of indeterminate gender, sat near the firepit and stared unblinking at Ryōtora.

The older man turned out to be Sekken's own servant, Jun, a wiry man with a receding hairline. The Phoenix put him to work moving some of his baggage out of the other room to make space for Ryōtora, while Ogano crossed his arms and glowered – a spectator in his own household.

Ryōtora felt like he should do something about that, but he couldn't figure out what. It took all his will not to stare at Ogano's square face, at Rin's stubborn chin, and wonder: *Could that man be my father? Could that girl be my younger sister?*

The governor hadn't realized, when he assigned Ryōtora to

handle matters in Seibo Mura, that he was sending him back to the village he'd been born in.

Because no one spoke of such matters. Ryōtora prayed that no one here would recognize him – or if they did, that they would have the sense to keep it to themselves. The last thing he wanted was for Asako Sekken to catch wind of that history. Ryōtora was already going to have enough to do, finding out the cause of the disturbances and putting an end to them, without adding an overly curious Phoenix to the mix.

Better if I get him out of here, Ryōtora thought. Then deal with the problem and leave as soon as possible.

But he doubted it would be as simple as that.

CHAPTER TWO

For the first time in months, Sekken's sleep was undisturbed.

He woke around dawn, disoriented; it always took his mind a few moments to catch up with his body in waking. All the more so now, when he half-expected a phantom weight on his chest, invisible bands locking his body tight. But he could move freely, and the only other creature in the room was the Dragon shugenja lying on a second futon just out of arm's reach.

He let out a slow, steady breath. A night without troubles. What did that mean?

Headman of his village Ogano might be, but his house was still a simple rural structure, built more to resist winter's trials than to provide elegant surroundings. The room Sekken and Isao Ryōtora slept in had no translucent paper screens for its outer walls, only solid wooden shutters, which let in almost no light. *Warded somehow?* Sekken wondered, before dismissing it. He'd slept in plenty of warded rooms since his problems began, and none of them had protected him. Some isolated Dragon peasants were unlikely to know techniques the Isawa did not.

At this point a night of peaceful sleep felt luxurious. Yawning,

Sekken scratched his fingernails through the thin stubble along his jawline and stretched, heels dragging across the tatami matting beneath his futon.

The shreds of light seeping in through the cracks around the shutters were pale enough that he knew it couldn't be long after sunrise. This was one of the many ways he'd never fit in well with the more courtly sorts; during his education, his peers had teased him that if he wanted to wake so early, he should go train with the bushi. While Asako scholars weren't as idle as the Doji, who were rumored never to rise before noon if they could help it, they weren't required to beat the roosters out the door, either.

But Sekken roused naturally early, and always had. "Blessed by Amaterasu Ōmikami," his mother liked to say. Even when he slept poorly, he woke at dawn.

The shugenja at his side showed no sign of such blessings. Sekken hoped the man wasn't always as monosyllabic as he'd been the previous night – though to be fair, if Sekken had shown up looking like a wet kitten, only to find another samurai there to witness his embarrassment, he too might have been a little curt. Isao Ryōtora's hair had dried in the night and now fanned out across his futon and the tatami mat below; Sekken almost put his hand on it when he pushed himself upright. It softened the cut planes of the man's face, which last night had looked as unforgiving as the mountains themselves.

Ryotora probably wouldn't thank his unexpected roommate for rousing him early. Sekken got silently to his feet and retrieved his kimono from the bar he'd shoved through its sleeves last night, tying his sash with a simple knot. Hakama and a short robe would be better in a place like this village, but his baggage was somewhere else – wherever Jun had put it.

The door out to the living area squeaked as Sekken slid it open, and he winced. Fortunately, Ryōtora showed no sign of stirring. Sekken hastily stepped out onto the polished floor and shut the door behind him.

Ogano's wife was descending the steep wooden steps that led to the farmhouse's loft. She and the rest of the family had relocated up there last night, except for Ogano; he took the larger tatami room with Jun and the shugenja's two servants. When she saw Sekken, her foot missed the bottom step, and she almost slipped. He lunged forward instinctively, but she caught herself, attained the safety of the floor, and promptly knelt on it, bowing her face to the boards. "Forgive me if I disturbed you, my lord."

The accent of deep-mountain Dragon peasants was different from the accent of deepmountain Phoenix peasants, but Sekken could follow it well enough. His first assignment after his gempuku had been with a scholar who studied the dialects of Rokugan. She said that the words to some ancient songs showed a change in Rokugani pronunciation in the thousand years since the great Kami fell – a borderline heretical claim to those who insisted the Empire had attained perfection under its early Emperors and thereafter ceased to change, or those who felt that any deviation from the ways of their ancestors was an unforgivable lapse. It was a silly thing to object to, but his superior got in an argument with the wrong Matsu at court one day, and Sekken's family had to call in favors in a hurry to keep him from being exiled along with her to a backwater posting.

He'd fallen down the well of his thoughts, as he so often did, and Ogano's wife was still on the floor. "You didn't wake me," he said. "I always get up early. Will I be able to get breakfast here, or…" His voice trailed off. Inns were as unknown as the ocean to this place, and it wasn't like the monasteries he'd visited, where everyone ate in a common refectory. If he couldn't get breakfast in this house, he didn't know where he would find it, unless he wandered outside and found some kind of berry bush. Jun was a faithful servant, but a miserable cook.

"I was about to stir up the fire," the woman said. She was still on the floor, which was absurd – but belatedly, Sekken realized she probably saw a samurai once a year, if that. She didn't know what was absurd and what wasn't.

"Please get up," he said. "You don't have to bow like that, especially not if I'll be living here while I'm in Seibo Mura. You'd never get anything done."

She scrambled upright, bobbed an awkward little bow, and shoved her feet into the rough straw sandals that waited on the earthen floor. To avoid making her feel even more awkward as she worked, Sekken found his own sandals and went outside.

After the darkness of the house, the early morning light lanced into his skull, but he took a slow breath of the cool mountain air and tipped his face upward, welcoming Lady Sun's touch. When he opened his eyes, he found a stupendous view all around: the rugged peaks of the Great Wall of the North, here thickly furred with trees, there baring great stretches of rock to the sky. A waterfall plunged over a precipice to the west, and, not far to the north of that, the ruins of a shrine clung to the mountainside, as if placed there for the purpose of enticing a painter.

Sekken hadn't brought any paints or suitable inks with him. But he could make some charcoal sketches, and paint the scene when he returned home. Though that would lead to people asking him where the scene was, and then he'd either have to lie – pretending he'd invented the view – or admit he'd gone well beyond where he ought to be.

I have permission to be in Dragon lands, he thought defensively. What his travel papers actually said was that he could visit Quiet Stone Monastery, to use the library there. Not an obscure village three-quarters of the way to Yobanjin lands.

He found a plain ribbon inside his sleeve and used it to tie his hair back, then set out for a brisk walk around the village. It would work up his appetite and give the headman's wife time to make breakfast. Sekken passed the village well and wondered what the bathing facilities here were like – or if there even were any. He very much doubted there was a bathhouse here, but he might be able to hope for a hot spring.

Unsurprisingly, he wasn't the only one awake. The peasants gave him awkward glances and even more awkward bows as they went to fetch water from the well or shouldered tools of various kinds. He saw much less activity than he would expect, though; Seibo Mura seemed to be a very small village.

Not entirely in ways that could be blamed on the disturbances, either. The house he'd seen the day before, the one that had burned down – that was definitely a recent problem. Other houses, though, seemed to have fallen into disuse and ruin years before, judging by the caved-in shingle roofs and the moss painting their walls. On the northern edge of the village he found one house that had become nothing more than a mound of brambles, barely recognizable as a former structure at all.

It suggested that whatever misfortunes were going on here, they might have their roots further back in time. A generation, at least. Much more recent than what he'd found in the monastery's library, but much older than Sekken's own troubles.

For months an *inugami* had been haunting his sleep, the dog spirit sitting on his chest while invisible bands of metal bound him tight, and it had defied all attempts to banish it. The search for answers as to why had led him to Quiet Stone Monastery and the records there… and then, while he was researching, there came three nights where the inugami barked at him without respite.

Three nights that later turned out to correspond exactly with the first round of disturbances in Seibo Mura.

It seemed too much to be a coincidence. As soon as word reached the monastery of what had happened in the mountains, Sekken set out immediately, not waiting for any kind of permission. On his way north, he suffered through three more nights of barking, almost one month after the original incident. He'd wondered even then if it meant a renewal of the problems in Seibo Mura, and wasn't surprised to learn that it did.

Clearly witchcraft was at work in the village. But until Sekken knew more – most particularly, why *he* of all people had been dragged into this – he would go on pretending his interest was purely idle, and see what the Dragon shugenja uncovered.

Directing his steps back toward the headman's house, he began to notice other, less ordinary things. Next to one of the thick-walled storehouses, a rowan tree that ought to have been in full leaf was withered and bare, as if struck by frost, though summer was well underway. One farmhouse's door bore deep gouges in the wood, only slightly faded by the passage of a week or two. The waterwheel of what he presumed was the millhouse was broken – and not just broken, but shattered, as if struck by an unthinkably powerful blow. Two men were working to build a replacement, their steady hammer blows punctuated by some kind of working chant.

No – not a working chant. A shift in the mountain breeze brought their words to Sekken's ears.

Shoshi ni kie. Shoshi ni kie.

The mantra of the Perfect Land Sect.

Sekken tensed. That heresy, here? It wasn't the witchcraft he'd expected – though he supposed that nothing prevented a peasant from being a seeker of the Perfect Land *and* a witch. The sect claimed Rokugan had entered the Age of Declining Virtue, and they blamed samurai for that fall. They also believed their mantra would help them escape the wheel of rebirth, freeing them to pursue enlightenment in some mythical paradise created by Shinsei, rather than seeking it through proper study in the mortal world.

When one's theology was wrong to begin with, a further step into ancient magical practices would hardly be unexpected.

He almost strode forward to denounce the men. It was the accent that stopped him: the rural Dragon speech that almost slurred the final word into a single syllable, *kye*. He wasn't in Phoenix lands… and in this clan's territory, the Perfect Land Sect wasn't illegal.

He scowled and made himself walk onward, as if he hadn't heard. But inside, his thoughts whirled.

Back at the house, there was no sign of Ryōtora having risen, but the headman's wife had breakfast ready. Sekken wondered if she, too, sought the Perfect Land. Had the whole village gone heretical? That was often the case, the Phoenix had found. Even those peasants who still followed the forms of orthodox Shinseism saw no harm in chanting the kie as they worked – because they were too unlettered to understand the harm.

Sekken knelt silently at the table as she served his meal. She'd fried up some kind of little fish and served it alongside a bowl of pungent barley miso soup. No rice, he noted. A deliberate insult to her unwanted guest? It was the kind of thing a Perfect Land follower might do. But she'd used what he suspected were her best bowl and plate. It was probably another signal of this village's poverty – or just the perennial problem of living in Dragon Clan lands, which were hardly prime agricultural terrain. Still, he would expect at least the headman of the village to eat rice.

Despite his troubled mood, a faint groan from behind the screen that closed off the sleeping room made Sekken grin. From the sound of it, his reluctant roommate was an even more reluctant riser.

But he wiped away his grin long before the door finally squeaked aside to reveal Isao Ryōtora. It was impolite to admit one had heard anything that happened behind closed walls, and he already had the feeling the shugenja was a stickler for manners.

To his surprise, Ryōtora showed no sign of having dragged himself awake. The man looked perfectly well composed, if one allowed for the slightly rumpled state of his kimono and hakama, which had suffered that undignified wetting the night before. Ryōtora bowed at the sight of Sekken, and hesitated only a moment before joining him.

The headman's wife hurried to bring him soup in a less fine bowl, with an expression that suggested she'd been hoping Sekken would finish his own in time for her to rinse it out and re-use his bowl for her other samurai guest. Ogano's bowl? Sekken assumed so. The headman must have risen and left while Sekken was out, because his sandals were no longer lined up on the earthen floor.

"Good morning," Sekken said cheerfully. "I hope I kept my promise and didn't sprawl at you in the night." He used to do that kind of thing, winding up halfway off his futon by morning. The hauntings, and the feeling of metal-bound limbs that accompanied them, had put a stop to that. But there had been no haunting last night.

Ryōtora looked like he would dearly prefer not to be having any conversation at all this soon after rising, but he answered politely, in a deep, rich voice that would have done well at court. "You did not trouble me in the slightest."

"Wonderful. We're off to an excellent start." Sekken was babbling, which he did when he was nervous. Fortunately, Ryōtora didn't look like he was in any state to even remember that travel papers were a concept, much less ask to see someone else's. "I heard you say last night that the governor of Heibeisu sent you. Is that where you live?"

A sizzle of oil heralded another fish frying, presumably for Ryōtora. The shugenja's answer was stiffly formal. "I am itinerant. My father lives in Yōmei Machi, and I travel there each year for the Bon Festival, but I maintain no home of my own. I go where my duties take me."

"And what might those duties be? Do you swoop about Dragon lands like your clan's namesake, smiting spiritual problems wherever they rear their heads?"

Ryōtora's suspicious gaze seemed to be weighing Sekken for mockery. Finding none, he said, "No. I… visit outlying villages, which otherwise would never see a shugenja. Ordinarily, though, the work is much quieter than this."

The brief hesitation gave away the existence of a deeper answer, but not what it was. The Dragon tended to be far too tolerant of heterodox theologies, claiming that each person must be permitted to find their own way, but that didn't mean they were utterly lacking in heresy-hunters of any sort. Maybe Ryōtora's duty was to keep an eye on fringe sects, making sure nothing too dangerous was taking root in the hinterlands – like the Perfect Land.

"What of you?" Ryōtora said, after the headman's wife served up his fish. "What duty has your lord assigned you?"

He either wasn't very good at hiding the accusing note in his voice, or didn't care to try. Sekken said, "I'm a scholar of spiritual matters. Not gifted at speaking to the kami, as you are, but at least a student of such things. I was studying at Quiet Stone Monastery when we heard of the troubles here." It was true without being the whole story – an art every courtier learned. Let Ryōtora think him an idle dabbler; it was safer that way. Until recently that *had* been his life, and as soon as he resolved his problems he looked forward to returning to it.

"So you decided to come see the troubles for yourself. Or perhaps you think the Dragon incapable of handling the matter?"

I'm not an Isawa. Sekken kept the thought behind his teeth. Ryōtora was a shugenja, trained by the Agasha family; he would have memorized prickly defensiveness toward Phoenix interference along with the lists of suitable offerings to the kami. Instead he said mildly, "I wasn't aware the problem was a recurring one. News of only the first disturbance had reached the monastery when I left. But since it is, I believe it would be a failure of Compassion not to offer what aid I can. Do you not agree?"

Ryōtora stiffened as if Sekken had slapped him. Had his mother perhaps been a Lion? All samurai were expected to abide by the ethical code of Bushidō, whether they were warriors or not... but some of them took it more seriously than others, weighing every action against the seven virtues, and taking offense when anyone questioned their own. Dragon usually weren't that prickly, though.

The headman's wife finally stepped outside, leaving the two of them alone. Sekken didn't know how long she would be gone, so he spoke rapidly, in a low voice. "It may aid your investigation to know the Perfect Land Sect is in this village."

Ryōtora's chopsticks paused in the middle of tugging apart the fish. "That's hardly unusual."

His tone was more suited to Sekken announcing that some of the villagers were carrying on illicit affairs with people they weren't married to. "You don't find that suspicious?"

"How so?" Ryōtora stared at him, honestly perplexed. "You think it has something to do with the troubles here?"

Every reply Sekken could think of sounded rude even in his own head, so he confined himself to a nod.

Ryōtora went back to pulling apart the fish. "Thank you, Lord Asako, but I doubt your theory. The Perfect Land has found followers in many Dragon villages, without any of them suffering the kinds of attacks Seibo Mura has seen. I'll certainly keep an eye out for any sign of trouble from that quarter – the more militant believers can cause problems, it's true – but I'm sure the cause lies elsewhere."

How can you be sure? Sekken wanted to ask. Perfect Land believers wanted to overturn the order of the world. It wasn't hard to imagine them so disturbing the spiritual atmosphere that something went awry.

He felt irritation and impatience rising like bile, and made himself breathe evenly until they subsided. One good night of sleep wasn't enough to erase the strain of these past months, but that strain didn't justify getting off on the wrong foot with the local authority. And the status of the Perfect Land Sect was a long-standing point of contention between the Phoenix and the Dragon.

Poking his finger directly into that bruise was a bad way to begin.

"Forgive me," he said, offering Ryōtora a seated bow. "I have spoken thoughtlessly, and in haste. Please allow me to retract my words."

Then inspiration struck. "Instead I should say, I defer to your authority here, and I only hope you will accept my knowledge and assistance in dealing with these troubles."

His eldest sister, trained as a bushi, had taught him the trick of throwing someone to the ground: first you resisted, and then you gave way. There was no audible *thump* as Ryōtora metaphorically fell, but the man's answering bow amounted to the same thing. "That is generous of you, Lord Asako. Once I have had a chance to begin my investigation, I will let you know how you may assist."

How my family would stare. Sekken didn't actively dodge responsibility; he didn't have to. His parents and his sisters had all achieved influential enough positions that he, the youngest child, had the unthinkable luxury of more or less doing what he wanted. Another man in his position might have dissipated himself with drinking or gambling, but since Sekken's preference was to bury himself in ancient scrolls, everyone let him be. It meant he wasn't exactly in the habit of volunteering for work.

But he needed Ryōtora and everyone else to see him only as a helpful visitor, brought here by compassion, and staying because it would be churlish to walk away.

And if he had some task to carry out, it would give him the cover he needed to conduct his own investigation – into the dogs of the village, into the witches who might be using them, and into the followers of the Perfect Land. Those things had to be connected in some fashion, and Sekken would find out how.

CHAPTER THREE

Ryōtora wasn't especially subtle in separating himself from Asako Sekken after breakfast, but then, he wasn't trying to be. A failure of the virtue of Courtesy, perhaps – but the last thing he wanted was a stranger watching over his shoulder as he began his investigation.

For now, Sekken was busy trying to arrange water for bathing, after being disappointed to find the local hot spring had dried up the previous year. Meanwhile, his manservant and Ryōtora's ashigaru were working out the logistics of their accommodations now that it was no longer nighttime and raining. That manservant had a pony, too, and Sekken himself had a proper horse; what they were all going to eat, Ryōtora didn't know. The horse especially. It wouldn't fare as well as the mountain ponies on the rough foraging available around Seibo Mura, but the villagers hardly had grain to spare for a samurai's fine mount.

The best solution was to solve the problem here and leave before feed became an issue. To that end, Ryōtora went in search of Ogano.

His ankle ached from its twisting yesterday and his head felt like a bag of sand in the piercing sunshine, but he was used to the latter. Mornings had always been difficult for him, ever since childhood. Years of early rising had failed to change that; every day was a struggle, dragging himself off his futon when his body just wanted to sleep.

But it didn't matter how hard it was. His duty demanded that he get up, so he did.

Haru, Ogano's wife, had told him where to find the headman – and why. Ryōtora paused on the edge of the village's cemetery, his gaze sweeping across the headstones of the family plots. They were well carved; Seibo Mura was primarily a mining village, and clearly some of the people here worked stone for artistic purposes as well.

Some of the graves were overgrown, though, as if no family had come to tend them in years. Others were all too fresh. Here and there Ryōtora saw the bright wood of a commemorative marker, far too clean and new at this time of year, when the Bon Festival was still three months off. One plot didn't even have a headstone yet; Ryōtora wondered who it belonged to, that they had no ancestors here in the village.

And what of my own ancestors? Which of these graves holds their ashes?

Ogano wasn't hard to find. His family had been the leaders of Seibo Mura for generations, and so their grave had the largest and most elaborate monument. The current headman knelt in front of it, but his hands weren't clasped in prayer. Instead he just stared wearily at the stone, hardly blinking.

Although he must have seen his samurai guest coming up the path, he hadn't moved. Ryōtora's jaw tensed. It wasn't inherently polluting for a shugenja to walk into a cemetery – he cleaned his adoptive family's grave each year alongside his father, as a son should – but it was rude of Ogano not to rise and greet him. Especially when the conversation they needed to have wasn't exactly appropriate for this quiet place.

But Haru, apologizing for her husband's lack of courtesy the night before, had explained. Ogano's younger brother Ogura had died during the second round of attacks. The fresh dirt in front of the headman showed where the urn with his ashes had been interred.

Courtesy. Compassion. The tenets of Bushidō had guided Ryōtora since childhood, and they gave a clear answer now.

He approached quietly and knelt at the grave, placing a stick of incense in the small holder in front of the headstone. A whispered invocation to the fire kami lit it, the smoke vanishing almost immediately in the mountain wind. Ryōtora placed his palms together and prayed for the swift journey of Ogura's soul through Meido.

When he lowered his hands, Ogano said, "We did the best we could with the funerals. But my brother's soul is probably wandering lost."

Ryōtora frowned. "No monk has come to see to your dead?" The Brotherhood of Shinsei routinely sent monks through the rural areas for that purpose, so that bodies would not have to wait too long for proper rites. He assumed one would have come through even so remote a place as this by now.

Ogano jerked his chin at the new grave, the one without a headstone. "He's over there. Thought he could deal with the problems. Got himself killed instead."

Even at the height of summer, the wind was cool enough to raise the hairs on the back of Ryōtora's neck. "I see. I… will do what I can for them." Funerary tasks were usually left to the Shinseists, because death was a source of spiritual pollution, which interfered with prayers to the Fortunes and the kami. There were no corpses here, though, and Ryōtora could cleanse himself of any lingering impurity afterward. The dead of Seibo Mura, on the other hand, could do nothing for themselves.

His offer earned him a grunt from Ogano. It sounded less hostile than before. Ryōtora said, "Let us go someplace we can speak, and you tell me what has happened here. From the beginning."

Ryōtora had read the account in Heibeisu, but that had been a summary, written by someone who believed the disturbance was over. The description he'd gotten of the second round of attacks had been both incomplete and garbled: the messenger had left Seibo Mura after only one day of three, and spoke incoherently of chaos and "monsters." Ryōtora needed the full story.

The first night, at the beginning of the full moon more than a month ago, hadn't seemed too serious. People heard strange sounds, both in and around the village: footsteps in lofts or empty rooms, banging on the walls, splashing or the rattle of spilled beans, in places where there was no water and no fallen beans. Singing in the woods, and the voices of people who later turned out to be somewhere else entirely. One person reported the clash of a gong – but no such instrument existed in Seibo Mura.

The second night, things got worse. Dishes smashed themselves, and paper screens tore. The length of fabric Haru was planning on turning into a new winter jacket for Ogano took flight around the room and tried to strangle her. No one was seriously hurt, but the entire village panicked and turned to their headman for guidance.

Ogano wasn't spiritually wise. He didn't say that part to Ryōtora, but it came through in how he related his tale. Up until that point, his duties as headman had involved settling disputes between the villagers and making sure they delivered their shipments to Heibeisu twice a year. He'd done his best to address the situation, though. That day they made offerings to every Fortune and spirit that seemed at all relevant, from Jizō, the Fortune of Mercy, to the kami of their hearths and fields. Because the worst troubles had occurred inside houses the previous night, Ogano advised everyone to sleep outside, with people taking turns to keep watch.

That was the night the monsters came.

Ryōtora had brought his portable writing kit with him and took notes as Ogano talked, but the kit's wad of ink-saturated moss ran dry before the man finished. Pressed for details on the "monsters," he described a dizzying array of creatures ranging from the bizarre to the terrifying: walking masses of hair; a giant head; an enormous cat with two tails, each tipped with eldritch fire. The villagers fled into their storehouses and barricaded the doors, but two of those who were caught in the open died.

The next day, Ogano dispatched the best runner in the village to Heibeisu. The fourth night everyone took refuge in the storehouses… but nothing happened. Nor the night after that, and so on until Mirumoto Norifusa arrived.

Norifusa, it seemed, hadn't told anyone in Seibo Mura what his conclusion was. The report he wrote back in Heibeisu, though, suggested it might have been mass delusion. The local mines produced cinnabar and realgar, which Ryōtora knew well were dangerous ores; working with cinnabar had killed one of his Agasha sensei. Norifusa presumed some kind of venting from the mines was responsible for the chaos.

But while such things could damage both the body and the mind, they didn't cause hallucinations. Nor could they possibly explain what followed one month later.

This time there was no prelude. After days of peace and stability, the monsters struck without warning. The burned house Ryōtora had seen went up on the first night, and a woman whose hook-filled hair moved on its own tore apart one of the inhabitants when he escaped the flames. An invisible whirlwind similarly shredded the village blacksmith, who nearly died. Something that looked like a cross between a bat and a monkey was found stealing the breath from a grandmother, whose deafness meant she was sleeping through the chaos; she survived because her granddaughter chased the creature away.

The next day, after Ogano dispatched his runner again, a handful of the villagers decided to leave Seibo Mura. Days later, one of the children discovered their bodies hanging from the trees a short distance to the south.

His brother Ogura and the monk died on the third night. The monk, Yugaku, had met Norifusa on the latter's journey to Seibo Mura, and he chose to stay after the samurai left, hoping to bring some serenity back to the village. When that serenity shattered, he and Ogura agreed to find the source of the problem and subdue it.

Both of them were dead by morning, their bodies bent into a rictus by poison.

At the beginning of his tale, Ogano spoke in the flat, dull voice of someone rendered numb by the trauma he'd suffered. As he went on, reliving that trauma made him more animated, fright and horror and fury braiding themselves together. When he got to the death of his brother, though…

Silence fell, except for the mountain wind and the faint sounds of the village below. Finally Ogano said, "That's it. That's what happened. And it will happen again, if you don't stop it."

Ryōtora didn't doubt him.

After Ogano left, Ryōtora remained on his boulder, looking out over the village and trying to master his feelings.

He'd maintained his composure while the headman was talking, because it would be both a loss of self-control and a dereliction of his duty to Ogano if Ryōtora showed the full extent of his horror – and his fear. But what the man had described… it went far beyond anything Ryōtora had ever faced, or knew how to address.

He deliberately clenched his hands, then made them relax. *Courage. Duty.* He was far more prepared to deal with such things than the villagers were. If they could maintain that much cohesion in the face of such threats, he must do no less.

The creatures Ogano described sounded like yōkai. But that didn't get him very far; saying "this was caused by supernatural creatures" was like telling a patient "your symptoms are caused by a disease." Which creatures? And why?

What baffled him was the sheer *array*. Ryōtora couldn't identify everything Ogano had described – Ogano hadn't given enough detail to identify many of them anyway – but it made no sense for so many different creatures to show up in the same place at the same time. A traveler might encounter a nure onna on the bank of a river, or a faceless nopperabō along a deserted road, or an akaname in a filthy bathing chamber; he didn't encounter all three of them, and dozens more besides, in a mountain village that had never done anything to attract such supernatural attention.

It sounded like an eruption of influence from Senkyō, the enchanted realms that existed alongside the mortal world. Most likely creatures of Sakkaku; that group of yōkai liked to play tricks on people, and sometimes the tricks became lethal. But he couldn't discount the possibility of Yume-dō, either. Ordinarily people only touched the Realm of Dreams in their sleep… but if it somehow bled through into waking life, the villagers' fears could have manifested as terrible monsters.

Perhaps. If the villagers knew tales of all these yōkai – though given how obscure some of them were, he doubted that.

Or perhaps they had offended a kami. But which one? If the mines had somehow disturbed the kami of the mountain, Ryōtora would have expected different consequences: a cave-in, maybe, or crops failing. The earth kami weren't known for indulging in capricious trickery. But he wouldn't expect any air kami around here to be powerful enough to cause something like this.

Regardless, at least he had avenues of inquiry to follow. He could ask whether anything unusual had happened in the days leading up to the first incident, and question the villagers for more specifics on the yōkai, to see if he could discern any kind of pattern in them. He'd also promised Ogano that he would place wards – probably not necessary yet, as the attacks had so far happened only on the three nights of the full moon, but he didn't want to take any chances.

Because Seibo Mura was valuable to the Dragon Clan. The cinnabar mined here was used to make vermilion pigment, useful particularly in crafting beautiful red lacquerware, which the Dragon traded all across the Empire. And the alchemists among the Agasha had many uses for the quicksilver they extracted from that ore.

The clan's policy for the last generation or more had been to consolidate its declining villages, relocating peasants from remote areas into more central and productive lands. Ordinarily, a place as isolated as Seibo Mura would have been high on the list for consolidation. But before Ryōtora left Heibeisu, the governor had said he was thinking of moving peasants *into* the village, to increase cinnabar production and make up for the declining population there. Ryōtora would not find a welcome waiting for him in Heibeisu if he instead evacuated Seibo Mura… but if he couldn't solve this issue before the full moon, then for the sake of the people here, he would have to do exactly that.

And hope the problems didn't follow them south.

Closing up his writing kit and tucking the scribbled sheaf of paper into his kimono, Ryōtora prepared to head back down to the village. As he rose, though, he caught sight of Asako Sekken standing outside Ogano's house. The Phoenix was looking toward a cluster of women washing laundry in a large tub.

The wind was from the wrong direction for Ryōtora to hear anything, but he'd been in enough isolated villages to know what Sekken must be hearing. Followers of the Perfect Land often chanted the kie to provide a rhythm while they worked.

Over breakfast this morning, Ryōtora had ascribed Sekken's suspicion merely to the usual Phoenix prejudice. Now, watching him watch the peasants, a worse possibility occurred to Ryōtora.

What if he's an Inquisitor?

Ryōtora's sensei had run afoul of an Inquisitor once, which was the only reason he even knew the name. Many clans had groups dedicated to stamping out heresies, but the most secretive of them all were the Phoenix Inquisitors. Their target was not merely simple heresies like the Perfect Land or the cults of Lord Moon, but truly blasphemous practices – like the blood magic known as mahō.

Ryōtora had been thinking of the disturbances in Seibo Mura as some kind of spiritual accident. He'd never considered that someone might have done this on purpose.

He felt as if someone had placed a dagger of ice against his heart. Ryōtora knew very little about mahō; he didn't want to know more. Its use tainted the mahō-tsukai with the corruption of Jigoku, and the stories whispered that even familiarity with its principles tempted one to reach for that power. But he did know that Jigoku's taint, once embedded in a person or place, could spread.

Down in the lands of the Crab Clan, where they fought a constant war against creatures from Jigoku far worse than simple yōkai, sometimes that meant slaughtering whole villages and burning them to the ground to root out the taint. If such a thing took hold here…

Ryōtora jerked his shoulders, trying to dislodge his unease. It was a theory, nothing more – one that wouldn't have even crossed his mind if Asako Sekken hadn't been in Seibo Mura. If someone *had* caused this, it didn't necessarily follow that they had done so by means of mahō. And even if blood magic were at work in the village, he was leaping well ahead to assume that stopping it would mean destroying everyone and everything here.

Another clench and release of his hands helped to steady his thoughts. *One thing at a time.* The bodies of the dead had been cremated – a precaution, Ryōtora remembered, that an Emperor had instituted centuries ago to prevent mahō-tsukai raising corpses from their graves – but he needed to make sure their spirits had moved on, lest they too begin to haunt Seibo Mura. Then he needed to create wards. Then question people, and find answers.

And pray to the kami and the Fortunes that any Spirit Realms influencing this place had no connection to Jigoku.

CHAPTER FOUR

One of Sekken's sensei used to hit him with her fan every time he turned to look at something, rather than using his peripheral vision. As he stood outside, gritting his teeth at the sound of some washerwomen chanting the kie, a breeze carried a giggle to his ear. He didn't turn, but out of the corner of his eye he saw a cluster of three young women, watching him from beneath a nearby tree.

Such courtly subtleties weren't really needed here. Sekken faced them properly and nodded, and they burst into giggles again, one ducking behind her friends.

From what he could see, they ranged in age from a girl too young to have passed her gempuku yet if she were a samurai, up to one who could have had a daughter almost that age, if she'd started early enough. Too old to be mooning after a visiting samurai; she ought to be married by now. Not that marriage necessarily precluded mooning – but in Sekken's experience, rural villages tended to be stricter about that sort of thing than the jaded society of court.

By the standards of that society, Sekken was no beauty. He

was too bony, and not good at the kind of elegant innuendo and double meaning that won praise at court. When he alluded to poetry, it was usually something too old and obscure for others to catch the reference. Still, he was a samurai in his early twenties, which meant he had good skin and long hair and all his own teeth. It wasn't the first time village girls had come out, in what he presumed were their best clothes, to try to catch his eye.

It was, however, the first time their laughter had a tinge of desperation to it. Attracting a samurai lover always meant the chance of favors and valuable gifts… but in this place, at this time, it might mean he would take his lover with him to safety when he departed.

If Sekken were inclined to take any of them as a lover – which he wasn't, for a host of reasons beginning with their gender. He began walking, hoping they would take the hint and leave him in peace. Otherwise he would have to say something, and even if these rural bumpkins didn't realize how embarrassing that would be for all involved, *he* would know.

He chose his direction at random, and realized too late that Ryōtora was descending the path ahead, from what looked to be the village cemetery. Turning away would be far too obvious, so Sekken bowed when the other man came within range. "I heard you were talking to the headman. Have you learned anything of use?"

Ryōtora hesitated, then said, "It's clearly an infestation of yōkai. The question is why – and why such a bizarre array – and once that is known, how to put a stop to it. But first, I must see to the dead."

Sekken recoiled. "Don't tell me they haven't cremated the bodies yet."

"Oh, they have. Unfortunately, there was no one to see to the rites. I will have to settle their spirits, or the village risks an infestation of ghosts along with everything else."

His words were almost flippant. His tone was anything but. "Will that pollute you spiritually?" Sekken asked, frowning. "Obviously you won't be touching the bodies, but even so…"

"The stain will be minor at worst," Ryōtora said. "And there is no one else here who can do it. I believe it would be a failure of Compassion not to offer my aid. Do you not agree?"

A near-perfect echo of Sekken's own retort that morning. For a man who apparently spent his days traveling the hinterlands of Dragon territory, Ryōtora was quite good at the art of verbal combat. For one heartbeat Sekken teetered on the edge of offense; then he chose, very deliberately, to instead give a rueful chuckle and an acknowledging bow. "Indeed. Then you will need to purify yourself afterward, I imagine. I saw a splendid waterfall when I stepped outside this morning; would you like me to ask whether there's a path that leads there?"

"No, thank you. I can take care of it myself."

Sekken waited. Ryōtora was very good at keeping his expression serene, but tension showed in his body, hinting at the argument being carried out within. Sekken could guess at its content. The Dragon didn't want an outsider present at all, much less involved in this situation. But time was already slipping through Ryōtora's fingers; in fifteen days, at the next full moon, the chaos would presumably return. Delay now could mean disaster later.

Finally Ryōtora said, "I'll be telling Ishi and Tarō to begin gathering stories from the villagers, so that I can piece together a more organized account of what's happened here. But they aren't scholars, and you are. Can I ask you to write up what they learn?

What creatures have been seen and where, and what they were doing."

Sekken bowed almost before Ryōtora was done talking. Not only had the Dragon taken him up on the offer of assistance, but the task was easy enough even Sekken could do it.

In fact, it opened the door to suggest something even more useful – for them both. "Gathering stories will go faster with three instead of two," Sekken said. "That way, I won't be sitting idle while I wait for them to be done." Animal spirits like inugami were included under the general header of "yōkai." He could search for any such thing here, without it seeming unusual.

He added, "Would you like me to note my own guesses as to the names and natures of the yōkai? I've read about them at great length. I may be able to identify what's appeared here."

Ryōtora nodded. "That would be useful. Now, please excuse me – I have funerals to conduct."

Back at Ogano's house, Jun had unpacked the saddlebags. Sekken changed into hakama and tied his hair back again – certain strands always wanted to slip free of their tail – and smiled to himself. *That would be useful,* Ryōtora had said. Not something Sekken was accustomed to hearing.

Now he had to decide how to approach his task. If he'd been the only one questioning the villagers, he would have arranged himself at the table here and had the villagers come to him one by one. Less effort on his part, and they shouldn't complain at the disruption to their work, when the point of the exercise was to save them from monsters.

But Ryōtora's ashigaru seemed to assume that their master wanted them to visit people wherever they might be. Sekken had to grant that would seem less like a tribunal than having people called before a set of three questioners. Unfortunately, it would also mean going to the mines, to the fields lower in the eastern part of the valley that provided food for the village, and into their houses.

He certainly didn't want to go into the mines. In the fields, he would have a difficult time taking notes, unless he simply gave up and sat in the muck. Which left the houses.

On the bright side, it offered him more chance to observe. Did any of the households keep an unusually large number of dogs? Witches usually weren't solitary; the whole family had spirit familiars, passing them down from one generation to the next. Would any of them try to hide things from his gaze? How many people in Seibo Mura sought the Perfect Land?

Houses it was. He sent one ashigaru to the mines and the other to the fields, and set out through the village.

Before the first hour was up, he regretted that decision.

He'd passed through villages before, but he'd never paid much attention to them. And in paintings, this kind of life looked simple and bucolic. The reality turned out to be simple enough, but as for the bucolic part...

However dark and inelegant Ogano's house seemed, it was palatial compared to the rest of the village. The headman of Seibo Mura was the only one who owned tatami mats; everyone else made do with wooden planks or, in the very poorest houses, nothing but packed earth. They slept all together in tiny enclosed rooms that were hardly more than boxes – which would be warm in the winter, he imagined, but must be stifling in the summer, and noisome regardless of season. The upper floors beneath the steeply pitched roofs were used for curing meat, of which the peasants seemed to eat an appalling amount, and the smell permeated the whole structure.

Their behavior was no better. The first man he questioned burst into tears halfway through his story, in a display of emotion that made Sekken embarrassed for them both. Peasants weren't held to the same standards of composure as trained courtiers, of course, and certainly the man had been through a great deal – but even so. Quite a few people cried, though none of them as loudly and dramatically as that one, until Sekken wanted to crawl under the nearest table to escape it.

Some of the discomfort came from his own end. Although Sekken thought of his indigo-dyed cotton hakama and cloud-printed kimono as simple clothing, they would have been festival finery for anyone here other than perhaps the headman. Even his writing kit, finely carved and lacquered with vermilion, was probably worth more than everything some of these people owned. They might mine the pigment here, but they couldn't afford to use it.

He took refuge from those thoughts in the tasks at hand – both the one Ryōtora had given him, and the one he'd set for himself. Quite a few of the peasants owned dogs: tall, sharp-eared and thickly furred, not much different either from the hunting dogs he'd seen in Phoenix lands or from the inugami haunting his sleep. Some of the dogs barked at Sekken, but only in the way any guard dog might bark at a stranger. None of them behaved in ways that suggested they might be a witch's bound spirit.

Sekken wasn't surprised to find many of the reports muddled, people giving contradictory accounts of what had happened when and to whom. But he found that kind of challenge soothing. Taking meticulous notes in tiny handwriting – he'd brought a limited amount of paper with him, and didn't want to run out – he began to get a sense of what had happened in Seibo Mura.

Ryōtora was right to call it a bizarre array of yōkai. Dozens of creatures, and most of them didn't belong anywhere near here. The jami was appropriately characteristic of the mountains, but the hyōsube belonged in the sultry climate of the south, and the kerakera onna was a creature of towns, being created from the miserable lives of prostitutes.

Not that the peasants knew most of those names. The people of Seibo Mura were accustomed to blaming illnesses on the baleful influence of jami – and true enough, in the household that told Sekken about seeing a ghostly blue thing, like a tiger but with no hind limbs, everyone was sick. Many people in Seibo Mura were, because multiple yōkai could cause disease; one young man, a fellow called Fubatsu, was feverish enough that he couldn't even rise from his bed. The other yōkai, though… there was no reason for these people to know about them, much less ever see one.

And for every yōkai that made sense, there were a dozen that didn't. The charred beams of the house that had burned down showed clear signs of having been eaten, as if a basan had been at them – but why would one of those mystical birds leave its home in an isolated bamboo grove to harass human beings, instead of vanishing the moment someone came near? Why would an ao nyōbō, born from the death of a failed court lady, be found in a village whose closest brush with the elegant world of court was probably Sekken's own arrival?

Then there were the things he couldn't identify. Sekken couldn't tell whether those were due to the panic of the events, muddling the observations and memories of the survivors, or whether some of the yōkai harassing Seibo Mura were so obscure even he had never heard of them.

Or perhaps something had interfered with their memories. Sekken wasn't aware of anything that could do that… but in one house he found a young woman who had lost her memory entirely.

She was one of the three that had been giggling at him earlier, the one in the middle age-wise. Her mother had apparently found her and dragged her back home, worried to the bone about her daughter's condition. "Are you also a shugenja?" the mother said, reaching for Sekken's sleeve as if to clutch at it. He stepped back before she could. "You're a Phoenix, ain't you? Can you bring her memories back?"

"I am a Phoenix," he admitted, "but not a shugenja. Tell me what happened."

A boy – the girl's brother, he assumed – hurried forward with a cushion for Sekken. Trying not to think about how dirty it might be, and almost grateful for the dim light that made it difficult to see stains, he knelt on it. The padding inside was so flat it was hardly softer than the packed earth beneath.

The mother wrung her hands and said, "It was during the last full moon, on the final night. We were in the house, with the door barred shut, but–"

She choked on the words, and the boy patted her shoulder, making encouraging noises. "I'm sorry," the woman said, rubbing her arms as if she were cold. "Even remembering it – we all got terrified. We were afraid before, but not like that. We panicked and started tearing at the beam we'd used to brace the door, even though we knew those things were out there."

"Buruburu, perhaps," Sekken murmured. It was too dark in the house to make a note, but his memory was well trained. "Invisible, generally, and they cause fear." They weren't the only yōkai who did, but he'd found that people seemed oddly reassured by him putting a name to the horrors they'd faced. As if that shrank them somehow, turning them into a known problem with a known solution.

Of course, the difficulty with that was, people immediately expected him to *have* a solution. "Is that what took Aoi's memories?" the woman asked eagerly. "Do you know how to get them back? She didn't even recognize me when we found her – her own *mother* –"

"Tell me what happened after you became afraid," Sekken said. It wouldn't divert her for long, probably, but it would at least delay him having to admit he had no idea how to return someone's lost memories.

The son took up the story. "We ran. Pulled the door open and just scattered. I went toward the stream, and there was this girl there, covered in wet leaves and such. She had hold of Yoshi and wouldn't let him go."

Sekken had already spoken with Yoshi. He'd apparently gotten into the clutches of a nure onago – which, fortunately for him, was less dangerous than the related nure onna. "But your daughter," he prompted the woman. "Where did she go?"

"We don't know," the mother said, stroking the girl's hair. "I didn't see; I was too busy running. The next morning we found her by the mill. Just sitting there, like nothing had happened."

The mill was built alongside the stream, a short distance up from where the brother had seen Yoshi. In the dark, though, he might not have seen his sister – definitely wouldn't have, if she'd been on the far side of the building. And while some of the yōkai described by the peasants were huge, most were human-sized or smaller. Something could have been happening at the mill without him seeing.

But that didn't tell Sekken what creature could have taken the girl's memories.

He turned his attention to her. She'd sat quietly through the whole conversation, hands clasped in her lap, gaze demurely on the ground. It wasn't just the polite deference of a peasant in the presence of a samurai. Most people felt awkward when discussed by those around them as if they weren't there, but she didn't even look at her mother or brother. Nor did she fidget with her hands or shift position. Sekken's own sensei would have given her full marks for composure and patience.

What had the mother called her? Aoi, that was it. "Aoi, you may look at me."

She lifted her gaze to his. Not directly – she gazed up at him through her lashes – but she showed no hesitation. He had the unsettling feeling that, along with her memory of her family, she'd forgotten the entire social structure of Rokugan, the gulf that separated peasant from samurai.

"Tell me what you remember," he said.

She shook her head. "Nothing. It was morning, and I was sitting by the mill. Then a man found me, and he called me Aoi. So I thought that must be my name. He shouted for other people, and they came running." A small movement of her hand indicated her mother and brother. "These two hugged me and began weeping. She called me 'daughter.' They told me what had happened, but I really don't recall anything from before that morning."

Her voice was low and melodious. She spoke carefully – and

with only traces of the accent that marked the speech of the other two, or for that matter, the rest of the villagers. Under other circumstances, Sekken might have suspected her of trying to mimic courtly manners, to sound as elegant as possible in order to appeal to the visiting samurai.

But everything about that felt off. She was being elegant, yes, and a little flirtatious… but unless some random traveler had taught her fine manners, this wasn't how he'd expect a young woman from the back corners of the mountains to angle for a man's interest. Nor was she showing a fraction of the concern Sekken would expect from someone who couldn't remember anything before the last month.

"Will you come outside with me?" he asked.

Aoi stood without protest, and all four of them filed out into the bright sunlight. Sekken made a show of taking her pulse and examining her eyes, as if he were any kind of physician, capable of diagnosing an ailment by such measures. Mostly he was observing Aoi's behavior. She stood as straight as a young tree, and neither flinched nor blushed when he touched her, though she drew closer than the process required. In a voice pitched only for his ears, she said, "You're very kind to help me like this. I'm sorry for worrying you."

She had him worried, all right. But not, he suspected, in the way her mother wanted.

Three possibilities presented themselves. The first was that some yōkai unknown to him had indeed interfered with this young woman's memories: possibly just clouding them, but more likely eating them. Plenty of yōkai fed on fear or laughter or devotion, and a few of the more dangerous ones consumed the life essence of their victims. No memory-eaters had appeared in any of the scrolls Sekken recalled reading, but admittedly, that would be only fitting.

The second possibility was that Aoi was, for reasons of her own, lying to her family. The mother didn't seem abusive, but Sekken had only observed them for a brief time – or perhaps the abuser was somewhere else in the village. She might, by feigning amnesia, be trying to escape whatever situation she was trapped in.

The third was that she'd become possessed.

"Has she been ill since then?" he asked the mother, who shook her head. "And has she been eating normally?" This time he got a nod.

He'd never seen a case of possession himself, only read about them. Suiko could do it, though they more commonly drained their victims of blood – and there had indeed been such a victim in among the village's dead. Furthermore, Aoi had been found on the banks of the stream, and suiko were a more dangerous kind of kappa, likewise associated with water. Then again, there were other yōkai who fed on blood, so it was no guarantee… especially not when he had another answer ready to hand.

Fox possession was well known throughout Rokugan. It could happen for a number of reasons – one of them being the active malice of a witch.

Aoi's situation didn't match the symptoms of kitsune possession. She had no fever, no odd appetites, and her mother surely would have said something if her appearance had changed. What did possession by an inugami look like, though?

"Let me try something," Sekken said, and went back inside for his satchel.

With the small knife from his writing kit, he cut a narrow strip of paper, appropriately sized for a talisman. Then he wet his brush and wrote on it, *There is nothing magical about this message.*

"Place this under your pillow when you sleep," he said to Aoi. "I fear you are very vulnerable right now, and it may help protect you."

He handed her the strip, politely turned so the writing faced her. Aoi accepted it with a bow. Most of the peasants in Seibo Mura would be illiterate, with only the headman and perhaps a few others knowing enough to handle the necessary records, but those possessed by kitsune sometimes gained the ability to read.

Did her expression flicker as her gaze fell on the message? Even with all his courtly training in reading the behavior of others, he couldn't be sure. If Aoi knew the "ward" was a hoax, she did a very good job of hiding it. The mother immediately knelt in thanks, yanking at her daughter's kimono until she knelt as well. Brushing off their thanks, Sekken escaped as rapidly as he could.

CHAPTER FIVE

Ryōtora had conducted funerals before. He couldn't travel into the hinterlands of the Dragon mountains – places without monks or priests of their own, or "monks" and "priests" with so little education they couldn't even recite a sutra – and not eventually wind up in a situation with a dead body and a spirit that needed to be ushered on to Meido.

Not that he ever touched the bodies. Even the most isolated settlements usually had an outcaste family living on the fringes, tasked with handling all kinds of polluting substances. In the one village that had recently lost its outcastes to disease, he'd been forced to order a peasant man to wash and dress the corpses for cremation and place them on the pyre. Afterward Ryōtora had purified that man along with himself, but he suspected the poor conscript been shunned forevermore by his neighbors.

A difficult situation, and not one Ryōtora had ever felt good about. But the alternative was to break imperial law and risk an unquiet ghost.

At least here the bodies were long gone. The outcaste family had survived, and they had cremated the dead, according to tradition and law. The issue was merely the lack of proper prayers for the spirits of the deceased.

Gathering the names of the dead and their surviving kin, then carrying out the rites, took him much of the day. It was unsettling work in more senses than just the spiritual one; people were tearfully grateful for both his assistance and the assumption that his arrival meant they would now be safe. Meanwhile, he couldn't help wondering if any of the looks he was receiving, any of the whispered conversations outside his hearing, meant that anyone had noticed a resemblance between him and someone in the village. None of the faces struck him as especially familiar – but would he be able to recognize it himself?

That was a personal concern, and far less important than helping these people. At noon Ryōtora stood in the cemetery with the families of the dead gathered around him and recited the sutras, praying the lost spirits on their way to Meido. When the last of the villagers was finally done thanking him, he wanted nothing more than to purify himself and then walk a circuit around the village, looking for signs of the Spirit Realms, before the sun set. To his irritation, though, he turned and found Asako Sekken approaching again.

The fan in the Phoenix's hand and the smooth, gliding stride of a courtier looked wildly out of place in Seibo Mura – though managing the latter while ascending the stone-pocked slope below the graveyard was an impressive achievement. That elegance was a facade, though, as soon became clear.

"Pardon me for troubling you," Sekken said, flicking his fan open and bringing it up to shield his face, "but I think you ought to know. I suspect one of the young women here is possessed."

Ryōtora listened, fighting the urge to pinch the bridge of

his nose, as Sekken described the strange changes in Aoi. All concealed by the fan, as if he feared some gossipy Crane courtier might be watching – and as if the peasants would respect the polite social fiction that said anything which was not seen was also not heard. The ever-present mountain wind was a better shield against eavesdroppers than the fan it nearly blew out of Sekken's hand.

When the Phoenix was done, Ryōtora said, "If she *is* possessed – by a kitsune or anything else – then we should have some sign of it tomorrow, when I put up wards around the village. For now, do nothing to tip her off. Or her family." He wasn't sure whether to be irritated by Sekken's trick with the "talisman," or to applaud his cleverness. Possibly that depended on whether it wound up causing problems, alerting a yōkai that someone was aware of its presence.

"Tomorrow?" Sekken said, more sharply than the word deserved.

Ryōtora's headache was getting worse. "Yes, tomorrow. I'm not going to attempt any wards, or anything else that depends on the goodwill of the kami, until I've purified myself and searched the land around the village for spiritual disturbances. Which I will wind up doing in the dark if you keep me here much longer."

He'd been too curt. It wasn't *that* late in the day, and even an unwanted Phoenix interloper deserved better courtesy than that. Before Ryōtora could apologize, though, Sekken bowed. "Forgive me. I let my eagerness carry me away."

Eagerness wasn't the description Ryōtora would have given it. There was no merit in arguing, though – not when it let them both save face. Ryōtora sighed and said, "No, the apology is mine. I asked you to carry out a task, then failed to thank you for the information you brought. I…"

He couldn't admit to this stranger how much the funeral had cut at him. Ryōtora had only dealt with single losses before, not the massed grief of a village. And even the familiar rhythms of a sutra had failed to distract him from the question pulsing beneath: was he praying for the spirits of his own kin? Were any of the dead women his mother or grandmother, any of the men his father or brother or uncle? Was there some loss he should be mourning more personally?

Isao Keijun is my father. In memory and in law: Ryōtora had been far too young to remember anything of the life he once had in Seibo Mura, and formal adoption meant leaving any previous family behind.

That didn't mean any surviving relatives would feel the same way. And if Sekken found out…

Underneath everything, where he shouldn't even let himself admit to its presence, there was a crawling sense of shame. Shugenja were adopted out of peasant families sometimes; everyone agreed that if the gift of speaking to the kami appeared in such a child, then it was a clear sign of Heaven's favor. Most clans – including the Phoenix – even convinced themselves it was evidence of samurai ancestry a generation or two back, on the wrong side of the blanket. Sekken might be startled to know Ryōtora came from such origins, but he wouldn't be appalled.

Except that adoptions of that kind happened *after* the child displayed the gift. Not with an infant scarcely one year old, too young to speak even to his fellow humans.

That was what made Ryōtora so curt now. The strain of the funeral, not knowing who in the crowd he might be connected to, and then the fear that Sekken might learn the truth. Twin failures, first of the tenet of Honesty, then of Courage. And the fact that hiding the truth was necessary for him to uphold Duty was poor comfort.

He'd been silent too long. Sekken peered at him in concern. "Truly, I wasn't offended. Can I… assist you in your purifications somehow?"

His purifications were going to involve stripping down to his loincloth and standing beneath the waterfall in meditation, waiting for the kami to cleanse him of pollution. The only "assistance" Sekken could offer with that would be–

Ryōtora's pulse skipped in its pace. Hokumei had made a similar offer, once. Except Hokumei had done it deliberately, with the light of mischief dancing in his eyes.

Sekken had no such intention. And it was inappropriate for Ryōtora to even think of such things, when he had so much else that demanded his attention.

He fumbled his way through a refusal, hoping it sounded more polite and less muddled than it did to his own ears. Then he escaped, stopping only long enough to grab the towel from his baggage, before heading up the trail Haru said would take him to the waterfall.

He found a ladle atop a boulder at the waterfall's base, the long-handled sort used to pour water over one's hands and head and rinse out one's mouth. That small purification would be insufficient for him right now, though; he removed his kimono and laid it over another stone, then waded barefoot into the stream.

At least the icy water was good for quelling troublesome impulses. The wind combed the strands of the cascade apart each time it gusted, but enough fell in a steady pattern that Ryōtora was able to find a good spot, balancing atop a slick rock, the water beating on his shoulders until they went numb. He interlaced his fingers in a prayerful mudra, closed his eyes, and focused on letting the water kami wash him clean.

By the time he felt purified, all sensation was gone from his hands and feet. Ryōtora had to step carefully back to shore, lest he slip and hurt himself on the rocks. Even the light breeze made him shiver as he toweled himself dry, and he rubbed more vigorously to restore warmth to his body.

Once he was dressed again, Ryōtora went down to Ogano's house to fetch some supplies, then set out at a brisk pace. From Ogano's descriptions, it sounded like the yōkai were originating from the northeast of Seibo Mura – not surprising, given the negative associations of that direction under the principles of geomancy. If there was some kind of thin spot in the veil between the mortal realm and Senkyō, then finding it and sealing it should put an end to the disturbances.

His ankle began to ache again as he hiked across the slopes surrounding the village, despite frequent pauses to light incense and commune with the local kami, searching for any hint of otherworldly influence. Nothing seemed out of place, and Ryōtora had to wonder if the issue only manifested during the full moon, as that was when the yōkai had attacked before. If so, he'd have to wait for the next round before he could do anything about it – a prospect he didn't relish at all.

The sun was touching the western peaks when he stopped to survey the area. Its light caught something he'd seen from the village: the ruins of a shrine, partway up the southern face of the mountain at whose foot Seibo Mura crouched. Ogano hadn't mentioned anything happening there during the disturbances… but still, Ryōtora couldn't rule out the possibility that it was somehow connected. With a sigh, he bent to tighten the straps on his sandals, then began searching for a route up to the shrine.

It proved to be the same path he'd taken to the waterfall, off to the west of the village. No wonder there was a ladle for purification: the villagers would pause there before continuing upward. Ryōtora passed under a torii arch, leaning semi-drunkenly to one side and propping itself up on a nearby tree. It looked like the work of time and weather, not yōkai malice.

Arriving at the ledge above, he discovered the shrine hadn't been ruined for long. By the looks of it, an earthquake was responsible for its collapse, and likely the state of the torii as well. *Probably the one last fall,* Ryōtora thought – he'd felt that one all the way to the west in Yōmei Machi.

The shrine wasn't large: just two buildings, one of which looked like it had been the hut for the shrinekeeper's family. Half of that second structure had fallen down the mountainside, along with a cascade of stone and earth, leaving the remnants clinging to that portion of the ledge. The other building was presumably the shrine proper, but its roof and walls had caved in.

Where was the shrinekeeper? Ogano hadn't mentioned any such person in his tale. Had they been among the dead Ryōtora prayed for? Or had they perished in the earthquake? It had happened at night, and might have caught them sleeping.

The hairs rose on the back of Ryōtora's neck, and he whirled.

A man was standing at the head of the path. "Sorry. I didn't mean to startle you."

He'd neither leapt back in defense, nor bowed in apology. "Who are you?" Ryōtora asked, his voice harsh with surprise.

"Masa," the man said, after a brief hesitation.

Ryōtora recognized him now. He'd been at the funeral, though which of the dead belonged to him, Ryōtora couldn't recall. Not a yōkai, though. Sekken's concerns over Aoi had gotten to him.

Masa nodded at the shrine. "Fell down last fall. In the earthquake."

"Why haven't you rebuilt it?"

"Meant to," Masa said. He had the laconic speech Ryōtora had heard from a hundred other mountain peasants, as unflappable as the mountains themselves. "Got started on gathering the materials. But we needed things from down south. Ogano was going to get them when he took the late-summer shipment."

Cinnabar and smaller quantities of realgar, mined here and delivered to Heibeisu. According to the governor there, they brought it out twice a year, half the adults of Seibo Mura leaving to drag the caravan of center-wheeled barrows to the city, then returning with the supplies they couldn't make in their own village. "Are you the shrinekeeper?"

Masa shook his head. "Whole family went in the earthquake. Don't worry, though. We had a monk to pray them on, back then."

"And the kami of the shrine?" Ryōtora turned to look once more at the collapsed structure. The murk of twilight was beginning to overtake this area, aided by the trees towering above. "Was anything done for it?"

"We make offerings. Ain't Saiun-nushi causing these problems."

Mount Saiun was the peak on whose slopes Ryōtora stood; Saiun-nushi, therefore, would be the name used here for the kami of the mountain. But that connection was eclipsed by the realization of what was bothering him about Masa's manner: the lack of any hint of deference. Masa didn't seem hostile – much less as confrontational as Ogano had been – but he didn't bow, or use polite speech, or call Ryōtora "my lord," the way he should.

However many followers the Perfect Land Sect had in this village, Ryōtora was willing to bet Masa was one of them.

But he'd also said "*we* make offerings." It wasn't unusual; although what passed for orthodoxy in the sect decried the worship of the Fortunes and other kami, calling for absolute devotion to Shinsei, there were almost as many strands of Perfect Land Shinseism as there were villages practicing it. And many of them thought it only prudent to pay proper reverence to other forces in the world.

Venerating a spirit in a ruined shrine was marginally better than not venerating it at all – but only marginally. Even if Saiun-nushi weren't responsible for the disturbances, it would be less inclined to shield the villagers against them, when its shrine was allowed to stay in this condition. Ryōtora was about to say so when Masa said, "My lord…"

The shift to polite address would have told him this was important, even if the man's posture hadn't. Hesitation and desperation, warring against each other. "Yes?" Ryōtora said.

"My daughter," Masa said. "You… you performed her funeral today."

Ryōtora nodded. "I'm sorry for your loss."

"She ain't dead."

His certainty was as immovable as stone. "It may be difficult to–" Ryōtora began.

Masa cut him off. "I ain't just being hopeful. The outcastes, they didn't burn her body. Because we didn't find it. Others who went missing, we found them. Moro got stolen *after* he died, and something…" He shuddered, looking sick, "… something had been eating him. The people who tried to run, we found them hanging from the trees. But Chie? We never found her."

Ryōtora suppressed a shudder of his own. That might just mean her body was hanging somewhere else... or that whatever yōkai ate part of Moro had finished its meal with Masa's daughter. There was more than one kind of yōkai that found human flesh delectable – the influence of Gaki-dō, the Realm of Hungry Ghosts, bleeding over into the Senkyō realm from which many yōkai came.

"You have to believe me," Masa insisted. "You have to help. She–" He stopped, breathing hard, then abruptly knelt and pressed his forehead to the damp soil. "I'm begging you. Search for her. I don't know what took her, but I doubt it will bring her back."

The agony in his voice cut Ryōtora to the bone. Children were precious everywhere in the world, but nowhere more than in Dragon lands. For a long time now their fertility had been declining, so slowly that it took generations for anyone to notice. Families elsewhere in Rokugan could expect to have four children, five, more – not all of whom would survive childhood, especially not if they were born to the hard life of a peasant, but enough to be sure of their family line continuing. In Dragon lands, they counted it good fortune if they had three, an outright blessing if there were more. And far too many families had only two, or one.

Masa's voice was that of a man who had lost his only child.

Please, Ryōtora prayed to Saiun-nushi, *let him be right. Let her be only missing.* Perhaps she had run away, but unlike the others she'd escaped the yōkai and made it to another village. Or was hardy enough to be surviving in the mountains on her own.

Or she'd slipped through into a Spirit Realm. If the disturbances were caused by an eruption of creatures from Senkyō or Yume-dō into the mortal realm, it would be entirely possible for someone to fall through in the other direction.

At which point a great deal would depend on what she encountered there.

All of that was speculation. "How old is she?" Ryōtora asked.

"Sixteen."

Not a child, then. If she were a samurai, she might have passed her gempuku by now. Old enough to take care of herself. "When did she vanish?"

"On the last night, this past time," Masa said. His face was still downturned, palms pressed against the ground. "Or before. I told her to be home before nightfall, so we could protect ourselves. But she didn't come."

"If she vanished before sunset, then it's more likely that she tried to flee."

Masa shook his head. "We'd talked about it. She didn't want to run. Said we had to stay and help others. And if she changed her mind, she wouldn't have gone without me."

Nothing in Ogano's tale had implied yōkai troubles during the day. But if Sekken was right, there was one in the village right now, possessing Aoi. Ryōtora would have to look into that. Possession would mean the trouble wasn't solely confined to the night hours.

He could ask around to see if anyone had more information to back up Masa's conviction. Or make Sekken do it – assuming he let the Phoenix stay. The risk that Sekken might discover Ryōtora's connection to the village still troubled him.

One thing at a time. First of which was returning to Seibo Mura before night caught him here on the mountainside. The light was fading rapidly, and the trees veiled the path in shadow.

"Stand," Ryōtora said, and Masa complied. "Lead me back down to the village, and tell me more about your daughter."

CHAPTER SIX

The second night, like the first, passed without incident.

That shouldn't have bothered Sekken. If anything, he ought to have been glad for the undisturbed sleep, and relieved that whatever sent the inugami to plague him had – perhaps – given up.

But he remembered his childhood nurse commenting that she had always been most concerned when his sisters fell silent. That was inevitably a sign that they were up to some scheme which would cause a mess, get someone hurt, or both. The cessation of the haunting didn't feel like a reprieve; it felt like the next stage beginning.

At least I'll face that stage well rested.

This time he didn't surprise the headman's wife when he came out into the living area, but she still didn't have breakfast ready. Sekken went for another walk, hoping the bright morning air would clear his head and leave behind a plan for how to find the witch. Even if it was true that Aoi was possessed, and even if that possession was the fault of someone in the village, it didn't tell him how to find the culprit. Possibly Aoi herself could do that, once she'd been restored to herself – but possibly not.

In the meanwhile, he had more people to interview. With no sign of Ryōtora even after his breakfast, Sekken gathered his writing kit and paper and sallied forth to find the peasants he'd not gotten to the day before, because of the funerals.

He soon formed the opinion that a rural village was every bit as much of a brewing-vat for interpersonal drama as any samurai court. The only difference was how willing people were to admit it. Samurai carried out their affairs discreetly, with poetry written on scrolls whose paper and sticks were selected to elegantly inflect the message they carried; here, one peasant told Sekken to his face that Kuwa would untie her kimono for any man who brought her a gift. Which might be true, because supposedly one of her frequent lovers was Ashio, the man he'd interviewed yesterday, who'd been driven half-mad by the laughter of a kerakera onna – the yōkai more often associated with red lantern districts. When Sekken found Kuwa near the well, he saw her hair was chopped short, and he asked if it had been cut off by a kamikiri; she responded by hurling her bucket at a passing woman and shrieking that "that hag" had done it out of jealousy. Said hag proved to be the alleged lover's wife, and Sekken was doing his best to keep the two of them apart when Ryōtora's approach quelled the fight.

"Thank you," Sekken said, once peace had been restored. "I'm afraid I haven't quite finished gathering stories. I keep running into… interruptions."

Ryōtora shook his head. "That isn't why I came. Does your scholarship extend to things other than yōkai?"

"Many," Sekken said, grinning. "You'll have to be more specific."

Needling the Dragon shugenja wasn't wise. Something about that stiff bearing, though, just *begged* to be prodded a little.

Sekken's parents and teachers had dutifully instilled a sense of propriety in him, but he also knew that strict adherence to the tenets of Bushidō often made people inflexible – and that which couldn't bend was at risk of breaking. Not that he wanted to tempt Ryōtora into misbehavior; just that it might be good for the man if he smiled every now and again.

The faint compression of Ryōtora's fine mouth was more likely to be him tamping down a scowl than a smile. "The enshrinement rituals for a kami."

Sekken hadn't expected that line of inquiry, and it sobered him. "Are you hoping to enshrine a Fortune here for defense? That will be difficult if you aren't carrying it from an existing site. And all of those are far enough away that you won't get back here before the next full moon."

"An existing site, yes – but not like that." Ryōtora turned and lifted his chin, pointing at the ruined shrine Sekken had noticed the previous day. "That's the shrine to Saiun-nushi, the kami of the mountain. The villagers have gone on making offerings since it collapsed, but I think the kami should be moved to another location until that one can be rebuilt."

That place was supposedly still in use? Given its wrecked state, Sekken had assumed it was long abandoned. From a distance, it looked like an old ruin. "Is that the cause of everything here? The kami's anger?"

A thin line pleated the skin between Ryōtora's brows. "I don't think so – the timing is wrong. The collapse happened well before any of this began. But before I try to ward this place, I think the kami should be taken care of."

"Why ask me for help, and not the shrinekeeper?"

"Because the shrinekeeper is dead."

Like so many others. The amusement left over from the tale of the kerakera onna and the jealous wife burned away like mist. In his scholarly fascination with the range of yōkai showing up in Seibo Mura, Sekken had lost sight of the terrible suffering inflicted on this place.

All the terrible suffering I'm familiar with took place centuries ago. And none of it prepared him for dealing with a problem that was current and very likely to return.

But the question at hand wasn't quite Ryōtora's specialty, either. A shugenja he might be, but his kind were trained to invoke the elemental kami, the little spirits of earth, water, air, and fire, which were relatively easy to propitiate. More powerful spirits like that of the mountain were less predictable, and harder to work with. Sekken asked, "Will Saiun-nushi answer you?"

"I will do my best."

In hindsight, he could have predicted that answer without bothering to ask.

The patient hope in Ryōtora's eyes both buoyed Sekken and weighed him down. For the second time since arriving in this village, his knowledge might be useful… but that meant someone *expected* him to be useful.

He scraped together his knowledge, hoping it would be enough. "Then you have two ways to do this. One is to create a daughter shrine – in essence, to leave the kami where it is, but also to enshrine it somewhere else, and have everyone make their offerings there." Sekken paused as an idea came to him. "Even if the collapse happened a while ago, there's a chance it's specifically the kami's ara-mitama that's causing this. I have to imagine the roof caving in didn't do anything good for the geomantic balance there. Perhaps the problem has built up over time."

The line between Ryōtora's brows was still there. "Part of the ledge fell… it's possible. Are you suggesting we enshrine the ara-mitama separately?"

It wouldn't be unheard of. The rougher, more violent part of a kami's spirit had been known to cause problems, and providing it with its own shrine often eased that tension. But Sekken frowned, finding the flaw in his own reasoning. "That would leave the nigi-mitama neglected back in the original shrine, though. Right when they need its protection the most." Even if Saiun-nushi wasn't causing the disturbances, the villagers were going to want to petition its harmonious side for aid. "You could still try to propagate its spirit into a new shrine. But if the point is to get it out of the collapsed building, you're better off moving it entirely. Have you ever done that before?"

Ryōtora's jaw tightened. Then he said, "I know the principles. But… no."

The uncertainty in Ryōtora's low voice was for Sekken alone, and it startled him. It seemed wholly at odds with the man's unyielding demeanor. But Ryōtora forging ahead as if he knew exactly what he was doing could add to the village's troubles, if he made a mistake and angered the kami of the mountain. And who else could he share his doubts with? He could hardly show any such weakness to the people he was trying to protect.

That gesture of trust touched Sekken, even if the only reason for it was that he was the only other samurai for miles in any direction. He just wished it didn't remind him of the limitations of his own knowledge. He'd never re-enshrined a kami, any more than Ryōtora had.

Then an idea came to him. "You don't mean it to be a permanent move, do you? Only until the shrine can be rebuilt."

"Presuming it gets rebuilt at all," Ryōtora said. "If I can't put an end to the disturbances this next full moon…"

A moment before, he'd said *we*. Now it was back to *I*. But Sekken could hardly fault the man for taking the responsibilities onto his own shoulders, when they were in Dragon Clan lands. While Sekken's idea wouldn't remove that burden, he hoped it might take a little weight off. "Then just treat it like a festival."

He'd confused Ryōtora. The shugenja frowned, opening his mouth to ask how that could work – and then understanding dawned. "You mean, not removing it from its current shintai and putting it into a new one."

"Moving the shintai itself," Sekken confirmed. "Just like you would do for a festival. If the village has a portable shrine, you could even leave it inside there."

"Or build a hokora." Ryōtora was still looking at Sekken, but his attention had gone straight through. Probably envisioning the small shrines that decorated the edges of roads throughout Rokugan and clung to the outskirts of larger shrines, especially in rural areas. "I'd want to protect it, though. Set up a sacred enclosure around it."

"Then you'll need rope, and… hmmm. You're unlikely to find a sakaki here; wrong climate." Those trees were hard enough to find in the milder weather of Phoenix lands, and usually grew in groves tended by shugenja who could keep the atmosphere warm enough for them.

"Cypress," Ryōtora said. "It's common around here."

Some courtiers prized the subtle dueling of poetry or wit. Sekken had always preferred the back-and-forth of ideas, unraveling some puzzle or developing a new theory. This was the first time he'd experienced that dance where its end result would be practical, and he couldn't hold in a smile. Ryōtora's demeanor didn't crack nearly so far, but the tension that seemed to always wind him tight eased a bit. Sekken wondered if it ever went away entirely, or if Ryōtora's concern for propriety always kept him on edge.

Perhaps after these troubles ended, Sekken would have the chance to find out. Always assuming he didn't get thrown out of Dragon lands, when someone noticed he wasn't where he was supposed to be.

"Thank you," Ryōtora said. "Can I ask you to look into whether they have a portable shrine? And rope. I could try to salvage from the current shrine, but I'd rather disturb the site as little as possible."

"Where can I find you, once I know the answer to that?"

"If you'll tell me which one is Aoi's house, I thought I might go examine her."

"It's–" Sekken stopped himself before he could give directions. "Not very pleasant in there. If you'd prefer, I can go find her, and bring her to the headman's house."

Ryōtora brushed the offer away. "There's no need. An examination at Ogano's will attract attention, and if she's lost her memories I imagine she's had enough of people whispering around her. If she's possessed, as you suspect, then I would prefer not to endanger my host."

And I'd prefer you to examine her somewhere I can see. If Ryōtora succeeded in driving the possessing spirit out of Aoi, Sekken wanted to observe every detail: whether it was an inugami, whether it fled in a particular direction, whether it could give him any clues to his own situation.

But he didn't want to say any of that. The fight between Kuwa and her lover's jealous wife was only one of the points of tension he'd observed while questioning the villagers; unsurprisingly, Seibo Mura was boiling over with suspicion, each peasant wondering if their neighbor was responsible for everyone's misfortunes. Small sins that would have passed unremarked in normal times now became cause for blame. One man accused his rival of stealing more than his share of barley from the granary; another told Sekken that his cousin habitually left the doors on his family altar open at night. The last thing Sekken wanted to do was give anyone a foothold for suspecting his own connection to witchcraft.

So he merely said, "Let me show you the way."

En route to Aoi's house, he thought of a path toward his real suspicion, without going directly at it. "Has it occurred to you that there might be an untutored shugenja in the village? This place is so remote that few samurai would have passed through, but it's always possible."

The path was rough, with great depressions where something unspeakably heavy seemed to have hopped along. Ryōtora stumbled and almost lurched into Sekken before righting himself. "My apologies. My sandal caught against a stone."

"It's quite all right. I know it's an indelicate thing for me to imply." Did Ryōtora have a by-blow of his own somewhere? The touch of relaxation that had come when they discussed moving the kami of the mountain was gone as if it had never been.

Ryōtora said, "I will keep that possibility in mind, but I doubt it."

"The gift is rare, it's true," Sekken mused. "But that doesn't rule out other ways to disturb the spiritual atmosphere."

"If you are suggesting again that the Perfect Land Sect is responsible for this, then I will remind you again–"

"Not that," Sekken said. He still didn't agree with Ryōtora's certainty, but that wasn't the target he aimed for. "Merely that there could be other… unorthodox practices here. The rural areas of Rokugan hold many superstitions a proper priest would frown at. Even things picked up from Yobanjin. We aren't that far from their lands." In theory contact with the northern barbarians was strictly limited, and the mountains certainly presented a substantial barrier – but not an impermeable one.

"I will consider it," Ryōtora said stiffly. "We are near the edge of the village. Which house is it?"

"Oh! This one." Sekken indicated the house to their left, and Ryōtora bowed in thanks.

Also in dismissal. There was no graceful way around it; Sekken either had to walk away or speak up. "Would you mind if I stayed? I know you asked me to inquire about materials for moving the shintai, but…" He hesitated, feigning a degree of embarrassment. Or rather, feigning a different reason for the embarrassment he actually felt. "The mother wanted so much for me to help her daughter. I know I can't do anything, not like you – but I'd like to offer what help I can."

At first he thought Ryōtora was going to refuse. But Sekken could practically read the scroll of the other man's thoughts: the tag on the scroll said *Bushidō,* and it was unfurling past the headers for *Courtesy* and *Compassion.*

"Very well," Ryōtora said, and knocked on the weathered wood of the door.

CHAPTER SEVEN

Ryōtora was surprised that Sekken wanted to assist with Aoi. The man clearly wasn't accustomed to spending time in rural villages, or interacting with peasants outside of the clearly structured confines of a servant's duties; he kept referring to Haru as "the headman's wife," though Ryōtora had used her name several times in his hearing. The sudden concern was unexpected enough that Ryōtora wondered briefly if Aoi had caught the courtier's eye.

She was pretty enough for it, he supposed. Not the polished beauty of a court lady, but the simple, fresh appeal of youth and health. If Sekken was attracted to her, though, he hid it extraordinarily well – so well, in fact, that he made no real attempt to interact with either Aoi or her mother, Fūyō. He merely stood to one side, hands tucked inside his sleeves, as Ryōtora introduced himself.

Which meant that responsibility for explaining the situation fell to Ryōtora. After some consideration, he chose not to say outright that Aoi might be possessed; that seemed too likely to make everyone panic. Instead he said, "You must have noticed how many people in the village are sick right now. Many yōkai can cause fevers and other illnesses – and in some cases, the illness is actually caused by something the yōkai places *in* the body."

"Or a yōkai that literally goes into the body," Sekken offered, in the exact opposite of helpfulness. "There are creatures, like small bugs–"

"Thank you, Lord Asako," Ryōtora said quellingly. When the Phoenix fell silent, abashed, he turned back to Aoi and Fūyō. "My point is, if something like this has happened here, then removing the influence of the yōkai might restore your daughter's memories."

The mother tried to bow to the floor, but Ryōtora caught her before she could. "Please, don't thank me for anything yet. This is just a theory. In order to test it, I will need to examine her."

Aoi promptly offered up one slender wrist for him to take her pulse. Ryōtora pulled his sleeve over his hand, for propriety, then laid his fingers on her skin, but it was mostly for show. He was no physician, able to diagnose blockages of *ki* or elemental imbalances from the subtleties of someone's pulse. The physical signs of possession he was looking for were the things Sekken had asked about already – changes of appearance or appetite; a sudden ability to read – and one other thing, which he could think of no delicate way to bring up.

If delicacy proved impossible, he would simply have to be direct. Releasing Aoi's wrist, Ryōtora said, "Sometimes these ailments leave signs on the body. I... will need to look at your skin."

The contrast between the mother's reaction and the daughter's could not have been more stark. Aoi promptly reached for the sash binding her kimono, while Fūyō flung herself between them, arms outstretched so that her sleeves formed a wall. "*My lord!*"

Ryōtora bowed his head. "You have my word that I mean nothing inappropriate by this request. Of course you will be permitted to oversee the process, so that you can be certain of your daughter's safety. I will keep my hands covered throughout. And we can conduct the examination discreetly, so that no one in the village spreads any gossip about this matter." In a rural settlement like this one, bathing was probably done communally, without any separation of genders – at least, it would have been before their hot spring failed. But nakedness in a routine context was very different from nakedness in an unusual one.

Aoi put one hand on her mother's shoulder. "It's all right. The samurai is a respectable man. I am grateful that he's offering to help."

Fūyō's jaw set in a mulish line, but in a contest between her sense of propriety and her concern for her daughter's well-being, the latter won out.

The real problem turned out to be lighting. Inside the house was far too dim for Ryōtora to see what he was looking for. Outside, of course, all the world would be able to see. "The headman's house?" Sekken suggested, but Ryōtora shook his head. There was no faster way to ensure that the whole village would know.

"Just tell her what to look for," Fūyō said. "I'll look anywhere she can't see herself."

If Ryōtora had trusted Aoi to report honestly, that would have been a good solution. Should she truly be possessed, though, she had every reason to lie. And the mark was capable of moving – in fact, that was part of what identified it as a mark of possession. Aoi wasn't acting like someone with a fox inside her, but Sekken was right; something about her behavior seemed off. She was too calm, too elegant in her speech and movements. Ryōtora was tempted to try exorcising her anyway, just to see if it helped. Any such action, though, would leave her stained for life in the eyes of her fellow villagers. He didn't want to do that unless it was necessary.

Finally he said, "We'll just have to build up the fire in here. It will be hot, but you'll only have to endure it for a little while."

Aoi smiled shyly. "Well, at least I won't be wearing a lot of clothes."

Her mother smacked her shoulder for the impertinent joke and went to gather firewood. Ryōtora sang softly for a moment, offering his melody to the air kami, and asked them to waft as much of the smoke as possible upward, so it wouldn't sting his eyes. "Shall I stand guard outside the door?" Sekken offered.

"That will only draw more attention," Ryōtora said. Aoi had already unfastened her kimono and stood with it loosely clasped about her, waiting for the firelight. "But if you insist on staying, then perhaps face the wall."

One of Sekken's eyebrows arched. "Am I not also a respectable man?"

He didn't seem like the sort to leer. Too preoccupied with knowledge, perhaps, to the point where he lost sight of the feelings of others, peasants especially – but that was hardly uncommon among scholars. Ryōtora used to chide Hokumei about that. His lover had never understood why Ryōtora took it so personally.

Until the day he *did* understand.

Ryōtora said, "This is not about your virtue, but the dignity of the patient. And Fūyō's peace of mind."

Sekken acknowledged this with a bow. When Fūyō returned, he faced the door without complaint, ready to intervene if someone should try to enter unexpectedly.

Feeding the fire one branch at a time, Ryōtora encouraged the fire kami to blaze up, the air kami to carry their smoke away. Soon the inside of the house was stifling, and his under-kimono began to stick to his skin. He almost envied Aoi when she slipped off her own clothing and stood bare next to the fire.

"Please be quick, my lord," Fūyō muttered.

It would hardly be polite to tell her his only interest in her daughter's body was intellectual. Ryōtora removed a pair of silk gloves from his sleeve, pulled them on, and took one of Aoi's arms, running his hands over her skin. Her other arm curled protectively across her breasts – but he didn't think she was truly embarrassed. Instead it was more elegance, drawing attention to her unclothed state by the feeble attempt to cover it.

In short, she was attempting to be flirtatious.

The only thing to do with that was to ignore it. Ryōtora kept his demeanor impassive as he searched her back, her other arm, her legs. Aoi was pliable in his hands. At no point did she turn oddly, as if trying to keep something out of sight. He also kept watch out of the corner of his eye, looking to see if anything slid away from his gaze. That was one of the most undeniable signs of possession: a migratory lump under the skin, which slipped out of any attempt to grip it, and fled if pricked with something sharp.

But he found nothing. Fūyō, watching like a hawk, said nothing. And Aoi – who ought to be worried about this, if she truly did have a kitsune or some other yōkai possessing her – was cooperative throughout.

"There is no sign of a foreign presence," he said at last.

Fūyō wasted not an instant in flinging the kimono back over her daughter's shoulders. Aoi, of course, took her time in donning it once more. "What does this mean?" Fūyō asked.

Ryōtora wished he had an answer to that question. "In one way, this is good news, as it means there isn't a yōkai present outside the nights of the full moon. So you need not fear the attacks resuming any time soon. But it does mean your daughter's memories haven't been restored. I have plans for helping to restore spiritual balance in Seibo Mura; together we can pray to Saiun-nushi to help her."

Aoi touched her mother's shoulder again. "Would you get me some fresh water from the stream? I am parched, after this heat."

Since her daughter was fully clothed again, Fūyō said, "Yes, of course. Pull the fire apart, so we can save some of the wood for later." She hurried out the door.

No sooner had she departed than Aoi folded herself gracefully to the floor. "I know you say the yōkai will not return yet – but I don't feel safe here. Please, I beg you, take me away from this place."

Ryōtora bent to lift her to her feet, and was unsurprised when she clung to his arms after that was done. "I understand your fears, and I promise you, I'm doing everything I can to make certain you and your family will be protected." Should he tell her that he'd been considering evacuating the entire village? No – he still wasn't sure that was a good idea, or if it would only bring the danger down on their heads while they were caught in the open. "I will be warding Seibo Mura before the full moon. And Lord Asako is a scholar of such matters; he knows many things about yōkai, and can no doubt suggest other defenses, specific to the creatures you've faced."

A sidelong glance elicited a nod from Sekken, but Aoi wasn't looking at him. Her gaze was fixed on Ryōtora. "I could never trust an outsider as much as a Dragon samurai."

Sekken made a small, miffed noise. Ryōtora pried Aoi's hands off his arms and said, "Then trust me. I will keep you safe."

He infused his voice with as much confidence as he could. Doubts had no place here; admitting to them would only weaken his resolve. He'd been given a gift he did not deserve, when Isao Keijun took him out of this village: however much his adoptive father spoke of spiritual merit raising him to the rank of samurai, Ryōtora knew that if he had truly deserved to hold that status, he would have been born to a samurai family. The only thing he could do was to strive his absolute utmost to live honorably – and if that meant dying honorably in pursuit of his duty, then so be it. Perhaps in his next lifetime, the Fortune of Death would make him a samurai in truth.

Aoi bit her lip. Then new words burst from her. "There's a mahō-tsukai in the village."

Ryōtora's bones turned to ice.

"Ogano doesn't want anyone to know," she said. "He's afraid of a panic. But I heard him talking about it to Masa – during the last full moon, one of the corpses got up and was moving around. And everyone knows some of the bodies have been drained of blood. Even if the yōkai don't come back for days, you can't leave me trapped here with someone using mahō."

It felt like someone had placed the tip of a spear between Ryōtora's shoulderblades. He was afraid to turn and look at Sekken… but Fear was one of the Three Sins, and he had to look eventually.

But the Phoenix didn't look angry, or implacable, or any of the things Ryōtora feared and expected. Instead he seemed skeptical. "Did they say it was mahō?" he asked. Aoi nodded vigorously. Still, Sekken only frowned in doubt. "It could be, I suppose. If that were the case, though, I'd expect something other than an eruption of yōkai that for the most part have no connection at all to Jigoku. And it doesn't require mahō to explain what Ogano saw; quite a few yōkai drink blood. Some of them even animate corpses. Bakeneko, for one."

Aoi clenched her fists. "How can you take this so lightly?"

That was what Ryōtora wanted to ask. If Sekken was an Inquisitor, he'd expect the man to react far more strongly to any hint of blasphemous magic in Seibo Mura. But Sekken merely shrugged. "I've been gathering reports from your neighbors for the last two days. They're all afraid, and mahō is a common bogeyman. Don't misunderstand me; if that *is* the problem here, then I'm very worried indeed. Look at it from another angle, though: if that's the work of a mahō-tsukai, then you have both a mass of rampaging yōkai, *and* someone who has somehow figured out forbidden magic. Because I don't see how the latter can explain the former. But the former can explain the latter, as I've already said."

His voice was calm – almost distracted, as if half his attention was on tracing out the lines of possibility within his own mind. Then Sekken came back to himself, and although Ryōtora had done his best to keep his thoughts from his expression, whatever Sekken saw there caused his attention to sharpen.

Ryōtora turned away before Sekken could say anything more. "Aoi. Speak to no one of this. I will look into it – I take your fears seriously – but I agree with Ogano; we cannot have you starting a panic. It would be all too easy for your neighbors to begin seeing each other as the enemy. Right now we need everyone working together against this problem, not tearing themselves apart. Do you understand?"

Grudgingly, she bowed.

Ryōtora left the house before Fūyō could return with more demands that he help her daughter. He set off with a rapid stride, but not fast enough to prevent Sekken from catching up with him.

"What was that?" the Phoenix asked. He sounded more bewildered than angry. "The look you gave me in there – I know you'd prefer I weren't here, but I truly am trying to help you. Poor though I may be at that."

They were close enough to the edge of the village that nobody was able to listen in. Ryōtora halted and said, "Someone brings up the possibility of mahō, with a Phoenix 'scholar of spiritual matters' standing right there, and you're surprised I was concerned?"

Sekken goggled. His response came out in a strangled whisper. "You… What, you thought I was an *Inquisitor*?" The disbelieving laugh that followed dragged his voice up to normal levels. "I'm a layabout scholar from a wealthy family whose elder sisters have already taken care of our political needs, leaving me free to spend my time reading and calling it 'work.' My knowledge of mahō ends at being able to tell you the Battle of Stolen Graves was in the sixth century. The year 510, to be precise."

Of course he corrected his own imprecision. Courtiers were good at bending their words, but Ryōtora had no doubt that Sekken was being absolutely sincere: he was a mere scholar. Not someone following rumors of disturbances as part of a duty to stamp out Jigoku-tainted blasphemy.

The tension inside Ryōtora had been growing like a bow bent to its fullest draw, but now that archer eased his grip. "I… The possibility of mahō occurred to me yesterday. And if that's what is going on here…"

"Then it might be necessary to obliterate the entire village and everyone in it. I understand." Sekken's hair had fallen in his eyes; he brushed it away with one long-fingered hand. "I meant what I said, though. It wasn't just to reassure that girl. This *could* be blood magic, but it could also just be yōkai."

"Aoi," Ryōtora said. "Her name is Aoi."

Sekken blinked in surprise. "I know."

"You know, but you almost never use their names. The headman is Ogano. His wife is Haru. Aoi's mother is Fūyō. Peasants may not hold as high a place in the Celestial Order as samurai, but they are not faceless creatures, either."

"No, if they were faceless, they'd be nopperabō." Sekken grinned at his own yōkai humor, then sobered when Ryōtora remained impassive. "Yes, of course. I… Well, to be honest, I'm accustomed to spending my time in libraries. So either in cities, or in monasteries. Not rural mining villages with no monks, and you the only samurai in sight."

Ryōtora said dryly, "I couldn't tell."

A delighted smile spread across Sekken's mouth. "Did you just make a joke?"

That riposte was the kind of thing Ryōtora might have said to Hokumei; it had slipped out without him thinking. But Sekken wasn't Hokumei. For one thing, Hokumei would have reacted much more harshly to the suggestion that mahō might be at work in Seibo Mura.

Kitsuki Hokumei had seemed so light-hearted and jovial when they first met. It had taken some time before Ryōtora realized that Hokumei's manner hid an astonishingly sharp mind, even by the standards of his lineage. When their mutual attraction brought them together… Ryōtora realized that eventually Hokumei would put together the clues of his past. He'd thought it better to admit the truth first.

Perhaps it *had* been better. But it still hadn't saved him from the flaying edge of Hokumei's condemnation.

Sekken's alarmed words broke him from that reverie. "Sir Ryōtora, forgive me. I shouldn't have called your words into question."

Ryōtora managed a shake of his head. "No, no. You said nothing wrong. Only my own thoughts, weighing on me."

It wasn't fair to Sekken, comparing him to Hokumei, letting the bitter taste of that memory stain him as well. The Phoenix was not Ryōtora's lover, and never would be. Once or twice Ryōtora had caught Sekken's gaze lingering on him… but even if Sekken's interests inclined in his direction, such diversions were a luxury Ryōtora couldn't afford. All his energy was – had to be – devoted to Seibo Mura and its problems.

Even once that was dealt with, he would not merit such attention. Not in this lifetime.

With delicate diffidence, Sekken asked, "Is there anything I can do to lighten those thoughts?"

Ryōtora clenched and relaxed his hands, then straightened his back. "Whether Aoi is right or not, I think the priority must still be dealing with Saiun-nushi. Once that's done, I can ward the village."

"So I need to go ask about the portable shrine," Sekken said, nodding. "Also rope. I remember. And I'll write up a list for you of what I've learned so far. Not all of the yōkai have weaknesses that I'm aware of, but some of them do. Maybe there will be a pattern amid the chaos, once I have the list in front of me." He sounded astonishingly eager.

"Thank you," Ryōtora said, and bowed deeply. "Whatever trick of karma brought you to this place, I am glad not to be dealing with this threat on my own."

CHAPTER EIGHT

Seibo Mura *used* to have a portable shrine.

It wasn't the kind of thing Sekken had imagined. He was used to enormous palanquins, larger than a cart and so heavy they took dozens of men to carry, carved on every surface and painted in a riot of colors. In hindsight, he should have realized this village wouldn't have anything like that; it would have required practically every able-bodied adult to shift, and nobody would have been able to get it down the mountain path even so.

But all of that was a moot point, since the shrine was now a pile of splintered kindling.

"The headman told me it was smashed on the last night of the first full moon," Sekken told Ryōtora after viewing the wreckage. "Ogano. My apologies."

He still wasn't sure why the issue of names affected Ryōtora so deeply. It was perfectly polite to refer to someone by their title – though Sekken admitted to himself that manners hadn't been at the forefront of his mind, and perhaps he had taken it a little far. But the look on the man's face when Sekken made that joke about nopperabō… as if Sekken had somehow wounded him personally.

Perhaps Ryōtora had a peasant lover? Or more than one, given that he'd said his duties took him through many villages. No, not that; Sekken couldn't imagine anyone so upstanding visiting a string of lovers as he traveled, whatever their rank might be. Or even a single one – not when that would mean allowing himself to stray from the path of duty. He'd displayed not the slightest shred of interest in Aoi, even as the girl all but threw herself at him.

Whatever the reason, Sekken was making an effort to use the villagers' names more often. He certainly knew a great many of them, after collecting their tales. One of the exercises from his training days had involved being introduced to a room full of his fellow students, all with invented names, and having to recite them back to his sensei afterward; this was a much larger list, but the association of names with yōkai incidents made them far easier to remember.

Ryōtora had looked discouraged at the news of the broken shrine, but now his brow furrowed. "Targeted destruction, do you think? Did the yōkai specifically aim to break it?"

"I don't think so," Sekken said. "They were smashing a great many things that night. Nothing I've heard yet suggests that they made a deliberate effort to go after it. Ogano kept it here in the village, rather than up at the shrine proper, because there was no room to store it up there; everything else in that storehouse got smashed too."

Targeted or otherwise, it presented a problem. Ryōtora said, "Without a portable shrine…"

Sekken shrugged. "How fancy does it have to be? They have carpenters here, I'm sure. You focus on preparing for the ritual, and I'll see how fast they can build a new one."

Ogano directed him to the village carpenter. On his way to the man's house, Sekken tried to recall why the name was familiar. It wasn't on the list of people he'd interviewed. As he lifted his hand to knock on the door, he remembered: Masa was the one Ryōtora had told him about, who claimed his daughter Chie had been taken by the yōkai.

Then Masa opened the door, and Sekken realized something else. Masa was one of the two men he'd seen working on the mill's broken waterwheel – and chanting the kie while he did so.

Sekken forced himself not to frown. By now it was clear that at least half the village sought the Perfect Land, if not more; he could hardly avoid working with them. "Are you the carpenter Masa?"

A wary nod was his only response. Sekken continued, saying, "Your headman Ogano told me where you live. You may have heard that Sir Ryōtora is planning to move Saiun-nushi down to a temporary shrine here in the village? But the portable shrine is broken, so we need something to carry the shintai."

Already he was making plans for what to do when Masa refused. Some followers of the Perfect Land became reckless, even actively suicidal, because their lives were so wretched that the paradise they believed Shinsei had created for them was far preferable to anything in the mortal realm. Given the troubles in Seibo Mura, Sekken wouldn't be surprised if people here were beginning to think in similar terms… or were simply uninclined to do anything a samurai said.

But just as the silence stretched out to an unbearable point, Masa nodded. His pause hadn't been reluctance; it had been him thinking. "Got some beams that will work for the base. Won't be hard to split some panels for the walls. Decoration, though –

that's harder. Don't want Saiun-nushi being offended because it's too plain."

Sekken's surprise must have shown, which was a shocking lapse on his part. Masa cocked his head to one side. "You thought I wouldn't help?"

Calling it out like that was rude – but what else could Sekken expect from a man whose greeting bow had scarcely been more than a nod? And apparently the rough atmosphere of Seibo Mura was getting to Sekken, because he chose to answer with similar directness. "I know you seek the Perfect Land. I'll admit I'm surprised to find a man of your spiritual inclinations showing such attention to the worship of a mountain kami."

"Believing in Shinsei's promise don't make offending a kami any less stupid. Particularly at a time like this."

"But your leader discourages or even outright forbids the veneration of the Fortunes," Sekken pointed out.

"What leader?"

The unexpectedness of that question left Sekken briefly at a loss for words. True, the Perfect Land was much less centralized than the orthodox orders of Shinseism; it had no monasteries, no ranked hierarchy of monks. But it did have a leader, the inheritor of the erroneous sutra that laid out the details of Shinsei's supposed promise. "You – How can you not be aware of this? How did your beliefs come to this village, anyway?"

Masa's one-shouldered shrug dismissed the question. "Been here since before I was born. I think somebody brought the kie back from Heibeisu, a long time ago. The kie is all we need; don't see how a leader would help much with that."

This barely even qualified as *religion*. Sekken might not like the Perfect Land Sect, might condemn their beliefs as heretical…

but Masa and his neighbors seemed to have reduced it to nothing more than mere superstition. He supposed it was preferable to them all becoming suicidal in the hopes of an escape from their woes, but his scholarly soul was offended by the sheer lack of rigor.

Masa clearly considered the topic over and done with. He scratched his ear and said, "Where are the broken pieces? Want to make sure I get the size right. Nawaro was the one who always put the shintai in and took it out again. Never seen it myself."

Nawaro, Sekken presumed, was the dead shrinekeeper. He would be the only person permitted to interact directly with the shintai – and even then, the divine vessel would be wrapped in fabric or encased in a box, hidden from touch and view.

Assuming the people of Seibo Mura managed to get that much right. At this point, Sekken was prepared to believe they might throw any point of tradition or orthodoxy off a cliff.

He led Masa to the ruins of the storehouse where the portable shrine had been kept. Once the fragments were laid on the open ground in something approximating their original configuration, Masa measured them with his gnarled, heavy-knuckled hands, mumbling under his breath. Sekken made a point of standing far enough back that he couldn't hear whether it was numbers he was committing to memory, or a chant of *Shoshi ni kie*.

To distract himself, he gazed around the village. They were beginning to get some onlookers – including Aoi, who appeared to have escaped Fūyō's grip. She was watching Masa work with an unreadable expression on her face.

Sekken trusted that Ryōtora would have found the telltale lump, had there been one. Still, he couldn't shake the feeling that there was more wrong with Aoi than just her lost memories. When she'd begged to be taken away before the next full moon, she hadn't said a word about the safety of her mother and brother. It might just be the unconcern of someone who couldn't remember her life with her ostensible family… but it bothered him.

He'd forgotten to use his peripheral vision instead of looking directly. When Aoi noticed Sekken watching her, she slipped away.

Masa finished his measurements and straightened up, noticing his neighbors gathered around. Raising his voice, he said, "Saiun-nushi's going to need another home. If you got something carved that ain't broken – or even if it is – bring it here."

A murmur ran around the scattering of people, and several of them set off immediately. When Sekken was gathering stories, he'd noticed that for all their general poverty the villagers had a surprising amount of decoration on their belongings. Crude work most of the time, by the standards of samurai art, but some of it was remarkably fine. And the splintered pieces of the portable shrine had also been carved.

Masa had one of those pieces in his hand. Holding it up for Sekken to examine, he said by way of explanation, "Winter here gets long."

And the villagers apparently got bored. One by one, they began to return, bearing tables and chests and rakes and other tools Sekken couldn't even identify, all of them carved to one degree or another, even if it was only with a cross-hatching of lines or curved shapes suggesting flowers. Masa sorted through them, nodding at some and dismissing others.

Sekken stood out of the way, feeling simultaneously useless and like it was his responsibility to oversee the process, even though he knew nothing about carpentry. Which more or less summed up how he'd felt since arriving in Seibo Mura – no, since meeting Ryōtora. He'd come here only wanting an explanation for – and an end to – his inugami haunting, but seeing Ryōtora work to help people made him want to do the same.

The only things he'd managed to contribute so far, though, were his skills as a scribe and a dead-end suspicion regarding Aoi. He wanted to do more. When Ryōtora thanked him outside Aoi's house… for a moment, it had made Sekken feel like his efforts mattered. Like *he* mattered. Unlike the rest of his family, he didn't manage a famous library or advise an important daimyō or protect the life of an Isawa shugenja with his blade, but he'd found a place where his knowledge could be of real, practical use.

Maybe of enough use that Ryōtora would even smile for once.

The wind brought shreds of a conversation to his ears. Two women whispered a short distance away as they watched Masa work. Sympathy for the carpenter… and that gave Sekken an idea.

He had no notion how to track someone taken by a yōkai. Plenty of them were kidnappers, usually targeting either children or young women; unfortunately, in many cases the reason to steal them away was to eat them. Days had passed since Chie's disappearance, so the odds that she was still alive were low. Still, he could at least try to establish whether the man was right – whether Chie might have survived that night.

According to Ryōtora, the last time Masa had seen his daughter was before sunset on the final night. By then the villagers knew they would have to barricade themselves in for safety, or the best approximation of it they could manage. Chie, however, hadn't returned when she was supposed to. Sekken began to circulate, asking questions – but his nascent theory that she'd tried to flee before sundown was undercut when Tsubame, one of the old grandmothers, told him she'd seen the girl.

"You're sure it was her?" he asked. "Not someone else in the village you might have mistaken for her?"

"Don't have all that many girls her age here," Tsubame said tartly, before adding a belated, "my lord." In her case he didn't think it was Perfect Land insolence; just the habitual authority of an old woman speaking to a young man. "And I'd recognize that–"

She cut off abruptly. "That what?" Sekken prompted her.

"That robe," Tsubame said. "I'd recognize that robe anywhere. Tattered like a beggar's, I tell you, but she liked it too much to give it up – but she's dead and gone, and it don't matter now what she wore. Poor Masa."

He'd heard that refrain from a dozen people already. It seemed Masa was a widower, and had lost other children before Chie. His daughter was the only thing he'd had left. No wonder he clung to the hope that she'd survived.

Sekken pounded his thigh with one fist. *I know so much… and none of it does any good.* Not a single scrap of his knowledge could help to lift that poor man's grief.

It was that feeling of uselessness as much as anything which made Sekken volunteer to go out the next day with the villagers cutting down a cypress tree to use in the re-enshrinement ceremony. Ryōtora was wholly occupied in preparing for his own part, purifying himself in the waterfall and then praying to Saiun-nushi, attempting to establish a rapport before the kami was moved. It didn't take a shugenja to appease the spirit of a tree before it was felled – the villagers were accustomed to carrying out those small rituals themselves – but Sekken hoped he might find signs in the forest that would help make sense of this entire situation, or give some hint as to where Chie might have gone.

The actual loggers were two men, one older and one younger. *Heigo and Daizan*, Sekken reminded himself, entertaining visions of saving the village and then capping that achievement by introducing every single resident of Seibo Mura to Ryōtora by name, in syllabic order. With them came Ishi and Tarō, Ryōtora's attendant ashigaru, to help carry the tree once it was felled. Finally, rounding out their party, there was the girl Rin, the one who'd guided Ryōtora into the village when he arrived. Her stick-thin arms wouldn't be much use in the heavy labor, but Sekken gathered that she was a deadly shot with her sling, and knew the surrounding terrain well enough that she could guide them to the ideal tree.

"What kind of rocks are good against yōkai?" she asked him as they set out. Like many of those in Seibo Mura, she didn't call him "Lord Asako" or "my lord," but in her case it seemed more like youthful oversight than an ideological point. "Round ones? Dark ones? Light ones? Do they need to be blessed?"

Jade rocks, Sekken thought. There was no point in saying it, though. The villagers didn't have any jade. Instead he said, "If you have any with holes in them, that might be lucky."

Rin brightened. "My grandmother used to use those for loom weights!" Then her face fell. "But I'm not sure where they went after she passed away. Nobody weaves here any more; we just get cloth from Heibeisu."

"It seems like the village has been in decline for a while," Sekken said. "Do you have any idea why?" Although Rin was young, she might have heard tales.

She merely shrugged. "That's just the way it is. Not just here; my father says it's the same in Heibeisu. I'm going to look for some rocks with holes."

With the energy of burgeoning youth, she leapt up the path as fleetly as a deer. Sekken frowned after her, wondering. He'd heard, even back in Phoenix lands, that the Dragon weren't thriving lately. It was a point of political contention, because they'd begun making marriage alliances with the Unicorn to their west, and the Phoenix and the Unicorn were often in disagreement. But it was one thing to say the clan wasn't thriving, and another entirely to look around Seibo Mura and calculate it had at best half the population it once possessed. Some of those were recent losses, but not all.

And they had so few *children*. That was what had been niggling at him, Sekken realized. Chie was all Masa had: very well, he appeared to be a widower, and sometimes families lost most of their children to disease or misfortune, or simply were never blessed with many to begin with. But almost nobody here seemed to bear names like Hajime or Ichirō, indicating they were their families' firstborn sons – much less anybody called Gorō, because he was the fifth boy. Sekken hadn't actively counted when he was gathering stories, but he doubted many of the families in Seibo Mura had more than three children, and quite a lot seemed to have fewer.

Was it a clue to the yōkai problem, or merely an unrelated issue? What did any of this have to do with the inugami, and why hadn't the damned thing appeared since Sekken got to the village?

He didn't mind questions. But he hated questions he couldn't begin to answer. If his knowledge and his intellect were the only resources he could offer here, then he wanted them to be good for *something*.

It put him in a bad mood. By the time Rin brought them to her chosen cypress – thin and straight, and not too tall – Sekken had no tolerance for irritations. He managed not to fidget with impatience as they tied a sacred rope around the tree and thanked its spirit for its sacrifice, but when the loggers began to time their axe-swings to the chant of *Shoshi ni kie*, he intervened.

"This is being cut to call down the spirit of Saiun-nushi," he said. "You should be praying to that spirit as you work, not asking Shinsei to save you from the work of enlightenment."

The surrounding trees blocked enough wind while allowing the sun to penetrate that the air was warm, but the atmosphere chilled as if an autumn breeze had cut through. "Begging your pardon," the older logger said at last, sounding not at all apologetic, "but we've put our trust in the Little Teacher for years, *and* respected Saiun-nushi at the same time. You're a stranger here – Lord Asako."

His use of the title was anything but respectful, and in his mouth Sekken's family name might as well have been an insult. Sekken stiffened. "Have you considered that perhaps your difficulties have come about *precisely because* you chant an empty mantra as you work, instead of focusing your devotion where you should?"

"You saying the Little Teacher ain't worthy of our devotion?"

"You're not supposed to *worship* him," Sekken snapped.

He was ready to deliver an entire theological lecture right there on the mountainside, about the difference between honoring Shinsei and his teachings and praying to him for direct intervention like just another Fortune, when Ishi stepped between him and the loggers and bowed. A proper bow, and when he spoke, his voice was placatory. "My lord, the kie is good for timing the axe-blows. Like blacksmiths chanting while they hammer steel, or women singing as they pound mochi. It keeps the spirit strong and makes sure the men don't risk each other's safety. We've prayed to the tree's spirit, and we can pray to Saiun-nushi as we carry the trunk back to the village… but for now, will the kie do any harm?"

Blacksmiths' chants and mochi-pounders' songs were often prayers – *real* ones, not the wasted breath of the kie. But Sekken was suddenly aware that he was standing a very long way from Seibo Mura and his own servant, with two armed ashigaru, two loggers with axes, and a peasant girl reputed to be the best shot in the village with a sling.

He didn't think they would attack him. When all was said and done, though, the only power he had to compel them to obedience was his status as a samurai. Elsewhere in the Empire that power was substantial, and if he chose, he could have brought heavy consequences down upon their heads for this insolence. But here, with him an outsider, talking to followers of the Perfect Land? That status carried about as much weight as dandelion fluff.

"Do what you must," he forced himself to say. Inwardly, though, he vowed to talk to Ryōtora again about the Perfect Land. Their beliefs might not be the cause of the yōkai disturbances – but it was entirely possible they had something to do with the withering of the entire Dragon Clan.

CHAPTER NINE

As the last rays of sunlight were cut off by the mountains, Ryōtora knelt in front of the ruined shrine and closed his eyes in meditation.

He'd been doing this since forming the plan to relocate the kami of the mountain, leaving the physical preparations to others. Sekken was overseeing the construction of a new portable shrine; Haru had organized the village children to fold strips of paper into the zigzag streamers that would hang from the sacred ropes and other tools of the ritual. Some of the men were building a cairn of stones to the northeast of the spot Ryōtora and Sekken had chosen for the temporary shrine, in the hopes that the symbolic mountain would improve the geomantic balance of the area and forestall whatever was bringing the yōkai down upon Seibo Mura.

Ryōtora sometimes wondered if the presence of the Phoenix Clan, in the northeastern part of the Empire, protected the whole of Rokugan from the baleful influence of that direction. Though the biggest threat to Rokugan was the Shadowlands, the Jigoku-tainted regions lying to the Empire's southwest, past the lands of the Crab Clan.

It had taken the threat of repercussions if he lied to make Ogano admit to seeing an animated corpse. Aoi hadn't made it up. But plenty of people had also seen a nekomata, a two-tailed cat related to the bakeneko that could likewise puppet the dead. In Sekken's considered opinion, that was the cause of the incident – not mahō and the forces of Jigoku.

Ryōtora prayed he was right.

Regardless of whether it stopped the yōkai incursions, the stone cairn would be a good spiritual measure, making the new location as pleasant as possible for Saiun-nushi. The responsibility for maintaining a shrine tended to be passed down within a family because that way they were known to the kami, and it to them – which was important when placating a kami required knowledge of its likes and dislikes, its habits and quirks. Some of that percolated out to the general community; for example, Ogano was able to tell Ryōtora that they always carried the portable shrine as smoothly as possible, rather than swaying it from side to side and bouncing it up and down. In other places that was done to amuse the kami, but in Seibo Mura it increased the risk of earthquakes. There were undoubtedly other secrets, though, which Nawaro, the late shrinekeeper, had taken to his grave.

Which was why Ryōtora had to leave much of the work in other people's hands and spend his own time meditating next to the ruins of the old shrine. He purified himself first in the waterfall, bathing rather than making do with the ladle, then climbed the path to the broken mountain ledge, where he did the one task which he, as a shugenja, could do more rapidly than anyone else here: familiarizing himself with Saiun-nushi, and making himself familiar to the kami in return.

Quick, however, was a relative word when it came to the kami of a mountain. They were powerful spirits of earth, solid and heavy, and their sense of time bore no meaningful relation to human perception. In one sense Ryōtora was glad that this mountain wasn't a volcano; dealing with the instability brought in by fire could be very dangerous. On the other hand, it might have allowed him to move faster.

He hoped, in the depths of his mind, that he'd chosen the right way to use his time. That moving Saiun-nushi would do some good – enough to justify the decision to do *this,* instead of something else.

Locked in communion with the mountain, another part of him merely shrugged. These moments were less than an eyeblink. If the people here died, others would come – or not. It hardly mattered. The mountain would endure.

But the mountain receives offerings from the people, Ryōtora thought. Not with words; the air kami delighted in language, but the earth thought in simpler terms. *Without them, you will be alone.*

That prospect didn't bother the mountain. Saiun-nushi had all the companionship it required, from the deer and the trees and the grass and the worms. And it had a duty, too; the role of the earth was to sustain everything around it, to be the foundation that held up the world.

Still… that world included the village, the people with their offerings.

Dawn touched Saiun-nushi's awareness before Ryōtora's, Amaterasu Ōmikami laying a delicate finger on the peak long before the lands below felt her warmth. Through his communion with the mountain, he tracked the glow down the slope, until it reached where he knelt in front of the shrine. Ryōtora opened his eyes and clapped his hands in thanks to the kami, then bowed forward with his forehead to the ground. All night he'd been steadily flexing his feet under him to keep his legs from going utterly numb, but when he stood they felt like they belonged to a stranger: two foreign and somewhat painful appendages, putting the rest of him very far from the solid, reassuring ground.

He watched his footing carefully as he descended to the waterfall. There he found six men waiting, hands clasped and heads bowed under the torrent, dressed only in their loincloths. A wand with paper streamers waited for Ryōtora on the rocks nearby. He called the men out of the waterfall and swept the wand over their heads, cleansing them of impurities. These six would be carrying the portable shrine; it was almost as important for them to be pure as Ryōtora himself. He didn't know four of the men, but Masa and Ogano completed the set.

They shrugged into short jackets and headed down the path after Ryōtora, to where other people had gathered. The constrained environs of the shrine's ledge meant it wasn't possible to bring the whole village up to the shrine, the way they might do elsewhere; only some of them would participate directly in the ritual. Rin and a younger girl were going to serve as the shrine maidens today, and several other villagers bore the trays of food and sake to be offered to the kami. The new portable shrine waited on the ground next to them. Ryōtora purified them all with another wand – offerings and shrine as well as the people – then led them back up the path.

There he carried out a second purification, using a cup of water and some of the village's precious stock of salt. One of the villagers beat a steady rhythm on a drum. Finally Ryōtora faced the shrine, took a deep breath, and clapped his hands.

Apart from communing with the kami, there was one task he couldn't risk assigning to anyone else. Nobody had dared to dig about in the wreckage for the shintai, the divine vessel that held the presence of the kami; they feared accidentally touching it with their unclean and ignorant hands. From his meditations, though, Ryōtora knew where to look. He'd found a finely crafted and somewhat battered red lacquer box beneath the fallen beams, which he'd promptly covered with one of Sekken's silk kimonos.

Now it was that brightly colored spot to which he addressed his prayer, inviting Saiun-nushi to be present in its divine vessel.

But the mountain did not move.

Not because his prayers were wrong, the offerings insufficient. Because Ryōtora was not of Seibo Mura.

I am, he thought. *I was born here.*

Mere words, and the mountain did not think in words. It responded to what lay in his heart. While Ryōtora might *know* he came from Seibo Mura, he had no memories of the place. Blood might bind him to someone here, in the village or in its graveyard, but he didn't know who. And he did not think of them as his people.

His serenity rippled as Hokumei's voice rose up like a vengeful ghost in his mind. *No matter what you call yourself, you aren't truly a samurai.*

His old lover was right. Ryōtora had known it his entire life. However much that knowledge cut at him, though, it had been nothing more than a dry fact until he came here and faced the reality.

I am a son of Seibo Mura, Ryōtora said to the kami. *I accept responsibility for these people, because some among them are my kin.*

I will give whatever I must to protect them. For their sake – for our sake – I beg you.

So deep in communion with the kami, he felt its great force rise up into the shintai. The weight of the mountain solidified beneath him, holding up the world, serving as the great table upon which they laid the small bowls of food and drink, the great stage upon which Rin and the other girl danced to the beat of the drum. The kami would need the strength given by those offerings: it was about to go on a journey.

When the dance was done, the drum fell silent, leaving only the rush of the wind, and Ryōtora prayed again. To Saiun-nushi… and to his unknown ancestors, the men and women of this village who had made their offerings to the kami of the mountain in generations past.

Then he tied a scrap of white cloth over his mouth and donned his silk gloves, to protect the shintai from any pollution he might still carry. When this was done, he stepped forward, drew aside Sekken's kimono, and lifted the box that held the shintai.

The villagers had been able to tell him what to expect, from their experiences carrying it inside the portable shrine. The shintai and its sheltering box were just barely within Ryōtora's strength to carry. But no one else could help him with this: everyone knelt with their faces to the ground, averting their gazes as he took the sacred treasure from its resting spot.

He hadn't wanted to disturb too much of the fallen shrine. Now, too late, Ryōtora realized he should have cleared a path for himself. Unsteady with the weight in his arms, he picked his way across the rubble, sweating whenever something shifted beneath his foot. His ankle had mostly recovered, but if it gave way again… He couldn't suppress a gasp of relief when he attained the reassuring stability of open ground, and then hurried to place the shintai within the new, portable shrine. It was a makeshift thing, beautiful despite that – or perhaps because of it. Ryōtora knew from Sekken's reports that Masa had assembled it out of donations from the whole village. The old one might have been more elegant, but this one was a symbol of the community itself, coming together to embrace their resident kami.

In the silence of the mountain wind, he closed the doors and bowed once more to Saiun-nushi. The hardest part was done. Now would come the festival – if anyone in Seibo Mura could muster the enthusiasm for such a thing, with the threat still looming in their future.

The six bearers didn't lift the portable shrine all the way to their shoulders yet. First they had to make their way down the path, calling out instructions to one another as they struggled to keep the small palanquin as level as possible. Six was more than enough for the weight, but necessary to maneuver it around the hairpin turns of the path, watching carefully to make certain the projecting beams upon which it rested didn't catch against the trees. Ryōtora, leading the procession, had to make himself stop glancing back to verify that nothing had gone wrong yet. *They've done this before.* And Masa had made the new shrine as close to the measurements of the old as possible.

Finally they attained open ground, with the village spreading out below them. A drumbeat began to sound, much deeper in tone than the hand drum they'd used during the ritual on the mountain, and the wind carried a faint melody to Ryōtora's ears: the waiting villagers, raising their voices in praise to Saiun-nushi.

The shrine-bearers hoisted their burden to their shoulders and began a circuit of the village. First they walked all around the outside, making sure to include every house within the shape described by their path; then they began making their way through the village proper. At each door they paused and the relevant household bowed to the shrine, re-introducing themselves to the kami and asking for its blessings and protection. Meanwhile, the others sang and danced and beat small drums, and if the atmosphere was more desperate than festive... they'd just have to hope it was enough.

Ogano's house was the first place they stopped, at his insistence. He'd already tried to demand they place the new, temporary shrine right next to his house, saying that was the "heart" of the village and therefore the only proper spot. It was clear that he wanted himself and his family to be the first ones protected – that he thought, as headman, he *deserved* to be the first one protected – and that he assumed proximity would help. Sekken had done a marvelous job of burying the man's protests under a flood of learned-sounding arguments about geomancy and how the placement of the temporary shrine in a different location would improve the flow of energy through the whole area, Ogano's house most definitely included. Halfway through he'd lost even Ryōtora, who couldn't tell how much of it was legitimate, and how much was soothing nonsense.

The placement of the shrine was certainly based on real principles. As the sun climbed in the sky, they finally finished visiting every inhabited household, and turned the palanquin toward the chosen site, where Sekken waited.

It stood near one of the abandoned houses, on a stretch of open ground. The spot was easy to see from a distance, because one of its features was a tall pole, the trunk of the cypress recently felled for the purpose. Just as the paper streamers of the purification wand served to attract impurities, removing them from the ritual's participants, the wooden column would serve as a holy tree, attracting the energy of the mountain kami to this place.

But first it had to be prepared. Sekken had erected four smaller poles around the perimeter, with twisted straw ropes connecting them, forming a square – the symbol of the earth. Larger zigzag streamers hung from these. Together they made a sacred enclosure, and a new home for Saiun-nushi.

There hadn't been time or sufficient supplies to build even a hokora, a small shrine. Most of the suitable wood they had available went to building the palanquin, which was necessary to move the shintai from its usual location. Instead they'd set up an eight-legged platform, a larger version of the small table Ryōtora might use for a ceremony. The bearers carried the portable shrine to that platform and laid it down, then backed away, bowing.

It would do no good to bring Saiun-nushi all the way down here if the new home for the kami was uncomfortable or displeasing. So even though Ryōtora was light-headed with hunger and lack of sleep, it was time for more offerings, more purifications. Dishes of salt and water, fish and pickled radishes, a flask of sake for Saiun-nushi to enjoy at the end of its long journey. The scents called forth an embarrassing noise from Ryōtora's stomach, but the only person close enough to possibly hear was Sekken, and he kept his expression impassive enough for court.

After the long prayer was complete, Sekken bowed and handed him a basket of rough scraps of hemp fiber. For this final purification, there was no drumbeat, no chanting, no music: only the rush of the mountain wind as Ryōtora scattered them to the east, south, west, north, and finally to the center, throwing a handful over the table of offerings and the shrine itself. The wind gusted as that last one left his grasp, flinging many of the pieces back over Ryōtora instead.

A defect of his spiritual power, failing to remove the last traces of defilement from this place? A message from the air kami, that it was Ryōtora himself who needed a final cleansing? A rejection from Saiun-nushi, saying he was unworthy to perform this ritual? Or just the caprice of luck?

He didn't know. He was only grateful that the villagers had been bowed to the ground as he threw the hemp, and only Sekken had seen.

One by one, the villagers approached to offer small evergreen branches to the kami. By the time they finished, Ryōtora regretted suggesting that every single one of them old enough to walk should do so, rather than just the elders of the village, the way it would normally be. He was swaying on his feet as he covered the dishes and the sake and prayed one last time, preparatory to bidding Saiun-nushi farewell. The shintai was the kami's divine vessel, but it would be folly to try to keep it continually present in that physical object.

Maybe it was related to the hemp scraps being blown back in his face. Maybe it was the strain of dealing with a powerful and unfamiliar kami. Maybe it was just that Ryōtora didn't serve in a temple, and hadn't undergone this kind of fasting and vigil since his student days.

He called out, using his voice to release Saiun-nushi from the shintai. And as he sensed the rushing energy of the kami's departure, his own energy left him, and he fell.

CHAPTER TEN

Judging by the way Ryōtora kept his gaze averted after the ceremony, he was embarrassed. Sekken wasn't sure why. True, he'd toppled over at the end of the ritual – but he'd just moved the spiritual embodiment of a mountain, on no sleep and no food. Ryōtora, however, seemed to view this as evidence of weakness on his own part. Sekken would have told him it was hardly some personal failing, if he'd thought it would do any good.

He also would have suggested Ryōtora rest. Except Sekken could fill in the counterargument for himself: they had no reason to believe moving Saiun-nushi to the temporary shrine had solved the underlying problem. And with the days slipping by, no one could afford to spend time on a nap.

At least he made sure Ryōtora got his share of the food that had been offered to the kami, when it got divided among the villagers in a meager feast. None of the sake, though. That would only encourage him to sleep.

As the sun drifted toward the horizon, Sekken was back in Ogano's house, copying out his notes in a form Ryōtora would be able to follow. The ceremony had used up much of his stock of paper – *and to think, Jun questioned whether I needed so much,* he thought wryly. So far, no pattern had emerged among the yōkai, unless the fact that none of them were benevolent qualified. Even then, though, there were creatures like the basan, the bird that had eaten part of the burned house. Not actively benevolent, but not malicious, either. Mostly they were just shy, disappearing as soon as they realized a human had noticed them. The one in Seibo Mura had stayed, though.

Ishi and Tarō arrived as he was finishing his own notes. This was the first chance he'd gotten to collect their reports, gathered from the villagers that worked in the mines and the fields. It was more of the same, confirming some of the incidents Sekken had recorded and adding a few others, though sometimes the timelines contradicted each other. "Multiples of some yōkai?" Sekken murmured, tapping the end of his brush against his lip. "Generally there seems to have been just one of each. More likely just people being confused. Understandable, given the chaos."

"It sounds like it," Ishi agreed. "Except for the black birds. There was definitely a whole flock of those at once."

"Crows?"

He shook his head. "Smaller. About the size of a sparrow. And only one person heard their call. Ona's husband Hideo – they flocked all around him, flew into his sleeve, and he said they were chirping so loud he could barely hear, but Ona didn't hear anything."

Sekken almost blotted his page. He set his brush down very carefully and said, "Was her husband attacked by a dog or a wolf soon after?"

Ishi was too stolid to show surprise on his face, but he rocked back on his heels. "Torn apart. How did you know?"

"Yosuzume," Sekken said, trying to sound as if it were of no particular interest. "Night sparrows. They're not dangerous on their own, but they're an omen for what follows: the okuri inu."

A type of dog spirit – a very malevolent one. It usually followed travelers on dark mountain roads, waiting for them to stumble, savaging them as soon as they did. Sure enough, Ishi went on to relate how Ona and her husband had tried to run for safety, but Hideo tripped over a stone jutting from the soil. In an instant, the dog had been upon him.

Sekken picked up his brush and took notes by reflex, while his thoughts raced elsewhere. The okuri inu stories gave instructions for how to protect oneself against them: when you stumbled, you had to immediately sit down and say something about how it was a relief to rest for a moment, pretending to have done it on purpose. They also said that if you got out of the mountains without dying, you should turn and thank the dog for escorting you, as if it had intended to be helpful.

Then, when you got home, you were supposed to put out a dish of food for the okuri inu.

The rituals for binding an animal yōkai to oneself as a familiar also involved offering them food.

It wasn't a firm connection. Okuri inu were black all over, and the inugami that had been haunting Sekken was shades of cream and brown. The creature that stood on Sekken's chest in his sleep and barked at him was a far cry from the one that had torn apart Ona's husband.

But it was the only dog-like yōkai he'd yet heard of in Seibo Mura.

When Ishi was done relating the tale, Sekken said, "I need you to do something when we're finished here. Try to find out –

discreetly – whether Hideo had any particular enemies in the village. Or outside of it, come to that, if he helped take the cinnabar to Heibeisu."

Ishi had good enough manners not to ask questions. Sekken could see it hovering behind the man's teeth, though, so he said, "Yes?"

"You think this was aimed at Hideo?" Ishi said.

It was an impertinent question, but also a fair one. Sekken sighed. "No – especially given that the disturbances continued after he died. The yosuzume and the okuri inu, though… those are different from the others. Which might be a clue."

Ishi bowed. When he and Tarō were done relating what they'd learned, Sekken sat alone with his notes, wrestling with his conscience.

He ought to tell Ryōtora. Not just about the okuri inu, but also the inugami that had been haunting him. There *had* to be a connection there; it couldn't be coincidence that the spirit had become so aggressive during the nights of the attacks.

Only he'd arrived in Seibo Mura, and the haunting had promptly stopped. What was he to make of that?

Possibly that the witch controlling the inugami wanted him here, and now that he'd come, they were satisfied. For what purpose, though? And why Sekken, of all the possible targets? Nobody had paid particular attention to him since his arrival. If anything, they'd ignored him: the unwanted outsider, intruding on private trouble without the excuse of duty. Almost the only time anyone spoke to him, apart from Ryōtora, was when Sekken started the conversation.

Of course not. It would be far more suspicious if they did. Rin excepted, peasants didn't randomly chat with samurai. Not unless they were attempting to sell something – and the closest anyone had come to that was Aoi, playing the coquette whenever she saw him about the village.

He sighed, started to chew on the end of his brush, then laid it down, appalled. He hadn't indulged in *that* bad habit since before starting his training.

His thoughts were dancing around the one he didn't want to face: that he ought to tell Ryōtora. Maybe the Dragon would see how this all fit together, when Sekken himself couldn't. At a minimum, he ought to know that while mahō might not be likely here, the witchcraft of binding familiars could be.

But reluctance still dragged at Sekken. When the inugami first began haunting his dreams, he'd mentioned it to his family. His parents initially thought it an omen of some kind, and sought interpretations. When those interpretations turned up nothing useful, and the dog kept visiting him every night, they tried to have it banished with repeated exorcisms. All very much in secret, of course; his sisters' matches had been good enough that nobody was in a rush to get Sekken himself married off, but they didn't want to scare away prospective spouses by letting it be known he was suffering some kind of spiritual ailment.

Still, word had gotten to Asako Fukimi, an elderly scholar from Ukabu Mura. She came to see Sekken without being invited, and told him the dog was probably the familiar of a tsukimono-suji: a witch.

Sekken had heard of it before, but only in passing. "Isn't that just peasant superstition?" he asked.

Fukimi shook her head, wisps of mist-white hair dancing with the movement. "An ancient practice, from before the Kami fell to earth in Rokugan. Very rare, now; few people even know how to bind a yōkai to their family line any more. So yes, superstition in the sense that most of the time when you hear someone talking about it, they're just jealous of their neighbor's success or blaming their own misfortune on someone else. There are real witches, though. I arrested one, back when I was a magistrate."

"It's illegal?" Sekken asked.

"What he was using it for was," she said.

It was difficult to imagine the elderly Fukimi as a magistrate, with her hands trembling so much she couldn't even hold a brush any more. That didn't stop her from reading, though, and her memory was prodigious. She told Sekken she'd learned what she knew about witches from a Dragon who'd visited Ukabu Mura decades before. Sekken's second sister made some inquiries on his behalf, and in time the answer came that the magistrate once known as Kitsuki Ieyori had retired to Quiet Stone Monastery, not far from the border with Phoenix lands. He was dead now – truly dead, not merely in the sense that a man who retired from duty as a samurai and took holy vows was dead to his former life – but he'd passed his final years writing, and the monastery had his works.

More favors. Permission to travel to Dragon lands. And then–

"Is that the list?"

Sekken knocked his brush off its rest and busied himself blotting up the ink smear it left on Ogano's table. "Yes. It's complete now – as complete as I can make it, anyway."

Ryotora looked exhausted, and one sleeve of his kimono still had a smudge of soil and grass from where he'd slammed into the ground when he fell. Sekken wished he'd been standing close enough to catch Ryōtora; surely even that man's sense of propriety couldn't object, not if it saved him from planting himself in the dirt.

When Sekken started to rise, Ryōtora waved him back and knelt, setting down his own writing kit and his seal. Next to the vermilion lacquer of Sekken's kit, his bronze one looked battered and travel-worn: an uncomfortable reminder that even the samurai of the Dragon Clan were often poor compared to their Phoenix neighbors.

Sekken handed the list to him with a seated bow, then tried not to fidget while Ryōtora read it over. The seal drew his eye. He'd assumed the shugenja's given name was written with the characters that meant "son of the tiger," but it turned out the second half was instead an archaic character for "northeast," usually pronounced *ushitora*.

Yes, and your own name is written as "ancient wisdom." But are you being wise?

"Thank you for glossing these," Ryōtora said with a rueful sigh, laying the paper on the table. One blunt fingertip tapped the tiny characters Sekken had inked in above the names. "Without that, I wouldn't have recognized how to pronounce some of these."

"Yōkai names get very strange," Sekken admitted. "But I spent some time in service to a woman who studied archaic forms of language. It's proven useful in my research."

"Has that research given you any insights here?"

Half the truth was better than none at all. Sekken touched the wooden end of his brush to the okuri inu in the list. "This is the only thing that stands out to me as possibly meaningful. Have you heard of tsukimono-suji?" Ryōtora shook his head, and Sekken wasn't sure whether to be glad of that or not. "It's a kind of ancient witchcraft, passed down in families. They bind animal spirits to serve them. The okuri inu could potentially be a witch's familiar."

Ryōtora frowned. "Bind? The way the Unicorn do, with meishōdō?"

"It's a different ritual. You don't need the true name of the spirit, and you don't bind it into a physical talisman, the way meishōdō practitioners do. And you don't have to be a shugenja to make it work." *Just like with mahō.*

The tightening of Ryōtora's jaw was almost certainly him making the same comparison. The Dragon didn't frown upon the binding techniques of meishōdō the way the Phoenix did; as with the Perfect Land, they were too tolerant of unorthodox practices, even when those practices treated kami like common servants. But the echo of mahō… that, even a Dragon would find worrisome.

Ryōtora's gaze roved down the list again. "There aren't many animal spirits here, though. No kitsune, no tanuki… there are some itachi, at least."

"Kama itachi," Sekken said. "Those are a guess. *Something* cut Isamu bloody, and nobody saw what did it; sickle weasels would fit the evidence."

"So you think this could be the active work of someone in the village – just not a mahō-tsukai." Ryōtora laid his hand flat, fingertips pressing into the table. "I was hoping that wouldn't be the case."

"I believe there might be such a person here," Sekken said cautiously. "Whether they're responsible for all of this… I've never heard of a witch causing this degree of chaos. Usually they're selfish, making their neighbors suffer misfortune while they enjoy prosperity."

Ryōtora rolled up the list and tucked it into his kimono. "Maybe the witch made a mistake."

•••

That night Sekken didn't sleep well, but not because an inugami troubled him. Instead he stared at the shadowed ceiling, listening to Ryōtora's steady breathing just an arm's length away, turning theories over in his mind.

From what he'd seen, rural peasants were all incurable gossips – nearly as bad as courtiers. He expected them to whisper amongst themselves if someone here were a witch. Fukimi had told him such people were disliked and distrusted by their neighbors, because their ancient magic involved binding and commanding yōkai, not propitiating them the way shugenja did with the kami. And the most common use to which they put their spirit familiars was profit.

In all Sekken's conversations with the villagers, no one had stood out as being unusually prosperous, nor resented by their neighbors for their success. The only person who came close to fitting that description, with a fine house and tatami mats and four healthy children, was Ogano.

If he was the witch… then Sekken, like an innocent fish, had swum right into that net and asked if he could stay.

But his prosperity wasn't proof of witchcraft. Village heads were usually the most successful men and women in their settlements. Then again, using witchcraft to attain that status would make sense – and Ogano's family had held the leadership of Seibo Mura for generations.

Was Ogano unpopular? Certainly people were angry at him *now*; the failings of the headman were a constant refrain in the conversations around the village. But that was to be expected in any disaster, when the person in charge failed to prevent suffering and loss. The peasants had even spoken disparagingly of the Mirumoto samurai sent after the first month. The blame directed at Ogano had sounded more like grievance at his leadership failings, not the righteous fury of people calling out the witch in their midst.

Still, he was the best candidate Sekken could see. Those who kept spirits bound to them were often emotionally unstable; hadn't the headman railed at Ryōtora – his social superior, and the man who'd been sent to help him – the very night Ryōtora arrived? And he was clearly wealthier and more successful than anyone else in the village. Admittedly, he'd lost his brother – but as Ryōtora said, maybe he'd made a mistake. And the haunting stopped the night Sekken arrived in Seibo Mura … which was the night he began sleeping under Ogano's roof.

Sekken's pulse quickened. He'd slept deeply and dreamlessly these past few nights. Deeply enough that he wouldn't notice if Ogano crept into the room to work some kind of foul magic over him?

Ryōtora would have to sleep through it too. Sekken knew by now, though, that Ryōtora didn't wake easily.

The more he thought about it, the more it began to make an incomplete kind of sense. There were only two gaps in the chain of Sekken's logic – but both of them were large enough to trouble him.

The first was how the witchcraft could explain the broader troubles in Seibo Mura. Witches could cause possession, or misfortune in the vein of failed crops and sickly children; they didn't bring hordes of yōkai down on a town. Sekken briefly entertained the notion that Ogano was somehow a new witch, and the eruption of chaos was caused by a failed attempt to bind a spirit to his service, before dismissing it. The timing didn't work: Sekken's own haunting had begun months ago, long before the disturbances here.

That haunting was the other gap. Why Sekken? He'd found a partial answer to that in the records of Quiet Stone Monastery. Like many who lived on the western side of Phoenix lands, his ancestry crossed the border in several places; a few of his forebears had been Dragon. One of them, Mirumoto Kotau, was referenced in the writings of Kitsuki Ieyori as being reputed to descend from a lineage of inugami witches.

Ancient history – so ancient it was more legend than anything else. Kotau had lived in the fifth century; the only reason Sekken even knew his name was because he'd been moderately famous for driving back an incursion from the Yobanjin beyond Rokugan's northern border.

But it meant Sekken's own bloodline was tainted with witchcraft. And if the inugami haunting him had something to do with Seibo Mura… then it might mean he himself had a connection to this village.

If Ogano was a witch – or if anyone in Seibo Mura was – he might be Sekken's own distant kin.

It ought not to matter. Only a Lion could recite his full ancestry back six hundred years, and Kotau's purported inugami heritage was even older than that. In the early days of the Empire, the Celestial Order hadn't been as well established in Rokugani society, and peasants who did great deeds might be adopted into clans as samurai. But Sekken's family took pride in their ancestry, their reputation, their influential position in the Phoenix Clan. He couldn't stand the thought of them knowing about this stain.

He couldn't stand the prospect of Ryōtora's growing warmth turning chill.

Because Ryōtora was the first person to make Sekken feel like he mattered. Even his past lovers had been mere idle diversions:

a brief sharing of pleasure, but nothing deeper than that. Sekken hadn't wanted more, not from his lovers, not from his assigned duties, not from anything. He'd counted himself lucky that no weight rested on his shoulders.

Now it did… and for all that it frightened him, Sekken also liked the feeling. Ryōtora's strength of character made *him* feel stronger. He wanted to go on the way they were, not risk this inugami situation driving them apart.

Sekken rolled onto his side. Ryōtora had left the shutters ajar for fresh air; the setting crescent of the moon cast just enough light into their room for him to make out the shugenja's profile, stern even in sleep.

No one has to know, Sekken thought, his fingers tensing against the futon. *About the witch, yes – but not about me. It isn't necessary for them to know.*

There was no way for them to find out, either. Jun wouldn't talk. The only other person who might know was the witch, if he or she had sent the inugami after Sekken deliberately. So he had to find them and expose them before they could do anything more.

With that resolved, he slept, and woke, and went for his usual morning stroll around the village. It wasn't until he turned his steps back toward Ogano's house that he realized a dog was following him.

A dog no one else reacted to. A dog he'd seen dozens of times in his sleep, standing on his chest until he could barely breathe for the weight.

It's back.

CHAPTER ELEVEN

The house was quieter than usual when Ryōtora woke the next morning. The only person who seemed to be present was Haru, and she excused herself immediately after serving Ryōtora breakfast, hurrying out the door. By the time he had finished eating, Sekken still hadn't returned, which made Ryōtora uneasy. The pattern of Sekken's early rising and morning walk, followed by breakfast together, had lasted for long enough to take on the air of a comforting routine. Having that disrupted was troubling.

Before he could make up his mind whether to go look for the Phoenix, Haru hurried back in and immediately bowed to the floor. "Sir Ryōtora, my nephew's fever has grown worse. My sister fears he will die of it. Please, I beg you – will you come see to him?"

According to Sekken's notes, it seemed like every third yōkai could bring disease. It was no wonder half the village had fallen sick. In most cases, though, the illness was minor, or else bad enough that the victims had passed before Ryōtora arrived in Seibo Mura. Fubatsu was the exception, lying in bed with a fever that refused to abate.

A bad enough fever could damage the mind, even if it didn't kill. "At once," Ryōtora said, and rose.

Stepping outside, he almost ran bodily into Sekken, who was looking over his shoulder as if someone was following him. "Is everything all right?" Ryōtora asked.

"Yes, of course."

It was clearly untrue – but challenging that type of polite lie was rude. Sekken gathered himself and said, "Where are you hurrying to? Has something happened?"

"Fubatsu's fever," Ryōtora said, setting off again. He wasn't sure which house in the village was his destination, but Haru wouldn't dare to interrupt his conversation with another samurai; by moving, he gave her tacit permission to start walking again, and forced Sekken to follow them both. "I need to ward the village today, but he may not be able to wait."

"Quite right." Sekken's long legs kept pace easily, while Haru scurried like she wanted to run and didn't quite dare. "You… haven't noticed anything odd this morning, have you?"

Tension laced through his question, and Ryōtora cast him a sidelong glance. "I only just left the house. Odd in what manner?"

"Spiritually." Sekken lowered his voice. "What we discussed last night."

Witchcraft. Ryōtora wasn't sure what to think of the prospect. On the one hand, if Sekken was right, then finding the witch would presumably end the problem. On the other hand, he'd seen what happened in villages where people decided that one of their neighbors was responsible for their misfortunes. Given the scale of the losses here…

Sekken was still waiting for an answer. Ryōtora said, "Unless Fubatsu's turn for the worse counts, no. Why?"

He caught the Phoenix casting another glance over his shoulder. When Sekken realized, he gave an embarrassed grin. "Just my own nerves making me jump at shadows, then. My apologies."

Ryōtora wasn't a courtier, trained to draw people out through the subtleties of conversation. He didn't even have time for a blunter approach, because Haru arrived at an open door and bowed the two samurai through it. Every portal in the house was open to the breeze, as if even the faint warmth of a mountain summer was too much right now. Fubatsu lay shaking and delirious on a pallet, with Haru's sister Hina fanning him helplessly.

Ryōtora knelt at her side and questioned her in a gentle voice about Fubatsu's condition and the steps she'd taken. "We give him as much water as we can," Hina said, "but it doesn't do any good."

That wasn't surprising. Fire and Water were opposed elements, and Fubatsu clearly had a massive imbalance of the two. Merely pouring water down his throat wouldn't correct it. While Haru took over the task of fanning and Sekken watched intently, Ryōtora placed his hands on either side of Fubatsu's head, not quite touching, and began to chant in a low monotone.

His palms rapidly heated as if it were a boiling kettle between them instead of a human body. The imbalance had grown *very* bad; his mother was right to be worried. Left unchecked, it would kill him within a day.

The answer was to strengthen the Water within him. Ryōtora formed an image in his mind: a deer-scarer like the villagers used out in their fields, with a bamboo tube on a pivot slowly filling with water until it tipped, then rocked back once more to clack against a stone. If the water kami strengthened Fubatsu, Ryōtora promised through his communion, then the family would build a deer-scarer for them in thanks.

It wasn't an unusual request. Ryōtora lacked the medical expertise of a dedicated physician, but traveling in the hinterlands meant this was far from the first time he'd been asked to heal a feverish patient. And the water kami gladly complied.

But no sooner did they flood into Fubatsu's body than the fever burned them out again.

The heat in his palms was becoming too much. Ryōtora sat back on his heels and shook his hands, trying to cool them. "I've never seen a fever like this."

Sekken closed his eyes, as if he could read his own notes on the inside of their lids. "He was trying to defend others during the chaos, and fought several different yōkai. He attacked a hihi with a mattock – not a bad idea, that; if he'd gotten it in the forehead instead of the shoulder, he might actually have killed it. A nozuchi; that's likely where the fever came from. But Sai also helped him attack that one, and she recovered from her fever. There was also… a yamajijii? No." Sekken's eyes flicked open. "A hiderigami. My apologies; they both have only one eye and one leg, so they're easier to confuse than you might think – though the former are all male and the latter, all female. But that might explain it."

Ryōtora had read through the notes, but they were brief; Sekken didn't have enough paper to contain everything he knew, nor enough time to write it. "Hiderigami also cause fever?"

"Drought. And extremely hot weather. My guess is that its influence has worsened the fever from the nozuchi."

He'd hoped that knowing the cause would make the problem easier to solve. If the hiderigami had been present, Ryōtora could have tried to banish it – but in the absence of any present threat, and with the water kami too weak to overcome its power, how was he supposed to bring Fubatsu's fever down?

"Your pardon, my lords." Haru's voice broke into his thoughts, and he turned to see her bowing low, the fan momentarily set aside.

"You have an idea?" Ryōtora asked.

"It's something Lord Asako said the other day, when he was questioning Kō about the monster that tried to steal her baby girl away."

Sekken lit up like a festival lantern. "Yes! It was an ame onna. I wondered briefly if she might have been responsible for the storm the night you arrived, until it became apparent that none of the yōkai have lingered in the village. Her power might counteract this. But…"

"But none of the yōkai have lingered," Ryōtora said, as the festival lantern guttered and went out.

Unless I try to summon one.

Not even to save Fubatsu's life would he do that. The risk was too great, and Seibo Mura was already in enough danger. But Haru was still bowed low. "My lords – Kō tore some of the rain woman's hair out when they fought. Would that be of use?"

Ryōtora's gaze met Sekken's. After a moment, Sekken said, "I've never heard of anyone trying it… which is no reason not to try now."

This time Haru did run, hiking up her kimono to give herself freedom to move, while her sister went back to fanning Fubatsu. Haru returned not long after, with Kō right behind her. Even days after the attacks, the hair was still wet, spilling cold water over Ryōtora's hands to drip steadily onto the floor. That unnatural touch made his skin crawl, but under the circumstances, it was a good sign.

He laid the hair across Fubatsu's brow and began to chant once more. The water kami in the hair were as powerful as a stormcloud, and angry. This wasn't like an ubume, the ghost of a woman who'd died in childbirth; the ame onna wasn't a former human, nor driven by grief. She was simply malicious, stealing away children so others would mourn. Fubatsu wasn't a child, but he was Hina's son, and the water kami from the ame onna's hair were willing to settle for his death.

But their sodden chill was answered with a wall of searing heat. The powerful fever created by the nozuchi and the hiderigami wanted to burn away all moisture, all rain. If either Fire or Water won, Fubatsu would be lost. If, however, Ryōtora could make them balance each other out…

With a hiss, steam began to rise from the hair draped across Fubatsu's brow. The waves of heat and cold, wet and dry that had pulsed between Ryōtora's hands abruptly settled into a damp warmth.

He let out an unsteady sigh and lifted the now-dry hair away. Fubatsu's trembling had ceased, and he was beginning to sweat – a very good sign. "I believe that did it," Ryōtora said. "My thanks to all of you."

The villagers immediately began bowing and insisting it was all his doing, but he meant what he'd said. Without Sekken's knowledge, Kō's courage in fighting the ame onna, and Haru's quick thinking to connect the two, all his prayers would have been for nothing.

Ryōtora left as soon as he could after that, so that Haru could tend to Fubatsu, and her sister could get some much-needed sleep. Outside, Sekken said, "That was fascinating. Will you think me a terrible person if I admit that I can't wait to write a record of this when I get home?"

It made Ryōtora laugh. "No, not at all. In fact…"

He stopped, but Sekken cocked his head to one side. "In fact?"

"You keep reminding me of someone I once knew," Ryōtora admitted. "A… good friend."

He couldn't keep a note of regret from his voice. Sekken bowed slightly, and Ryōtora knew the Phoenix had assumed the friend in question was dead. But correcting that mistake would only make things more awkward.

Instead he blotted his damp brow with his sleeve and said, "I still have to ward the village."

"After what you just did? Not to mention the ritual yesterday?" Sekken dismissed those objections before Ryōtora could. "Never mind. You have the endurance of a horse, and I admire it. Not to mention the honor of a Lion."

It stung far harder than it should have, when Sekken meant it as a compliment. Stiffly, Ryōtora said, "I can only aspire to do my best."

In truth, he would have been glad for a rest. But after that, he couldn't sit with Sekken, feeling the twin serpents of truth and unanswered questions gnawing at his spine. Fubatsu was only a little younger than he; was his patient his brother? Was Hina his mother, Haru his aunt? Ryōtora was beginning to pray he would resolve the disturbances and get out of Seibo Mura before he learned the answer.

Because if not, then he didn't know what he would do. Duty would call him back to the life he'd been assigned – the life he didn't deserve, no matter how hard he tried to live up to it. Would it be better to turn his back on that and take up the humble existence that should have been his? Or would that only compound his failings when he came before the Fortune of Death, that he'd refused the obligations his adoptive father had given him?

Compared to wrestling with such questions, it was almost soothing to work on warding the village. Ryōtora had asked the carpenter Masa to make small stakes of wood from the broken carrying beams of the portable shrine, which he'd painted with phrases from various sutras. He retrieved these from Ogano's house, then began to walk a circuit of the village, following the route that seemed to work best with the geomantic flow of the terrain. Periodically he stopped to hammer one of the stakes into the ground, praying to the kami of the four material elements to protect the village against malignant spirits.

As he went, he began to notice something odd.

He'd walked the ground of the village before, communing with its spirits to search for any weak spots that might be allowing passage to the Spirit Realms, and had found nothing. That hadn't changed.

But something else *was* there. Not the influence of the Spirit Realms; this was here in the mortal realm, in the elemental kami of the physical world. Ryōtora felt like someone attempting to cut a path through what he'd assumed was trackless forest, only to find he was re-cutting a path that had been there long before.

No, even that wasn't correct. The path was still there: faint and wavering, but present. Only it wasn't a path; it was a ward.

Someone had warded Seibo Mura before him.

Ryōtora paused in his circuit, easing himself onto an overgrown boulder. The exertion was making his heart beat faster than it should; Sekken had been right to question whether he had the stamina for this, just as he'd been right to dismiss that concern.

This was work Ryōtora *had* to do, whether he felt up to it or not.

But it was easier than it would have been otherwise, because he wasn't building a wall from his own prayers alone. There was a foundation already in place, far deeper and stronger than anything he could create. Whoever had laid it was a master of warding invocations.

No such master existed in Seibo Mura, Ryōtora was sure of that. A child just discovering their ability to talk to the kami would never be able to craft something like this. Nor was it the kind of thing Sekken's proposed witch might do. It felt simultaneously old and new, in ways he couldn't explain. The kami along this boundary had been doing the work asked of them for long enough that even the earth acknowledged the span of time as meaningful, and the air simply took it for granted as the natural state of things. But it wasn't something that had been created once and then decayed.

He closed his eyes and sank deeper into his communion. *Who asked you to do this?*

The question was meaningless. The kami were capable of recognizing people after a fashion, but they couldn't give him a name, and even the water kami – usually the most reliable source of images – had no answer for him. It was what they did; it was what they had always done. Their job was to–

Ryōtora knocked his satchel with its remaining wards off the boulder. *Their job is not to keep something* out. *It's to keep something* in.

He slid off the boulder to retrieve his satchel and stayed kneeling for a moment, light-headed. His own ward was meant to repel the yōkai that kept attacking Seibo Mura – but the ward he'd found had the opposite purpose. It was meant to *contain* something.

Which makes no sense at all.

As he began to rise, he noticed something else. The boulder he'd been sitting on was deeply buried in grass, the overgrowth almost obscuring a trio of characters carved into its face. When Ryōtora pulled them away, he found the boulder wasn't simply a random stone – which he should have realized, with it sitting alone in this meadow, no other large rocks in sight. It was a marker stone: the type of thing usually placed at a branch in a road, or just outside a settlement, to inform travelers of the name of the village ahead.

But this wasn't the path to Seibo Mura. Ryōtora had passed that a little while ago, not far to the east. When he glanced around, however, he recognized the route by which he and the ashigaru had descended into the valley. It looked like it had once *been* the path, before its erosion had presumably led the villagers to find a new route.

The characters carved into its face weren't quite right, though. On the map Ryōtora had studied in Heibeisu and the report he'd read from Mirumoto Norifusa, Seibo Mura had been written with characters meaning "Twilight Star Village." It had struck him as a remarkably poetic name for such an out-of-the-way place. This stone, however, gave a different name. He recognized the second character as the one for "forget" – *bō* instead of *bo* – but the first one was unfamiliar to him.

Ryōtora stood, brushing dirt and bits of grass off his hands, and shouldered his satchel once more. Whatever might be going on here, he still thought his own ward was a good idea. And he had a feeling Sekken would be able to solve that linguistic puzzle for him.

•••

Walking the full circuit took him most of the day, and the food he'd brought with him proved woefully inadequate to his appetite. Over dinner that night, in between stints of devouring his meal with indelicate enthusiasm, he told Sekken about what he'd found with the ward – and nearly made the Phoenix forget his own meal in the process.

"A ward to keep something *in?*" Sekken echoed, baffled. His chopsticks dipped until they hit his plate, then stayed there as if they were propping him up while he thought. "That makes absolutely no sense with what we've seen. Unless someone meant to trap people here as prey for the yōkai – and now it sounds like we're back to mahō again."

"But people have left," Ryōtora pointed out. "Ogano was able to send a messenger boy to Heibeisu, after the second round of attacks started."

"Not everyone had as much success. There were those found dead nearby."

"Where were they found?"

Sekken chewed on his lower lip. "Good question. Within the bounds of the ward you found, or outside it? I don't know, but we can ask."

"And then there's this." Ryōtora got out his writing kit, then realized he had no paper to hand. Too impatient to go find some, he pushed his sleeve up and inked the characters onto his forearm. "I found what looks like the marker stone for the village, along what used to be the path here, but it had a different name. What's this first one?"

Sekken peered at his arm in the dim light of Ogano's house. Ryōtora was abruptly glad that none of Ogano's family ate with the samurai, nor did the ashigaru nor Sekken's servant Jun. There was only Haru to serve them, and she had retreated upstairs. They were alone as Sekken's breath ghosted over his skin.

"It's an old character for 'chain,'" Sekken told him, straightening up. "Pronounced the same as the modern one, *se*."

Ryōtora cleared his throat and covered his arm once more. "So not Seibo Mura, but Sebō Mura. Not Twilight Star Village, but–"

"Forgotten Chain Village? Chain and Forget Village? What a peculiar name. I'm not surprised it got changed in the records; differences of vowel length are easy for someone to mishear or misremember. And once the samurai have written it down a certain way, that's the official name forevermore."

"The question," Ryōtora said, "is what got chained. What someone laid that ward for."

Silence fell. Ryōtora continued to shovel food into his mouth, while Sekken stared into the dimness of the house's working area, beyond the reach of the wooden floor and the lamp.

At last the Phoenix said, "This is unrelated to those questions, and perhaps unrelated to Seibo Mura – Sebō Mura – at all. But the Perfect Land…"

Ryōtora stopped eating. Sekken held up one placating hand. "I'm not going to suggest again that they're behind what's happening here. As you said, there are other villages where the sect has a foothold, and yōkai aren't attacking; here the sect has been around for decades, and yet these problems are new. I think a witch is a far more likely explanation. Or whatever is being contained by that ward."

"Then what troubles you about them now?" It was clear that *something* did. Had Sekken had an altercation with a believer today?

Sekken hesitated, one bony fingertip tapping the table. When he finally answered, he almost seemed to have changed the subject – but Ryōtora feared otherwise. "While I was at Quiet Stone Monastery, I noticed that it had room to house at least twice the number of monks resident there now. At the time, I simply assumed it had fallen into disfavor for some reason. Such things happen."

Ryōtora's stomach tightened. His appetite gone, he laid down his chopsticks and listened as Sekken went on.

"Here in Seibo Mura," he said, "I see the same thing. Abandoned houses – abandoned long before these troubles – and families with remarkably few children. Rin told me the same is true in Heibeisu."

Sekken glanced down. Then he gave a small, seated bow. "Please forgive my rudeness in asking. But it's known outside of Dragon lands that your clan is not thriving. What I've seen here, and at the monastery… is it this bad everywhere?"

No one had ever told Ryōtora outright not to discuss it. They didn't have to; the reclusive habits of the Dragon meant that relatively few of their people traveled outside their own borders, and the forbidding terrain of their mountains meant most visitors were just as glad to visit a few accessible trading towns. They thought nothing of not being permitted to travel through the interior. Where would they go – north to the lands of the Yobanjin? To either side the Dragon had the Phoenix and the Unicorn, two clans that were often at odds anyway. It took no particular effort to ensure that contact with outsiders was limited.

And those who undertook such duties understood that they must not show weakness to their neighbors.

Ryōtora's own duties usually kept him very far away from foreign samurai. He'd never been given orders on this point.

Lying outright was contemptible, and he would be terrible at it if he tried. Refusing to discuss it would amount to an admission that Sekken was correct… but it was the best course available to him.

He couldn't bring himself to do it.

That wasn't the strictures of Bushidō talking. Honesty was the only tenet that argued in favor of confessing, and it would be satisfied by simply declining to speak of the matter. But whatever impulse of curiosity had brought Sekken to Seibo Mura, the man was working hard to help – working on behalf of a village and a samurai who weren't even a part of his own clan. He'd shown no sign of wanting to leave. Ryōtora had gone from being wary of his presence to more grateful for it than he could bring himself to admit. Stonewalling Sekken's query, however correct it might be, seemed like a poor way to repay his generosity.

Your attraction to him is clouding your judgment. You want a closeness you can never have, and you're allowing that to sway you from the right path.

But Ryōtora had been born a peasant. He didn't have the strength to make himself do what was right.

Sekken was drawing breath to speak again, almost certainly to withdraw his question. Ryōtora said, "Yes."

The breath came out again in a quiet rush. "I thought it might be. That's… I'm very sorry to hear it. And again, please forgive my impertinence in suggesting this, especially as I'm sure I'm not the first to think of it. But is it possible that the spread of the Perfect Land has something to do with *that*? Could their… beliefs be undermining the spiritual health of your clan?"

Ryōtora assumed the word he'd replaced with "beliefs" was "heresy." Sekken could hardly be blamed for his suspicion; the

Dragon willingness to tolerate the Perfect Land was one of their main points of conflict with their neighbors to the east. To the Phoenix – widely regarded as having some of the wisest spiritual minds in the entire Empire – the Perfect Land's teachings were a false path, and deserved only to be stamped out.

The two of them could have a theological debate over it. He suspected Sekken would enjoy that: all the finer points of history surrounding the founding of the sect, the questions over its originating sutra, the probability or improbability that the Little Teacher had sent a second teaching to Rokugan, centuries after the conversations with the first Emperor that eventually became the *Tao of Shinsei*.

But discussing that would do nothing to help Seibo Mura, nor the Dragon Clan. So Ryōtora cut instead to the points that would actually answer Sekken's question. "If that were true, we would see a greater decline in the eastern half of our territory, where the Perfect Land is more widespread. We do not. If it were true, we would see a greater decline among the peasants than among samurai, who never follow the sect's teachings without first giving up their status. We do not. And if it were true…"

Sekken waited in silence, not prodding. Ryōtora couldn't tell if he'd persuaded the man or not.

"If it were true," he said quietly, "then we would see the decline beginning only after the followers of the Perfect Land gained a foothold in our territory. We do not."

The house was still. Several heartbeats passed before Sekken asked, even more quietly, "How long has this been going on?"

"Our scholars have pored over records in an attempt to answer that question. The decline is a slow one; pinpointing its beginnings is difficult. But they think it began over a century ago."

Ryōtora was grateful for Sekken's courtly training. It meant the other man's expression remained smooth, his gaze unaltered by this revelation. In that moment, Ryōtora did not think he could have borne any sign of horror or pity.

Not when there was one detail he was keeping back, one thing even Sekken could not be permitted to know. The duty of the Isao vassal family, the duty Ryōtora ordinarily carried out, was to examine the souls of peasant children and weigh them for spiritual merit. Those who showed enough promise were taken and raised as samurai – because if any group of Dragon showed a greater degree of withering than the rest, it was those at the top of the Celestial Order.

That could never be known outside their own borders. Showing weakness would be bad enough, but letting the Lion, the Crane, the *Phoenix* learn that the Dragon were upending the Celestial Order in such fashion? That some undisclosed number of samurai had been born as peasants? That would be disastrous.

Fortunately, Sekken made no further inquiries. He merely sat with his head bowed for a long moment, before nodding once, as if he'd won an internal argument. Then he shifted back from the table and made a full bow to Ryōtora, his hands forming a long-fingered triangle beneath his brow. "Sir Ryōtora. In my arrogance, I believed that I had thought more deeply about these matters than you. I was wrong, and I apologize for putting you to the effort of explaining to me."

"Please, Lord Asako – you don't need to bow like that." Ryōtora reached out without thinking, touching Sekken's elbow to encourage him to rise.

For an instant he felt warmth under his fingertips. Then,

horrified, he snatched his hand back and bowed as well. "Forgive me. I should not have."

It was how he would have reacted to Hokumei – but here it was an inexcusable gesture of familiarity. They'd only met a few days before. This wasn't a bath house, nor were they drinking. Sekken's family held far higher status than his own.

But Ryōtora's hands kept wanting to reach out. To touch Sekken, to share that warmth, to relax into comfortable familiarity. In his weakness, he craved the companionship and affection he'd once enjoyed with Hokumei.

In his peripheral vision, he saw Sekken's hand twitch, as if to reach for Ryōtora's own elbow. Then a laugh came from above. "Please get up. Otherwise we're going to waste half the night here in a duel of bowing and embarrassment. I'm not offended that you touched me; I'm not the Emperor or some sacred shintai. And while I'm still wishing I had never broached this subject with you, I am glad I haven't so badly insulted you that you've decided to order me out of Seibo Mura."

Ryōtora made sure to bring his expression under control before he sat up. Friendly courtesy, nothing more. "I have no intention of ordering you anywhere. You're trying to help. I can't tell you how grateful I am for that." The governor of Heibeisu shouldn't have sent Ryōtora with only two ashigaru to assist him… only he didn't have anyone else to spare.

"And I am grateful to you for giving me the chance," Sekken said, with oddly heartfelt sincerity. "Let us agree that together, we will solve this mystery."

CHAPTER TWELVE

Sekken was ordinarily cautious when he got up in the morning, so he wouldn't wake Ryōtora. But he must have made too much noise in rising and getting dressed, because when he finished tying his hakama around his waist, he turned to find Ryōtora sitting upright on his futon, bleary-eyed and half-sensible.

His fingers itched to brush the other man's hair out of his face. Their conversation the previous night… Ryōtora's willingness to trust him with such important truths had taken Sekken's breath away. And then their silly little dance, Ryōtora trying to help him up, then being so embarrassed by his own presumption.

Sekken wanted to tell him it was no presumption at all. But if even touching someone with casual familiarity made Ryōtora apologize with his face to the floor, he'd be shocked to hear that Sekken would welcome more. And he would say, rightly, that this wasn't the time for such things.

No, Ryōtora wouldn't hide behind a tactful deflection like that. Courtesy was a tenet of Bushidō, but so was Honesty. He would say outright – and politely – that he wasn't interested.

Ryōtora lost a battle with a yawn. "My apologies," Sekken

murmured in the soft tone one used toward a person tottering on the edge of wakefulness. "Go back to sleep."

"No… I shouldn't sleep so late."

He'd heard that note in Ryōtora's voice before, but never quite so nakedly exposed. It was the dreary sound of a man despairing at his own irreparable failings – as if, by not rising the instant the first rays of sun crested the horizon, Ryōtora was as contemptible as the most idle layabout.

Who made you so harsh on yourself? Here in the pale light of dawn, it was all too clear that Ryōtora's sense of honor wasn't a matter of aspiring to a greater purity of soul. It was a cane he used on his own back, thrashing himself for any perceived weakness. *Was it your mother? Your father? A sensei? Who persuaded you that if you cannot be perfect, then you are worthless?*

Asking would only shame him. Still in that gentle tone, Sekken said, "You need your rest. Tell me what you need done, and I'll see to it."

Ryōtora had pushed himself as far as a kneeling position, and was looking around as if unable to remember where he'd put his kimono. His hair slipped further until it covered one eye. "The stone. Ogano – I was going to ask him. And about the dog."

Despite the disjointed delivery, Sekken was able to reconstruct his meaning. "The stone" meant the road marker that gave the name of Sebō Mura; "the dog" was the inugami. Last night, after they finished dinner, he'd shared his theory that Ogano might be the witch. Ryōtora had agreed with his reasoning, though he also agreed there was no proof.

Not yet, at least. "I'll ask Ogano about the name of the village. And I'll see if I can catch him out with regards to the inugami. My sensei did train me for that sort of thing, you know." Sekken tied his hair out of the way and added, "Go back to sleep."

"I'll join you soon," Ryōtora said, as if he hadn't heard that last comment. Sekken decided not to argue, but slipped out on quiet feet. With any luck, Ryōtora would topple back over as soon as he was alone.

Haru didn't seem to be out in the main part of the house. Sekken called quietly up the staircase that led to the dark loft above, trying not to disturb Ryōtora further, but got no response. He'd hoped he could ask her where Ogano might have gone.

I'll try the cemetery first. The headman seemed to visit it every day, tending the grave of his brother. Or doing something more sinister? Though the proper hour for evil matters was the Hour of the Ox, shortly after midnight, not in the bright light of early morning. Sekken wondered if it would be worth staying up tonight to see if anyone visited the graveyard when they shouldn't. At a minimum, it might give Ryōtora an opportunity to enjoy being the alert one, while his companion stumbled about half-asleep. Even if Sekken hadn't preferred scholarship to politics, his sensei might have pushed him toward it, since he handled late-night entertainments so poorly.

He smiled to himself as he nudged his feet into his sandals. When all of this was done, perhaps he could persuade Ryōtora to take a day or so in Heibeisu. They might go to a play together. Or enjoy a night of drinking, before Ryōtora went on to his next important task… and Sekken went back to his very important stack of scrolls to read.

The smile faded. *What do you think that night of drinking would accomplish?* Even if Ryōtora was attracted to men, he was the sort to admire virtue, hard work, meaningful contributions to the Empire. Not the petty scribblings of a frivolous scholar.

In Seibo Mura, though, Sekken had the chance to achieve something more than petty scribblings. *Sebō Mura,* he thought as he left the house. *If the headman doesn't know, then who?* It was entirely possible the knowledge had been lost somewhere in the intervening centuries since the name changed. Or last year, when the shrinekeeper died.

He glanced around and scowled when he saw the inugami again. Why was it appearing in daylight now? Sekken appreciated the unbroken sleep, but not the shadow that had consequently attached itself to his heels.

Shouts drifted to his ears, carried by the mountain wind. That wasn't usual; the morning melody of Seibo Mura was chickens, crying children, and the creak of the well pulley. Sekken squinted into the brightness and saw a knot of villagers down the slope, gathered around–

Apparently he won't be hard to find. Ogano had his back to the side of Ashio's house and his arms crossed over his chest, half belligerence, half defensiveness. As Sekken hurried in that direction, he began to pick out words – chief among them, phrases like *your fault.*

Among the villagers he saw Ona, the woman who had lost her husband to the okuri inu. She was weeping and trying to lunge at Ogano; Haru was holding her back. "–brought this on us all, killed my Hideo with your evil dog, and for what? So you can have a fine house and tatami mats–"

Sekken swallowed a guilty curse. *How did they find out?*

"This is nonsense!" Ogano snarled, arms clamping harder against his chest as if that was the only way to keep from unleashing his fists. "You dare accuse me of doing this? I lost my *brother*–"

It was the wrong tactic. At least half the people facing him had lost family; given the kinship links that undoubtedly tied the members of this village together, probably all of them had. Sekken interposed himself before the situation could get any worse and put on his very best samurai air, the posture and tone of voice that said *none of you would dare touch me.* Hopefully it would be enough to protect him. "What is going on?"

"We found him," Ona spat over Haru's restraining shoulder. "You're trying to find the witch, ain't you? And here's Ogano with his wealth and his power – *he's* the one responsible for it all. Take him!"

"But he's known all along." That came from another face Sekken recognized: Heigo, one of the loggers who'd cut down the cypress for the re-enshrinement of Saiun-nushi. He wasn't furious and red-faced like Ona; his eyes were cold as he stared at Sekken. "He's been sleeping in Ogano's house this entire time. Both of them have. Enjoying the witch's hospitality, while the rest of us live in fear."

And this is why you don't let the Perfect Land into your territory. Under their philosophy, the samurai were at fault for everything, their moral failings the decaying root from which all other troubles sprang. Was that why Ryōtora judged himself so strictly – because he'd drunk too deep from the well of the heretics' judgment?

That was a question for later. Right now, Sekken faced down Heigo, hoping his fear didn't show. In his peripheral vision he saw the inugami at the fringes of the crowd, darting back and forth as if trying to find a way through the press. "You assume far too much. And someone has been eavesdropping on the private conversations of samurai."

"Your privacy ain't worth more than our lives!"

He couldn't tell who'd shouted that. The crowd was growing, every soul in Seibo Mura headed their way. Sekken raised one hand, hoping to quell them. "We have theories, nothing more! Which we kept to ourselves in the hopes of preventing exactly what you see right now: all of you turning on each other in suspicion, lashing out when you should be holding strong together."

The shouts rose instead of subsiding. Sekken was neither an orator nor a commander; he'd never been taught to control a crowd. He no sooner attempted to answer one accusation than another layered itself atop his words, drowning him out. When a sudden surge burst through the crowd, he almost bolted – but to his inexpressible relief, it turned out to be Ishi and Tarō, spears in hand. They planted themselves in front of Sekken and Ogano, weapons held at the diagonal, so their shafts were ready to form a fence as needed.

Then the ground gave a quick, sharp shock beneath everyone's feet. Silence fell, the villagers clutching one another as if expecting the earthquake to continue.

"You will stop *right now*."

Like aspen leaves fluttering in the wind, the crowd turned. Between their pivoting bodies, Sekken caught sight of Ryōtora: his kimono hastily thrown over the under-robe he'd slept in, his hair loose and tangled, his feet bare on the short, trampled grass. He still looked like he would rather be anywhere other than vertical and outside, but now it worked in his favor, making his aspect more forbidding.

Causing a local earthquake helped, too.

"There is no proof against Ogano, only supposition," Ryōtora said. "If he has done anything wrong, we will discover it.

Meanwhile, the first person to raise his hand to Ogano, or to his wife, or his children, or anyone connected with him, will suffer the consequences. The same goes for any of your other neighbors. You are forbidden to fight with each other. If strife breaks out here – if the people of Seibo Mura cannot remain strong – then I will not be able to save you. Because you will destroy yourselves before the monsters can. Do you understand?"

Of course they understood. The question was whether they would heed him. For now there were quiet mutters of assent, but Sekken knew better than to trust that would hold. He remained tense as Ishi and Tarō encouraged the crowd to disperse, Ona spitting at Haru's feet after she wrenched herself free.

"What nonsense!" Ogano blustered once the most hostile people were out of earshot. "Me, a witch! I don't even know what they're talking about!"

The inugami waited nearby, standing with all four paws braced. Either Ogano was very good at pretending it wasn't there, or he genuinely couldn't see it. Only Sekken could. "You deny binding a dog spirit to your family line? Or inheriting one from your ancestors?"

"I..." Ogano goggled at him. "A *dog spirit?* I hate dogs! They bark, they shed, their claws tear up the tatami–"

Sekken had expected a denial, but the prosaic nature of Ogano's response took him aback. No protestations that he had suffered as much as anyone, or noble claims that as the headman of his village he would never do anything to harm it. Instead he was concerned for his straw matting, as if that were a powerful counterargument against engaging in witchcraft.

Glancing at Ryōtora, Sekken saw his own thoughts mirrored in the shugenja's eyes. *Not Ogano, then. But who?* Haru, possibly, though Sekken hated to think it of her. She'd been so concerned for her nephew Fubatsu the day before.

In fact, Fubatsu was at her side now. Sekken didn't remember seeing him in the crowd around Ogano; by the look of the young man, he shouldn't even be out of bed yet. Haru was gripping his elbows to keep him steady as he whispered something to her, an urgent expression on his face. Then she looked stricken, and her gaze went to the cluster of the three of them, Sekken and Ryōtora and Ogano.

After transferring Fubatsu to a nearby sapling for support, she hurried over to their group, hesitating a longer distance away than manners alone called for. Then she knelt on the ground and bowed her head. "Sir Ryōtora, may… may I speak with you privately?"

She was afraid. Sekken could see it in the way her fingers dug against the trampled grass. Afraid of her husband? Maybe Sekken had dismissed Ogano's guilt too readily. A peasant could be as accomplished of a liar as a samurai; better, even, since peasants weren't expected to follow Bushidō.

Ryōtora pushed his hair out of his face and said, "Ogano, return to your house and stay there. Don't let anyone in who isn't family or one of your guests. I'll be there in a moment."

Ogano still looked furious, and his bow was minimal at best, but he obeyed.

Haru glanced up briefly, then ducked her head low again. "Please, my lord, I beg you for privacy."

The only people still close enough to hear were Fubatsu and Sekken. Ryōtora said, "Lord Asako has been assisting me in dealing with these troubles. I know he's an outsider to our clan, but whatever you have to say, he may hear it."

Yet still Haru hesitated. As if she desperately wanted to argue, but couldn't quite bring herself to contradict a samurai. And she was still afraid.

Fubatsu let go of the sapling and lurched a few unsteady steps toward them, then dropped to his knees so heavily that Sekken winced. In a voice still hoarse with illness, he said, "Sir Ryōtora – it's him. The Phoenix is the witch."

In circumstances of great emotional distress, it was possible for a person's spirit to leave their body as an ikiryō, a living ghost.

For a brief moment, Sekken thought he knew what that must feel like.

He was still standing with Ryōtora and Haru and Fubatsu, but his body felt very far away. As if something had popped him out of contact with his flesh, and the rest of him might be carried off by the wind. Ryōtora was staring at him, and Sekken wanted to say *that's absurd,* but his mouth no longer seemed to belong to him.

Then he was back, and Fubatsu had one hand on the ground to keep himself from tipping over, with the other raised unsteadily to point. Directly at the inugami waiting a little distance off.

"There's a dog there," Fubatsu said. "I saw it yesterday, when you came to heal me. I thought I imagined it because of the fever. But then I heard everyone talking about a witch, and spirit familiars, and – and this morning when I came outside for fresh air, I saw everyone gathered here. And the dog. Standing not far from the Phoenix. It keeps *looking* at him."

That was true. The dog had ignored Ogano, and paid no attention to Haru, either; all its attention was fixed on Sekken. Just like Ryōtora's was.

"Lord Asako," Ryōtora said, his deep voice suddenly stiff with formality. "What do you have to say to this?"

Too many answers wanted to come out of Sekken's mouth at once. He supposed it was only typical of him that the one which beat the rest out the door was, "How can you *see* it?"

Ryōtora shifted position. Orienting himself so that he faced both Sekken and the place Fubatsu was pointing to, where the dog stood. "Is this true?"

"The hihi," Sekken said inanely. His mind was still clinging to the part of this situation it liked, the puzzle of how Fubatsu could see the inugami when no one else could. "The yōkai you hit with a mattock. You must have gotten some of its blood in your mouth when you fought. Stories say it grants the power to see invisible spirits. Also it makes an excellent red dye." As if that mattered to *anything*. But as long as he was babbling about scholarly inconsequentials, he didn't have to face the growing coldness in Ryōtora's gaze.

"Fubatsu. Haru. Thank you for bringing this to my attention. Please go find Ishi and Tarō and tell them they're needed back here."

Haru wasted no time in springing to her feet. As Fubatsu rose, she visibly mustered her courage and said, "I don't want him in my house any longer. Because of him, my husband was attacked."

"Have you already forgotten that I also put myself *between* your husband and his attackers?" But Sekken was talking to her retreating back; she clearly felt she owed no deference to him any longer. Far too late, he called after her, "I'm not a witch!"

Then he pivoted to Ryōtora, hoping he didn't sound as desperate as he felt. "I'm not a witch. You don't need the ashigaru. I mean no harm to you or anyone here, I swear on my ancestors…"

Ancestors like Mirumoto Kotau, who might indeed have been a witch.

Some part of that doubt must have shown on his face. Ryōtora abruptly linked his hands together and chanted, and the inugami yelped once. Then Sekken knew, by the change in Ryōtora's expression, that he too could now see the dog.

If Sekken had to be accused of witchcraft, he might have hoped for a more imposing familiar. Now that he was paying attention, he saw the inugami was standing with all four paws braced and its head drooping, as if something had exhausted it. Not Ryōtora's invocation; Sekken was pretty sure it had been like that before.

"Go ahead and banish it if you want," he said drearily, feeling more than a bit like the dog looked. "Maybe you'll have more luck than the others did." Bragging rights for the Dragon, that one of their own succeeded where the Isawa failed.

That startled Ryōtora. "You've been trying to have this creature banished?"

"For months now. Well, after a while I gave up on that, and instead I started trying to figure out why it was haunting me. If I'm a witch, it's not by choice."

Like Ogano and his precious tatami mats, it clearly wasn't the protest Ryōtora had been expecting. Disheveled and confused, he ought to have looked charming – but Sekken honestly thought the shugenja had never seemed more imposing than at this moment.

He was looking at Sekken like he mattered, all right. But not in the way that had once made Sekken feel warm and strong inside.

"You owe me an explanation," Ryōtora said at last. His jaw was still set in an uncompromising line. At least he was giving Sekken a chance, though, instead of condemning him on the spot. "We'd better go somewhere less public, and then you start talking."

CHAPTER THIRTEEN

Haru didn't want Sekken in her house any more, and Ryōtora couldn't blame her. Furthermore, that place wouldn't be private unless Ryōtora ordered Ogano to leave, scant moments after confining the man there in the first place.

Instead he sent the ashigaru to patrol the village for any further trouble, then took Sekken up onto the hillside above the village, the spot near the graveyard where Ogano had first told him about the events in Seibo Mura. He didn't intend it as a reminder to Sekken of what had happened here – it was merely an open spot where they would see any approaching people long before they drew close enough to hear – but if it had that effect, it might not be a bad thing.

He knew something that might be relevant to the problems here. And he didn't tell me.

Sekken appeared… smaller somehow, as he arranged his hakama beneath himself and sat. Whether he realized it or not, ordinarily he carried himself with an air of confidence and authority – one born not of literal rank, but rather the privilege of his upbringing. That first night, he'd said his mother oversaw the famous Kanjirō Library in Sheltered Plains City; other comments in the days since had made it clear that quite a few members of his family held influential positions throughout Phoenix lands. Sekken wore that influence like a splendid cloak. But now it was gone, and he seemed ashamed.

Which wasn't the same thing as guilty. The tale he related to Ryōtora didn't clear matters up; if anything, it muddied the waters even more.

Not because Sekken told it poorly. His training came through in how he spoke, laying out the events in a way that managed to be both enlightening and affecting. Ryōtora had never personally experienced the paralysis he spoke of, the metalbound immobility of his body in sleep, but Sekken made him feel the suffocating terror of it. Night after night, with an inugami standing atop him, its teeth a mere snap away from his throat.

The same inugami that now sprawled on the grass nearby, its head down but still watchful. "In daylight it doesn't seem as intimidating," Sekken admitted, pausing briefly in his narration. "Not to mention that it's behaving differently now. I have no idea why."

That was a question for later. "Continue," Ryōtora said, and Sekken did.

Ryōtora held himself impassive, but inside he bled. Even with such a short acquaintance, he thought he'd come to know Sekken. Now he saw an entire side to the man whose existence he'd never suspected. A side Sekken had kept hidden.

Just like you thought you knew Hokumei.

It was easier to let out his anger than any of the other things he felt. When Sekken finished, Ryōtora said, "So this entire time –

every hint you've dropped about 'strange magical practices' and thinking a witch might be responsible – it's been because of the inugami."

"Yes," Sekken said.

"Why didn't you *tell* me? Why point to an innocent man as a suspect?"

"I genuinely thought he might be guilty!" Sekken protested. "*Someone* must have sent this thing after me. I didn't summon it; I didn't even know spirits could be bound this way until Asako Fukimi told me about tsukimono-suji. And Ogano seemed like the most likely culprit. For that matter, we still don't know for sure that he's innocent."

"That isn't the point." Ryōtora's shoulders ached with tension. "You had information I needed. The whole time I thought you were helping, you kept this secret from me. I trusted you, and you betrayed that."

"I–"

Whatever answer Sekken had been going to give, he cut it off short. Then he bowed to the earth, and this time Ryōtora felt no impulse to make him rise. "I have no excuse. It was my own weakness, nothing more."

No excuse – but Ryōtora still needed an explanation. "What weakness? Did you think me so short-sighted that I would immediately blame you, even though you were nowhere near this place when the troubles began?"

He could barely hear Sekken's reply, addressed as it was to the ground. "It was because of Mirumoto Kotau. And because witches bind the spirits to their family lines. If the inugami has something to do with Seibo Mura, and it has something to do with me… then it may mean I am related to a family here."

Sekken stopped again, and the poised arrangement of his kneeling bow sank lower, his forehead touching the earth. "I have no excuse."

He didn't have to say anything more. Ryōtora could imagine the rest for himself. For a samurai like Sekken, the idea of being related to peasants was an unspeakable disgrace. Even worse if they were hereditary witches, of course – but his shame wasn't for his connection to that samurai ancestor said to come from a tsukimono-suji lineage. It was for any connection to this tiny, rural village.

The village Ryōtora himself had been born in.

You knew what he would say if he found out. Be glad that he hasn't. And stop yearning after what you will never have, and do not deserve.

"Rise," Ryōtora said at last, because he couldn't leave Sekken bowed like that forever, and it was clear the Phoenix was going to stay there until told otherwise.

Sekken kept his head bent as he straightened. "I know I have betrayed your trust. But please permit me to go on helping, in any way I can. Whatever my connection to these incidents may be, I owe both you and the people of this village my best efforts in stopping them. Confine me if you must, but do not send me away."

Sending him away hadn't even crossed Ryōtora's mind. Sekken was still a piece of the riddle, and no matter what he'd done, Ryōtora still needed his help. The villagers, on the other hand…

"By now everyone in Seibo Mura will know about the inugami," Ryōtora said. "They were willing to turn on Ogano, who is one of their own; you have only your status as a samurai to protect you." *And me.* It wasn't personal feelings talking – at least, not only. It was Ryōtora's responsibility to protect a guest in Dragon lands.

Sekken nodded. "And Haru won't let me into the house. Somewhere outside the village, perhaps? I survived the trip here; a few days in the mountains will do me no harm."

That wasn't necessarily true. Even if the yōkai didn't return before the full moon, there were plenty of ordinary predators and other hazards in the wild. "Part of the shrine is still standing," Ryōtora said, after brief argument with himself over whether he was being too soft. "You can shelter in what's left. With Saiun-nushi moved down into the village proper, no one has reason to go up there." That didn't answer the question of what to tell everyone about Sekken and the inugami, but Ryōtora needed more time to consider that – time without the weight of Sekken's regretful gaze on him, muddying his thoughts even further.

"I will go there at once," Sekken said, bowing. "Please look after Jun."

His servant, who had spent most of his time since arriving in Seibo Mura taking care of his master's mount and belongings. Would people turn on him, in the absence of Sekken himself? "I'll send him with supplies for you," Ryōtora promised.

Then Sekken left, striking out across the slope to reach the path up to the waterfall and the shrine without first descending into the village, with the inugami following at his heels. Ryōtora resolutely did not watch him go.

Ryōtora half-expected to find the mob re-forming outside Ogano's house, but it seemed his shameful display of temper had made an impression. People went about their business – with sullen and suspicious looks, true, but they let the matter rest. For now.

In dealing with Sekken, he'd completely forgotten that he'd rushed outside half-dressed. It was only when he reflexively moved to step out of the sandals he wasn't wearing that Ryōtora remembered he was barefoot. Jun, crouched outside the house like Haru had thrown him out – which she probably had – brought him water to wash his feet.

While scrubbing the dirt off, Ryōtora explained to Jun what had happened, and where Sekken had gone. "You might be safer with him," he said at the end. "I know it's inconvenient, but…"

But the alternative was worse. Jun nodded. *You won't have to be there long,* Ryōtora thought. Assuming all went as it had before, the next round of disturbances would be starting in just eight days. Inugami or no inugami, he doubted Sekken would want to stay for that.

While Jun packed up his master's belongings, Ryōtora dressed himself properly, then searched Ogano's house, the headman watching with his jaw clenched tight. As Ryōtora expected, he found no signs of anything untoward. Of course, Ogano might have cleared those out days ago – but he doubted it. Whoever was responsible for the inugami targeting Sekken, they must have a reason, and Ogano's only reaction to his Phoenix guest had been annoyance.

When the search was done, Ryōtora sat down with Ogano in the living area and said, "Are you aware of the name of this village changing? It was once called Sebō Mura, instead of Seibo Mura."

Ogano shook his head, mouth still clamped shut.

"No old tales from your grandparents?" Ryōtora pressed. "Or is there someone else in the village who might know – some storyteller or lorekeeper?"

"Nawaro," Ogano said. "Who kept the shrine."

And now was dead. Ryōtora sighed. "No stories about something being… *held* here?" Another shake of Ogano's head.

"What about inugami? Or witches? Has anyone here been accused of witchcraft before?"

Again and again, the answer was no. Ryōtora didn't think Ogano was hiding anything; it would have been in his best interests to throw suspicion onto someone else, if he'd had any grounds for doing so. He truly seemed to know nothing.

Who *would* know? Ryōtora pinched the bridge of his nose, then made himself put his hand down. He couldn't show weakness to anyone, not when they were looking to him for salvation. If Sekken were still around…

He pushed that thought aside. "Tonight, before sunset, I need to address the whole village. When everyone is back from the mines and the fields."

"Yes, my lord."

"Until then," Ryōtora said grimly, straightening his spine, "I need you to help me work out how to prepare for the evacuation of Seibo Mura."

Any attempt to bring the whole village through the mountains would be a nightmare. The peasants managed the trip twice a year, when they took their loads of cinnabar and realgar to Heibeisu, but that was with the strongest and healthiest adults pulling the wheelbarrows. They were used to hardship. So many residents were ill, though, while others were elderly, or very young. They could use the barrows to carry food and some makeshift tents, with those who couldn't walk far riding atop the loads, but where would they camp? They couldn't all sleep under the barrows, the way the usual transport crew did. And Ryōtora knew from his own trip that there were precious few places flat and hospitable enough for the whole village at once.

"Not to mention that they'll want to bring other things," Ogano told him. "Family altars. Treasured keepsakes. Anything they don't want the monsters to smash. They won't like being told to leave those behind."

"They'll like even less being here when the yōkai return," Ryōtora said grimly. He had no reason to think anything he'd done had forestalled that. And if there was going to be an evacuation, it needed to happen well ahead of the full moon, so that people had time to get away.

Still, he knew there would be strong objections. Ryōtora had more than a few of those himself; the more he considered the situation, the more potential problems he saw. He could loan them his pony, and commandeer Sekken's mounts – but even finding enough water for everyone might be a problem. While creeks ran everywhere through the mountains, many of them were at the bottoms of small ravines that would be dangerous to climb down.

It would be a risky journey under normal circumstances. And if the yōkai didn't remain in Seibo Mura, but followed them south…

Thinking about the yōkai possibly following reminded him. "The people who tried to flee, and were found dead," Ryōtora asked Ogano. "Where were their bodies?"

Without going there in person, it was difficult to pinpoint the location, but Ryōtora was fairly certain the spot Ogano described was within the bounds of the old ward he'd found. It wasn't proof; lacking anything to compare against, it might just as easily have been outside that line. The rest of the disturbances had been centered on the village – but that was where the people were. *Still, is that what the ward is for? To keep the yōkai here?* Except it was an ancient ward, and the yōkai were a new problem.

He hated trying to think through on his own. Sekken was the one who enjoyed puzzles. Ryōtora didn't dare go up to the shrine, though. Not yet. Not until he'd spoken to the villagers… and gotten his own feelings under control.

The villagers came first. As the sun began to set behind the mountains, Ryōtora gathered them together near the temporary shrine for Saiun-nushi. That was the last time the village had felt anything like unified, during their tiny festival. It seemed as if months had passed since then, rather than two days.

Ryōtora laid out the situation as honestly as he dared. Not the evacuation plan – that would only encourage people to start fleeing now – but the inugami, Ogano, Sekken, the possibility of a witch. "I have found no evidence that either of them is guilty, nor anyone connected with him," he said, as forcefully as he could. "In fact, I have found no evidence that *anyone* in Seibo Mura is guilty of such practices. You know each other; you've been neighbors for years. In a place like this, such a thing can't easily pass unnoticed. The attacks you've suffered aren't a simple matter of a failed crop or someone gathering suspicious wealth. The problem lies deeper than that.

"Which is why I need your wisdom. You know the stories of your own village; your history lives in your minds. The old name of this village is not Seibo Mura, but Sebō Mura – a name that speaks of chains and forgetting. I believe that may hold a clue to what is happening. And someone long before me laid a kind of ward around this place, traces of which still remain. If you know anything that might shed light on those two things, then for the sake of yourself and all your neighbors, tell me."

Silence answered him. He could see the peasants shifting

position, glancing at each other; here and there someone leaned to whisper to another person. But no one spoke up.

"Anything," Ryōtora said. "However far-fetched or fragmentary it may be."

That was a mistake – but a necessary one. In Ryōtora's experience, every village had at least one self-appointed expert who had to know something on every topic, even if that "something" was invented on the spot. Seibo Mura had two, and they disagreed. Still, Ryōtora listened patiently, at least for a while. When it looked liable to degenerate into an endless argument, he announced that people could come to him one by one at Ogano's house. Then he escaped.

The problem was, he had no way of knowing whether anything he heard was accurate, let alone useful. Ryōtora had vaguely hoped that it would feel like opening a puzzle-box: something would shift, and suddenly the whole thing would come open and reveal the answer to him. Instead he felt more like he was trying to reassemble the portable shrine, and all he had was a pile of splintered kindling that might or might not have even come from that structure in the first place. One person said his grandmother had once been chased back from the hot spring by a "demon dog" that sounded somewhat like the okuri inu Sekken had told him about; another claimed Seibo Mura actually had a guardian dog, which was supposed to bark to warn people about impending rockfalls, while a third said that no, the tradition was that as long as there were dogs in Seibo Mura, the cinnabar mine would continue to produce valuable ore. A few generations back, there had been a rōnin accused of a crime who hid out in Seibo Mura; was that perhaps what the "chain" bit meant? Then the villager telling that story belatedly realized they might be held responsible for harboring a criminal, and tried very ineptly to claim it hadn't been Seibo Mura after all; it was some other village off to the west.

None of it helped. Ryōtora went to sleep with a head full of useless information and woke up no more enlightened than before. The only thing he could be half-sure he'd accomplished was to talk people down from attacking Ogano or Sekken.

Sekken himself remained the best clue – one Ryōtora should have investigated more closely. Him, and the inugami. Sending them away yesterday morning had been weakness, Ryōtora's inability to face his own conflicted feelings. He would not be so weak today.

It was self-spite as much as anything that made him leave the house without breakfast, heading directly for the waterfall and the shrine above. Too late, Ryōtora realized it would have been better if he'd taken the time for that… because then he might have arrived after Sekken left the waterfall.

Ryōtora knew very well that the Phoenix wasn't accustomed to hardship. It wasn't part of a courtier's training, the way it was for bushi or shugenja, because their duties didn't require them to toughen their bodies or purify their spirits. And Sekken had made a comment or two about how chilly the nights here were, even though it was the height of summer.

But now Sekken stood underneath the relentless cascade of snow-cold water, one hand clasped over the opposite fist, meditating. He must have been frozen to the bone. That concern, however, was Ryōtora's second thought, coming well after the first – which was not so much a thought as transfixion at the sight of the water streaming over Sekken's bare shoulders and chest.

Heart suddenly beating too fast, he wrenched his gaze away and found the inugami was still there. Was it his imagination, or did the dog look even more listless than before? It lay with its muzzle atop crossed paws, eyes slitted and watching Ryōtora. Nothing in its posture seemed hostile, and Ryōtora, trying to think about anything other than Sekken's body, found himself reflecting that if this was a witch's familiar, it was being remarkably placid.

"Sir Ryōtora."

Sekken's greeting was barely audible over the small thunder of the waterfall. Ryōtora didn't quite turn to face him, but he got far enough to see that Sekken had moved out from under the cascade, arms now clamped over his chest for warmth as he waded toward the bank. Ryōtora stepped away from Sekken's piled clothes, even though he hadn't been very close to them in the first place, and waited until the Phoenix had toweled himself off and thrown his kimono back on.

"My apologies," Ryōtora said in a rough voice once that was done. "I thought to find you at the shrine."

"I didn't expect you to come looking for me. That water is shockingly cold, isn't it? I'm not sure how you stand it." Sekken laughed, awkwardly. "You're wondering why I was doing that. I thought… I don't even know. I felt the need to be purified, I suppose."

Lies weren't the kind of pollution the water kami could remove. But Ryōtora understood the impulse, subjecting oneself to hardship in the hopes of grinding the weakness out.

It never seemed to work.

"Let's talk somewhere quieter," he said, still not looking at Sekken. He used the ladle to perform a brief purification, prayed for equanimity, and headed for the shrine.

CHAPTER FOURTEEN

Sekken had barely slept the previous night. He could blame that on a variety of factors: the discomfort of lying on the floor without tatami or a proper futon to cushion him; the uneasiness of being in a ruined shrine whose remaining roof might collapse on him at any moment; the jug of thick farmhouse sake – halfway to alcoholic porridge – that Jun had acquired by mysterious means and brought to ease his master's isolation. Sekken had managed to drink only a few sips of it before the texture made him stop.

More than anything, though, his rest was forestalled by two things: the watchful presence of the inugami, and the memory of Ryōtora's expression when he learned the truth.

The dog spirit didn't seem to particularly mind being on sacred ground. Was it still sacred, Sekken wondered, with Saiun-nushi's shintai removed down to the village? Perhaps not. The inugami had paced around the wreckage for a time, whining deep in its throat, before lying down as if the effort of walking was too much. When Sekken got up from his own failed sleep, though, the dog insisted on following, paws dragging with exhaustion.

Sekken's own feet dragged, but for different reasons. The hot shock of betrayal in Ryōtora's gaze – and then the cold distance that descended soon after. Every effort to sleep had been thwarted by Sekken's own mind, spinning out hypothetical conversations with Ryōtora, explanations, justifications, new stagings of the reveal wherein Sekken handled the entire thing a thousand times better.

Visions of the past where he told Ryōtora sooner, and things never came to this point.

It was a masochistic impulse as much as anything that sent him to the waterfall at dawn, to stand under the icy flow and pray to any benevolent spirit that might be listening. And maybe it had done some good, because when he opened his eyes, Ryōtora was there. Not angry, but… Sekken wasn't sure what name to put to the man's expression. Whatever it should be called, it eased the spot inside Sekken that had been knotted tight since the previous morning.

Not that he could expect much to be easy going forward. Sekken hadn't realized how much Ryōtora had begun to relax around him until the man reverted to being unreadable stone. They climbed the path in silence, and Sekken had to fight the urge to fill it with useless words.

The inugami whined again when they got to the top of the path, possibly in protest at the exertion. Ryōtora hesitated, then crouched, looking at the dog. "This seems like the best clue. You indicated that others have tried to banish it before, with no luck… but have you tried to communicate with it?"

"An Isawa tried. He preferred cats, though; maybe that's why the dog refused to answer." Sekken was reflexively taking refuge in humor, and made himself stop. "If you're willing, it might be worth trying again. Things have changed: the inugami used to only appear to me at night. Now it's here in the daytime, and it looks…"

"Tired," Ryōtora said. "Yes. And you said it didn't appear at all after you arrived in Seibo Mura, until just recently. So that's two changes."

It didn't have the comfortable flow of their previous conversations, but it was better than silence, better than sitting up here alone. Better than going back to being useless. "Something to do with the ward you found?" Sekken ventured. "Though if it's designed to keep something imprisoned here, I'm not sure why it would keep the inugami *out* – not to mention that it managed to haunt me in Sheltered Plains City. On top of that, it seems to be staying here even though you've warded this place against yōkai. What a paradoxical creature."

"And none of that explains why it would haunt you, of all people. I know you theorized that you might be related to someone here – but if that's the case, then so are all members of that branch of your family. Not to mention others besides."

Ryōtora delivered that part stiffly, not looking at Sekken. Trying to avoid giving insult, perhaps. "Well," Sekken said, "if you can get the dog to talk, we might get some answers."

With no particular care for the state of his hakama, Ryōtora sat cross-legged on the dirt, facing the inugami. The spirit looked briefly at Sekken, then couched itself a short distance from the shugenja, as if it knew what was coming. "It doesn't seem malevolent," Ryōtora said, shaking out his sleeves.

Sekken felt embarrassed, even though he doubted Ryōtora had meant it as a criticism. "It was a good deal fiercer before, when it came at night. But you're right. Now it seems… more sad than anything else. I almost feel sorry for it."

"That might be of use," Ryōtora said thoughtfully. "Sit between me and the inugami – not directly between, but a little to the side, so I can see you both."

There was enough space between the shugenja and the spirit that Sekken wasn't directly next to either of them, but they formed a small triangle instead. Once he was settled, Ryōtora said, "Breathe as if you're meditating, and try to let go of your thoughts."

The resonance of his voice was like a deep-toned bell, helping Sekken do as instructed. His wet hair had soaked the back of his kimono, and he was still half-frozen from the waterfall; any time the wind gusted, a bone-deep shiver tried to set in. But he'd found a measure of clarity standing under the flow, and it returned to him now. A feeling of stability – as if, after months of walking on unsteady ground, he had good solid stone beneath him at last. *Maybe it's the influence of Saiun-nushi, lingering in this place.*

The inugami whined again, more insistently than before. Its head dipped several times; was it communicating somehow with Ryōtora? The shugenja was as motionless as a stone himself, except where the wind tossed strands of his hair about. He stared unblinking at the inugami, and only that feeling of clarity kept Sekken from giving in to the urge to ask what was happening where he couldn't see.

Then, with no warning, Ryōtora said, "It wants to show us something. You… It wants to show *you* something."

On his words, the inugami attempted to scrabble to its feet, but it didn't quite have the strength. Without thinking, Sekken rose to his knees and slipped his hands under its body, helping it up. It was the first time he'd touched the spirit of his own will, the first time he'd touched it waking. The fur and the flesh beneath it weren't quite warm: more like the memory of warmth, a scent lingering when the incense itself was gone. But if he'd expected some feeling of peril or malevolence, he found none.

Ryōtora stood as well, but kept his distance. The dog moved toward the wreckage of the shrine, where it had been pacing the previous night, looking back over its shoulder every step or two until Sekken rose and followed. When it got to a particular spot, it pawed weakly at the fallen beams and roof tiles and whined again.

Sekken looked at Ryōtora, but the shugenja only shook his head, baffled. "I don't know. It isn't communicating in words. You'll have to dig."

If it meant helping Ryōtora, he'd dig through this mountain with his bare hands – but he hoped he wouldn't have to. Sekken's sleeves caught on the wreckage as he tried to lift pieces away, and he didn't have a cord to tie them back; he realized belatedly that Jun was nowhere in sight. Probably down in the village, getting food. Sekken wound up shrugging out of his kimono entirely, letting it dangle loose from his hakama as he heaved broken tiles and rafters out of the way. The exertion warmed him at last, though his damp hair kept falling forward in an irritating fashion.

He was just starting to wonder if he would even know when he found what he was looking for – and also whether he should pause to grab a knife and hack his damn hair off; it could be an offering to Saiun-nushi – when his hand touched a board and the inugami barked once, very loudly.

The board was thick, and pinned beneath a heavy beam. This had been a shrine in the old style, built out of whole logs as much as shaped lumber, and Sekken wrenched something in his shoulder trying to get the board out. When he hissed in pain, Ryōtora came forward to help. Together they managed to drag it free.

"It's a board," Sekken said, stupid with breathlessness.

Ryōtora said, "Turn it over."

The wood thudded into the dirt as it landed. The other side proved to be carved with characters; it must have been the decorative plaque that hung at the eaves when the shrine still stood. The outward-facing surface was badly weathered, and any paint that had once filled in the grooves was long since gone. Sekken had to trace them with his finger to make them out.

"Ingyō Jinja," he said. "Assuming the pronunciation hasn't changed since this was carved."

"The shrine wasn't marked on the map in Heibeisu; I think it's too small to have an official name. Signet Shrine? But the second character you traced looked different."

Sekken ran his fingers down the grooves again. "It's the same *in* as in 'signet,' yes. But the second part – that's just the character for 'journey.' Journey's Seal Shrine? Sealed Journey Shrine? That's an even odder name than Forgotten Chain Village."

"Chains," Ryōtora said. "Seals. I suppose they fit together – the idea of something being held here. The yōkai? But why an ancient ward and an ancient shrine, and then this new problem?"

Yōkai. Ingyō.

That last syllable echoed in Sekken's mind like a temple gong, and he whispered a disbelieving curse under his breath. *Yagyō.*

Ryōtora crouched at his side, brow knitted with concern. "What is it?"

Sekken stared at him. "The Hyakki Yagyō. Except – that doesn't make any *sense*. Because it isn't *real*."

"The what?"

Ryōtora's duties had him traveling through the hinterlands of Dragon territory, not enjoying the cultured life of the city.

And the Dragon were hardly renowned for their enjoyment of literature anyway. Sekken said, "The Night Parade of a Hundred Demons."

He shot to his feet, one hand raking his damp, tangled hair out of his face. "It's a… a *literary trope.* The kind of thing you see in Scorpion picture scrolls, or, or… I've heard the Crab perform draw-lot plays about it, very silly ones where the actors have to pay a forfeit if they pull out the name of a yōkai they don't know. There's no such thing as the Night Parade!"

"Yagyō," Ryōtora murmured, looking down at the shrine's weathered, barely legible plaque. "Ingyō. Not a journey being sealed… a parade, being locked away."

Sekken found himself staring at the inugami. It had slumped down again when he found the plaque, but now it lurched up and came to his side. The phantom coolness of its muzzle nudged into his palm, a feeble gesture of encouragement.

Ryōtora said, "Real or not – tell me about the Night Parade."

"I don't know if it's literally a hundred yōkai," Sekken said. They'd moved a little distance away from the shrine, to a spot where the sunlight came through; it was warmer there, though not so much that he hadn't pulled his kimono back up. The inugami lay flopped with its head in Sekken's lap, apparently deciding that, now that Sekken had found the answer, he could be treated as a human pillow. "There was a… no, not a Bayushi artist. Shosuro? Soshi? I get those two families confused more often than I should. I think it was a Shosuro–"

"Lord Asako."

Ryōtora's patient voice called him back from the edge of that hole. "You're right; it doesn't matter. Some Scorpion artist did a whole series of paintings of the Night Parade, and he did exactly one hundred of them, but that might just have been artistic tidiness. It's sort of a catalogue of yōkai, including a few he may just have made up. Other versions show some of the same yōkai, some different. If there's a set composition for the Night Parade, I don't know what it is."

He paused to let Ryōtora pull his writing kit out of his kimono, but the wad of moss in it proved to be too dry for use. Sekken scrambled up and ran to fetch his own. Once the loaned brush was wet and Ryōtora had a scrap of paper laid across a flattish rock, Sekken continued. "There isn't much of a story to be told. The Night Parade is just a bunch of yōkai rampaging through a place – usually a town, and usually at midsummer. Some versions say it's led by a creature called Nurarihyon, but not all of them agree on that, and even the ones that do depict Nurarihyon a bunch of different ways. Like I said, it's a literary trope – at least I assumed it was. So people feel free to make up whatever they like."

"What do these things say about how you defeat it?"

"You *don't,*" Sekken said. "You just survive it. There's a very old kyōgen play from Crane lands – hasn't been performed for several hundred years, I think; it went out of fashion – that makes the Night Parade out to be this fun bit of chaos, everything topsy-turvy for a little while before order reasserts itself. But based on what's happened here, I think the truth is closer to the versions that say it brings death and destruction. Even *seeing* Nurarihyon is supposedly enough to kill a person on the spot… which is why no two artists depict him the same way."

The movement of the brush faltered. "If that's true, then he could kill the entire village."

The entire village was at risk anyway; plenty of the yōkai were dangerous. Sekken understood what Ryōtora meant, though. If Nurarihyon had walked through Seibo Mura when people were fleeing for their lives, there would be hardly anyone left now.

"I don't think he's appeared," Sekken said. "Yet, anyway. The first round of disturbances started off small, just noises and animated objects. It's gotten worse over time."

"Which means he might show up during the next full moon." Ryōtora gripped the brush hard enough that Sekken feared it might snap in his hand. "And I have no idea how to defeat – or imprison – a yōkai I can't look at."

Blindfolded, I suppose. That was one facetious answer Sekken managed to keep inside. If Ryōtora thought it was necessary, he would do exactly that.

Instead Sekken said, "I wouldn't recommend trying. Better to move the people here to safety. There's enough time to get everyone well away from Seibo Mura before the full moon, if not all the way to Heibeisu. And since the ward is keeping the Night Parade trapped here–"

"I'm not sure it is, though." Ryōtora glanced over his shoulder, toward the ruined shrine. "I told you it feels like it's fading. If the shrine is part of it somehow, I'm betting the earthquake last autumn weakened the barrier. I had thought the two weren't connected, because the timing was wrong, but you said the Night Parade is a summer phenomenon. Maybe that's why the delay."

Sekken had begun to pet the inugami without even really thinking about it, scratching behind its ghost-soft ears. Now his hand stilled. "The *timing*. I… am a prize idiot who should not have been let out of school."

Ryōtora's head whipped around so fast his hair fell into his eyes. "What do you mean?"

"This spirit," Sekken said, dragging his fingernails through the dog's fur, "started haunting me right after we felt a little tremor in Sheltered Plains City. That would have been – let's see – the third day of the Month of the Dog."

He'd never asked when exactly the earthquake struck Seibo Mura. *I should have.*

Ryōtora's jaw tightened. "So the earthquake broke the shrine, which freed the Night Parade. And the dog was trying to warn you. I don't think that's a witch's familiar; I think the story I heard last night, that Seibo Mura has a guardian dog, is closer to the truth."

"But it *is* a familiar," Sekken said. "The Isawa we consulted was able to figure out that much, though not who it belonged to. It's definitely someone's bound spirit."

"Then why is it trying to help?"

That was an excellent question. Sekken thought about it, continuing to scratch gently as he did. Finally he said, "This is an ancient practice – something people used to do more often before the Fall of the Kami. Maybe back then, it wasn't always used for personal gain. Maybe the owner is a… a benevolent witch of some kind."

He had no idea if the inugami could understand him, but it huffed softly and turned its head so he was scratching a different, and apparently better, spot. Its tail thumped a few times in pleasure.

Sekken still didn't know why the inugami had chosen him, of all people, to drag all the way to Seibo Mura. His tsukimono-suji ancestor had been a Mirumoto; surely there were samurai in

Dragon lands it could have called on instead? Unless that family line had died out. He remembered the magnitude of their decline, and felt a chill far deeper than that of the waterfall.

Then he heard a voice calling his name. "That's Jun," Sekken said, easing out from under the inugami. It made a mournful sound at the loss of his lap. "You should get back down to the village and let them know what you've learned. I'll stay here and see if I can't remember anything else useful." *Three easy methods for killing Nurarihyon with your eyes closed. Surely I've read something like that somewhere.*

"No," Ryōtora said, also rising.

"No?"

The shugenja attempted to brush the dirt off his clothing, then gave it up as a lost cause. Sekken wasn't much better off, after digging in the ruins of the shrine. "I can't afford to waste time climbing up here every time I need to talk to you. I apologize for the inconvenience, but we need you down in the village. You're simply going to have to pack up your things and bring them into Seibo Mura again. I'll convince Haru to let you back in."

CHAPTER FIFTEEN

If the ward was weakening, could it be strengthened again? That question chewed at Ryōtora as he waited for Sekken to change into clothing not dirtied by digging in a collapsed shrine, then while the two of them descended once more into Seibo Mura, followed by the inugami. Rebuilding the shrine might help – but that would take a long time. And if the ward had somehow been bound up in the specific architecture of the building, Ryōtora had no idea how to recreate that. He would have to write to his superiors in the Agasha, and perhaps also to the Isawa and even the Asahina of the Crane. Or the Yogo, down in Scorpion lands; one of their schools trained renowned wardmasters.

You'd have to write to every shugenja school in the Empire. You have no way of knowing who might hold the key to this puzzle.

All of that would take months, even a year or more. Time the people in Seibo Mura didn't have.

Sekken walked silently at his side, but the silence was no longer as fraught as it had been. He seemed deep in his own thoughts. Ryōtora knew he should still be angry at Sekken; if the man had just shared information about the inugami sooner, maybe they would have found the plaque in the shrine before now. But the regret in his eyes had been all too clear, and in the face of that, it was hard for Ryōtora to cling to his feelings of hurt.

It had been easier when he was angry. Then he hadn't wished quite so intensely that he could be honest with Sekken himself.

Drawing in a deep breath, Ryōtora cast about for something they could discuss. Before he settled on anything, he saw a woman running across the trampled grass and dirt of the village towards them.

"Sir Ryōtora!" It was Fūyō, the mother of Aoi, the girl who'd lost her memories. She flung herself down onto the ground, breathless. "You must come, please."

"What's happened? Please, get up."

Fūyō obeyed without hesitation, reversing direction into the village. "It's my daughter. I don't know what's wrong with her, but she's getting worse. Please…"

Ryōtora was already following, Sekken at his heels, the inugami lumbering along behind. *Getting worse.* Fubatsu had gotten worse, due to a confluence of effects from the yōkai he'd encountered. The dog spirit seemed to be getting more and more tired, though they didn't know why. Now Aoi.

Fūyō led them to the house, but stopped outside and wrung her hands. "She's been acting strangely for the last two days. Scratching at herself like there's bugs all over her, wailing that she has to get out of here – but she won't even leave the house to get water. I didn't want to trouble you, when you've already done so much to try to help her–"

"You did right to tell me," Ryōtora said. He wished she'd told him sooner. The last two days… What had happened in the last two days? It felt more like two years. He'd moved Saiun-nushi down into the village – no, that was three days ago. Finding out about the inugami had happened the day before. Two days ago, he'd healed Fubatsu.

And warded the village against yōkai.

Catching the edge of Sekken's sleeve, Ryōtora drew a few steps back from Fūyō and spoke in a low voice. "When did the inugami start behaving this way?"

"Showing up in daylight? I noticed when I went for my walk the morning after the re-enshrinement."

"Did it look tired then?"

Sekken frowned in thought. "It's hard to say, because I was used to seeing it sitting on top of me at night, not walking around. Definitely not as tired as it is now… but perhaps a little? You're thinking this has to do with your ward."

Ryōtora was grateful for his quick mind. "Possibly. But the problem with that is–"

"The Night Parade has only been attacking at night, during the full moon. So how could Aoi be affected?"

"And she's not possessed. I'm certain of that."

"Not possessed in the ways we're familiar with, at least. Let's take another look."

Fūyō slid open the door and bowed them inside. It took Ryōtora's eyes a moment to adjust to the darkness of the farmhouse; at first all he could detect of Aoi was her rapid, strained breathing. Fūyō moved past him to go to her side, and then he spotted her: a dark huddle in the far corner, wedged into the gap between a barrel and the wall.

Behind Ryōtora, the inugami growled.

"Daughter?" Fūyō whispered. "It's all right. The samurai are here. Sir Ryōtora and Lord Asako have come to help you."

"Make him go away," Aoi moaned, not uncurling from her huddle. "The Phoenix. He's an outsider – I heard someone say he's a witch. He has a dog spirit as his familiar. He's cursed me; I'm sure of it."

"I managed to curse you before I even arrived?" Sekken said, in the lazy drawl of an arrogant courtier. "How talented I am. Or is it just the latest development in your condition that you blame on me?"

Aoi hissed at him. "Don't mock me, witch!" Then her demeanor softened as she turned to Ryōtora, her face a pale ghost in the shadows. "Please, you have to help me. Send the witch away, and take me to safety. I… I will do anything for you. I will be your servant. Your concubine–"

"Aoi!" Fūyō's scandalized cry rang through the small house.

Gesturing at Sekken – and the inugami – to stay back, Ryōtora came forward and crouched next to Aoi. When he reached for her wrist to take her pulse, she clutched his hand. "Please," she whispered, barely loud enough for him to hear. "You know it isn't safe here. They're coming back, in just a few days. We should all leave, shouldn't we? While we still can."

It was the first time she'd spoken of him taking anyone but her out of Seibo Mura, and it had the air of someone fishing for an argument he might find more persuasive. She wasn't worried about other people, her own family included. Granted, she didn't remember Fūyō or anyone else; they were essentially strangers to her. But even for strangers, showing no concern except for their possible use as a bargaining chip was remarkably cold.

He pried her hand loose and took her pulse through his sleeve. Fast and thready – much weaker than it ought to be. Her eyes were wide, and in the dim light they looked black, the pupil consuming all the brown. The inugami growled again, and this close, Ryōtora felt Aoi flinch.

His mind was whirling. He had a suspicion… but to test it in front of Fūyō would be cruel. How to separate the two, though? He couldn't lie, even if it would make things easier. Neither would it be kind to simply order Fūyō and Aoi to do as he said, with no explanation.

Where could they go? Not to the temporary shrine he'd constructed; ordinarily Ryōtora would consider that the ideal place, but it would be far too public. Back up to the old shrine? Ogano's house? No, because he wanted Sekken there, and didn't want to handle the arguments with Haru right now. Just away, then. Out of the village, someplace others weren't likely to see.

Ryōtora stood up. "I will have Lord Asako leave. Not Seibo Mura, but this house – it's clear that he's causing you distress. Lord Asako, may I ask a favor of you?"

He took the precaution of stepping outside, and even then, he stood close enough that he could murmur directly into Sekken's ear. "Can you obtain more rope? And more paper streamers for it?"

Tools for a new sacred enclosure. Sekken's head moved in a tiny nod. In an equally quiet voice, he said, "Where should I bring them?"

"There's an old hemlock near the boundary stone I told you about. Don't go to the tree itself just yet; wait nearby with the rope."

"Give me a little while," Sekken said. He set off immediately, with the confident stride of a man with purpose. The inugami lingered, its gaze on the house, but eventually it followed the Phoenix.

Back inside, Ryōtora found Aoi had emerged from hiding and was trying to tidy up her appearance. Sweat had glued strands of hair to the sides of her face, and her sash had gotten turned partway around; she was in the middle of untying it. Fūyō hurried to stand between the young woman and Ryōtora. As he'd opened the door, Ryōtora had heard what Fūyō was saying: "*Shoshi ni kie. Shoshi ni kie. Shoshi ni kie.*"

So, she too sought the Perfect Land. No wonder she loathed the idea of her daughter leaving with Ryōtora, much less becoming his concubine.

He passed some of the time Sekken had asked for by questioning Aoi about her symptoms. She described them as a feeling of dread, the impending approach of the monsters weighing on her like it was trying to crush her breath out. Her appetite had dwindled, Fūyō added, and she'd been unable to do any work in the house. But her symptoms had definitely begun when he laid the ward around the village – not just the same day, but after the ward's completion.

When he judged he'd given Sekken enough time, Ryōtora said, "I would like to try something, if I may. Fūyō, will you entrust Aoi to me? As before, you have my solemn word that I harbor no improper intentions toward her. Nor will I take your daughter away from Seibo Mura without giving you an opportunity to say goodbye."

Fūyō looked deeply unhappy. But she was also worried for Aoi's well-being; in the war between those two impulses, which would win out? Reluctantly, she said, "Of course you should do whatever you think best, my lord."

"Thank you," Ryōtora said. Silently he added, *And I'm sorry.*

Aoi was already heading for the door. Gritting his teeth, Ryōtora followed her out.

•••

For someone who had been ill, Aoi walked fast. Ryōtora couldn't help but compare her nervous energy against the inugami's drooping head and heavy paws. Aoi behaved more as if she were standing on a hot stone and wanted to get off it as soon as possible, while the dog behaved as if it were dragging some weighty burden and couldn't go much farther.

Perhaps her energy was simply due to enthusiasm. Ryōtora had told her they were going southward out of the village; the line of the ward lay well beyond the southernmost buildings, but even the prospect of heading in that direction seemed to fire her up. Ryōtora had to hurry along in her wake, and hope Sekken was waiting for them there.

When they got to the old hemlock, there was no sign of the Phoenix. Ryōtora called for Aoi to halt. "This is far enough."

She didn't hide her disappointment very well. One hand rose to rub at the opposite arm; then she switched sides, the nervous scratching Fūyō had mentioned. But then she forced herself to relax and smiled at Ryōtora, drifting closer to him. "I'm glad you brought me out here. Away from my mother."

Ryōtora stepped back, out of reach. "I meant what I said to her. Among other things, I'm not in the habit of taking advantage of peasants."

Aoi dipped her chin, looking up at him through her lashes. "Is it really taking advantage, if the woman offers herself to you?"

"Yes," Ryōtora said firmly. "Because I am a samurai, and you are not. Even if a peasant voluntarily became involved with me, the imbalance of power between us would make it unfair. They wouldn't be free to leave whenever they wanted. Any such relationship is inherently unequal, with the power resting in the samurai's hands."

This time when she crossed her arms, it was to pout. "Are you always so virtuous?"

"I strive to be. And that is a second reason why I would turn down any such offer: because it would be nothing more than me giving in to my own desires. If I had any, which I do not."

Aoi sniffed in disbelief. "No desires at all? I don't think any human alive can say that."

"No desire for women," Ryōtora said. "Which is the third reason I have no interest in you."

She made a small, curious hum. "Is that so? Well… that explains a great deal."

He hadn't meant to say so much. If Sekken wasn't here yet, he should keep Aoi talking, buying time for the Phoenix to arrive. If Sekken *was* here, this wasn't a conversation he wanted to be having – not where the other man could listen in. Not anywhere, really. He could see the curiosity building in Aoi's gaze, and knew she was going to ask questions he didn't want to answer.

Questions he didn't *have* to answer. He owed her nothing at all. And fortunately – or perhaps not; the blade cut both ways – Aoi's head came up with a sudden hiss. Sekken, Ryōtora realized, was unused to creeping around in the forest. He didn't think to take the direction of the wind into account.

"Liar!" she snarled at Ryōtora, and tried to bolt. But the inugami was there, appearing out of the underbrush, and if it was still tired it showed no sign of it now. The spirit bared its teeth at Aoi, and she bared hers back at it, shrinking away.

"I lied about nothing," Ryōtora said, shifting to block another avenue of flight as Sekken appeared behind Aoi. The trap wasn't a tight one; she might still escape. "I said I would have Lord Asako leave the house, and I did. I told you I wanted to try something, and I do. I want to confirm my suspicion. The fourth and final reason I have no interest in you is that I'm fairly certain you aren't Aoi."

She tried to bolt. The inugami leapt at her, jaws snapping, and she shrank back. The coil of straw rope over Sekken's shoulder was more like twine, but that was all right; it meant he'd brought a substantial length of it. He swiftly tied one end around a tree trunk and unspooled the coil until he could wrap it around a second tree, then a third – forming a lopsided box around Aoi, while Ryōtora and the inugami herded her against the old hemlock, trapping her within the line of the rope.

When she saw what he was doing, she shrieked. All attempt to behave like an innocent peasant girl was gone; her hands were spread like claws, her posture feral. She made one last lunge for safety, but Ryōtora caught her with an arm across her waist, knocking her to the ground. She raked at him with both hands, drawing blood from his jaw, but he kept her down long enough for Sekken to close the square around them. A handful of paper streamers fluttered in the wind.

"You aren't possessed," Sekken said from outside the enclosure. Aoi scrambled to her feet and into the center of the space, as far as she could get from the sacred rope. "But I was right to suspect you. There are no yōkai that steal memories. The reason you don't remember anyone in Seibo Mura is that you *are* a yōkai: a shapeshifter, taking on Aoi's form to masquerade as her."

Behind Aoi, Ryōtora laced his fingers in a mudra and began chanting under his breath.

Sekken shook his sleeves out, undoing the minor disarray of his exertions. "So I now have three questions. What are you? Did you kill Aoi? And why are you, of all the members of the Night

Parade, able to stay in the village outside the full moon?"

At that last question, Aoi's eyes went wide. She was still staring at Sekken in disbelief when Ryōtora called on the spirit of the old hemlock tree to lend him its strength. Then the creature masquerading as Aoi yowled, twisting in on herself – and abruptly changed.

Where the young woman had been, there stood an enormous black cat with a long, sweeping tail.

"First question answered," Sekken said. "You're a bakeneko."

CHAPTER SIXTEEN

The bakeneko bared her teeth at Sekken and hissed, tail lashing back and forth. He could see the long claws curving out of her toes to dig into the earth. The thin line of rope seemed to be holding her in for now – but if she leapt for Ryōtora…

The shugenja hadn't backed away. Not that it would make any difference if he did; the bakeneko was the size of a snow leopard, and could easily cover the small space of the enclosure in a single pounce. Sekken wished Ryōtora would duck under the rope – or would that weaken or undo whatever he'd done to her? Sekken didn't know. Everything had seemed like a fascinating intellectual exercise until this moment, when he came face-to-face with an angry monster cat.

He'd read countless scrolls and books about yōkai. They were rather different outside the safe confines of a library.

"Let me out!" It seemed the cat could still talk, even in this form. Her voice was thinner than Aoi's, a little higher pitched. But the complete lack of deference was still there, and made far more sense now. Of course a cat wasn't impressed by a mere samurai.

"Not until we have more answers," Ryōtora said steadily. If he was afraid, he showed no hint of it. "You're the one responsible for that animated corpse, aren't you. The one you told us about, trying to persuade us there was a mahō-tsukai in Seibo Mura."

Her fangs were easily as long as Sekken's little finger, and bone white. "That wasn't my doing!"

"Why should we believe you?"

The bakeneko started to pace toward Ryōtora, and the inugami growled. It had abandoned its show of strength, allowing its head to sag once more, but at no point had it turned its attention away from the cat. The bakeneko sidled away from it, fur rising. "Get that *thing* away from me."

"No, I think this one is quite useful," Sekken said. "You haven't answered the question."

"I'm supposed to have a civilized conversation with people who just stripped me bare, while trapped in this spot, with a different ward telling me I'm not welcome here and should leave at once, and yet *another* ward binding me to stay?" She hissed again.

Ryōtora said, "Whether the conversation is civilized or not is beside the point. Why should I believe that you didn't desecrate a corpse?"

Her tail lashed again, and then the bakeneko turned so her rump was facing first Ryōtora, then Sekken. At first Sekken assumed she was just being rude – until she said, "How many tails do I have?"

Seeing Ryōtora's confusion, Sekken replied, "One, not two. You're not the nekomata seen during the attacks. So what? Nekomata may be more evil than bakeneko, but that doesn't mean you're good."

She lifted her lip at him in delicate contempt. "I don't claim to be good. But I am more a creature of Chikushō-dō than Sakkaku."

"A virtuous animal spirit," Ryōtora mused.

The creatures that called Senkyō home had varying allegiances. Sekken said, "'Virtuous' might be going a little far in this case. But you at least acknowledge the Celestial Order, and hope for eventual reincarnation as a human?"

"I certainly don't make corpses get up and dance for my entertainment. Filthy habit." She licked briefly at one paw and rubbed it over her head. It was simultaneously an expression of disdain, and an echo of the way she'd scratched at herself before. She really was uncomfortable here.

"Then who did?" Sekken demanded.

"Someone more inclined toward Sakkaku, obviously."

Ryōtora's voice sank in pitch, like a warning rumble from the earth. "I don't want to force answers out of you. But if you do not begin to cooperate, I will."

It was the same demeanor he'd shown toward the villagers when they went after Ogano, and all the more effective because it didn't come from a place of anger. Ryōtora's sense of compassion extended even to an inhuman creature like a bakeneko. But when that current tried to flow in two directions at once, then Ryōtora would sacrifice whatever mercy the yōkai might deserve for the sake of the people he was duty-bound to protect.

She felt it, too. Her fur fluffed slightly, but she settled her haunches onto the ground and wrapped her tail primly around her feet. "My mother."

A snort of disbelief escaped Sekken. The tip of the bakeneko's tail twitched in irritation. "Yes, I have one. We start as ordinary cats, you know. With dams and sires and littermates. All the latter are long dead – they didn't live long enough to become yōkai – and few kittens ever know their sires, but my mother became a bakeneko before me, and then in time her tail split and she became a nekomata. Before you can ask… no, she and I do not get along."

He supposed it was plausible. The part about bakeneko starting out as normal cats was common knowledge; he'd just never thought about the possibility of familial connections among them. "Is she also in the village?"

"No." Another twitch of her tail. "Not until the full moon."

When the Night Parade returned. "Lord Asako's third question," Ryōtora said. She hadn't told them yet what happened to Aoi, but Sekken feared that was the least urgent of the three. "How are you able to stay in the village, when the rest of the Night Parade seems to be exiled?"

Her ears flicked in what Sekken thought might be amusement. "Isn't it obvious?"

Judging by Ryōtora's expression, it wasn't at all. But Sekken suppressed a groan as he saw the error in his own reasoning. "You aren't a member of the Night Parade."

"Just a poor, innocent cat caught up in this net. If you'd had the decency to take me only a little further south, past the bounds of that stupid confining ward, I would have been long gone. One less problem for you to deal with."

One more problem unleashed on the world, Sekken thought. Even a virtuous bakeneko was often middling at best. This one certainly didn't seem to be interested in helping anyone, any more than she had to.

Ryōtora seemed no more convinced than he was. "An innocent cat… who happens to be the offspring of a nekomata. And from the sound of it, your mother *is* part of the Night Parade."

The cat sighed. "Fine. My curiosity got the better of me – will you believe that, at least? I saw everyone streaming across into the realm of mortals, and I wanted to see what was going on. So I followed them. Only then I couldn't leave! I truly want nothing more than to get away from this, before–"

She stopped, ears flattening. "Before what?" Ryōtora prompted.

Sekken thought back to the speculation he and Ryōtora had shared. "Before Nura–"

The bakeneko yowled so loudly that Sekken clapped his hands over his ears and the inugami started barking back at her. "Don't say that name!" she snarled.

"I already have," Sekken said cautiously, wondering if he'd made a serious error. "When we realized that the – is it safe to name the phenomenon? – that the chaos in Seibo Mura was the Night Parade of a Hundred Demons. What did that do?"

She got up and paced a circuit around the enclosure, staring out at the surrounding forest. "If you're lucky, nothing. He's still confined – I think. I hope."

Which explained why Nurarihyon hadn't appeared during any of the outbreaks so far. "What can you tell us about him?"

"Me? Very little. He's…" The bakeneko sat down again, but she was restless, shifting position again and again. "You humans tell stories about creatures like us to scare each other. To make children behave and travelers be wary. We yōkai? We tell each other stories of *him*."

A bogeyman for yōkai. Sekken thought briefly – irrelevantly – of the reports he could write when he got back home. *I'll be Rokugan's foremost expert on the Night Parade.*

Only if he got home safely, though.

"Then tell us what you do know," Ryōtora said.

Still the cat hesitated. Ryōtora stood for a moment, looking at Sekken, but this time Sekken couldn't guess what he was thinking. Then Ryōtora said, "Here. As a gesture of good faith."

Sekken took an involuntary step forward when Ryōtora went to the corner where he had tied both ends of the rope to a smaller tree. The inugami growled low in its throat. But Ryōtora held up a placating hand, then untied the rope and began coiling it up, reversing the circuit Sekken had made around the trees.

The bakeneko's fur sleeked down again, and she washed herself vigorously. "Your ward is still telling me to go away," she complained, but it sounded more querulous now than hostile. "Fine. Sit down – make that dog stop growling at me – and I'll tell you what I can."

The inugami sat with its head in Sekken's lap again. Sekken wasn't sure when exactly the spirit had gone from being a terrifying curse to an odd sort of companion; it was a gradual process, he thought, beginning when it appeared in daylight, and reaching a new equilibrium after it showed them the plaque bearing the name of Ingyō Jinja. He wondered if it had a name.

"Do *you* have a name?" he asked the bakeneko as Ryōtora finished setting the rope aside and paused to thank the kami of the hemlock for its assistance.

"Of course," she answered. "Are we friends now, that I should tell it to you?"

"Your choice," Sekken said with a shrug. "It depends on how much you object to being called Neko-chan."

As he'd hoped, the cute diminutive irritated her. "You may call me Sayashi."

Better than calling her by the name of a dead girl. Sekken assumed the real Aoi was dead. While Masa might believe his daughter Chie had only been stolen away, there was no proof he was right, nor that anyone else had been spared. Sekken still wanted to know if the bakeneko was responsible for that.

Ryōtora was right, though: getting information on Nurarihyon took priority. The shugenja settled down on the other side of the inugami's sprawled limbs and said, "Sayashi. It's time for you to talk."

Her claws dug gently into the earth, as if for comfort. "He's been imprisoned for… oh, a long time; we don't bother to count years the way you mortals do. And time doesn't always pass the same between the realms, regardless."

"Imprisoned by whom?"

The flick of her ears had the air of a shrug. "Why should I know? Some mortal. A very powerful one, I presume, or they would have never captured him. No one in Senkyō knew where – well, perhaps someone did. But they have no reason to share. It isn't as if anyone particularly mourned his loss."

If he was a bogeyman to yōkai, that wasn't surprising. Sekken buried his fingers in the inugami's fur and closed his eyes, imagining what they knew and what they surmised laid out before him like the broken pieces of a pot. Trying to see how they fit together. "You say N… *he* has been imprisoned. What about the rest of the Night Parade?"

"His imprisonment was their freedom."

The pieces flipped themselves around. Sekken opened his eyes and found Sayashi grooming herself again. Ryōtora said, "You mean … they aren't all trapped here."

"Not like he is," Sayashi confirmed. "He's been summoning them each night when the full moon rises. They have to come, and they can't leave this place until it sets; then they go back to Senkyō. But I'm not bound to him, and I missed my opportunity to leave."

"So why do you need me to take you across the boundary? It sounds like you came here from Senkyō; why not simply return there with the rest of them during the next full moon?"

Her tail lashed in irritation. "Do you *want* me here in the village when they start rampaging again? I may call myself part of Chikushō-dō instead of Sakkaku, but that's hardly a permanent allegiance. If I see them having fun, tormenting the mortals … I might just be tempted to join in."

It was a bluff. Not *false*, Sekken thought; Sayashi absolutely was willing to contemplate tossing virtue aside and aligning herself with those who took delight in causing trouble for humans. But that wasn't her actual reason.

"You're afraid of *him*," he said. "The one you don't want me to name."

Sayashi's tail puffed up involuntarily, and she licked it down again with a hasty tongue. "Not … afraid. But I have no interest in becoming part of the Night Parade. And if I ride along with them when they leave …"

"Then you might get trapped in a different way," Ryōtora said, understanding. "I have no more interest in seeing that happen than you do. When we're done here, I'll do what I can for you."

Sekken's hand tensed. "One moment. We haven't yet established whether this bakeneko is a murderer."

"I'm not," she snapped.

"Is Aoi dead?"

"Yes." Sayashi showed no particular regret at the statement; he wouldn't have believed it if she had. Still, her casual lack of concern felt like a slap. "But I didn't kill her. She died trying to save some other girl – a friend of hers, I presume."

"What girl?"

She could have taught lessons to Crane courtiers about how to look disdainful. "How should I know? It's been tiresome enough, trying to learn the names of those who are still alive. This all happened just before dawn, when I was trying to avoid the others. I was up a tree, and I saw them dragging the girl along – a whole pack of them, with her in their midst. Aoi was stupid for running at them. The raiju shot itself through her and she dropped dead." Sayashi sniffed. "She was lucky. The sarugami wanted to claim her as a prize, and that would have been much worse for her. But the others said no, they were only going to take the one they already had."

The one they already had. Sekken looked at Ryōtora, and found the shugenja's eyes wide. Could Masa have been right about Chie?

"This other girl," Ryōtora said. "Was she about sixteen?"

"She might have been. I'm not good with human ages. Older than a child, but I think not so old that she had kittens of her own yet."

It wasn't proof, but it was the best they were likely to get out of Sayashi. "Why were they taking her?" Sekken asked. "If it was as food, there would be no reason for them not to take a second victim. Or even if they were just going to torment her."

Again her ears flicked. "I don't know. I was mostly concerned with making sure they didn't see me – especially since my mother was among them. We don't exactly get along. But it didn't seem like the usual sort of amusement."

Sekken racked his brain, trying to think what use yōkai might have for Chie, beyond the obvious. Something specific to the Night Parade? The stories didn't mention anything along those lines… but then, the stories weren't written as factual accounts. How long ago had Nurarihyon been imprisoned? Centuries, at the very least; maybe even before the dawn of the Empire.

"After that," Ryōtora said. "What happened to Aoi's body?"

"I didn't eat it," Sayashi said, with such a great air of dignity that Sekken suspected she *had* eaten corpses at some point in the past. His stomach curdled. "I dragged it off into the forest and buried it. I could tell I'd missed my chance to leave, and sooner or later someone was going to comment on the enormous black cat skulking about. My best option was to disguise myself." Her whiskers twitched. "In hindsight, I should have taken on the appearance of the one they kidnapped. That would have been less effort."

Ryōtora's voice was flat and hard. "The effort you went to is not our concern. Aoi deserved proper rites. We're fortunate she hasn't been haunting the village."

That was unquestionably true. A body not cremated, and her family not even aware they should be mourning? Aoi wouldn't have been included in Ryōtora's prayers, either. Sekken said, "You may not have killed her, but you hardly acted in accordance with the tenets of Chikushō-dō. Should we really be helping this creature?"

Sayashi surged to her feet, teeth bared. "That one promised he would aid me. If he breaks his word…"

She clearly hadn't been paying much attention to Ryōtora's character, if she thought that was likely. Sekken should have known better than to even suggest it himself. Ryōtora said, "I have no intention of breaking my word. But before I do anything for you, you're going to show me where Aoi is buried."

CHAPTER SEVENTEEN

Perhaps Sayashi did have some decency in her, because she'd gone to the effort of burying Aoi deeply, where animals wouldn't dig her body up and tear it to pieces. Ishi and Tarō did the work of digging to find that, because Ryōtora didn't want anyone from the village to know exactly what had happened, and coming anywhere near that task himself would be profoundly polluting, at a moment when he couldn't afford to be weakened.

He knew they'd located the body even before it became visible. After so many days in the ground, the smell was overpowering. Sekken retreated a step, gagging, and Ryōtora beckoned him around to stand upwind of the makeshift grave. *I should have thought to do that from the start.*

"What are you going to do now?" Sekken asked in a low voice, as the ashigaru paused and wiped their brows. Their square faces were carefully expressionless, but Ryōtora could tell they weren't happy with being assigned this work. If he ordered them to exhume the body completely, they would probably obey… but it wasn't the kind of work peasants were supposed to do. "If you call the village's outcastes here to deal with this, word will probably get out. And you certainly can't cremate her without everyone knowing. But leaving the body where it lies–"

Ryōtora shook his head before Sekken could even finish that sentence. "No, that isn't an option. But the problem goes deeper than that. What am I supposed to tell Fūyō?"

Sekken clearly hadn't thought that far ahead. Now he grimaced. "You've seen how volatile the situation is. Telling them there's been a yōkai hiding in their midst all this time…"

It would be disastrous. Unfortunately, it was also the truth. How was he supposed to balance those demands? Even if Ryōtora were willing to lie, he had no plausible story to give. He couldn't claim he'd sent "Aoi" south, not on her own. And he could hardly waste the help of Ishi or Tarō on the pretense that the ashigaru was escorting one lone villager. Could he pretend the young woman in Fūyō's house had actually been her daughter's ghost? He seemed to remember hearing some tales like that. The mere thought of trying to lie to a grieving mother, though, made him loathe himself beyond words.

Sekken would probably do it for you. The man was hardly a Scorpion, ready to sacrifice decency in the name of pragmatism at a moment's notice, but he was better with words than Ryōtora was. And the calculation was there in his gaze, whether the greater good would be better served by hiding the truth about Sayashi.

"Pardon me, but… I couldn't help overhearing."

The oddities of speech Ryōtora had noticed in Aoi's voice – her lack of a rural accent; her elegant turns of phrase – seemed to be Sayashi's own manner of speaking, now accompanied by the self-confidence of not having to hide her identity. She looked like Aoi again, because Ryōtora hadn't wanted to test Ishi and Tarō's equanimity in the face of a cat large enough to tear them apart, but she'd abandoned even her flawed pretense of being a humble peasant girl. Now she sidled up to the two samurai. "I might be able to assist with one thing."

"Oh?" Ryōtora said neutrally. He'd been careful in his promise to her; he'd said he would do what he could for her. Not what she had asked for. His intent was to banish her back to Senkyō, rather than unleashing her on the outside world.

"Cremating the body," Sayashi said. "I don't quite understand these concerns you humans have about defilement, but if I have the principles correct, it might be a problem for you to call on the fire kami to burn a corpse. Would it help if I took care of that for you?"

Ryōtora's immediate, uncharitable thought was that she meant to "take care of" the body in some blasphemous fashion. But at his side, Sekken made a small noise of understanding. "Fire… and your kind are known for – ahem. Interfering with funerals."

"That's kasha," she said with affronted dignity. "Who are very *thoroughly* of Sakkaku, if not Jigoku itself. I'm not proposing to steal the body. Only to provide the necessary flame, without need for stacks of wood or a shugenja's prayers."

"A bakeneko's tail can start fires," Sekken explained to Ryōtora. "I've never heard of one assisting in a funeral – usually it's house fires they're responsible for – but I can't see any reason why it wouldn't work."

Whether it *could* work and whether it *should* were separate questions. Ryōtora was torn. Fūyō deserved a proper funeral for her daughter, not one conducted in secret with the aid of the same yōkai who had consigned Aoi to an unmarked grave in the forest. But the people of Seibo Mura couldn't spare the time for a proper funeral, not when the evacuation needed to begin soon if they were to reach safety. Nor could Ryōtora accept the risk – much less the contempt – of leaving Aoi's remains uncremated.

"Will it trouble you to dig up the body?" he asked quietly.

Sayashi shrugged. "No more than it troubled me to bury it."

He swore Ishi and Tarō to secrecy and sent them away. Then Sayashi reverted to her true form and finished exhuming the corpse, while Sekken cleared an area for her to lay it in and Ryōtora prayed quietly. This was different from what he'd done after arriving in the village; this time the mortal remains were there, and he imagined he could feel the impurity of it settling upon him.

But it wasn't his imagination that he heard a whisper at the end. A young woman's voice, saying, *Find Chie.*

Ryōtora couldn't expect the kami to respond to him after that. Instead he went back to the waterfall, not quite believing it was still the same day that Sekken himself had been there. By now it was afternoon, the hours slipping through his fingers like grains of rice. *I'm finding answers – but still no solutions.* And the Night Parade was coming.

At least that worry kept him from feeling too self-conscious as he stripped down, handing his clothing to Sekken rather than setting it on a boulder. Sayashi had returned to Aoi's guise once more, in case any villager came to the waterfall, and she was failing to hide her impatience for Ryōtora to be done with his purification. When he came out, he found his clothes draped neatly over a tree branch and Sekken sitting nearby with his fine vermilion writing kit, making a prayer strip. The inugami slept at his side. "Will this do?" the Phoenix asked, holding the paper up for Ryōtora to see.

His calligraphy was beautiful, at once elegant and bold. And while Sekken might not be a shugenja, his learning stood him in good stead. The sutra quote inscribed on the strip wasn't the one Ryōtora would have chosen – probably it was favored by Isawa-trained shugenja – but it would suffice. "Yes, thank you," Ryōtora said. He dried and dressed himself hastily, all too aware of Sayashi's sardonic gaze. She clearly hadn't forgotten what he'd said right before revealing her as a bakeneko… nor was it much of a challenge for her to connect that to Sekken. He prayed that whatever virtuous instincts she had would keep her from saying anything.

Once his hands were dry, Ryōtora took the prayer strip and held it between his palms, calling silently upon the kami. Then, in one swift movement, he reached out and pressed it against Sayashi's forehead, shouting for her to be gone from the mortal realm.

He felt like his hand struck a tightly woven net. It gave a little beneath the pressure, then rebounded; the prayer strip fluttered free and drifted to the ground. The inugami whined, as if in pain. And Sayashi was still standing there.

She hissed and twitched her shoulders, as if trying to dislodge something. "I thought you knew how to do this! Did you not purify yourself enough first?"

"Maybe it would go better if you were in bakeneko form," Sekken said. "I'll watch the path and tell you if anyone's coming."

Ryōtora repeated the banishing on the black cat, but with the same result – including the inugami's protest.

He said, "It isn't me. It's the ward on this village. I hoped that direct action by a shugenja would be enough to send you back to Senkyō, but apparently not. And I think…" He looked at the inugami, which had hunched in on itself. "This dog spirit must be part of it. I wondered if my own ward might be at fault for its exhaustion – but what if instead it's sustaining the *old* ward? Can you let her pass?"

That last was directed to the inugami, even though he wasn't sure if the creature could understand him. Its only response was to put his head back down on its paws, exhausted.

"I think that means 'no,'" Sekken said. "Well, she wanted you to get her physically across the boundary. Maybe that will work better?"

But it didn't. They went to the line Ryōtora had walked before when he laid his own ward, and both Ryōtora and Sekken stepped across it with no difficulty. When Ryōtora tried to take Sayashi with him, though, the unseen force of the ancient ward wouldn't let her by. He tried pulling her, pushing her, walking at her side, praying to the inugami and the elemental kami – none of it worked, and only made both Sayashi and the dog yowl in discomfort. "Stop, *stop!*" she cried at last. "At this rate you'll get me out of Seibo Mura by killing me and sending my spirit down to Meido instead."

She sounded genuinely miserable. Ryōtora bowed to her in sincere apology. "I would not have made my promise if I'd realized I wouldn't be able to fulfill it. You have held up your end in good faith; I regret that I cannot do the same."

Suddenly light-headed, he sat down. Sekken paced nearby, hands locked behind his back. "The old ward is keeping you here. I don't think a dog spirit is capable of creating such a thing on its own; whoever put that ward up is presumably the person who trapped the leader of the Night Parade. Is there any way to call up their ghost?"

"I don't even have a name," Ryōtora said, fighting the urge to drop his head into his hands. "I can try, but…"

Sekken seemed to focus on him at last, and he crouched in front of Ryōtora. "But you're as pale as a ghost yourself. We've been out all day; you haven't eaten since breakfast."

Ryōtora forbore to mention that he hadn't eaten breakfast, either. "We don't have time for–"

"For what? Keeping up your strength? I'd say we don't have time for you *not* to do that."

The concern heated Ryōtora's cheeks, and he ducked his head to hide it while Sekken turned to address Sayashi. "My friend here will object to this solution, but I think that for the time being you need to keep up your masquerade as Aoi. We have no way of getting you out of Seibo Mura, and you can't hang around with people knowing you're a bakeneko – that really *will* get you killed."

He was right; Ryōtora did object. He also agreed with Sekken, though. Right now, Fūyō's loss had to come second to the safety of the village. Time he spent explaining what had happened to her daughter would be time he didn't spend protecting everyone else.

There was one thing he could do, though. Ryōtora laid his palms against the ground and reached for the kami he'd invoked when he laid his ward. With a prayer of thanks, he bade them cease their efforts. Sayashi breathed a sigh of relief as that ward faded. "I may need to renew it before the full moon," he warned her. "For now, though, it seems to be causing more trouble than good."

"That's enough for now," Sekken said, physically helping Ryōtora to his feet. "Haru can exile me again if she wants, but first I'm going to bring you back."

•••

Haru didn't exile Sekken. Ryōtora wasn't entirely clear on what explanation he gave her; it came out muddled not only because he was tired and hungry, but because his thoughts were crammed full of all the things he knew and all the questions he still hadn't answered. At least he managed to avoid simply ordering her to comply. While that would have been his right, it wouldn't have led to harmony.

Not that harmony would matter for much longer. Once he'd devoured a bowl of thick country noodles, Ryōtora met with Ogano privately and said, "Tomorrow morning, I need you to announce the evacuation of Seibo Mura. We won't leave until the next day, but this will give people time to pack up what they need."

Ogano's hands twisted around each other. Ryōtora could see his doubts; they both knew how much difficulty and danger there would be in traveling south. Nor could Ogano, as headman, be happy with abandoning his village. Peasants might not follow the moral code of Bushidō, but that didn't mean they were incapable of understanding concepts like duty.

He wouldn't be held at fault for it, though. That would fall on Ryōtora, once they reached Heibeisu.

My orders were to deal with the problem here. Not to run away from it. Arguably, leaving was a failure of both Courage and Duty.

But in Dragon lands these days, there was another consideration – one that superseded even Bushidō, though he could justify it under Duty and Compassion. With his clan's dwindling population, they could not afford more deaths like those Seibo Mura had already suffered. If it was a choice between facing the danger and possibly losing the whole village, or preserving their lives by fleeing, he had to choose the latter.

Sekken came to sit with him after Ryōtora dismissed Ogano. Having companionship was comforting, but it felt like yet another failure on Ryōtora's part that Sekken was clearly able to read his black mood. In a gentle voice, the Phoenix asked, "What do you want me to do?"

The inugami hadn't followed Sekken inside. The central post of Ogano's house had a ward on it, purchased from a temple in Heibeisu, that was meant to keep hostile spirits away. Did that mean the dog counted as hostile? The ward hadn't kept the Night Parade out. Ryōtora said, "Haru is willing to let you stay here tonight, but… did the inugami trouble you last night, when you slept at the shrine?"

"I barely slept," Sekken admitted, then let loose a cracking yawn as if to underscore his sincerity. "It stayed close to me, though, if that's what you're asking."

"More or less, yes. I don't think removing my ward did anything to help it – which makes sense, if the cause of its exhaustion is the weakening of the *old* ward. I don't know if you can do anything to strengthen it –"

"But you want me to sleep outside. I can do that." Sekken yawned again. "I don't think I'll have much trouble sleeping, even if Haru dumps me on the ground with no pillow. Maybe the dog will talk to me in my sleep."

Ryōtora's experience of communing with the inugami had been that it was non-verbal. Then again, until recently, Sekken's experience of it had been that it only appeared at night. "At this point, I'll hope for anything."

Then Ryōtora groaned. "I haven't yet told Masa about Chie. When he finds out… he's not going to want to evacuate."

Sekken didn't point out that Ryōtora could simply choose not to tell the carpenter what they'd learned. Again, there could be virtuous justification for it; Masa's life was not his own to throw away in pursuit of his missing daughter, any more than Ryōtora's was. For both peasants and samurai, their lives and their service belonged to their lords.

But this wasn't like delaying telling Fūyō what had happened to Aoi. There was a chance that Chie could be rescued – if only he could figure out how.

Which meant figuring out why she'd been taken in the first place. *It didn't seem like the usual sort of amusement,* Sayashi had said. Could Chie somehow be part of the–

"I didn't think you knew that sort of language," Sekken said dryly. "I take it by your sudden profanity that you've thought of something. Can I help?"

"We were looking for a witch," Ryōtora said. He'd shed his outer kimono in anticipation of staying indoors for the remainder of the night; now he put it back on, yanking impatiently when one of his hands got caught in the deep pocket of the sleeve. "But we didn't find one. What if that's because the yōkai took her?"

Sekken echoed his curse. "It's as good an explanation as any we've come up with. But that sort of witchcraft is usually bound to a family, and I didn't notice anything odd happening around Masa."

"Still," Ryōtora said, "he might know something. This can't wait until morning. Let's go talk to him."

CHAPTER EIGHTEEN

The village was silent as they hurried across its grounds. The moon was only half full, but the light it shed across Seibo Mura felt ominous enough – a harbinger of what was to come.

Generally speaking, Rokugani offered up their prayers only to Lady Sun, not to Lord Moon. He was a figure of madness and wrath… which, Sekken supposed, was appropriate to the context of the Night Parade. He prayed silently to Amaterasu Ōmikami to restrain her husband, and to illuminate the path to their answers.

No miraculous beam fell on Seibo Mura, but he didn't expect it. Instead he led Ryōtora to the small hut where Masa lived, which showed only the faintest glow around its solid door.

"Our apologies for disturbing you," Sekken called out in what he hoped was a reassuring voice. "It's Asako and Isao. We have questions for you, and they're too urgent to wait for morning." He stepped on the urge to add, *We promise we're not shapeshifting yōkai.* That wouldn't reassure anyone, and the last thing he wanted was to raise suspicions about Sayashi-Aoi.

Ryōtora spoke up as well. "It has to do with your daughter, Chie."

That got Masa's door open. The carpenter gestured for them to come in, and slid the door shut practically on Sekken's heels. Sekken wondered if he could see the inugami, and was trying to close it out. If so, he failed; the dog preceded Sekken, as if scouting for trouble.

Masa's house was small, but cleaner than Fūyō's. He didn't have any tatami, and only seemed to have two cushions, which he gave to his samurai visitors. "You've found something?" he asked.

The hope in his face was almost painful to see. Ryōtora said, "After a fashion. I have confirmation that the yōkai took her, but not why. And where that's concerned… you must have heard the accusations that Lord Asako is a witch."

It was an uncomfortable thing to say to a peasant, putting Masa in a position where he either had to lie in response to one samurai, or accuse the other of blasphemous deeds to his face. Then again, as a follower of the Perfect Land, maybe he wouldn't mind doing the latter. It surprised Sekken when Masa found an admirably politic path between those two traps. "I also heard my lord's declaration that it isn't true. I believe you wouldn't associate yourself with someone who couldn't be trusted."

"There *is* an inugami haunting him," Ryōtora said, and gestured to where the spirit lay almost flat on the floor. "Can you see it?"

His gesture had been a broad one, not pointing directly at the dog. Masa's gaze swept the area without even the slightest hitch that might indicate a pretense of blindness. "No. I… have no gift for spiritual things."

"What about your daughter?" Ryōtora asked. "Is there any chance that she could have bound herself to such a spirit?"

Masa's entire body was rigid with tension, and had been since they entered his house. It could have indicated deception. But

Sekken believed the bafflement in Masa's voice when he said, "If she did, I don't know it. You… You don't think she *caused* this, did you?"

Pain laced through that question, and Sekken took pity on him. "Not in the slightest. If anything, we think the inugami is trying to defend Seibo Mura against the yōkai. Which might be why they took your daughter, if she's connected to it. Is there any chance that might be true? Any legend connecting your family line to someone famous in Seibo Mura's history? Any strange omens around her birth? Any chance she can speak to the kami, or that she has some other kind of spiritual gift?"

Masa bowed his head, not in respect, but in turmoil. "No. Nothing like that. If anything of the sort was going on, she didn't tell me."

Sekken forbore from asking him how well he knew his own daughter. A widower with only one surviving child; they might have been very close, or they might have been estranged by grief. But then inspiration came. "We know Aoi was – is – a friend of hers. Is there anyone else in Seibo Mura that she might have confided in?"

"Rin," Masa said. Sekken remembered her; the girl with the sling. "The two of them loved to wander the woods together."

To Ryōtora, Sekken said, "I know where Rin's house is. But her family was very nervous about having samurai around. Masa, would it be possible for you to bring her here?"

The carpenter was on his feet without even waiting for Ryōtora's approval. Not that Ryōtora would have argued; his agreement followed Masa out the door. "I could have asked that question sooner," Ryōtora said, one hand curling in frustration. "But–"

"But you were trying to help the entire village, and had no reason to think helping one missing girl might make a difference to that," Sekken said gently. This was no time for Ryōtora to sink into self-recrimination. "Especially when the most likely answer was that the girl was already dead."

She still might be. But he hoped, for Masa's sake as well as the village's, that she wasn't.

Masa returned quickly enough that he must have run the whole way there and the whole way back, with Rin not far behind. "Chie is alive?" she said, only belatedly remembering to sketch a bow in their direction.

"She may be," Ryōtora said cautiously. "It depends on why she was taken. Can you think of any reason why the yōkai would have found her worth kidnapping? Not the usual reasons yōkai take people, but something more. Did she have any spiritual gifts, any connections with an inugami – anything to mark her out?"

"I don't know about any spirits." Rin dropped cross-legged onto the floor, looking doubtful. She didn't so much as glance in the direction of the inugami; it must be invisible to her, too. "But she didn't really have problems during the first full moon. Which might have just been luck, and I told her that. When the problems came back, though, she told me that she thought she was protected. And she wanted to use that to help people."

"Protected?" That came from Masa, who was staring at her.

Rin drew back from his gaze. "That's what she claimed. It must not have been true, though, if they took her."

Ryōtora leaned forward, fingers white against his knees. "What kind of protection? Did she refer to any kami – Saiun-nushi, an ancestor, *anything?*"

"It might have been Saiun-nushi," Rin said, chewing on her lower lip. "I didn't think of this before, but… last fall, after the earthquake, she found some kind of charm up in the ruins of the shrine."

Masa growled in frustration. "I told her not to go up there! It wasn't safe."

"She said she saw lights," Rin murmured, shrinking in on herself. "She wanted to know why."

"Spirit lights?" Sekken asked, his thoughts suddenly springing to life. There were many kinds of such things, going by a dozen different names in different parts of Rokugan. They appeared in forests, mountains, fields, over the sea; sometimes they were the spirits of departed humans, while sometimes they heralded the approach of some kind of spirit.

And there was at least one poem, written by a Togashi poet, that spoke of them as being a warning sign of the Night Parade.

Rin nodded mutely. Ryōtora said, "This is important, Rin. What was this charm she found?"

"I don't know," Rin said. "She never showed it to me. She said it might be the shintai of something, and people shouldn't see it. But she kept it on her."

It wasn't the shintai of Saiun-nushi. That had been loaded into the portable shrine and brought down to the village, and it was far too large and heavy to be anything Chie could have carried around. But–

The muscle jumping in Ryōtora's jaw was almost certainly him biting down on another curse. Sekken could guess why. It wasn't uncommon for a shrine – even a small one – to house more than one kami.

Could Ryōtora have overlooked another spirit during his

communion with Saiun-nushi? Sekken wasn't a shugenja; he didn't know for sure how such things worked. But if he'd been focused on the solid weight of the mountain – if this hypothetical other kami had a different nature, such that it didn't register on his earth-attuned awareness…

"Not tonight," he said to Ryōtora, drawing baffled looks from both Masa and Rin. He had learned to read past the man's lack of expression, and knew what the shugenja must be planning. "No good comes of conducting rituals at a shrine in the middle of the night. We'll go at dawn." Ryōtora needed rest, too… but Sekken wasn't going to shame him by saying that in front of the peasants.

He half-expected Ryōtora to argue. Instead the shugenja offered a small bow to first Rin, then Masa. "Thank you. This may be a vital clue. And I promise, we will do everything we can to get Chie back."

Once outside, Sekken said, "I'll wake you at dawn."

"Before, if you can," Ryōtora answered. "I've wasted too much time already."

"Do you think what Chie found was actually a shintai?" Sekken asked, after he and Ryōtora had used the ladle at the waterfall for a simple purification.

Dawn was beginning to pierce the trees, casting its thin light on Ryōtora's face. The man looked half a ghost, like he only had one foot in reality. With anyone else, Sekken might have doubted the wisdom of trying to commune with an unknown kami under such conditions – but he trusted Ryōtora's determination to see him through.

"I thought they were usually bigger than that," Sekken added, as Ryōtora shook his hands dry.

Ryōtora's mouth bent in thought. "The wrappings and containers they're put in are usually larger. But the shintai within them... who can say? If the container broke, she might have found the divine vessel itself."

"And that wouldn't hurt her?" Shintai were conduits for the power of a kami. Ryōtora had spent hours preparing to handle Saiun-nushi's, because unlike the dead shrinekeeper he wasn't known to the spirit of the mountain. And he was a shugenja, trained in mind and in spirit for such things.

The shake of Ryōtora's head said he didn't know. "Or maybe what she found wasn't the shintai. Maybe there was a nemuranai in the shrine."

Sekken should have thought of that himself – except that a simple village like this one was the last place he'd think to find a major nemuranai. Rather than being conduits for some external entity, those objects drew their power from the awakened spirit of the thing itself. It could happen to any item that was used for long enough, especially a century or more; scholars debated whether yōkai like hahakigami or furu-ōgi were meaningfully different from awakened brooms and fans, or whether they were merely a variant on the same principle, that gained not only awareness but the ability to move on their own.

That, however, was quite different from a nemuranai that could protect its bearer from yōkai, or keep them trapped in a certain place. Such a relic was the kind of thing a high-ranking lord would keep as a renowned treasure, or donate to a shrine to improve his karma. A *significant* shrine, not some out-of-the-way building in an obscure corner of Dragon lands.

At least this time he and Ryōtora had come prepared. Ishi and

Tarō had followed them up the path at a respectful distance; now they stepped forward to pour water over their hands and heads. They would do most of the heavy lifting, helping Sekken dig through the rubble for clues while Ryōtora attempted to make contact with the unknown kami.

It seemed almost like a contradiction in terms. There were kami no human had ever documented, and kami in shrines that had been neglected for so long that their nature was forgotten. This one, though, seemed to have been kept *secret*. When the villagers of Seibo Mura made offerings here, it was to Saiun-nushi only. Yet the whole point of enshrining a kami was for it to receive the worship of its community. Why enshrine something, and then not tell anyone?

All the answers Sekken could think of were unsatisfactory – but they made him worried for Ryōtora's safety.

Unfortunately, there wasn't anything he could really do to protect the shugenja. Sekken had two swords, like any samurai, but he only carried his wakizashi. And that had been sitting with his baggage most of the time, because Sekken's skill with it ended at being able to draw the blade without yanking the sheath out of his sash. He was no kind of warrior. Nor a shugenja, able to speak with the kami directly. Nor even a monk, with great spiritual wisdom. He was just a scholar… and scholarship was useless when there was no information to work with.

If his brain was of no use, at least his body could do something. Sekken tied his sleeves back and went to work alongside Ishi and Tarō, heaving wreckage out of the way in search of anything that might shed light on the secret kami. Mountain mornings were cool, even in the height of summer, but soon he was sweating and out of breath.

Most of the real lifting was being done by Ishi and Tarō, though, while Sekken contributed his knowledge of shrine architecture. In a larger site there would have been a separate building to house the shintai, but here there was only the one structure, plus the secular one the shrinekeeper's family had lived in. Which meant the shintai would have been in some kind of cabinet toward the back – and indeed, that was where Ryōtora had found the vessel for Saiun-nushi.

There were no auxiliary shrines set up near the building, not that Sekken could find. Would they have placed the second shintai below the first? Or behind it? Or–

He muttered a curse, smacking his forehead lightly with one palm. *Or you're looking for the wrong thing entirely.*

Shintai weren't always crafted things, wrapped and boxed and tucked away somewhere safe. Sometimes they were natural features, like trees… or mountains.

He almost would have expected that here, with the shrine being publicly dedicated to the kami of the mountain it stood on. But Ryōtora had definitely moved a shintai during the makeshift festival – and it must have been Saiun-nushi's, because Sekken couldn't imagine the shugenja could call a kami into a foreign vessel without noticing. The spirit would have refused to cooperate.

So did that mean the mountain had two separate kami? Or the shintai for the other one might be a tree, a boulder, or some other natural object. Usually those were marked with a sacred rope, though, and he didn't see anything like that nearby.

Sekken hated to interrupt Ryōtora's meditation, but he had to. He knelt in front of the shugenja and spoke quietly. "Have you sensed anything yet?"

Ryōtora's eyes drifted open. "I… Yes. I think so. It's difficult when I don't know what I'm looking for; there are kami everywhere in the world. But there's something more powerful here."

A chill crept across the back of Sekken's neck. "It just occurred to me. Is there any chance that what you're trying to communicate with is the creature Sayashi doesn't want us to name?"

He couldn't hold in a sigh of relief when Ryōtora shook his head emphatically. "No. There's no feeling of chaos to this, and from what we know of that creature, it absolutely would radiate such an aura. And what I felt isn't trying to break free. It's… hmm. Not sleeping. That's the wrong word."

"Otherwise occupied?"

Sekken meant that answer as half-facetious, but Ryōtora nodded. "I don't think it's quite aware of me. Have you found the shintai?"

Grimacing, Sekken explained his reasoning. When he was done, he said, "I don't suppose you're able to sense where it might be?"

Ryōtora's gaze was unfocused as he looked around. "Not the way you mean. But I think – it may not *have* one. Either what Chie took is indeed the shintai, or the other kami isn't exactly enshrined here. It's just sort of… present."

"That would explain why the villagers weren't making offerings to it. If that's the case, though, then what do we do?"

The unfocused searching became more directed. "We find a suitable yorishiro."

Something that wasn't a permanent shintai, but could become a kami's vessel for a time. Like the tree they'd cut down for the enclosure in the village, which was meant to draw a spirit's energies toward it. "Do you want another tree, or a rock?"

They couldn't afford to spend a day ranging around the mountains, looking for something suitable. Fortunately Tarō pointed out an interestingly shaped boulder near the ruins of the shine, which Ryōtora inspected and pronounced acceptable. He didn't sound confident, and Sekken didn't blame him; this wasn't supposed to be like perusing a list of marriage candidates and selecting the best of the lot. It was supposed to be more like the process by which the ancestral sword of the Phoenix chose the next Clan Champion: a serendipitous alignment of fate.

Still, if all they had was a boulder, they'd make do.

Ryōtora laid out the scant offerings they'd brought, then knelt in front of the boulder, breathing deeply and steadily. The ashigaru hung well back, but Sekken stood as close as he dared, trying to match his breathing to Ryōtora's. As if that would somehow help the shugenja bring the kami down into the stone. The inugami sat at his side, upright for once – though after a few moments it leaned hard into Sekken's leg. Sekken resisted the urge to give it a comforting scratch behind the ears, and directed his thoughts to the mysterious kami instead. *We need your presence. If you are defending this place against the leader of the Night Parade, we want to help. I beg you, make yourself known to Ryōtora, so that we can communicate with you. Pour yourself into a vessel in this world.*

Sekken wasn't a shugenja. He could pray, even hope for a shallow communion of sorts, but he couldn't achieve the deep connection of a shugenja. He'd never experienced the direct attention of a spirit.

Until now.

A skin-crawling feeling came over him – not of corruption or terror, but the same kind of awe-inspiring wonder he'd felt the first time he saw the shifting lights of the Elemental Dragons dancing across the northern sky at night. Ryōtora was right; there *was* another spirit here. One that had nothing of chaos or destruction in it.

It had heard their prayers. And it poured itself into a suitable vessel.

Sekken.

CHAPTER NINETEEN

Ryōtora felt the attention of the unknown kami. It wasn't the heavy, alien awareness of the mountain, thinking on a time scale in which his entire lifespan was scarcely the blink of an eye; it was more familiar than that. Not Earth, nor Water, nor Air, nor Fire, but all of those things together. And with them, something else: the element that was not an element, the absence that defined the presence of the other four. The Void.

A very *powerful* connection to the Void.

It's human, Ryōtora realized. Not a spirit of the natural world, not one of the primordial Fortunes, but the spirit of a human. One that, instead of descending into Meido to be judged and reborn in a new form, or lingering in the mortal world as a restless ghost, had transcended to become a kami.

He felt the moment its presence flowed down into a vessel – but not into the boulder he'd chosen as a possible yorishiro.

Ryōtora shot to his feet, hands outstretched. But it was too late. Sekken's body convulsed – and he thought of it in those terms, *Sekken's body,* because he knew with the unspoken instinct of his communion that the awareness now inhabiting that flesh, the entity that opened Sekken's eyes and looked at Ryōtora, was not the Phoenix scholar.

He dropped back to his knees and bowed low. Just because this kami had once been human didn't mean it was benevolent… and if he angered it, Sekken might be the one who paid the price.

"Revered kami," he said, his voice trembling. "You honor us with your presence. If there is some offering I can make which will be pleasing to you, name it."

With his face turned downward, he couldn't see anything but the moss and dirt and stone beneath him. He heard the quiet scuff of Sekken's foot against the ground, and then a long, drawn-out breath. As if the kami was testing out its host body, making sure it remembered how everything worked.

He should have seen the danger. People could be yorishiro, too – though usually not like this. High-ranking sumō wrestlers could hold that status, and there were rural traditions where a local medium called a kami down into a child. He'd seen it before. Yet he'd been thinking in terms of the natural environment, not a deceased human. Something like Saiun-nushi.

Sekken, forgive me.

"You are that one…" That was Sekken's voice, but not his manner of speaking. There was an odd cadence to its words as it tried again. "You are that one who called me forth."

"Yes, revered kami."

He heard a rustle, as of someone kneeling, and then a soft whine from the inugami. Not of pain; the dog sounded like it was trying to both seek and give comfort. "My poor friend," the kami murmured.

Ryōtora hesitated, then risked a question. "Are you the one to whom that honored inugami belongs?"

"Yes."

They'd found their witch at last. Not a villager; someone who had died untold centuries before. "Are you the one who imprisoned the Night Parade?"

"Lured them, ages ago. Only their leader lies trapped."

As Sayashi had indicated. That must be why no one had seen him yet, and Ryōtora silently thanked the Fortunes and this kami for that. "Please forgive my ignorance. But what is your connection to Asako Sekken, the man who now serves as your vessel?"

A long pause answered him. Then the kami said, "Will you forever stay like that? I cannot see your face. Sit up."

It sounded puzzled, rather than like it was granting him formal permission to release his bow. How long ago had that unknown person died? The etiquette of Rokugan might have been different then.

The Empire itself might not have existed then.

Now was not the time to ask questions about irrelevant history. Ryōtora straightened up and found Sekken's body now sitting cross-legged not far away, one hand stroking the dog with absent familiarity. Sekken himself had taken to petting it over the last few days, but always in a cautious fashion.

A brief glance over Ryōtora's shoulder showed him that Ishi and Tarō were still bowing. "They as well should sit up," the kami said. "That seems not comfortable."

The two ashigaru didn't look much more comfortable once upright. They kept their gazes trained on the ground, rather than staring at the possessed samurai now speaking in such an odd manner. Ryōtora thought of the boundary stone, carved with that archaic character for *chain,* and Sekken's previous assignment to assist a scholar who studied ancient forms of the language. Was Sekken still inside there somewhere, helping the kami translate to something more like current speech?

"This," the kami said, holding one hand up and studying it curiously. "As you asked. There is a connection… yes."

"Were you, in life, of the Phoenix Clan? Or the Dragon?" Sekken had a Mirumoto ancestor.

"Clans?" The kami seemed puzzled by this word. "Mean you… no, I recollect. Not the old tribes. Those who vowed themselves to the children of Lady Sun and Lord Moon. The ones who took their names held lands not far from here."

The earliest days of the Empire, then, when "Mirumoto" and "Agasha" meant not families, but the man and the woman who followed Togashi-no-Kami, the founder of the Dragon Clan. Or perhaps a little afterward; Ryōtora knew very little of history after the Day of Thunder, but he had a vague sense that the Empire as it was today hadn't sprung into existence overnight. How long had it taken before the scattered tribes of humanity all either joined the clans of the Kami, or migrated north to become the Yobanjin? Even Sekken might not know.

If he were sitting with me now, he'd have so many questions.

But the questions that mattered most, Ryōtora could ask for him. "Were you a shugenja? Could you speak to the elemental kami?" A tentative nod answered him, followed by a more confident one. "Were you an ishiken?"

Shugenja with the gift of working with the Void were exceedingly rare outside of the Phoenix, and not common even within their ranks. The term seemed to puzzle the kami again. "The Void," Ryōtora said. "Were you able to channel it in some fashion? You have a powerful connection to the Void now."

"I understand not what you mean," the kami said. "I am…" It gazed around, frowning. "My connection is to this place. And to this dog. And to this man."

Without warning, it reached into Sekken's kimono. A moment later it drew out the scholar's portable writing kit. A delighted smile spread across Sekken's face. "Ah. *This* is why."

Now it was Ryōtora's turn to be confused. The writing kit was much like his own, albeit more finely made, with–

"Vermilion lacquer," he breathed. There was more than one source of cinnabar in Dragon lands, of course, let alone in the Empire as a whole. But they'd wondered why, out of all possible descendants from the witch, Sekken would be the one haunted by the inugami.

A simple writing kit, lacquered with pigment mined in Seibo Mura, and owned by a descendant of the shugenja who imprisoned the Night Parade. That slender thread had drawn Sekken all the way from Phoenix lands to this place.

By way of the inugami. Sekken's body didn't have the exhausted look of the dog, but the way the kami sat seemed nearly as weary. Ryōtora said, "You have weakened recently, revered kami. Is it because the shrine fell? Or because something was taken from it?"

"Taken. Yes." The kami passed Sekken's hand over his face. "So many wounds of late. There was… a shaking. Saiun itself trembled. The fire stopped, and Nurarihyon woke. His breath slipped free. The amulet, gone. I reached out, I sent my friend… the Night Parade came. Their presence feeds him. Then someone took the mountain away."

Ryōtora's breath caught. "Saiun-nushi. I… I moved its shintai from here down to the village."

Sekken's hand trembled on the inugami's head. "Its strength no longer sustains me."

Guilt knifed through him. He'd thought that by re-enshrining the kami of the mountain down in the village, he was making Seibo Mura safer. Instead he'd torn away this kami's support.

The dwindling of the ward is my fault.

Ryōtora didn't even realize he'd bowed to the earth again until he heard the kami say, "Why do you do such a thing? I am no daughter of the Sun and Moon. Made from the tears of Amaterasu Ōmikami and the blood of Onnotangu Ōmikami, yes – in life – as all humans are, but no divine child, fallen to earth."

"I have weakened you," Ryōtora said, remaining fixed in his bow. "In trying to help, I have made things worse."

"Are they made better by you staring at the ground?"

No – but that wasn't the point. How could he show his face, when he'd erred so badly? But the kami's pragmatic response reminded him that his own sense of shame was an indulgence right now. Better that he find some way to undo his mistake than grovel uselessly in repentance for it.

He forced himself to sit back up, though he kept his gaze low. "If I return Saiun-nushi to this shrine–"

"It will help, but not undo," she said. The kami had spoken of herself as a daughter; it implied she had been female in life. "Saiun can support only. Even with the mountain, Nurarihyon will break free. Each time the Night Parade returns, he grows stronger."

"How long do we have?"

"Without the mountain, until the full moon begins. With it… until the end," the kami said simply. "I will not last beyond that."

Did she mean her ward? Or was the kami herself at risk of destruction? Ryōtora's orders were to protect Seibo Mura, not a kami the governor of Heibeisu didn't even know existed – but his duty as a shugenja was to protect the spiritual fabric of Dragon lands.

And of Rokugan itself. "What happens if he is freed?"

"As it was before. In the full moon of summer, the Night Parade roams free. Once it was everywhere, any place, without warning; no one knew if their village would be next."

Meaning that it could appear in Heibeisu. Or in Phoenix lands. Or in the imperial capital.

He started to bow again, then saw impatience in Sekken's face. The impulse to courtesy was deeply ingrained in him – but if the kami found that more irritating than gracious, the courteous thing to do was to refrain. Stiffening his back in an attempt to quell that reflex, Ryōtora said, "How did you imprison him, revered kami? I am also a shugenja, though without your knowledge and power. If I can restore the ward that holds him bound–"

The kami stood in the middle of his sentence, and for a moment Ryōtora feared he'd offended her. Instead she bowed to the west. "Spirits of the wind." Then north, toward the peak of Saiun. "Spirits of the earth." Then east – the waterfall? "Spirits of the water." Then south, toward Seibo Mura. "Spirits of the flame. But not any more."

Flame. In the village? No one had mentioned anything of the sort to him. There were lanterns, to be sure, and hearth fires… but a ward of this kind, he thought, would require a constant presence. The mountain was always there, and the waterfall, and in terrain like this it wasn't difficult to find a spot where the wind blew without ceasing. Fire, though, wasn't usually a permanent feature of the landscape. Not unless there was an active volcanic peak, or–

"The hot spring," he whispered. It had dried up after the quake, the movement of the ground somehow cutting off the vents that supplied heat and water.

The fire stopped, the kami had said. Then: *His breath slipped free.* The spirit lights Chie had seen. And then–

"You spoke of an amulet," he said, twitching as he instinctively tried to bow again. "Was that the element of Void in his imprisonment?"

She nodded Sekken's head. Ryōtora's heart twisted every time she moved like that, reminding him that the body he saw was being manipulated like a puppet. He prayed Sekken was unharmed in there, and that the Phoenix would understand the need to speak with the kami while they could – that Sekken would forgive him afterward.

He forced his thoughts back to where they belonged. "So what Chie took was part of the ward."

"More than that," the kami said. "Without it, you cannot face him. With it, you are safe."

Ryōtora's blood chilled. "So Sekken was right." In the stories, one couldn't even look at Nurarihyon without dying.

Was that why the yōkai had taken Chie? Perhaps they *couldn't* harm her… but they had to get her out of the village, because their master was coming.

He said, "The girl who took the amulet. Were you able to sense where she went?"

"Sideways," the kami said, making an elegant, obscure gesture with one hand.

"Into Senkyō?" When she nodded, he said, "There is a bakeneko here in the village who claims not to be part of the Night Parade. She wishes to leave so she will not be forced to join them, but I was neither able to banish her, nor to send her away from Seibo Mura. If it is your power that holds her here, would you permit her passage into the Spirit Realms? Her and… another person?"

The kami hesitated. This time Ryōtora bowed anyway, though he rose a moment later, rather than staying down as he delivered his plea. "If we are to stop the Night Parade, we must get that amulet back. And it is my duty to rescue the girl if I can. But I have never traveled in the Spirit Realms; I will need someone to guide me." Sayashi would be less than eager to help, he suspected. But if it meant breaking her mother free of Nurarihyon's control, and making it so that Sayashi herself need not fear being made to join their ranks…

"Goodwill is not in question," the kami said. "For now, they are kept out. But if I open the way now–"

"Then they might come through early." Ryōtora felt sick. He had no choice but to wait.

No matter which way he turned, he felt trapped. To defend against the Night Parade, they needed Chie, but to get Chie, they would need to risk the Night Parade. The presence of the other yōkai fed strength to Nurarihyon, and the kami wasn't strong enough to hold him for much longer. Because the hot spring had dried up, and the amulet was gone, and Ryōtora had, in his ignorance, moved Saiun-nushi out of place. That left only the waterfall and the wind to keep Nurarihyon trapped. And only a few days more before the chaos began again.

He was going to fail Seibo Mura, and his clan, and the Empire.

The kami knelt in front of Ryōtora. In her time, etiquette had been different; she showed no hesitation in laying her hand against his cheek. The touch was simultaneously comforting –

the kindness of the mother he'd never known – and a taunting offer of what he couldn't have, as Sekken's fingers cupped his jaw, Sekken's long-lashed eyes gazed at him from only a breath away.

"You are not alone," she said. In Sekken's voice, quiet but strong. "I have not failed yet. We have my friend, your followers, and the man who has given me this chance to speak. We have Saiun and the people of the village."

"I should send them away," Ryōtora whispered. "If the village is empty–"

"Then the creatures of the Night Parade will have nothing to occupy their attention save seeking out their imprisoned leader. They need a target. But perhaps not *all* the targets."

Evacuate part of the village – the young, the old, those who couldn't defend themselves well. Keep a small number in Seibo Mura. But Ryōtora had to go after Chie, and he had to take Sayashi with him; who would that leave to lead the defense here? Sekken was no bushi, much less a military commander. He would do it anyway, Ryōtora thought. But it might very well mean that Ryōtora would return to find Sekken dead.

Those were not concerns to trouble a spirit with. She was doing what she could; the rest was up to him.

"Thank you, revered kami," he said. The words came out barely audible.

Her gaze grew distant, and Sekken's hand slid from his jaw. Then she said, in a thoughtful, half-unsure tone, "Kaimin."

"Is that your name?"

"That is what they called me. Those who venerated Saiun, and kept the knowledge of my presence here. Kaimin… yes."

Sekken would have been able to reflexively identify what the name could mean. It might or might not have been her name in life; it might or might not even match with the language as it was spoken now. But it was good to have *something* to call her, other than "revered kami."

Ryōtora backed away on the rough ground and bowed low. "You have my gratitude, Kaimin-nushi. And I vow to you that I will give everything I have to keep the Night Parade and its leader imprisoned."

His ears heard only silence. The part of him that sensed the spiritual fabric of the world, though, felt the rush as Kaimin-nushi's spirit dissipated.

And then he heard the thump as Sekken collapsed.

CHAPTER TWENTY

"Now I know how you felt after moving Saiun-nushi," Sekken said, rubbing his face.

He hadn't been out for long. Just long enough for Ryōtora to rush to his side, so that the first thing Sekken saw when he woke was the shugenja's worried face. That had lasted long enough for Ryōtora to make sure Sekken hadn't suffered horribly during his stint as a temporary vessel for a kami, nor taken any permanent damage from it; then, predictably, Ryōtora was face-down on the ground, in abject apology for something he couldn't have seen coming.

Nor had Sekken himself anticipated it. He'd been too fixed on the assumption that his connection was to some living person in Seibo Mura. Besides, he wasn't a shugenja – not that one had to be, in order to encounter the kami, but Sekken wasn't in the habit of thinking of himself as the sort of person who came into direct contact with spirits.

He wondered if Ryōtora could guess at both meanings behind his comment. The first was that now he felt the bone-deep exhaustion of sustaining the kami's presence. According to

Ryōtora's account, all Kaimin-nushi had done with Sekken's body was move it around a little bit, but he felt as if he'd run to the top of the peak and back. The second…

The second was the embarrassment of having caused someone such worry. In the wake of Sekken's collapse, Ryōtora's usual composed mask had dissolved, and the anguish in his eyes had burned like fire. If Sekken had been able to move his arms in that moment, he would have reached up to touch Ryōtora's face, stroking the lines of worry away. But he'd been immobile, and Ryōtora wouldn't have welcomed such a gesture regardless.

The mask was back now, of course. And Sekken wasn't about to call attention to the slip; that would only make matters even more awkward. He'd focused on coaxing Ryōtora out of his bow, assuring him that everything was fine, that Sekken was glad to have been of use in communicating with Kaimin-nushi.

Sekken pulled his writing kit from his sash and turned it over in his hands. "This little thing," he murmured, shaking his head in disbelief. "It was a gift from my uncle, in honor of my gempuku. Not even my maternal uncle – no one with any connection to Dragon lands. But we have many objects with vermilion lacquer in our territory; we're fond of the color. I'm not surprised some of the pigment comes from here."

"Were it not for that," Ryōtora said in a flat, dull voice, "you would never have gotten involved in all of this."

"Then I should send my uncle a letter of thanks," Sekken answered, with deliberate lightness. He held up the kit and shook it gently at Ryōtora. "I know my presence has been an imposition on you, but I like to think it's also been at least a *little* bit useful."

"More than a little!"

He smiled at Ryōtora's hasty response. "If I've given you at least one moment of meaningful assistance, then I'm glad to be here. To be honest…"

At the pause, Ryōtora lifted his eyebrows in query. Sekken lowered the writing kit, looking down at it so he wouldn't burden Ryōtora with his feelings. "It's a little sobering to think that I've done more of significance in the last ten days than in my entire life before this point."

In his peripheral vision, he saw Ryōtora shake his head. Before the shugenja could voice his disagreement, though, Sekken held up one hand. "While I appreciate your confidence, I know my past better than you do. I used to think that my life was ideal – that I was lucky, having the opportunity to do more or less what I wanted, without any burden of obligation saying that I *must* do thus-and-such for the good of my clan. But while that may be pleasant, it's also hollow." He allowed himself a small laugh. "Ironic that my most important deeds in this lifetime will be in the service of another clan."

"And the Empire as a whole," Ryōtora pointed out. "Kaiminnushi indicated that the Night Parade used to ravage anywhere it pleased. What we do here will protect not only the Dragon and the Phoenix, but every clan from the Crab to the Unicorn."

It was a daunting prospect. Still, Sekken felt as if Ryōtora had helped him uncover a core of good steel inside himself… and he liked the feeling. Even with the danger looming over their heads, he had no intention of abandoning this battle.

"By now Ogano will have announced the evacuation," Ryōtora said. "I need to get back there and ask for volunteers to stay – people willing to risk themselves in order to keep the Night Parade's attention focused on the village, rather than on freeing their master."

Sekken rose, even though his legs still felt as if they belonged to someone else. "Lead on."

When the path down from the shrine brought them in sight of the village, Sekken's first thought was that someone had kicked an anthill.

It looked as if every resident of Seibo Mura was running around in a panic. As he and Ryōtora drew closer, though, he realized that what looked like panic was in fact surprisingly orderly. Several men were dragging out a series of wheelbarrows and lining them up in the heart of the village, with their front shafts propped up on barrels and crates so that the platforms would be level. While not as capacious as carts, they had the advantage of not needing oxen or horses to pull them, and their single wheels, jutting up from the center of each platform, were much more suited to maneuvering along narrow mountain paths.

Of course, the sight also made him think of certain extremely unpleasant yōkai: wa nyūdō, katawaguruma, severed heads and screaming women mounted on flaming wheels. None of those had been seen in Seibo Mura… yet. But the attacks had gotten worse with each passing night, presumably as Nurarihyon's ability to call his followers to him got stronger. Who could say what might appear next?

The main things being loaded onto the wheelbarrows' platforms seemed to be food and other vital supplies, not personal possessions. *Good,* Sekken thought. Those not capable of walking far – children, elderly, injured villagers – could perch atop those. Anything else people wanted to bring they would have to carry on their own backs. Which would, in turn, limit how much they tried to carry.

When he said as much to Ryōtora, the shugenja nodded. "I discussed it with Ogano. Though I'm surprised they're so willing to heed him, given the confrontation the other day."

"The weight of tradition is on his side," Sekken answered. "He is, after all, their headman."

But when they got into the village proper, they discovered it wasn't Ogano's doing. Haru stood near the wheelbarrows, directing people, answering questions, and chastising anyone who tried to slip their personal belongings in among the vital supplies.

Sekken's breath huffed out in a quiet laugh. "Perhaps peasants aren't so different from samurai after all. As usual, it's the lord's hatamoto that actually gets things done."

Ryōtora rubbed the back of his neck, smiling ruefully. "Indeed."

While Ryōtora went to talk quietly with Haru, Sekken hung back. He could still see more than a few unfriendly glances cast his way; word had circulated that he wasn't responsible for the problems in Seibo Mura, but people still wanted someone to blame. It was easier to turn on an outsider than their own headman. *And Ryōtora thinks I can lead them in defense of the village?*

He knew yōkai. That was the only skill he could offer here. But he wasn't even sure how much use that would be: while certainly he could tell people to turn away if they heard the song of an azuki babā, or not to lift their heads to look a mikoshi nyūdō in the eye, how many of them would remember that in the panic of the moment? Not to mention that most of the instructions for surviving an encounter with a yōkai assumed there was just *one*, acting in accordance with its own inhuman nature. Matters were quite different when it was the whole Night Parade, bound to Nurarihyon's service.

With a jolt, Sekken realized the inugami wasn't there. He'd grown so accustomed to having the spirit dragging in his wake that the absence was unsettling. In hindsight, it made sense; now that Sekken had communicated with Kaimin-nushi – or rather, had been the means by which Ryōtora communicated with her – there was no need for the dog to pester him any longer.

You spent months trying to get rid of that thing, he thought. *You should be glad it's gone.* He wasn't, though. The last few days had transformed the inugami's presence from a haunting to an odd kind of companionship. However tired the spirit might be, it would have been comforting to still have the dog by his side.

Ryōtora came back, with the particular stony expression Sekken interpreted as hiding nerves. "I've asked Haru to gather people so I can speak to them. Do you – ah – have any tips? I'm not used to making speeches."

"Most of my education in that regard is about speaking in court," Sekken said. "I don't think the literary allusions and flattering compliments based on research into some lord's lineage would be very persuasive to these people. What you really want is a Lion general, to rally the troops. Pity we don't have one here."

"Pity indeed," Ryōtora muttered, and Sekken regretted the attempt at a joke. Their situation would be much improved if they had *anyone* here with military leadership experience. Or even military training.

His next answer was more serious. "Just be honest and sincere. Two things you're very good at."

Now why did that make him flinch? Sekken wondered as Ryōtora nodded and stepped away. It was a genuine compliment.

Haru sent out runners, and soon what Sekken believed to be the entire population of Seibo Mura was gathered in the center of the village. Ogano was there, doing his best to look important, dressed in what Sekken assumed was his finest kimono; so was Fūyō. At first Sekken couldn't see "Aoi" anywhere; then he found her half-concealed behind the corner of a house. Sayashi was doing her best to look like a meek peasant girl, but she undercut that by shooting first Ryōtora, then Sekken, a look that might as well have been a banner as high as a house. *This is all well and good for these people, but what about me?*

The reason for her hiding became apparent when he noticed Fubatsu was also present, still unsteady from his illness and leaning on his mother for support. Sayashi had chosen a spot out of his line of sight. With the blood of the hihi in him, Fubatsu would be able to see her for what she really was; she must have heard about him spotting the inugami.

Then Sekken put such thoughts from his mind, because the villagers had all gathered, and Ryōtora began to speak. Not in the elevated, roundabout phrasings of a courtier addressing fellow samurai, but in simple speech that cut right to the heart of the matter.

Sekken didn't bother listening closely to what he said. All of it was known to him already. Instead he watched the crowd, trying to evaluate their reactions.

They were afraid, of course. When Ryōtora had first arrived in Seibo Mura, the assumption had been that, with the governor having sent a shugenja, all would be well. Yet days had gone by – in which Ryōtora did a number of useful things, true, but nothing which definitively banished the threat and made the village safe. He hadn't even been able to tell them why they were cursed with such troubles.

Well, now they had their answer. And it was far from reassuring.

The phrase "Night Parade of a Hundred Demons" elicited no flickers of recognition that Sekken could see. He suspected that after so long, even the shrinekeeper hadn't known about the village's ancient history. The peasants were, however, perfectly capable of comprehending the concept of "demons." And even though it was really just a frightening name for a phenomenon they'd already experienced, codifying it like that deepened their fear.

But for all his lack of experience in making speeches, Ryōtora did an admirable job of responding to that fear.

He spun them the tale of Kaimin-nushi: the ancient and heroic shugenja who'd lured the Night Parade to this remote spot, then bound its leader – he didn't use Nurarihyon's name, just in case – and set herself as his eternal guardian. He glossed over how that knowledge might have been lost in the intervening centuries, and instead characterized the people of Seibo Mura as Kaimin-nushi's helpers in that task. Sekken privately suspected that no one in the village had any blood connection to Kaimin-nushi's descendants – if they had, surely her inugami would have haunted *them* first – but that didn't stop Ryōtora from invoking them as the inheritors of her tradition. It was true enough not to violate the ethics of Bushidō, and it gave them pride, as an antidote to fear.

Then Sekken heard his own name.

Ryōtora was standing atop a wheelbarrow that hadn't yet been loaded with supplies, at the center of the crowd, so that everyone could see him clearly. Now he turned and bowed to Sekken. "Many of you have feared Lord Asako because of the inugami seen in his presence. Gonbei, you told me you had once heard a tale that Seibo Mura had a guardian dog. I tell you today that you're correct. The practice of tsukimono-suji is not always turned to personal gain and evil; in ancient times, it could be a noble art. Just as the Fortune Inari is attended by foxes, Kaimin-nushi has her attendant dog – the same spirit that Fubatsu has seen around our visitor.

"This is because Lord Asako is himself a descendant of the kami! Though he is an outsider to you, he's come to Seibo Mura because he was called here by Kaimin-nushi's inugami. He is not a great threat to you; far from it, in fact. He is instead your great ally."

Now all eyes were on Sekken. He was accustomed to maintaining his composure in court, but it was hard to draw on those habits when he stood on a patch of trampled grass with frightened peasants looking at him like some minor Fortune. *I'm just a scholar,* he wanted to say – but humility was neither useful nor advisable when trying to rally people to defend against the Night Parade. He finally inclined a small bow toward Ryōtora, which had the merit of giving him *something* to do other than fight the urge to squirm.

It seemed to be enough. Ryōtora went on to explain that Masa's daughter Chie had indeed been taken by the yōkai, and that an amulet in her possession had the power to protect its holder against the leader of the Night Parade. "In order to save Seibo Mura," he said, "it's of the greatest importance that we rescue Chie. To that end, this is what we'll do.

"The majority of you will evacuate, as you've been told. Once past the line of Kaimin-nushi's ward, you'll be safe from the Night Parade. The mountains are still dangerous – but you are the people of the mountains. These dangers are ones you know well, and I trust you to work together to reach Heibeisu safely. I'll send a letter with you, addressed to the governor of that city, requesting that he give you shelter until the threat here has been dealt with."

And also telling him what you've learned, Sekken thought. *Because it's still all too possible that we will fail to deal with this, and someone else will have to pick up that task.*

"But we can't all evacuate," Ryōtora said. "In order to delay the moment at which the Night Parade breaks free, we must keep the attention of the yōkai focused on this place. I therefore ask for volunteers: strong and brave people, who are willing to stand their ground against this chaos. Lord Asako will lead you in the defense of the village."

A murmur rippled through the crowd, and it sounded uneasy. Ogano, being the headman, felt free to speak bluntly. "What about you?"

Ryōtora said, "I will go into the Spirit Realms to rescue Chie."

The murmur grew instantaneously into a small roar. *Nobody* liked that idea, it seemed. Their one shugenja, the man the governor had sent to save them – and he proposed to leave just as the Night Parade arrived? The cries Sekken picked out of the noise didn't accuse Ryōtora of cowardice; nobody considered a journey into Senkyō to be the act of a coward. But they wanted, they *needed* him in Seibo Mura. Men and women who had been stiffening their spines to volunteer abruptly changed stance at the prospect of fighting the yōkai without Ryōtora at their side.

Sekken couldn't blame them. Quite apart from his lack of confidence in his own military skills, *he* didn't much relish the thought of facing the Night Parade without a shugenja's help. Descendant of Kaimin-nushi or not, he was definitely not leader enough to quell those fears, not when he shared them himself.

What could Ryōtora do about it, though? He kept his face

impassive, raising his hands to try to quiet the shouts so he could explain… but in the end, he faced an impossible choice. Chie had to be rescued, the amulet retrieved. The village had to be defended. And there was only one of–

Sekken was moving through the crowd before he could think, murmuring reflexive apologies as he shouldered villagers out of the way. Even after he'd drawn close, he had to raise his voice before Ryōtora could hear him over everyone else. "Send me instead!"

Those nearest to him heard the offer, and took up the cry. "Yes! Send the Phoenix to save Chie!"

Ryōtora's eyes went wide. Kneeling atop the barrow, he lowered his voice, so that at least the entire crowd wouldn't hear him. "Lord Asako–"

"Are you going to say it's too dangerous? Staying here is hardly safe either."

"Yes, but from here you can retreat if you have to."

Retreat: a polite, respectable synonym for *flee*. "With all that's at stake, I'm not likely to do that."

"You know yōkai better than I do–"

"And I also know the Spirit Realms. How much good does it do, being a shugenja there? Some, to be certain – but not nearly as much as it will do here. If we can't have you in both places, then the next best thing is to assign me the task that has less need of your particular skills."

"Yes, but…" Ryōtora hesitated, then scrambled off the barrow and caught Sekken's sleeve. Together they pushed out of the crowd to a spot where Ryōtora could speak without being overheard. "You know as well as I do that going into Senkyō after Chie is a gamble. Even if whoever goes is successful… it might not help Seibo Mura."

Sekken hadn't given it any particular thought. He'd had too many other things to consider, after he woke from his stint as a divine vessel. But it wasn't hard to see what Ryōtora aimed at. "You're worried about time."

The Spirit Realms didn't always move at the same speed as the mortal world. A human could spend a lifetime there and come back to find only a day had passed at home. Or sometimes it went the other way: even a brief trip across that border translated into days, months, years in the realm they'd left behind.

Whoever went after Chie might not come back before the end of the full moon. In which case the Night Parade might break free, and the amulet would be used not to protect Seibo Mura, but to contain the threat that once more ranged across Rokugan. And with how fickle the Spirit Realms could be…

He might leave behind everyone and everything he'd known.

But if Sekken had spoken up sooner about the inugami, Ryōtora might have had more time to prepare. Sekken had broken his trust, and put everyone in greater danger as a result. The consequences should be on his own head.

"You aren't a Dragon," Ryōtora said. "Your duty is to your own clan. I can't ask you to do this."

The intensity of his voice held more power than any courtier's crafted phrases. But in his eyes, Sekken saw something other than protest: hope, gratitude… and trust.

He answered simplicity with simplicity. "You don't have to."

Then Sekken turned, jogged back through the parted crowd, and leapt atop the barrow. Spreading his arms so that his sleeves fluttered in the wind, he declared, "I will go to the Spirit Realms in Sir Ryōtora's place!"

CHAPTER TWENTY-ONE

Nothing Ryōtora said would talk Sekken out of his declaration. Too much of the village had acclaimed him for it... and Ryōtora knew he was right.

More than anything, he wanted to tell Sekken to leave while he could. But that was the Three Sins ruling him: Desire in his attraction to Sekken, Fear in his worry that Ryōtora might never see him again, and Regret in his guilt that he hadn't solved the puzzle before now. That he couldn't find any solution that didn't require them both to risk death.

Confessing any of this to Sekken would only compound the problem. They had their duties; those should have the whole of their attention now. Ryōtora tore his gaze away from the Phoenix, busy writing a message for the refugees to carry to Heibeisu, and devoted himself to the task of preparing Seibo Mura.

He had a surprising number of volunteers to join the ranks of the defenders. Daizan, one of the loggers who'd gone to cut down the cypress tree for the temporary shrine. Gonbei, who'd told Ryōtora the story about the village having a guardian dog. Ashio, who according to Sekken's notes had been driven half-mad by the laughter of a kerakera onna, due to his affair with another woman in the village; Ryōtora had to turn him down, because Ashio's twitchy manner and disjointed speech cast doubt on the man's stability in a crisis.

Others he did his best to turn down, with no more success than he'd had with Sekken. Ona insisted on staying to avenge her husband Hideo, killed by the okuri inu. When Ryōtora attempted to point out that she had three children, the eldest at fifteen declared that he could take care of his younger siblings, and then all three children bowed to the ground to beg Ryōtora that their family be permitted justice. Ryōtora suspected that if the eldest son hadn't lost one arm in the collapse of a mining shaft, it would have been him staying instead.

He also didn't manage to turn away Rin. She demonstrated her skills by using her sling to knock a bird from a tree branch, then told him with the sort of impudence that could get her into trouble elsewhere in the Empire that even if he ordered her to leave the village, he couldn't stop her from sneaking back.

It was true, and better to bow to the inevitable than to encourage insurrection from the start. Even if he hated the thought of someone so young risking herself.

The last person in his line was the carpenter, Masa.

"I would have thought…" Ryōtora began, then hesitated.

"That I would ask to go with the Phoenix?" Masa's jaw tightened. "When Chie was taken, if I'd known how to get to her, I would have gone on the spot. But now…"

Ryōtora waited. For all that time was precious, he couldn't push this man, who was on the verge of losing everything he had left.

"Now," Masa said, steadying his voice, "I think my place is here. I don't know the Spirit Realms. I know Seibo Mura, though, and you… you'll need help."

It was all too true. "Thank you," Ryōtora said gently, and stood. "You can start by helping with defenses."

One other person stayed, because she had no choice.

"Aoi" told her mother and brother that she was going to help defend the village. "The only way I might get my memories back is if I find the yōkai that took them and confront it," Sayashi said, lying with a persuasive fluency that disturbed Ryōtora.

Especially when Fūyō tried to say that she didn't care whether Aoi never remembered her; all she cared about was her daughter's survival. *We're going to have to tell her afterward that Aoi died during this battle,* Ryōtora thought, feeling sick to his stomach. Then, on the heels of that: *No. When this is over with, she will have the truth. She'll hate me for it – but I must live with that.* It was all too tempting to slip into the trap of doing what was easy, rather than what was right.

Of course, that assumed he was alive to give her the truth. But if he wasn't, someone else could. He'd written up a report; it would go south with the evacuees, with strict orders that whatever else happened, it must reach Heibeisu. The Empire must be warned.

They couldn't depart yet, though. Before they did, there was one thing they had to assist Ryōtora with, because he couldn't do it on his own.

If the first "festival" had been a little subdued, the second was funereal. Moving Saiun-nushi out of the center of the village and back up to the mountainside shrine was necessary to prop up the failing ward – but it also reminded everyone that they might never return home, to their familiar rituals and local kami. The one saving grace was that Saiun-nushi itself seemed easier to bear, returning to its old home; this time Ryōtora didn't collapse afterward.

Which was a relief, because he had something else he wanted to try.

The question of whether to do it scraped his nerves raw. Ordinary invocations to the kami were fairly safe; they were handed down through generations of Agasha-trained shugenja, recorded and learned and taught to students because they'd proven to be a reliable way of getting a predictable result. What he was considering doing was a different matter entirely: an improvised request, following no set form, and directed toward some of the most volatile kami in existence.

The morning after the evacuees departed, Ryōtora went out of the village to at least assess his chances… and found Sekken lounging on a rock above the dry bowl that had once been Seibo Mura's hot spring.

"I figured you'd think of this," Sekken said when Ryōtora came into view. "I saw you working yourself up to it. You're going to try to restore this part of the ward, aren't you?"

He hopped down before Ryōtora could answer. "The rocks aren't warm – no more so than any other stone that's been in the sun for a few hours. Whatever connection this area had to the fire kami, it's gone."

"Cut off, perhaps," Ryōtora said. "Fire is oddly like water in that fashion. Where it lives in the earth, it flows along channels. The crater of an active volcano is the most obvious of those channels, but there are smaller gaps all throughout the mountains. And just as the flow of water in a spring can be severed by the shifting of the earth, so too can the flow of heat. If I can open it again–"

"Then eastern Dragon lands might have an exciting new volcano?"

More likely that they will have one charred shugenja. Ryōtora huffed a self-deprecating laugh and brushed his hair out of his face. "You have a very high opinion of my skill if you think I'm capable of creating that."

"I take the risk very seriously indeed." Sekken's smile undercut the claim of seriousness; he meant it only as praise.

Warmth and embarrassment churned together in Ryōtora's stomach. To hide it, he cast a glance at the dry bowl that had once been the spring. "You aren't going to try to talk me out of this?"

"'The mountains never learned to step aside' – isn't that how the Dragon saying goes? I'm nowhere near silver-tongued enough to persuade you. As it happens, though, I have no intention of trying. What you're doing here may be dangerous… but it's also necessary." Sekken bowed Ryōtora toward the stones, like a host inviting a guest in. "Is there anything I can do?"

Kneeling at the side of the empty spring, Ryōtora said, "Just stand back."

He lost track of both Sekken and time after that. He couldn't simply put himself in communion with the lost fire; it was too deeply buried, and the earth above it was sluggish with the newfound cold. Ryōtora was able to restore the flow of the water – that was relatively easy, with the same prayer he'd used to shake the earth under the feet of the villagers when they were attacking Ogano – but heat was another matter. He could coax warmth into the pool; he couldn't make it self-sustaining. Fire and Water stood in opposition, each annihilating the other. Getting them to coexist required a delicate balance, and he simply wasn't capable of drawing the fire back up to the surface in the necessary strength.

What finally broke him from his trance was the feeling of hands on his shoulders. He opened his eyes to find the hands belonged to Sekken, and were keeping him from slumping over. The Phoenix let go of him once he was upright, then bowed in apology. "I didn't want you going head-first into the pool."

"Thank you," Ryōtora said, reflex alone propelling the words out of his mouth. The light had shifted direction; it was mid-afternoon already. He hadn't meant to try for so long.

Sekken dipped a hand into the water, then wiped it dry. He didn't bother pointing out that it wasn't hot; Ryōtora already knew. Instead he said, "You still have time."

Time alone wouldn't be enough. But Ryōtora didn't say that.

"Come back to the village," Sekken said. "Ishi and Tarō should have some defensive plans for you by now, and Ona will have food."

With Fubatsu gone from the village, tied into the saddle of one of the ponies, Sayashi didn't have to keep out of sight. They'd told the other defenders that "Aoi" wouldn't be staying to fight the yōkai, but would go with Sekken into the Spirit Realms; this had the unfortunate side effect of freeing her from any responsibility to help out with the defenses, aside from making the occasional sardonic comment. Those made the others resent her, muttering amongst themselves that Aoi certainly had changed, and not for the better. But in their own way, her comments were helpful, because she knew more about yōkai than anyone other than Sekken – and her knowledge, unlike his, came from direct experience.

After one of those instances, Ryōtora and Sekken followed her out of Ogano's house. When they were safely out of earshot from the others, she turned around and snapped, "Now that everyone's gone, why not let me through? I see no reason to go on waiting. What difference does it make whether the Night Parade attacks now?"

"It gives them time to get farther away, and us more time to prepare," Ryōtora said, even as he wondered why he was bothering. Sayashi knew that, and didn't care.

The other reason, he didn't voice. They hadn't yet had a chance to ask her to be Sekken's guide through Senkyō. That was why they'd followed her now, and it might take all their remaining time to convince her.

But he hadn't reckoned on her quick wit. Examining her fingernails as if disappointed at how short and dull they were, Sayashi said, "Go ahead. I already know what you're going to say."

Sekken feigned surprise. "Are we so transparent?"

"Everything you know came out of a scroll," Sayashi said to him, with a sharp smile that didn't reassure at all. "And you expect to find that girl on your own, in the wilds of Senkyō? How laughable."

Ryōtora said, "You understand why we need her. Even if you don't care for the fate of this village, or for Rokugan, surely your own self-interest argues in favor of helping us."

"My self-interest?" In this form she had no tail to lash, but he could imagine it anyway. "Going anywhere near *his* people runs very much counter to that. Would you feel safer, sneaking up to an enemy's castle rather than running away?"

"If I knew the enemy would soon be pouring out of that castle to overrun the land, yes. Without that amulet, we can't face… *him*." Kaimin-nushi had shown no fear of naming Nurarihyon out loud, but she was a kami. Ryōtora judged it best to follow Sayashi's lead in this matter. "And if we can't face him, then soon he'll be free. Which means you'll have to fear him and his creatures everywhere you go. A smaller risk now gains you safety later."

Sayashi's lip curled. "*If* you succeed. You'll forgive me if I have my doubts."

While the two of them talked, Sekken had been watching quietly. Now he spoke up. "For all your objections, you haven't refused outright. In fact, you invited us to present our request. Which means that you *might* be willing – if we were to offer you the right incentive."

She merely smiled at him, and waited.

What could a bakeneko want? Some sort of gift? Or a bribe; the line between the two could be thin indeed, and given Sayashi's personality, Ryōtora felt the latter was the more apt term. It wasn't integrity that held him back, though. It was a complete lack of inspiration as to what might persuade her to help.

Sayashi laughed silently at them both. To Ryōtora she said, "Even your pet *Phoenix* can't figure it out. I guess he doesn't know as much about us as he thought."

"Phoenix," Sekken whispered, echoing the word she'd stressed. Then his eyes went wide.

Before Ryōtora could ask what he was doing, Sekken retreated two steps, to a more respectful distance. Then, with all the grace and dignity of a man in formal court, he knelt, brought his arms up, and bowed his face to the ground.

"Noble bakeneko," he said, his voice humble, "I beg you to grant me the favor of your assistance."

Ryōtora stared, struggling not to let his jaw drop. Showing such deference to a *yōkai* was –

It was an echo straight out of history. The divine founder of the Phoenix Clan, Shiba-no-Kami, had bowed to the mortal shugenja Isawa to beg his assistance before the Day of Thunder. Because of that, to this day, the Phoenix Clan Champion answered to the Elemental Council of the Isawa, rather than standing supreme.

Sayashi's voice was bright with delight. "Why, little Asako. Are you placing yourself under my authority?"

Her question and her mode of address made Ryōtora tense. Sekken said, "I will not betray my clan. But while we are in Senkyō, I promise to defer to you as I would to any other learned teacher – because I cannot deny that your wisdom there far surpasses my own."

"That's true enough." Sayashi paced around him with a leisurely stride, first glancing down at Sekken, then up at Ryōtora with a wicked grin. He held himself rigid, swallowing all the objections he wanted to make. As much as he hated to admit it, Sekken's guess seemed to be right: what Sayashi wanted was not some material incentive, but the pleasure of seeing a human defer to her whims. Sekken stood above her in the Celestial Order… but so had Shiba-no-Kami stood above Isawa. And yet he had knelt, for the good of all.

Sekken remained where he was, not moving. Finally Sayashi said, "Oh, very well. You plead so prettily; how could I refuse? I'll go with you into Senkyō."

"And help me rescue Chie once I am there, and help us both return to the mortal realm?"

"What do you think I am – some creature of Sakkaku, out to bend words? Will you demand a written contract next? I won't promise to help you with the rescue, if it looks too much like suicide. But I promise to help you find her. And if you're still alive after that, I'll even help you get home."

It was all they could hope for, and more than Ryōtora had feared they would get. Sekken rose, as smoothly as he'd knelt, and gave Sayashi a smaller bow. "Thank you, sensei."

Peasants weren't expected to follow the tenets of Bushidō. Ordinarily samurai spoke of that as a deficiency in battle: without a code of honor to strengthen their spirits, peasants were cowardly and prone to fleeing rather than upholding their duty.

It had its uses, though. As Ryōtora rapidly discovered, peasants had no compunctions about using dirty tricks of a sort no virtuous samurai would employ on the field of battle… but then again, their enemy was not another army of samurai.

Ishi and Tarō had some experience of combat, though mostly against bandits. They were able to advise Ryōtora on the best ways to control the terrain and maximize their own ability to act, while restricting the yōkai – as much as was possible, given the otherworldly abilities some yōkai had. The villagers, meanwhile, brought the expertise of hunters to the task. Sekken tied back his sleeves and helped out with preparations, even to the point of his hands blistering from the unfamiliar tools.

Ryōtora's preparations were of a different sort. The Agasha trained not only shugenja, but also alchemists; he wasn't an expert in the latter field, but he'd learned some basic techniques. Flash powder, used for theatrical effects, was nothing more than the dried spores of clubmoss, which grew in abundance around the village. And since the evacuees hadn't been able to take with them any of the cinnabar or realgar they'd mined during the summer, he was free to extract certain components from the ores. Not only could the arsenic from realgar produce acid and toxic vapors, but the quicksilver from cinnabar made an excellent offering to the kami – so long as he was careful in how he used it. Those materials could also poison the land and the water.

He couldn't set up everything he wanted in advance. Some things had to wait, in order to preserve the element of surprise. To some extent, though, he could commune with the small kami in and around the village and make offerings to them now, so that when the time came, they would respond more quickly. That could make all the difference in the heat of battle, when he wouldn't have time to propitiate them the usual way.

Sekken spent most of that time scribbling like mad, not on paper – they were almost completely out of that now – but with paint on some boards, writing out notes on creatures as yet unseen that might appear during the next set of attacks. Most of those notes were oriented toward telling Ryōtora what dangers to expect from them, not how to counter them; very few had specific weaknesses a person could exploit. Ryōtora finally stopped him when the notes threatened to become so extensive that they would be no use at all. "It doesn't help me to have the information," Ryōtora said, "if I'm busy looking for it while they're attacking."

"True." Sekken grimaced. "I just…"

He didn't have to finish that sentence. They both wished they could be in both places at once. They simply had to trust each other to take care of their half of the responsibilities.

Ryōtora trusted Sekken. He only hoped he would not let the other man down.

As the sun dipped toward the western horizon and the first silver edge of the moon began to creep over the peaks, Ryōtora waited with Sekken and Sayashi on the ground in front of the ruined shrine.

Masa had already bid them farewell, bowing to the ground in thanks – not the deference of a peasant to a samurai, but that of a father to the man who was risking himself to save his daughter. Then he'd hurried back down to the village, where Ryōtora would soon join him.

Twilight was a time of transition, between worlds as well as between day and night. The soft, uncertain light blurred everything, making Ryōtora believe that something *more* hovered just a breath away. He'd communed with Kaimin-nushi and knew she would aid in the travelers' passage; so would the kami of the mountain. Sayashi herself was a creature of Senkyō, and her presence helped to thin the veil. Sekken wouldn't have to wander through the mountains, hoping to stumble upon one of the places where the Spirit Realms bled over into the mortal world. He had Ryōtora's prayers, a mountain's support, the blessings of his ancestor, and a bakeneko to assist.

It was what he would do when he reached the other side that was in question.

Ryōtora could see Sekken searching for some kind of light-hearted comment to ease the tension, then discarding it. For his own part, Ryōtora feared that if he tried to say anything, all the words he was holding back would come spilling out. Words that had no place here, because they were the undiluted cry of his heart.

In the end, all Sekken said was, "I'll be back as soon as I can."

"I will hold the village as long as I can," Ryōtora said.

Sekken bowed, and Ryōtora bowed back. Then he turned and began to walk, with Sayashi at his side; and between one step and the next, they faded from view.

The full moon was rising.

CHAPTER TWENTY-TWO

A well-designed garden was meant to imitate a landscape, real or imagined, in miniature: large boulders for mountains, streams or channels of white sand for rivers, pools for lakes.

Crossing into Senkyō, Sekken felt as if he'd stepped out of a garden into the real world.

It wasn't that anything was bigger – not exactly. The mountain that loomed to the north didn't tower several times higher into the sky; the trees didn't grow to a size that dwarfed him. But everything was more *present,* suggestive of greater depth and complexity. As if his whole life he'd been living in a simplified representation of true nature, and for the first time he faced the thing itself.

The sheer wonder of it stopped his breath. Although his interest had always been more in scholarship than art, he found himself wishing he were a skilled painter or a poet, to capture this greater reality with color or words. *I would fail, and spend the rest of my life happy in the trying.*

A long, drawn-out sigh of pleasure broke him from his reverie. At his side, Sayashi bent to the ground, stretching like a cat; by the time she finished stretching, she *was* a cat.

She sat and scratched vigorously behind one ear with a hind paw, then licked her forefeet in turn, spreading her finger-length claws to give her tongue access to the spaces between. "You have no idea how good this feels," she said when she was done. "An endless month, pretending to be human! Not being able to stretch properly! And I was expected to be *awake* all day."

"My sympathies," Sekken said, with the sort of exquisite politeness that was, at its heart, a rebuke.

Her feline eyes regarded him with flat disdain. "Don't tempt me to go back on my word."

A spirit of Chikushō-dō shouldn't do such a thing, but Sayashi was only nominally of that allegiance. *As are all cats,* Sekken thought wryly. *They have to be able to dangle their tails to one side or the other at will.* Ironic, then, that nekomata – with their forked tails – were so firmly on the side of trickery and malice.

Such thoughts weren't useful right now. "My apologies, sensei," he said, with all the sincerity he could muster. Correctly guessing that she wanted deference would do no good at all if he couldn't follow through. "I am simply impatient to be on our way."

"Why?" Sayashi said, whiskers flicking. "You know that time here doesn't pass the same. A day here might be only a minute back where you come from."

"Every minute matters. And it might go the other way; each day might be a year."

"With that way of thinking," she sighed, "you'll never do well in Senkyō." But she climbed to her feet nevertheless.

Sekken gazed around. He recognized their location as being somewhat like the ledge that held the shrine, only without any sign of habitation or human touch – and lit by daylight, instead of fading into night. Through the branches he could see the seemingly boundless expanse of the northern mountains, grey stones and dark trees stretching off into the distance. The songs of birds and the rustling of unseen creatures in the brush ornamented the constant melody of the wind.

Somewhere in all of this, there was a human girl with a priceless ward in her possession.

He wished they could have brought the inugami with them. Sekken's traveling bundle held Chie's pillow, a battered little case stuffed with buckwheat hulls, because while they had no exact trail for a hound to follow, any creature with a sufficiently sensitive nose might be able to pick up her scent, if it got close enough. In this kind of place, "close enough" might be astonishingly far.

He just needed to find such a creature… and then persuade it to help.

From his studies, Sekken knew that areas which were only lightly settled in the mortal realm tended to be the homes of the most powerful spirits in Senkyō. None of those texts, however, told him how to find such things. "You must have come from near here," he said to Sayashi, "for you to follow the members of the Night Parade when they crossed over. What can you tell me about who rules this land?"

"You're also far too attached to human notions of space," she sniffed.

This time he wasn't put off. "I know it's possible to travel with extraordinary speed here, but the geography of Senkyō more or less mirrors that of Rokugan. Even if you followed the yōkai that were called to Seibo Mura a long way, you still traveled through this area. Who is the Great Tengu here? And are they of Chikushō-dō, or of Sakkaku?" Despite the name, it wouldn't necessarily be a tengu. Those great, bird-like creatures were revered throughout this realm, though, and so any yōkai or spirit that rose to a position of power over its neighbors was called a Great Tengu, just as major samurai lords were called daimyō, "great names."

Sayashi's tail lashed with irritation. "Chikushō-dō, and I will tell you nothing else. Unlike mortals, we don't gossip and whisper amongst ourselves. If you want to meet the Great Tengu, I will lead you; otherwise, choose your path, and let us be on our way."

What had her so on edge? Some crime against the local lord, perhaps. "I'm afraid any path I chose would be nothing more than random chance. And I would not want to give offense here by not paying my respects. Please, sensei, bring me to the Great Tengu." He bowed again, for good measure.

"Let's get this over with," Sayashi grumbled, and headed up the slope.

Sekken expected to be exhausted by the climb. He'd lived enough of his life at high elevations to have a good balance of Air in his body; he didn't become out of breath in the mountains the way lowlanders did. Weighed against that, though, was his generally sedentary life, where some moderate horseback riding was the most exertion he ordinarily got.

Here, everything was different. The air kami felt stronger, and the endurance of the earth seemed to rise up through his feet into his body. He climbed and climbed, following the elegant sway of Sayashi's tail, and had no sense of how much time had passed. It was still daytime – but was that even possible?

Human notions. He could hear what Sayashi would say if he asked her. Sekken clamped his jaw shut and climbed.

As he went, he began to hear whispers from all around him, too faint to make out. Whenever he looked for the source, he saw nothing. Until he remembered his sensei's lessons – his human sensei, not Sayashi – and looked indirectly: then he saw tiny, bark-brown figures perched on tree branches and roots, murmuring amongst themselves. Kodama, emerging from the trees they guarded to watch him go by.

It wasn't only the trees that seemed to be commenting on the human in their midst. Sekken began to feel as if every flower, every bush, every blade of grass was aware of his presence. He knew, intellectually, that everything in the world had a spirit, and furthermore that in Senkyō those spirits were awake to a degree the mortal realm could not even imagine... but it was a very different matter experiencing it first-hand. He began to understand why some orders of Shinseist monks refused to eat not only meat but even root vegetables, whose harvest meant the death of the plant. *I feel almost as if I should apologize to the rocks before I step on them.*

Then he looked at the enormous black cat ahead of him, and his perspective changed. *There are still predators here, and creatures whose place in the Celestial Order is to die to feed others.* Which was higher in spiritual merit, he wondered: the cat who ate the rabbit, or the rabbit whose life sustained hers? Orthodox theology agreed that virtuous demons reincarnated as simple animals, and virtuous animals as animal spirits; there had to be some monk or priest who had taken the question further and determined the relative merits of the different kinds of animals.

Sekken clung to that last thought. Someone had written about it. He would find what they had written. Which would require going back to the mortal realm. Senkyō was a seductive place, for all that it masqueraded as pure simplicity; indeed, that very simplicity was its lure. If he let himself, he would fall prey to his own desire to understand this place… and he would never leave.

Ryōtora is waiting for you. That was an even stronger rope to bind himself with. Even if their relationship could never be what Sekken wanted, he could still do this for Ryōtora.

But before Sekken could make good on that promise, he had to reach the top of this mountain, which seemed like it was going to stretch all the way into the Celestial Heavens.

"Who is this you've brought, Sayashi?"

Sekken would have sworn there was no one on the path before them, but out of nowhere a young woman had appeared a few paces ahead. Her hair fell like a waterfall of ink, all the way to the ground, and her kimono was simple but elegant, patterned with a design like raindrops. When she caught him looking at her, she snapped open a fan and hid behind it.

His mind promptly began cataloguing all the kinds of yōkai she might be – most of them malevolent. Was Sayashi actually of Sakkaku, and she'd led him into a trap?

The bakeneko yawned. "You're off-target, Shiwa. If you want to tempt this one, I suggest looking like a stone-faced Dragon shugenja."

Sekken hoped his surprise didn't show. Had his attraction been so obvious? Then he retreated a step as the young woman's form shimmered and became a good deal shorter. When that stopped, an otter stood on her hind legs before him, her thick fur sleek in the light. "I never was much good at imitating men," she sighed.

A kawauso. Tricksters, yes, but generally benign ones. "He wants to see the Great Tengu," Sayashi told her.

For no reason he could see, Shiwa laughed. "And *you're* bringing him? How delightful. I think I'll come along, just to watch." Sayashi growled, and the sound made the hairs on the back of Sekken's neck stand up – but the kawauso, who might well have been prey for a cat of that size, bounded up the path without any concern at all.

"Go on," the bakeneko said ungraciously, and Sekken did.

The otter led them to the very top of the peak, where boulders rose like pillars to form a kind of natural hall. Yōkai of various kinds ringed the place; for them to be here already, either they spent much of their time lounging about waiting for something to happen, or word of his approach had spread. Sekken suspected the latter. At the far end was a flat slab of stone, like a dais, which yet stood empty.

I didn't think to bring a gift. Sekken kicked himself mentally. His first journey as an envoy, and he hadn't brought anything for the local lord? Not that he knew what to bring, when the local lord might be anything from a weasel to a kappa to another bakeneko–

A flutter of wings arrowed out of the sky to alight on the stone dais. *The Great Tengu,* yōkai called their rulers... but this one was a good deal smaller than a tengu. In fact, it was smaller than Sayashi herself.

The bakeneko made a displeased noise deep in her throat, and Sekken could guess why. From the way Shiwa had greeted her, she was a member of this court – and the yōkai who ruled over her, the proud bakeneko, was a *crow*.

A three-legged one – a yatagarasu. Now Sekken understood the unvarying sunlight: yatagarasu were the crows of the sun. Their three legs were variously said to represent the Celestial Heavens, Senkyō, and the underworld; or the kami, humans, and animals; or even the Three Sins and transcendence from their grip. Certainly they were noble creatures; of all the yōkai he might have encountered here, this one was a fortunate omen.

He bowed deeply and held it, waiting for some official to announce him.

But this was no human court, with a strict hierarchy and officials assigned to every possible task. Sekken heard a mutter that sounded like it came from Shiwa, prodding Sayashi; when the bakeneko spoke, her voice was tight with affront. "Great Tengu, I bring you a human, Asako Sekken."

"Rise." The yatagarasu's voice was melodious, not a crow's harsh caw.

Sekken straightened. The Great Tengu said, "You are no hunter, crossed over while roaming the mountains. What brings you to my realm?"

Before Sekken could answer, Sayashi spoke up. Her reluctance had vanished as if it had never been. "That is my doing, Great Tengu. This human has bowed to me and acknowledged me as his sensei."

Only while we're in Senkyō, and only in matters related to this place, Sekken thought. He knew better than to say it, though. Sayashi had clearly realized she might gain prestige by boasting of her superiority over him; undercutting that would only antagonize her.

Besides, he didn't have to. The yatagarasu chided her, saying, "Sayashi, beware of pride. It was pride that cost you your status; if ever you have hope of regaining it, you must learn to bow your head."

For a heartbeat Sekken was reminded of Ryōtora, even though the Dragon shugenja was a deeply honorable man, and Sayashi was none of those things. *The mountains never learned to step aside – and cats never learned to bow.* The proud carriage of her tail faltered at the rebuke, though, and Sekken wondered what status she had lost.

"Lord Asako." The three-legged crow had transferred his attention to his guest. "You honor us with your presence, however it came to be."

"I am the one who is honored, Great Tengu," Sekken said. On impulse, he reached into his kimono and drew out his writing kit. "Forgive my poor gift, but I did not realize I was to be attending the court of a sun crow. I bring you this, made with vermilion from the village of Seibo Mura, which in the mortal realm lies at the base of your mountain. It is, after a fashion, an heirloom of my family."

He bowed and presented his writing kit. At a flick of the yatagarasu's wing, Shiwa took it from Sekken and presented it to her lord, who studied it thoughtfully. "Sebō Mura," he said.

Hope stirred in Sekken's heart. "That you speak that name, Great Tengu, suggests that you are aware of the village's significance."

"And that you bring me this gift, Lord Asako, suggests that you have a particular reason for coming to my court."

"I do," Sekken admitted. "But it is perhaps not the reason you expect."

In his experience, it was never a bad thing to pique the curiosity of someone from whom he intended to ask a favor. "Explain," the yatagarasu said, shifting forward on the flat stone of his dais.

Sekken tucked his hands into the opposite sleeves: a way of looking elegant and dignified, and also of hiding any tremor in his hands. "I was sent here by a noble shugenja of the Dragon Clan, Agasha no Isao Ryōtora, whose duty it is to protect Seibo Mura against the depredations of the Night Parade of a Hundred Demons. Even now – if too much time has not yet passed in the mortal realm – he fights to keep their leader contained. But Sir Ryōtora's battle is doomed to fail, if I cannot bring him what he lacks.

"The woman who stopped the Night Parade, revered now as Kaimin-nushi, had an amulet which protected the bearer against that leader. A peasant girl named Chie found it in the ruins of Seibo Mura's shrine. Because of this, the yōkai of the Night Parade kidnapped her away into Senkyō. Great Tengu, I come to ask your aid in finding and rescuing Chie."

Silence fell. The sun blazed down, not shifting in the sky. How fast was time moving? Had years gone by at home, or mere heartbeats? Was Ryōtora still defending Seibo Mura – was he still alive?

"Rescuing the girl," the yatagarasu said. "Not the village."

Sekken bowed deeply. "Great Tengu, if you wish to offer your assistance there, I would hardly refuse. But I recognize that I have little to offer you. Merely to ask for your help with Chie is an imposition; it would be the height of folly for me to assume you would risk your own people in the mortal world, when you have so little to gain."

Except, of course, for the continued imprisonment of Nurarihyon. Even a court of Chikushō-dō, however, could not be relied upon to act solely on the basis of virtue. Such purity could only be found in the Celestial Heavens – and the denizens of that place rarely intervened directly, lest their actions upset the delicate balance of the world.

"The girl is not far from here," the three-legged crow said. Before Sekken's hopes could rise, he added, "She has been given into the keeping of one who is neither a member of my court, nor a follower of the Night Parade."

Something about his tone said, *You should be afraid.* Knowing he wasn't going to like the answer, Sekken asked, "What creature guards her?"

"An ōmukade."

A giant centipede – but "giant" fell pitifully short of describing the reality. Their bodies could wrap seven times around a mountain; they were known to attack even dragons. No ordinary weapon could pierce the armor of their skin. Sekken knew precisely one tale of someone defeating an ōmukade; Daidoji Chizuru had shot it with an arrow coated in her own saliva, which was the creature's sole weakness.

He had not a drop of moisture in his own mouth.

"Rest for now," the yatagarasu said kindly. "You will need your strength when you go into the ōmukade's den."

CHAPTER TWENTY-THREE

The first thing Ryōtora heard was music.

Not the slow, elegant music of court or fine theater, nor the cheerful chanting and clapping of the folk tunes played at festivals. It was more like a mockery of the latter: almost tuneful, then unexpectedly discordant, full of clanging and harsh laughter that came from no human throat. The sounds echoed from the slopes around Seibo Mura, circling north, west, south–

"They're taunting us," Rin said, coiling and uncoiling her sling with tense hands. "Letting us know we're trapped."

"They're trapped, too," Ryōtora said, doing his best to maintain an appearance of calm. "More than we are. And we will make sure they stay that way. Gather close."

Everyone crowded inside the sacred enclosure that still stood at the heart of the village. He lifted a wand of streamers over their bowed heads – the last of Sekken's paper. This time, though, its purpose wasn't to purify them. Instead he prayed to the kami of the earth and the Fortune of Battle to make their hearts steadfast. What they had planned would fall apart in the blink of an eye if someone broke and ran, or cowered in hiding rather than doing their part.

His allies were only peasants, not samurai. But they were defending their homes… and Ryōtora was born of the same stock. He had to believe in the possibility of their courage, in order to believe in his own.

The music was getting closer.

"Go," Ryōtora said. "You know what to do."

As the villagers dispersed, he set the wand aside and began a new prayer, this one to the water kami. They answered readily, the air curdling into a thick, impenetrable fog.

The goal was not to fight – not until they had to.

Instead they answered trickery with trickery, chaos with chaos. The fog blanketing the village provided cover for Ryōtora and the villagers as they darted from place to place, luring the attention of the yōkai.

The torches and lamps they'd lit all around Seibo Mura went dark one by one as a bat-like nobusuma flitted about, blowing out their flames, then lit again as Gonbei circled around to light them again. Daizan was remarkably good at mimicking the sound of a crying baby; he wailed from inside Kō's house, then climbed up into the attic and out the window there, sliding down a rope while the ame onna came looking for the non-existent child. She was human-like enough to scream when she fell into the pit trap on the far side of the door. A barrel containing every drop of sake in the village must have lured the invisible whirlwind of the kama itachi, because when Ryōtora passed it on his way to break up a cluster of other yōkai, not a single drop remained at the bottom. He only hoped their response to inebriation was to curl up somewhere and go to sleep.

"Sir Ryōtora!"

The cry for help was stifled – Ona not wanting anything else to hear. Ryōtora changed direction, keeping to the wall of a house as he approached, so that at least nothing could sneak up behind him. Plenty of yōkai were able to imitate the voices of people, with enough precision to fool even those who knew them well.

But it appeared to actually be Ona, staggering along beneath the seemingly enormous weight of the small, hairy child clinging to her back. It cackled in glee, saying, "Give me a ride! Give me a ride!" Then it bent its head to chew on her scalp, and Ona yelped in pain.

Ryōtora's mind raced, trying to remember what Sekken had written about this one. There were many yōkai that got heavier and heavier, but depending on which one it was…

Ona stumbled, almost falling. She'd tripped over a protruding stone in the ground – one Ryōtora himself had tripped over a few days before. Even with the fog masking everything, he realized where they were. Ona's house was just a little further ahead.

"Go home!" he whispered.

She grunted with the effort, lurching forward. Ryōtora didn't quite dare to step forward and help her; he didn't know what that might do. Instead he followed, keeping watch all around for the signs of anything else approaching. By the time Ona made it to the entrance to her abandoned house, she was crawling on her hands and knees, her arms trembling with the effort. A final lunge got her to the doorpost, and clinging to it, she gasped out, "I'm home!"

Her unwanted rider cheered and clapped its hands. Then it vanished, and the sack that appeared in its place slid off Ona's back to clink heavily onto the ground. Ryōtora hurried forward and untied the sack. As he suspected from reading Sekken's notes, the creature was an obariyon, and the sack was filled with coins. He grabbed a handful for himself and shoved the rest at Ona, who was sagged against the post, breathing as if she'd climbed the mountain. "There's a kuchisake onna out there," he said. "If you throw the coins at her, you'll have time to get away."

Ona took the bag and shoved herself upright. "I'll make sure the others have some," she whispered. "Go – you're needed elsewhere."

Too many elsewheres. But at least their tricks were working. As Ryōtora hurried onward, a sudden flare of light to his left was one of the dummies going up in flames. One of the outdoor ones, dressed in a straw raincoat, because minobi had been among the yōkai seen in previous nights, and that was their preferred target. Veering away from that, he heard a desperate, hungry lapping, and peeked through the torn screen of a house to see a woman kneeling to lick up the lamp oil they'd spilled for her. But she knelt a long way from the oil, her neck extending like a snake's to reach the banquet.

Then he recoiled, swallowing his instinctive shout, as the holes in the screen suddenly filled with eyeballs that twitched and blinked at him.

Their diversions couldn't work forever, though. Some of the yōkai could speak; Ryōtora heard one of them howling that the bodies in all the beds were decoys, spare clothing stuffed with rags and leaves. The vicious jubilation of the yōkai lost its playful note and became angry. A furious shout from the vicinity of the well was so loud the force of it drove Ryōtora to his knees. *Yamajijii,* he thought. The creature Sekken had gotten confused with the hiderigami that had contributed to Fubatsu's fever.

Fever was the least of their worries right now. Shortly after the yamajijii's shout, Ishi came lurching through the fog, bleeding from his ears. When Ryōtora tried to speak to him, the ashigaru only shook his head in a daze, tapping his head to indicate deafness.

I have to get him to safety. If Ishi couldn't hear the yōkai coming, he was in even more danger.

There was a storehouse Ryōtora had designated as their stronghold, though he'd hoped not to retreat to it yet. It lay past the well, where the shout had come from; the yamajijii responsible for the cry was gone, and the well itself was shattered. As Ryōtora and Ishi hurried past, something rose up out of the wreckage – a woman, it seemed at first, with her arms bound behind her back. But then the rest of her emerged, as a long, writhing caterpillar body.

Before Ryōtora could even begin to chant, something cracked into the creature's head, sending it slumping back into the well. The projectile bounced and rolled to his feet: a small, round stone. Rin was on the rooftops somewhere nearby, using her sling to interfere as needed.

Ryōtora hoped the mud darkening her skin to thatch-brown was camouflage enough. Some of the yōkai could fly.

One thing at a time, though. He had to get Ishi to safety. The storehouse wasn't much farther; Ishi patted his shoulder, then pointed, indicating that Ryōtora should get back to the work of protecting others. With reluctance, Ryōtora nodded and turned away. If things were getting worse already, then he needed to–

Ishi screamed.

Ryōtora whirled to see the ashigaru floating off the ground. No, not floating – something had snared him and was lifting him bodily to the top of the storehouse. A shadow hulked atop the slate roof, thick-bodied and many-legged: a monstrous spider.

There was no time to wait for Rin and her sling, nor to see if this was the type of spider to drag its prey off for later consumption. Ryōtora dropped to his knees, one hand flattening itself on the earth, the other forming itself into a mudra aimed at the yōkai. The earth kami answered his prayer with the purity of sacred jade. Vibrant green light shot from his upraised hand to strike the spider, which shrieked in an inhuman voice before its convulsions toppled it backward off the roof.

Ishi remained where he was, dangling from the spider's silk. But one arm was free, and although he'd dropped his spear, he still had his knife. He drew it and hacked at the strands until he fell. By then Ryōtora was on his feet again. "Come on," Ryōtora whispered, forgetting for a moment that Ishi couldn't hear. More shouts and howls were headed their way, and fast. "It's a long time yet until dawn."

If Nurarihyon's followers had been associated with the months of winter, Ryōtora and the others would never have made it through that first night. But it was summer, and the nights were short; when dawn came, they were all still alive.

Not without cost. Ishi's hearing hadn't returned. Daizan's face and hands were blistered, from an encounter with something fiery none of them had a name for. A screaming horse head had dropped from the eaves of a house as Masa passed under, and now his skin burned with fever – but when Ryōtora tried to pray to remove it, Masa stopped him. "Save your strength," he said.

They needed Masa's strength, too. Ryōtora understood what he meant, though. Masa's fever wasn't as bad as the one that had afflicted Fubatsu, and a shugenja could only presume so much on the goodwill of the kami. Already he had asked so many things of them, and there were two nights still to go.

I don't know if I can do this.

In the sharp light of dawn, the chaos of the night before seemed like a bad dream. Except that Ryōtora's nightmares had never featured battles like this; when his mind tormented him, it was with Hokumei rejecting him in public, or his father. Or being cast back down to the ranks of the peasantry for his shortcomings. Or going before the Fortune of Death and being judged a blasphemous failure.

If he lived through this, he would have new nightmares to replace those.

He wasn't even sure if they'd killed any of the yōkai. The creatures *could* die; Sekken had assured him so. Or at least some of them could. But the members of the Night Parade were under Nurarihyon's control, and it was possible that their spirits didn't go on to Meido for judgment, but were bound to their master somehow.

His hands shook, and no amount of his usual trick, clenching and releasing, would make them stop. Rin sat with her knees drawn up to her chest and her arms clamped tight around them, rocking in tiny motions back and forth. Ona and Gonbei were side by side, shoulders pressed tight. Only Ishi and Tarō seemed unrattled – because only they had been in battle before.

Tarō coughed to clear a throat made rough by shouting and said, "We won't have it so easy tonight."

Several of the others shuddered. The first night had hardly been easy – but the Night Parade hadn't expected what they'd found, a village all but deserted, decoys and traps lying in wait. Come the second night, they would be focused on hunting down those who'd hidden from and tormented them. Ryōtora anticipated joining battle as soon as the sun set... and possibly not living to see the next dawn.

But we still have a few tricks up our sleeves, he thought, trying to draw strength from that.

Tricks that would require them to be well rested. "I know it's difficult," Ryōtora said, "but sleep if you can. It seems we can at least trust that the Night Parade is true to its name; the yōkai won't return until sunset."

Ishi and Tarō promptly lay down and were soon snoring. Their time in the Dragon army had clearly taught them to sleep when and wherever they could. Masa brewed some willow leaves into a tea for his fever and drank it, grimacing at the bitter taste. Ona walked off; Ryōtora thought about following her, but surmised that she'd rather have time alone. He headed in the other direction – because while they all needed their rest, they needed defenses first.

He'd held off on this stage because he wanted to take the yōkai by surprise on the first night. Now that they knew to expect organized resistance, survival would depend on limiting where they could enter the village. It wouldn't stop the ones who could fly, and others might well be able to infiltrate by other routes... but even if it only meant surviving for an hour longer than otherwise, that was better than nothing.

It took him until nearly noon to circle the perimeter Ishi and Tarō had laid out, praying and making offerings to the earth kami until the trees and bushes grew into an impenetrable thicket, or the stone itself rose up in a defensive bulwark. He finished on the southern side of the village, near the path that led to the hot spring. There a sudden thought struck him.

He hadn't succeeded at drawing up the fire kami that had once warmed the spring. But the hiderigami had worsened Fubatsu's fever because she was a creature of drought and intense heat, powerfully linked with Fire.

Could he use that somehow?

It would mean separating himself from the rest of the defenders for a time. If it restored one of the broken components of the ward, though…

Hope, however tenuous, made the coming night seem less impossible. Pondering ways to lure a hiderigami away from the rest of the Night Parade, Ryōtora headed back to Ogano's house, and what rest he could catch before sunset.

The governor of Heibeisu had sent Ryōtora to protect Seibo Mura.

There won't be much of it left, when this is done.

As he'd predicted, on the second night the yōkai came prepared not for mischief, but for battle. Rin's sling stones and arrows from Daizan and Ishi persuaded flying creatures not to attack directly, while the others circled the perimeter, looking for a way in. They found it in the gap between Kō's house and Tsubame's, where a blackberry bush hadn't quite grown dense enough to block passage.

Ryōtora had asked it not to.

Ona and Gonbei were waiting in those two houses, with giant fans woven of leaves. When they heard Tarō's warning whistle, they worked the fans as hard as they could, then bolted. As the yōkai began to press through and around the blackberry bush, Daizan and Ishi shot flaming arrows through the open windows of the houses… and the village's remaining flour stores, stirred into the air by the fans, exploded.

That was the last thing to be clear to Ryōtora for quite some time. Everything else was a terrifying flood, every new threat coming hard on the heels of the first, with only brief moments surfacing into clarity here and there. The severed, flying head of a nukekubi forced the rooftop defenders down to the ground, moving too fast for any of them to shoot it. A filthy child-like creature reached out from under one of the houses and yanked Masa's feet from under him, clawing him until he hacked at it with the axe Ryōtora had blessed for him. A massive ox that scuttled along on equally massive spider legs smashed through the flames, breathing a cloud of poison as it charged; Ryōtora prayed to the air kami to blow that cloud back upon the yōkai instead, but he didn't know if it did any damage.

The other things he'd prepared certainly did. The defenders lured yōkai into houses, then lit the arsenic compounds Ryōtora had prepared, filling the buildings with toxic smoke. Rin dumped a bucket of acid over an enormous severed head that was doing its best to crush Gonbei. Masa, chased by an old man with eyes in his hands, lit a dose of flash powder behind him, and the old man screamed as it blinded him.

But then Ryōtora had to turn his back on it all and trust the others would keep going – because he'd caught sight of the hiderigami.

Ishi and Daizan had dug a tunnel through the earthworks on the southern side of the village. Heart hammering like a festival drum, Ryōtora squirmed through the passage, praying the walls wouldn't collapse on him, and emerged into the relative quiet of the ground outside. The full moon lit his way as he hurried to the hot spring and the materials he'd prepared there.

Yōkai were a type of spirit. Not a type people ordinarily worshiped... but the lines between such things were often more a matter of practice than anything else. There was nothing preventing a shugenja from making offerings to a hiderigami.

He lit a coal and knelt, trying to still his body and his mind enough to form a prayer. *There is water here, and it is your nature to burn such things away. Come. I offer you this pool; sear it dry with your heat.*

The hiderigami was bound to serve Nurarihyon. But her service was destruction; offered the specific temptation of the spring, she could be lured away from other targets. With his senses attuned to the spiritual balance of the world, Ryōtora felt the wave of burning air as the hiderigami approached.

And his skin felt the burst of steam as she entered the spring.

He lunged to his feet. The hiderigami was too caught up in her battle with the water to notice him placing four talismans around the edge of the pool until it was too late. Ryōtora had promised her water, and he kept that promise – but he hadn't promised not to bind her there, weakening her power until it attained balance with the flow of the water kami into the spring. Nor that he wouldn't bid the earth kami to open up and swallow her, locking her deep within the stone.

For just an instant he stood at the edge of the spring, swaying, half expecting the hiderigami to burst free and undo his victory. But the prison held, and he couldn't stay to celebrate. Instead Ryōtora sprinted back north, through the tunnel, into the village, and arrived to find Ishi and Tarō battling a hag of some kind – no, not a hag. It was Ona, her hair wild, her hands curved like claws, and they were trying to hold her at bay without harming her. "She's gone mad!" Tarō shouted when he saw Ryōtora.

She's possessed. By what, Ryōtora didn't know, but they couldn't afford to lose even one defender. Nor could they afford to have both ashigaru caught up in fighting their own. At Ryōtora's plea, the earth rose up to clutch Ona, holding her immobile; then he drew a prayer strip from inside his kimono and touched it to her head, chanting the words of an exorcism.

What burst from her wasn't a kitsune or a bakeneko. It was a demon-faced woman, with tusks and a long nose like a tengu's. When Ryōtora shouted another prayer and struck her with jade's purifying force, she screamed and disappeared. *Dead? Banished?* Gone; that was what mattered right now, and Ona was herself again. He told the earth to let her go, and together they ran for the storehouse that would be their final defense of the night – and possibly their tomb.

The others were still fighting. Ryōtora shouted at them to follow, grabbed Masa by the shoulder when he seemed like he would go on fighting, and led the way.

Right into the trap.

A dead rowan tree stood a little distance in front of the storehouse door. Ryōtora maintained enough sense to look up into its branches as he approached, in case something was lying in wait there, but they were empty.

Empty – and alive. As Ryōtora and Masa ran beneath the tree, the branches thrashed into motion, stabbing downward at them. One branch wrapped around Ryōtora's arm and yanked him upward; two others stabbed through his stomach and his thigh. He couldn't hold in his scream. For a moment all he saw was pain, the world vanishing in a haze of red.

What dragged him back was Masa's voice, begging Ryōtora to save him.

Ryōtora's scream became a chant. He reached for the fire that lived within all wood – fire that only waited to be unleashed. His sensei had told him never to use this invocation in the grip of anger or fear… but such concerns were past him now.

The tree burst into flame. Heat seared Ryōtora's face, and his clothes began to burn where the flaming branches impaled him. Then he fell, hard, and he was burning, until someone beat at him with a cloth, putting the fires out, dragging him into the storehouse.

Darkness fell as the door slammed shut. The storehouse had no windows. Its walls were thick, and augmented by a ward Ryōtora had placed before sunset. It might last until dawn; it might not. Until then, they were safe–

And trapped.

CHAPTER TWENTY-FOUR

How could Sekken rest?

It seemed out of the question – and yet, he found he could. The sun bathed the mountaintop in gentle light, striking a perfect balance with the chill of the breeze, and the moss cushioned him like a futon. He didn't sleep, but he lay on his back, sighing as the tension drained from his muscles. It was like Sayashi had said: time moved differently here. What harm was there in taking a moment to breathe?

For him, no harm at all. For Ryōtora…

Sekken sat up like someone had just frightened him awake. A little distance away, Sayashi made a discontented noise. "Can't you just relax?"

"No," Sekken said.

"You human… you *samurai*. I prefer being a cat." She yawned, displaying sharp teeth.

Her constant air of disdain made him more pointed than he might have been. "Tell me, sensei – what status did you lose, and how?"

Those teeth gleamed when her lip curled back. "Wouldn't you like to know."

"I genuinely would," Sekken said. "You've helped me, and all you're getting in return is the satisfaction of me bowing to you. Which you seem to appreciate… but if I can do more for you, I will." He was mildly surprised to find it was true, and not just a polite courtesy. Though if being friendly persuaded her to help more than the bare minimum, he would hardly complain.

The tip of Sayashi's tail flicked. "You can't help with this. I doubt you even know what a marushime neko is."

He scoured his memory but came up with nothing, apart from the obvious conclusion that it was a type of cat yōkai. Sekken shifted into a kneeling position and bowed. "I would be grateful if sensei would instruct me."

As he hoped, the deference worked. With a sigh, the bakeneko said, "A marushime neko is… like those silly 'inviting cats' you people decorate your homes and businesses with, but much older. There aren't many of – them."

The hitch in her words was almost imperceptible, but not quite. *Of us,* Sekken guessed she had almost said. "You used to be a marushime neko?"

"I was *so good,*" Sayashi growled. The rumble in her throat was that of an angry predator. "I saved a man's life – led him away from an ambush. I changed the course of a war for the better. And when I died and went before the Fortune of Death, do you know what he said?"

Sekken shook his head mutely. Very few people remembered their experiences in Meido. They weren't supposed to… but cats rarely followed rules.

"He said, for my merit, I had earned the right to be reincarnated *as a human.*"

Contempt dripped from her words. It was orthodox theology;

humans were higher in the Celestial Order than animal spirits. To be reincarnated as one was indeed a reward. Sekken didn't ask, though, whether she had been intended for life as a peasant or a samurai. It was all too clear that Sayashi considered either one an insult.

Now it was not just the tip of her tail but the whole thing that was lashing. "I told him I had no interest in being anything other than what I was. And for that, he cast me down to be a bakeneko. Now that three-legged bird lords it over me, as if I passed up some great opportunity! To do what? Live my life bowing and scraping, worrying about reputation or where my next meal will come from, never with a moment of freedom? Look at you: you're about to go face an ōmukade, when any creature with a shred of sense would run the other direction. I certainly won't go with you. Meanwhile, you swallow your smallest pleasurable impulses for fear someone will punish you for having them. What kind of life is that? Short and miserable. Just look at your friend."

Ryōtora. Fear twinged up Sekken's back. Until the yatagarasu came back, he couldn't do anything more to help the people in Seibo Mura – but what if that delay killed them?

He could at least defend Ryōtora to this bakeneko. "Bushidō gives him strength."

"It bites at his hamstrings like a wolf," Sayashi said. "If he ever lets himself step off that path, the wolf will kill him. He can't even admit he lusts after you without his entire world shattering."

The world didn't shatter around Sekken, but it did spin briefly. "What?"

Sayashi's ears flicked in laughter. "You aren't as rigid as he is, but you're far more naive. You should read a wider variety of scrolls, *scholar*."

"I know what you mean," Sekken said through his teeth. "I've had lovers. But Ryōtora – he would never. He's–"

"Too virtuous? Exactly my point. He has to strangle everything he feels, or hide it if he can't kill it. If he doesn't, he'll hate himself. So he wants you, and you want him, but he pretends he doesn't, and you believe his pretense, and you both go on living miserable lives." Sayashi scrutinized one paw, then gave it a cursory lick. "Short ones, too, at the rate you're both going. And that was supposed to be my reward?"

"No," Sekken said.

The word burst out of him without pause for thought, and it stopped her mid-lick. "No? Have you not listened to a word I've said?"

"I won't argue that sometimes Ryōtora makes himself miserable, trying to live up to an impossible standard. But by doing so, he helps those around him – makes their lives longer and happier. That's what society is: people all doing their best to help each other, to make things better. We aren't as good about it as we should be; on that point, I suppose I agree with Perfect Land beliefs. We should try harder – samurai in particular.

"And that's why I'm about to go face an ōmukade. Because it will make Ryōtora's life longer and happier, and that of everyone who stayed to defend Seibo Mura. Or if not them, then everyone else who will be threatened by the Night Parade. If I don't do this, I might live longer myself… but I wouldn't be happy. I couldn't live with myself, knowing I hadn't even tried."

His heart was beating unexpectedly fast, as if that ascent of the mountain had finally caught up with his body. *Ryōtora wants me.* All the awkward formality, the excessive apology when he'd touched Sekken to lift him from his bow. It wasn't the stiffness of a man with room in his heart only for duty and propriety. It was the self-control of a man holding himself back from what he desired.

Sekken couldn't fail him. Not when it would mean leaving far too many things unsaid between them. Not when it would mean losing the chance to take Ryōtora's hand and say, *We can be stronger together.*

Sayashi had gone utterly still. On impulse, Sekken added, "*That* was what the Fortune of Death was offering to reward you with. Not a human form and human responsibilities. Other people to stand by your side. But if sensei is happier alone, I will not question her wisdom." He bowed again, and held it long enough to be an insult.

He received no reply. Only the faint sounds of a cat getting up and walking away.

The yatagarasu personally escorted Sekken to the entrance to the ōmukade's den.

"This can't possibly be how it goes in and out," Sekken said, eyeing the blackness of the cave entrance. It rose above his head, but not by much, and it was narrow enough that he could touch the walls to either side without fully extending his arms. "Either that, or they aren't nearly as large as I've been led to believe."

"They can squeeze through openings you would think too small for them," the three-legged crow said. "But no, this is too small even for that. I assumed you would prefer to go in by a less-traveled entrance."

He was right about that. Even more importantly, this passage would be a useful route for their escape – at least from the caves. After that… "Is it likely to follow me out here? Onto the mountainside?"

The yatagarasu shifted its wings in what Sekken imagined was the avian equivalent of a shrug. "Ordinarily it doesn't. But these are not ordinary times."

Looking at the cave, it was hard not to think that Ryōtora had been right – that *he* should have been the one to come to Senkyō, while Sekken remained behind to fight the Night Parade. Were ōmukade vulnerable to the prayers of shugenja? None of the stories he knew said one way or another. It was just the legend of Daidoji Chizuru and her arrow coated in spit.

Sekken had his wakizashi. In theory he had saliva, though every time he thought about confronting the monster in the mountain, his mouth went as dry as dust. That wasn't likely to improve as he went along, and he wondered if he should have anointed the blade earlier, before fear had him so firmly in its grip. Or did the saliva lose its ōmukade-slaying properties once it dried? The more he thought about it, the more inadequate those stories seemed. They left far too many questions unanswered.

"You will want a light," the yatagarasu said. He gestured with one wing, and a spirit light coalesced in mid-air, its flame a warm echo of the sun. "Unlike a torch, this will not burn out."

"Thank you," Sekken said. *My parents and my sensei would be very proud. I don't forget my manners, even when faced with almost certain death.*

But he couldn't die. Chie was in there, waiting for rescue. His family was back in Phoenix lands, waiting for him to return from his journey to rid himself of an inugami. Ryōtora was in Seibo Mura, waiting for Sekken to bring him the amulet that could save them all.

Before he could think of more ways this could go wrong, Sekken climbed the slope to the cave entrance, and let the mountain swallow him.

The spirit light hovered politely behind his right shoulder, casting its illumination ahead without blinding him. The tunnel opened up after a short distance into a larger cavern, though one still too small – Sekken hoped – for a creature the size of an ōmukade; there were two exits from that. "I don't suppose anyone at the yatagarasu's court has a map?" he muttered, then flinched as the stone echoed his words back at him. *Idiot. The last thing you want to do is alert the monster that you're here.*

He could think of it as a riddle to solve. That idea steadied him as he began to explore, tracing the various passages as they led him upward and down and sometimes back to where he'd begun, creating a map in his head. If it had been difficult for him to tell how much time had passed in the world outside, with the sun eternally overhead, here it was impossible; the oppressive darkness and the whispering noise of his movement made everything blur like a dream. He didn't even find himself growing hungry… which was good, because there was nothing to eat.

Then he began to hear a clicking – the eerie, unsettling *tap tap tap* of too many legs on stone.

The sound was deceptive. In this maze of caverns and tunnels, it was impossible to tell which direction it was coming from. But Sekken had left behind the small passages of his entrance and was now in areas so large his spirit light seemed like a tiny, pathetic spark by comparison.

When that spark illuminated an enormous scale up ahead, Sekken froze dead.

But it wasn't the ōmukade. It was the creature's molted skin, left behind like that of a snake. Even half-deflated, it towered above Sekken. He could barely work up enough moisture in his mouth to spit on it, but he tried to take heart from the way the spit sizzled and ate through the thick armor.

What heart he mustered, though, faded the moment he saw the ōmukade itself.

The passage he was following suddenly opened up, rising above and dropping steeply away below. The spirit light, after a moment of what Sekken could only interpret as hesitation, floated ahead of him, drifting through the blackness until its glow caught something below: the curved and coiled mass of a centipede so large, Sekken's mind refused to accept it as a living creature.

He put one hand to the hilt of his wakizashi for reassurance, but there was no comfort to be had there. The same sequence of images kept presenting themselves, like rehearsals for a very bad play: drawing his blade, spitting on it, charging downhill toward the ōmukade, heroically stabbing the thing… and then the ōmukade rolling over on top of him, crushing him flat and barely even noticing the small wound in its side.

The spirit light was moving again, continuing away from Sekken. Had it decided to give up on this foolishness?

No, it was showing him something else. A small alcove, high on the cavern wall. There was a bundle of rags there – rags which stirred at the growing light.

Chie. He managed to keep from saying it out loud. The peasant girl sat up, rubbing her eyes and squinting into the unexpected brightness. Then she reached out toward the spirit light–

–which zipped back across the cavern to where Sekken waited. Now he couldn't see the girl at all, but she would be able to see him. Sekken stood paralyzed, one hand still on his wakizashi. He couldn't just throw himself at the ōmukade; that would be suicide. Getting to where Chie had taken refuge would mean crossing the floor of the cavern, and praying the creature didn't rouse along the way. That seemed like suicide, too. *I'm not a warrior!*

Neither was Ryōtora, yet he fought when he had to. The thought of the Dragon shugenja steadied Sekken. He imagined the two of them sitting together in Ogano's house, discussing the problem over a meal as if it were some intellectual puzzle.

That was the answer. *If all you have is your brain, then use it.*

Sekken bowed in the general direction of where Chie hid and gestured as broadly to her as he could, indicating that she should wait. He could imagine the outrage and despair she must feel at seeing her one hope of rescue leave… but he couldn't shout an explanation across to her, and for the plan taking shape in his mind, he was going to need some resources he couldn't find in this cave.

Sekken retraced his steps as fast as he could, threading the subterranean tangle back to where he'd entered. When he emerged once more into the sun, it was as blinding to him as the spirit light must have been to Chie. Before his vision had even cleared, he heard the rustle of wings, and then he saw the yatagarasu standing before him.

"I found the ōmukade," Sekken said. "And I have an idea. I'm going to need some bamboo poles, a turnip, and a straw mat, if any such thing exists here." He swallowed with difficulty. "Also some water."

He wound up needing more than just water. The entire plan amounted to Sekken pinning his hopes on a wild speculation; given that and the size of the ōmukade, he wanted to take no unnecessary chances. The yōkai of the crow's court seemed to enjoy bringing him a variety of bitter and sour foods – and just in case, Sekken thanked each of those foods before he put it in his mouth. He didn't want to wind up trading his inugami haunting for some plant spirit taking offense at the callous treatment he'd subjected it to.

If this works, Sekken thought, putting the finishing touches on his masterpiece, *I am never telling anyone.* Daidoji Chizuru and her arrow made for a good tale. A bucket full of spit did not.

All the same, he was a little sad not to see that masterpiece in action. For all that he wanted to stay as far from the ōmukade as possible, in some ways it was worse to be crouched in impenetrable blackness at the mouth of the tunnel leading to its main lair, waiting for a pack of yōkai to do their part. He trusted the yatagarasu... but this called for some assistance from tricksters, and even those who pledged themselves to Chikushō-dō were a little bit unreliable.

With his spirit light doused, the darkness was practically a tangible thing, pressing down on him like a stone. Sekken felt like he was drowning in it, crushed by the shadows and the invisible bulk of the mountain overhead. He fought not to let his breathing grow loud, and strove to keep bestial terror from provoking him into bolting. He would only fall, hurt himself, maybe bring the ōmukade down upon him. How silently could the creature move? What if it crept up on him while he crouched there, utterly blind, and–

Faint sounds began to whisper through the caverns. Not the ōmukade moving; a voice. Sekken's voice – or rather, Shiwa's best imitation thereof. He'd been surprised when the kawauso told him, with a sly smile, that of course she knew the text of the Lotus Sutra.

It was the closest approximation he could manage of a shugenja's prayers. A giant centipede was unlikely to know the difference anyway; it just heard a human at the main entrance to its warren. There was no prey an ōmukade loved more than human flesh – a delicacy, perhaps, for a creature that lived in a Spirit Realm full of animals. Now Sekken most distinctly heard the thunderous clicking of its legs as its body uncoiled, and he stuffed one fist into his mouth to bite down on the whimper of sheer terror that wanted to burst forth. Every instinct wailed at him to flee, *right now*, the monster was coming…

But the sounds receded. The ōmukade wasn't moving toward him; it was going away.

Toward the main exit from the cave, where to all appearances a samurai was sitting cross-legged, chanting prayers to the Celestial Heavens that they might aid him in smiting the beast that laired within.

The initial test had been unnerving. The seated figure not only wore Sekken's kimono and hakama; it bore his face, down to the tiny scar under his chin where he'd split it as a boy. The hair was his – not merely in his style, but literally shorn from his head, because illusions worked better when they had a reasonable base to work from, and that and the clothing would guarantee the decoy smelled like a human. Underneath the illusion, however, was nothing more than a cobbled-together statue. The body was a tatami mat wrapped around a bamboo pole, like the dummies his eldest sister practiced her sword cuts on, and the head was a massive turnip roughly carved to resemble a face.

And hollowed out inside, so that it would hold every drop of saliva Sekken could produce.

The spirit light flared into brilliance as soon as the thunder of the ōmukade's passing receded into the distance. Sekken wasted no time in scrambling down the cavern's slope and running across its seemingly endless floor, looking about wildly for the alcove where Chie had been hiding. He couldn't see her; the spirit light wasn't large enough to illuminate both the far wall and the floor under his feet, and if it left him he would go sprawling two steps later. Sekken risked a stifled call: "Chie! Masa's daughter! I've come to–"

A scraping sound made him thud to a halt. *What if something else lives here? What if the ōmukade has offspring?*

"W- Who are you?"

The spirit light soared higher, shedding its light more thinly over a greater area. At the edge of visibility, Sekken saw a figure, crouched behind a broken stalagmite.

"Asako Sekken. Your father sent me to find you. I'm the one you saw earlier, across the cavern." He grimaced, gesturing at himself. "Though I know I don't much resemble it now." His hair was cropped nearly to the scalp, and in place of his kimono and hakama, the yōkai had only been able – or perhaps, only willing – to provide him with a rough robe made from undyed barkcloth. He looked more like some half-mad mountain hermit than a scholarly courtier.

She rose warily from her crouch and inched closer. "You're a Phoenix?"

"And very far from home."

Then he saw her properly, and he couldn't quite suppress a gasp.

The strong cheekbones. The straight brows, and the level-set eyes beneath them. The mouth, fuller on the bottom lip than the upper. Sixteen, and a girl… but put her in a silk kimono, and he would have accepted without question that her name was Agasha no Isao Chie, Ryōtora's sister.

But... she's a peasant.

One who flung herself suddenly at Sekken, clinging to his barkcloth robe like he was Shinsei himself, come to bring liberation from the suffering of life. After who knew how many days trapped in this cave with a titanic centipede, he couldn't blame her.

Then an inhuman sound tore through the air: part shriek, part growl, part insectile chitter. And the ground shook beneath their feet.

Sekken's own response was part curse, part laugh. "I guess it ate the turnip."

"The what?" Chie raised her head enough to stare at him.

"I filled–" He cut off his explanation, shaking his head. "I'll tell you later. If I'm as smart as I hope I am, I just gave that thing a very bad case of indigestion. Maybe a fatal one." The tremors grew stronger, and the noise louder. Sekken grabbed Chie's hand and turned back the way he came. "*Run!*"

CHAPTER TWENTY-FIVE

A human-faced, snake-bodied bird soared through the dawn sky, calling out mournfully, "Until when? Until when?"

Ishi bent his bow to shoot it, but Ryōtora put out one blistered hand to stop him. "Don't. It isn't part of the Night Parade." Sekken hadn't told him about this one; Ryōtora knew the story himself. The itsumade appeared in places where disasters were occurring, where the suffering of the people was unalleviated. He wouldn't have expected one little village with a mere handful of defenders to draw the attention of such a creature, but here it was.

Although Ishi's hearing still hadn't returned, the gesture was clear. He lowered his bow and bowed. As the ashigaru walked away, Ryōtora watched the itsumade bank toward the mountain and murmured to it, "You'll have more to weep over after tonight."

He was alive; so was Masa. The flaming branches had partially cauterized their wounds. When Ryōtora had knelt to pray to the water kami on Masa's behalf, though, the man had stopped him. "If you can heal, then heal yourself. The others need you more than they need me."

They need so much more than just me. That thought was distant now, like it came from the far side of the Empire. He'd burned through all his fear, leaving his heart full of ash. His little group had already done far better than he could possibly have expected. But they all knew how this was going to end.

Ryōtora didn't have to tell them to rest. He suspected that Rin, in her exhaustion, had fallen asleep even before dawn, heedless of the clamor outside as the Night Parade tried and failed to break in. Tarō and Gonbei helped Ryōtora shift Masa to a futon left behind by the evacuees, and then they too lay down and closed their eyes.

Leaving Ryōtora with Masa. He tried to invoke the water kami again, but the spirits were impatient with his repeated requests; all he managed was to ease Masa's pain a little. The man's life wasn't in immediate danger – not until nightfall, anyway. After that, he probably wouldn't need to worry about infection setting in.

"Thank you for everything you've done," Ryōtora whispered. His voice felt raw, as if he'd shouted far more than he recalled. "I'm sorry I didn't save your daughter sooner. But I trust that Lord Asako won't fail us."

Masa's burned hand rose as if to touch him, then settled once more. "You've done everything we could ask for, and more."

Ryōtora's eyes were as dry as dust. He should try to sleep… but something echoed in his memory, and he wouldn't be able to rest until he asked. Masa, screaming in agony, pleading for Ryōtora to save him.

Only he hadn't said *my lord,* nor *Sir Ryōtora,* nor even *Ryōtora.*

"You called me your son."

Masa's eyes squeezed shut, as if in pain. He said, "Yes."

All that time spent wondering, and trying not to wonder. The man lying before him, wounded and burned, was Ryōtora's father.

"That's why you stayed," Ryōtora said, forcing the words past the dam in his throat. "Instead of fleeing. And instead of asking to go with Sekken into the Spirit Realms." To rescue Chie – the sister he'd never seen.

"You needed my help," Masa said. "I have no right to call you my son; I gave that up when I surrendered you to Sir Keijun. But I couldn't abandon your side."

The dam burst. "Why? Did my f… Did he force you? I know peasants are compensated when samurai claim their children, but you're a follower of the Perfect Land. You have been since before I was born. Doctrine holds that this is the Age of Declining Virtue, and that samurai are the cause, that we… that they've lost their way, fallen from the true path of morality. Was it my mother who insisted? Why would you send me off to *pretend* to be a samurai, if they're so corrupt?"

Masa's lips were silently shaping the mantra of the Perfect Land, *Shoshi ni kie*. Ryōtora's breath came ragged, his composure hanging on by a fingernail. He'd never felt less like a samurai in his life, filthy, wounded, crouching in the ruins of a village he'd helped destroy, wanting nothing more than to break down and scream at the suicidal futility of this last stand.

Silence fell. The mantra, it seemed, was to help Masa gather strength to speak. He finally said, "Because I wanted my son to have a better life. Sir Keijun offered me money, but I didn't take it. He promised you would always have rice to eat, clean clothes to wear, a fire to warm you in winter. He promised to teach you. What father wouldn't want that for his son?"

"One who condemns the corruption of the samurai."

"Which is why I prayed every day to Shinsei that you would

grow up to be a good man. And he has answered my prayers."

Ryōtora couldn't hold back any longer. His smoke-fogged eyes burned as they flooded, tears slipping down his cheeks. "But I'm not a true samurai. If the Fortune of Death had judged me worthy of that status, I would have been born into a samurai family. Not here in Seibo Mura."

Masa whispered, "Whether you were born a samurai or not matters less than the fact that you're a virtuous and honorable man." This time he didn't abort the gesture; he reached out and laid his hand gently on Ryōtora's wrist. "Such people should be called samurai, wherever they come from."

His words were heresy. But they were also a balm, and for once Ryōtora felt no shame as he wept.

Although his legs dragged like they were made of lead, Ryōtora forced himself to climb the path to the shrine.

It was untouched by the chaos of the battles. All the stories of the Night Parade featured it rampaging through settled areas, not outside them – and perhaps the presence of the enshrined kami repelled them. Or perhaps, Ryōtora thought, Kaimin-nushi was actively hiding the shrine. She'd made it clear that a continued presence in Seibo Mura was necessary to keep the yōkai from seeking out Nurarihyon himself, and Ryōtora suspected that if that creature's prison had a physical location, it was here, at the shrine.

He sat on the ground in front of the makeshift shelter Masa had rigged to give Saiun-nushi a better home than a ruin, lit a stick of incense, and sank into the peace of communion. Inasmuch as he could find peace, when he was weary to the bone, and Kaimin-nushi's exhaustion went far beyond that. Ryōtora offered her what he could of his strength, and she took it, her spirit leaning on his for support. *It will not be long now.*

"Kaimin-nushi," Ryōtora said, his lips shaping the words without sound. "I restored the hot spring last night. Saiun-nushi has returned to its place. Is that enough?" Enough to keep Nurarihyon imprisoned past the end of this full moon. Sekken had said the Night Parade was a summer phenomenon; if they could hold out, would that contain him until the following year? Even if it didn't, buying the Empire one more month could make all the difference.

It has helped, the kami said. *But I know not if it is enough.*

He smiled, wearily. There was nothing funny about it, but still: he smiled. "That is the meaning of duty. To do what you can, and what you must, even if it is not enough."

Yes.

She had lived in the early days of the Empire, before the ways of the samurai were well established, but she understood. So did the peasants who'd stayed behind to defend Seibo Mura. They might not be samurai, but they understood holding their ground for the sake of others. Even if it meant their deaths.

Ryōtora wasn't alone. The spirit herself had told him that. And it gave him an idea – a brief flicker of hope, that what he had come here to ask might not be necessary.

"Kaimin-nushi. If it would help for me to be your vessel, then my body is yours. Possess me, as you did Sekken. Use my strength as your own. I was never trained for battle, and I lack your knowledge of the Night Parade, your familiarity with their master. You would be a better general for this defense than I could ever hope to be. If I could serve as the means by which *you* fight, then I give myself to you without hesitation."

A pause. And then… *Yes. Perhaps.*

Her presence increased from a tremor on the edges of his awareness to a pressure, then a crushing weight. It was as if the components of her spirit were trying to push their way through his own, making space for themselves where there was no space to be had. Ryōtora tried not to resist, tried to open himself as a conduit; he knew it was possible, because he'd seen it done. Not just with Sekken, but with mediums in rural areas across Dragon lands.

But it didn't work. The channel of his communion with her wasn't enough to let her flow into him. The weight receded, becoming mere pressure, then a tremor once more. *I cannot. We have no connection, you and I.*

Because while he was a son of Seibo Mura, she'd imprisoned Nurarihyon here long before the village as he knew it came to exist. Wild thoughts flew through his mind, of somehow using the cinnabar mined here to forge a link, the way Sekken's writing kit had allowed her to send her inugami to him. All that would accomplish, though, would be to poison himself with quicksilver.

And if he was going to die, there were better ways of doing it.

"Kaimin-nushi. When I asked how you trapped the leader of the Night Parade, you bowed to the manifestations of the elements surrounding Seibo Mura… but those alone were not an answer. Someone – you – had to act, to forge those disparate pieces into a chain that would endure for centuries. Even now, that would be an achievement, and my sensei taught me that in the early days of the Empire, the knowledge of shugenja was not as well developed as it is today." Only the Tribe of Isawa had practiced anything like the traditions of later shugenja, and even they had needed the light of Shinsei's wisdom to reveal the whole of what they touched. Other clans had taken generations to catch up.

Which meant there was only one likely answer. "Did you give your life to do it?"

Silence answered him at first. But Kaimin-nushi was still there; he felt her presence, weary but steadfast. Finally she said, *I thought at first to kill him. It would have been the better answer. But whatever he is… something akin to a Fortune, perhaps. A twisted and malevolent one. No power I could call upon would have been sufficient. So – yes. To make it strong enough, and to make it endure, the price was my life.*

Kuni Osaku had raised the waters of the Seigo River into an impenetrable barrier for seventy-three days to hold off the forces of the Shadowlands, buying the Crab Clan time to build their famous wall. Ryōtora had learned about her and other legendary heroes of Rokugan during his schooling: shugenja whose extraordinary deeds went far beyond the scope of a normal invocation. Kaimin-nushi should have been in that list… except that no one remembered her or what she'd done.

This part of the story had not been in the report Ryōtora sent to Heibeisu with the evacuees. If he could guess it, though, someone else could as well. At least future generations might learn her name.

And, perhaps, his own.

"Tell me how it is done."

He could feel her hesitation. *This is not merely an invocation, something one can learn and perform on command. My purpose was pure, my conviction unwavering. Had I held back even the smallest part of myself, I would have simply died, and nothing come of it at all.*

Was his own conviction strong enough? Ryōtora thought of the bushi he'd sometimes trained with, because the Dragon believed their warriors should know something of the spiritual, and their shugenja should know something of war. Those bushi had boasted about how they would behave when they got to the battlefield – until one of the sensei chided them, saying that courage was a metal whose quality could not be known until the first strike. It was easy enough to *imagine* oneself being heroic and brave. Until the moment itself came, that was nothing but empty words.

"I have to try," he said. "If I fail… at least I will go down into Meido knowing I did everything I could." The way a samurai should.

Then all you must do is offer yourself to the kami, Kaimin-nushi said. *Give the fire your Fire, the water your Water, the air your Air, the earth your Earth. Become nothing: become Void. Become the empty vessel that holds all of existence. Then all things become possible.*

It had the sound of the *Tao of Shinsei,* but Ryōtora didn't think it was a quotation. Merely a reflection of the truth within the Tao.

He hoped his understanding was good enough to put it into practice. And that, when the moment came, his will would not falter.

Ryōtora bowed low. "Thank you, Kaimin-nushi. For your past sacrifice, and your present effort. When I meet the Fortune of Death, I will praise your name."

He didn't tell any of the others what he intended. It would only pain his father, and perhaps give the others false hope.

Instead he gathered them together in the center of Seibo Mura, in the place where he'd temporarily enshrined Saiun-nushi. The rope of the sacred enclosure still stood, and the cypress yorishiro. Ryōtora purified the space and the tree, then the gathered defenders, warding them against malevolent spirits. He took the last of the village's salt and spread it in a line around the enclosure for good measure, making offerings and whispering prayers so that it would hold its place and not be blown away.

Daizan said uneasily, "If this is where we're meant to retreat to this time… it's awfully exposed."

"Not a retreat," Ryōtora said. "We're in no shape to fight now." Masa could barely stand; Ishi was still deaf; Daizan's right arm was broken. Everyone had burns, cuts, fevers, stomach pains from inhaling the toxic smoke Ryōtora had tried to poison the yōkai with. They wouldn't last an hour in battle, much less an entire night.

"You're mostly whole," Ona croaked.

Ryōtora shook his head. "Yes – but on my own, I won't be nearly enough. And we *have* to keep the Night Parade's attention fixed on us. By now they know to expect tricks, defenses, attacks from ambush. They're prepared. I think the only way to make them focus on us is to taunt them."

Rin saw where he aimed. "You mean you want us to sit in there all night. Let 'em see us, and hope that what you've done is enough to keep them out."

"If it were that alone, you'd be right to call it idiocy," Ryōtora said. "But I communed today with Kaimin-nushi. I think that, with her aid, I can –"

He'd been intending to say, *hold them off*. The lie stuck in his throat. *I can't die like a samurai if I'm dishonest with my allies.*

Sitting on the ground, the only thing Masa could touch was his leg. "Do what you can," he said quietly. "We'll stand at your side."

A knot tightened in Ryōtora's throat; he swallowed it down with difficulty. "You don't have to. I… I don't expect any who stay here to live through the night. Myself included. If you want to go, there's still enough daylight left for you to get some distance away. It might be enough."

Silence answered him. Then Rin shrugged. "Or it might not. I'd rather die standing than running."

Tarō said, "Our orders were to help you. Ishi and I won't back down on that."

On their own, some of the others might have left. But with the ashigaru staying, and Rin… and Masa. Ishi was deaf, and Tarō might not have noticed what Masa said during the chaos, but Ryōtora suspected all the people from Seibo Mura knew he was Masa's son. They might even have guessed before the evacuation. It might be why they had volunteered.

"We're not leaving," Ona rasped. Gonbei nodded, and then Daizan.

They had remained to fight because he'd asked them to. Just as Sekken had gone into Senkyō in Ryōtora's place. *I don't deserve this.*

But even if he was the immediate reason, it wasn't really about him. It was about everyone else, and the Empire.

There was peace in that thought. In the end, Ryōtora didn't matter. He could let go.

His only regret was that he'd missed his chance to be honest with Sekken. To admit the truth of his heart, even if he could never have what it desired.

Ryōtora bowed to each of the defenders, one by one, far more deeply than etiquette required. "May the Fortunes watch over us all."

CHAPTER TWENTY-SIX

I'm too late.

Sekken and Chie had run as fast as they could: out of the ōmukade's den, back to the yatagarasu, down the mountain to the place where, in the mortal world, the shrine of Seibo Mura stood. They could have chosen to cross over anywhere, he supposed; Sayashi was nowhere to be found, for all her promise to help Sekken get back home, but the three-legged crow was powerful, and within the area he called his domain he could allow or bar passage as he pleased. But in Senkyō, Sekken could run without tiring, and the same could not be said of his endurance at home.

Chie clutched the amulet in both hands: a simple wooden plaque, tall and thin, the kind of thing a priest might carry during a ceremony. Sekken couldn't identify the characters written on it, not without a lot of time and possibly a library to help, but he had no choice except to trust in its power. It was what Chie had taken from the shrine; it had to be the right thing, and it had to work. Anything else was unacceptable.

"Prepare yourself," the yatagarasu said – and then they were back in the mortal world, and it was snowing.

The cold that slapped Sekken's body was nothing next to the absolute chill in his heart. *Snow.* When he'd left, it was high summer. Even in northern Dragon lands, snow wouldn't fall that early. His endless, otherworldly day had lasted – how long? A month? Two?

It could be years.

Sekken fell to his knees. *Ryōtora warned me.* But somehow he'd been so sure he wouldn't fail like this, that of course he would come back in time. Because there were things they hadn't said. Because Ryōtora needed him.

Chie stumbled forward, shivering and clutching the amulet. Then her voice rose in a tight, horrified wail. "The village is burning!"

It pierced the fog of horror and brought Sekken lurching to his feet. Through a gap in the trees, he saw Seibo Mura.

Thick clouds matted the sky, blotting out the full moon. But lightning spiked here and there, and in the brief flashes, he saw a terrible creature soaring through the air: a nue, its body a hideous patchwork of monkey and tiger and tanuki and snake. One of the most terrible of all yōkai, a harbinger of absolute disaster. Below its slow flight, flames lit the scene like so many torches, revealing the distorted and capering bodies of dozens of yōkai.

All surrounding an open space in the center of the village, where Ryōtora had built the temporary shrine.

"We're not too late," Sekken breathed. The snow numbing his toes might argue otherwise, but–

A gust of frigid air struck him from behind. He knew before he turned what he would see: a woman with hair as black as a starless night and skin whiter than the moon itself. A yuki onna, as cold as the snow she was named for, who lived only in winter… or brought it with her wherever she went.

The merest touch from her hand would have drained the warmth from Sekken, but her attention wasn't on him, nor on Chie. She was facing the shrine, and she was laughing.

"While the others run and play, *I* have found you," she whispered. Her sleeves danced in the wind as she spread her arms wide. "You will be free, and I will be your most exalted servant – favored above all the others, your savior!"

Sekken lunged for cover, dragging Chie with him. He had his wakizashi, but a yuki onna wasn't an ōmukade, to be defeated by human spit; her bane was hot water, and he had no way of conjuring that.

Crouching with him behind a bush, Chie wordlessly held out the amulet. Would it protect him against the yuki onna, too? He'd had no chance to ask for details. The yōkai had been able to kidnap her, but they hadn't killed her. Even the ōmukade had left her alone. Sekken took the amulet in his left hand and slowly drew his sword with his right. *I'm not a warrior.* But he didn't have to be: even a scholar understood that if you hit someone enough times with a sharp blade, they would die.

Did that apply to a yuki onna, too?

He never got the chance to find out. Her exultant voice rose to a shout. "*Nurarihyon, I call you forth!*"

The ground began to shake beneath him. It knocked Sekken off balance, and when he reflexively caught himself with a hand against the ground, he dropped the amulet. Then a terrible cracking sound came from the shrine, like the mountain itself breaking in half–

–and then the ground went still.

Sekken squeezed his eyes shut. In the frozen darkness, he heard a voice speak, like a querulous old man… but colder than even the yuki onna's wind. A voice that was to malice what the vivid landscape of Senkyō was to the ordinary world.

"At last. Come with me, my dear."

Nurarihyon was free.

Sekken might not be brave, but he was stubborn.

When the warming air told him the yuki onna was gone – and Nurarihyon with her – he came lurching out of cover to find the inugami sprawled on the ground. He dropped to his knees at the dog's side and laid the amulet against its fur, as if that would do any good. The spirit wasn't breathing… but it had never breathed, except to bark.

"You can't be gone," he whispered. "This can't be over. Kaimin-nushi–"

He felt her presence. As tenuous as fog, compared to the force that had taken him over once before – but not gone. Sekken forced himself to breathe slowly, to calm his racing heart, to ignore Chie pleading with him to not just sit there but get up and *do something*.

In order to do something, I have to do nothing first. He had to be still. And empty. He had to be Void.

Kaimin-nushi's spirit flooded into him. Not enough remained of her to shove him aside the way it had done before; Sekken retained control of his body. Out loud, he said, "We have the amulet. Tell me what to do."

"I know you've got the amulet! We have to save whoever's down there!"

He ignored Chie, listening instead to the faint voice within. *My ward is broken.*

"Can you remake it?"

... I cannot.

If he'd only heard her words, hc might have despaired. This communion was not like ordinary speech, though; it was as much a thing of emotions and images as anything else. *She* could not. But someone else could.

"Ryōtora," he murmured.

He is in the village. The Night Parade gathers around. Nurarihyon is on his way there.

And Ryōtora didn't have the amulet. Sekken had thought before that the man would fight Nurarihyon blindfolded if he had to. If Sekken didn't get down there soon, Ryōtora might do exactly that.

"Who are you talking to?" Chie demanded.

It was too complicated to explain in full. "The spirit who made this amulet," Sekken said, rising to his feet. "I have to get it down into the village. You stay here–"

"No," she said, fists clenching. "My father might be down there!"

"I can't protect you."

"Then make me another amulet!"

He almost asked if he looked like a shugenja to her. Then knowledge flickered in the depths of his mind: Kaimin-nushi's knowledge, not his. He couldn't make something proof against Nurarihyon... but some amount of protection against yōkai, perhaps.

Except he'd given his writing kit to the yatagarasu, and had nothing to use for ink.

Blood – *definitely* not. The snow, rapidly melting now the yuki onna was gone, or water from the waterfall – but none of those would leave a visible mark.

"Mud," Sekken said, grabbing a broken piece of wood from the shrine, and ran down the path with Chie at his heels.

The soil near the waterfall was soft. He used the ladle to fetch water and mixed the two until he had a suitable consistency of mud; then, with the tip of his finger, he began to write on the broken slat, while objections yammered in his head. *I'm not a shugenja. Finger-painting is not proper brush strokes. The grain of the wood disrupts the lines.* All those reasons and more why this might not work. It was what he could do, though, and so he did it, praying to every Fortune and ancestor he could name that his makeshift talisman would have some power to protect Chie.

When it was done, he handed it to the girl. "Watch my back. And if anything comes after you, run."

"Let's go," she said.

"Can they leave yet?" Sekken asked as they descended, not sure whether he spoke out loud or in his head. By the look Chie shot him, it was out loud.

Kaimin-nushi's whisper was even fainter than before. *Yes. But the night is half spent, and Nurarihyon cannot target another place until the next full moon. When the moon sets, they will go into Senkyō.*

Where they would meet the yatagarasu. As powerful as the three-legged crow was, the Night Parade had once roved at will across the Empire. Sekken didn't think the Great Tengu and his people could stop Nurarihyon now.

But it meant he had the dubious benefit of knowing Nurarihyon wouldn't escape before he could get to the center of the village. He said, "When we–"

Chie's scream cut his words off. Sekken spun to find the girl pinned to the ground by an enormous black cat, and for one gut-wrenching instant he thought it was Sayashi. The broad black head was similar, and the fangs as long as his finger… but behind them, two tails danced like smoke.

A nekomata. Sayashi's mother. And by the looks of it, his makeshift talisman had done no good at all.

"Drop what you bear," the nekomata growled, "or I will pull this girl's entrails out and dangle her from them like a puppet."

Chie whimpered.

The amulet. "Come now," Sekken said, trying to keep his own voice steady, while his mind scrabbled for some kind of way out. "You're a nekomata. We both know that if I do that, you'll kill her, and then me. Or the other way around."

"You have my word."

"The word of a creature of Sakkaku?"

By way of answer, the nekomata bared her fangs and bent toward Chie's face. The girl was rigid beneath her, one hand gripping the talisman so hard it must be driving splinters into her palm… and Sekken, watching, realized something.

The nekomata was straining against an unseen force. She menaced Chie, but even though the merest flex of her toes could have sent her claws into the girl's shoulder, she hadn't harmed her. Only knocked her down.

She was bluffing.

And then a second shadow appeared out of nowhere to wrench the nekomata clear in a whirlwind of fur and claws and teeth.

He had assumed that he'd seen the last of Sayashi, when she didn't keep her promise to bring him back. But she must have followed him out of Senkyō – and now she and her mother were doing their best to kill each other.

I can't tell which is which, he said desperately to Kaimin-nushi.

The spirit had no answers for him. She had never been a warrior, any more than Sekken was. But he felt her power flow down into his blade, blessing it against spirits.

Then suddenly it wasn't two cats any more. It was one cat and one human: Aoi. As claws raked down her thigh, she wailed, "Kill her, my lord!"

Sekken leapt forward, sword raised. For the first time in his life, he felt the sickening impact of his wakizashi cutting through flesh and into bone.

"Aoi" dropped to her knees, her eyes going blank and lifeless. Then she collapsed, and where she had been, a two-tailed cat lay dead.

Panting for breath, all four paws braced against the ground, Sayashi said, "How did you know?"

Sekken's vision was going white around the edges, and the only functioning part of his mind told him that under no circumstances was he allowed to stick the point of his wakizashi into the ground and use it to prop himself up. Faintly, he said, "Because you've never once called me 'my lord.'"

Even if the makeshift talisman gave some protection, Sekken wasn't about to take Chie into the center of Seibo Mura. If anyone yet lived, they were either hiding or at the heart of the Night Parade, and merely opening her eyes near Nurarihyon would mean Chie's death.

"I'll guard the kitten," Sayashi said.

Now wasn't the time to comment on her change of heart. Sekken bowed and said, "If you get the chance to rescue anyone else–"

"Go."

Her growl held a predator's threat still. Besides, she was right. Sekken went.

Past burning ruins and shattered ground, toward the mass of yōkai. They weren't howling and laughing any longer; an uncanny silence had fallen over the village. Only Kaimin-nushi's watchful presence within him kept Sekken from fearing the worst: that Ryōtora was dead and their last hope was lost.

He held the amulet in front of him like a weapon – which it was. The yōkai felt its presence; as he drew close to their ranks, they turned and faded out of its path, hissing or snarling or making noises no human throat could produce.

Until he reached the center, and the figure standing there.

It took all of Sekken's courage to lift his gaze and look at Nurarihyon.

At first the leader of all this chaos looked like a courtly old man. Wrinkled with great age, and with a moustache drooping down like a catfish's whiskers, but his silk kimono resembled those Sekken had seen on ancient statues. It wasn't until Nurarihyon moved that Sekken saw his head was grotesquely elongated, like an enormous gourd set atop his shoulders.

He didn't snarl at the amulet, the way the others did. He just eyed it coldly, then transferred that attention to Sekken.

"You are neither warrior nor priest," he said, in that bone-chilling voice. "A mere pot to hold the last dregs of someone greater than you. So: you look upon me, as no one has for untold ages. It will do you no good. I have so many ways to hurt you."

"Come now." Inside, Sekken was quaking, but his words came out pleasingly steady. "We've only just met, and all you can think to do is threaten me? Allow me to introduce myself. I am Asako

Sekken, a courtier of the Phoenix. In the absence of any higher dignitaries of my clan, it falls to me to negotiate with you."

Nurarihyon's laughter bubbled up like nausea. "Negotiate? For what?"

"For the safety of my clan, of course. I acknowledge that you lead a fearsome army; it is therefore in our interests to seek–"

"There will be no agreement between us, worm. Your kind are pathetic toys, mere playthings for my followers. You have nothing I want."

But Nurarihyon had something Sekken wanted: his attention.

Past the leader of the Night Parade, inside the confines of the sacred enclosure, all of Seibo Mura's defenders were on the ground. Not bowing; they huddled face-down, their arms clamped over their heads, as if they feared any light creeping into their eyes and bringing death with it. Sekken couldn't even tell if they were still alive.

Except Ryōtora. He sat cross-legged, his hands on his knees, his back as straight as if he were in a temple. His voice was too soft for Sekken to hear the words he was chanting, but the serenity that emanated from him was almost a tangible thing, a cushion of air on which he seemed to float.

Sekken scrambled for more words, more time. "Nothing you want? Great lord of the Night Parade, I heard of you long before I ever came here. But not as the leader of a terrifying force – no, you were a *joke*."

Hisses and growls rose from the assembled yōkai, and an icy wind gusted from the yuki onna. Nurarihyon's wrinkled face crumpled into ugly lines of anger. Undaunted, Sekken said, "People don't remember what the Night Parade really is. You've become an amusing little motif, a way for artists to entertain themselves by drawing silly creatures dancing in the streets. They don't fear you any more."

"*They will,*" Nurarihyon snarled. And even with the talisman protecting him, Sekken nearly fell to his knees beneath the weight of that malice.

"I can help," he said, and now his voice did shake. "Tell the truth of your power. Remind people of what you are."

Looking directly at Ryōtora would only draw Nurarihyon's notice back to the very thing Sekken was distracting him from. He could only watch with his peripheral vision, waiting for some sign that the ward was nearly done–

Understanding came, heavier than the mountain.

I cannot. That was what Kaimin-nushi had said. Not because she was weakened, but because she was dead. She was a kami; she could make no offering *to* the kami, to bind the five elements of the ward back into a whole.

Something that powerful required the offering of a life.

It wasn't mahō. This was holy. Ryōtora was giving himself to the kami: his Fire to the fire, his Water to the water, his Air to the air, his Earth to the earth. Becoming empty. Becoming Void.

Within Sekken's heart, something broke. *No.*

Everything Ryōtora was doing was right. To give up one life for the good of the Empire – that was exactly what a samurai should do. And it was the only answer, the only way to trap Nurarihyon again. Distantly, he heard the creature speaking, the cruelty suddenly coated in honey: yes, he accepted Sekken's offer. If Sekken left the village, *immediately,* and promised to spread tales of the Night Parade, he would be safe. His home would never need to fear attack. His children would be blessed by all the good fortune yōkai could bestow.

Sekken could see through it. Nurarihyon was hoping he hadn't figured out what Ryōtora was doing, and could be talked into leaving Seibo Mura – with the amulet – before Ryōtora finished dying.

He didn't understand that Sekken would never walk away. And he couldn't allow Ryōtora to die.

Deep in the silence of his heart, Kaimin-nushi spoke. *He has to give all of himself, without reservation. He cannot hold anything back.*

Sekken said, *Then help me give myself to him.*

He'd said it back in Senkyō, when Sayashi complained about the reincarnation she'd refused: being human was about having other people to stand by your side. If his loss could save Ryōtora from losing everything... he didn't hesitate.

With the kami of his ancestor in him, Sekken felt the tidal wave of spiritual energy crash over Seibo Mura. Earth, Water, Fire, Air – Void – knitting together into a balanced whole, with Ryōtora as their vessel.

Then they were gone – and so was Nurarihyon. And the empty shell that had been Agasha no Isao Ryōtora began to fall.

Go to him, Kaimin-nushi said.

And they fell together.

CHAPTER TWENTY-SEVEN

There was something profoundly wrong with the world. Because when Ryōtora opened his eyes, the first thing he saw was Sekken, and Sekken was asleep.

That wasn't how it worked. Ryōtora never woke before Sekken.

Ryōtora hadn't expected to wake at all.

He tried to sit up, and another face suddenly appeared in his view. An unfamiliar man, who put his hands on Ryōtora's shoulders and said, "Don't move yet. Let me examine you."

The soft chant that followed told Ryōtora the man was a shugenja, and Agasha-trained. He tried to follow the meaning of the man's words but failed, his mind as sluggish as a half-frozen river. It kept sticking on the fact that he was alive: that he'd given himself to the kami, holding nothing back, and yet here he was.

After a moment the stranger finished chanting and helped him sit up. They were in Ogano's house, in the room where Ryōtora and Sekken had been sleeping since their arrival. "I am Agasha no Sawara Moriuji. I've been tending to you and the Phoenix. Do you think you would be able to move into the next room? If so, I can bring you food, and Lady Agasha Hatsuyo would like to speak with you."

"Sekken," Ryōtora said, his voice creaking like a rusted hinge. "Lord Asako. Has he woken up?"

"Not yet," Moriuji said.

Ryōtora wanted to shake Sekken's shoulder, to tell him the sun was up, and he should be too. The man's face was shadowed and slack, not at all like his usual self, and for some reason his hair was cut short. But Moriuji was trying to guide Ryōtora upright; he had to leave the Phoenix behind.

He also had to crawl, because he didn't trust himself on his feet yet. Moriuji slid the door open and shut it again once Ryōtora was through; then he bowed himself out to go find the woman he'd mentioned. Through that door Ryōtora glimpsed the rest of Ogano's house – or rather, what remained of it. The area with the tatami rooms was intact, but the rest had collapsed, as if a great hammer had struck it.

How much time had passed? Where had the other samurai come from? And what had happened after he–

Ryōtora's mind shied back from finishing that thought.

Moriuji returned with a bowl of miso soup and another stranger behind him, a tall woman in a practical traveling kimono and hakama. While Moriuji excused himself to continue watching over Sekken, the woman introduced herself as Agasha Hatsuyo, sent by the governor of Heibeisu to respond to the problems in Seibo Mura.

"I read your report," she said, sitting cross-legged on the other side of the low table. "And what little I could find on this Night Parade before we headed north. The peasants we found here–"

"Are they alive?" Ryōtora put down his empty bowl and bowed

as deeply as he could without falling over. "Forgive me. I should not have interrupted."

Hatsuyo brushed off his apology. "They're alive, though with one of the men it was a near thing. Fortunately, Sir Moriuji is a gifted healer. It's why the governor sent him with me."

Masa. Feverish, wounded by the tree – yes, he would have needed a shugenja's aid. Which peasants rarely received… but the Dragon could not afford to lose any more lives than necessary. And the service he and the others had given, defending Seibo Mura, would be rewarded with more than just a few prayers.

Hatsuyo said, "They were able to tell me some of what happened – up to the point of the earthquake, when you told them to cover their eyes and not look up until it was quiet again. Or until they were dead, though I believe that was the girl's addition, rather than something you said. She was also the one who looked up first and found you unconscious inside the enclosure, and Asako Sekken unconscious outside it, holding what I assume is the amulet you mentioned in your report. But in between those two things… all they know is that you were praying. I'm hoping you can fill in the gap."

"I can," Ryōtora said slowly, pushing through the fog in his head, "but not all of it. To be honest, I'm not sure why I'm alive."

She listened impassively as he explained. His intention to recreate the ward, even at the cost of his own life; his failure to do so until he felt the amulet's presence, the piece he had been lacking. In the midst of saying that Sekken must have brought it back, another thought caught up with him. "Which girl did you mean before? Rin, or is there another one – Chie?"

"Rin, but yes. The Phoenix rescued the carpenter's daughter from an ōmukade in Senkyō."

My sister. He hadn't put that into his report, because he hadn't learned about Masa until after the evacuees left, and it wouldn't be important to the governor anyway. Ryōtora could tell by Hatsuyo's level gaze that she'd guessed, though. She didn't say anything. The Dragon knew not to.

He tried to gather the scattered threads of his thoughts. "I believe I said in my report that Lord Asako is descended from the shugenja who originally ended the Night Parade. He was her vessel once before, and I think he was again; it caused him to collapse then, too. But not as badly as this. I don't know what he – they – did. I assume it's the reason I'm alive."

"It seems likely. But the Night Parade is contained once more?"

"The… leader is," Ryōtora said cautiously, unsure whether it was safe to say Nurarihyon's name. "I don't know about the rest."

Hatsuyo nodded. "I meant the leader. According to the peasants' testimony, the other yōkai scattered. There were still some around when Rin looked up, and a few of them went on destroying things, but by dawn they were all gone. Back into Senkyō, I presume, since I examined the perimeter you described, and found the ward is strong."

To Ryōtora's surprise, she shifted to a kneeling position and bowed all the way to the floor. "Thanks to your efforts, Sir Ryōtora. I will make certain that not only the governor, but both the Agasha and Isao daimyō and even the Clan Champion know of this."

"But…" He had to put one hand on the mat to steady himself. His thoughts were still slow, his body weak.

"But nothing," Hatsuyo said, rising. "I know you expected to die, Sir Ryōtora. Take it as a blessing that you did not. The Dragon Clan needs all its people, and most especially samurai like you."

•••

Masa and the others were living in one of the few houses still standing. Later that day, when Ryōtora had finally devoured enough soup and fish and rice that he felt strong enough to stand and walk more than a few steps unaided, he went to see them. Gonbei and Ona cleared out with remarkable speed, leaving him alone with Masa – and with Chie.

The resemblance between them was too obvious to miss. Obvious enough that Ryōtora had to assume every single person in Seibo Mura had guessed at his origins the moment they saw him.

"You both take after your mother," Masa said. "She passed away after Chie was born. I didn't expect I'd ever see you again, or that Chie would ever meet you."

Chie kept alternately ducking her chin in shyness and sneaking sidelong glances at him. She didn't seem to know what to say; Ryōtora felt the same. Everything he'd been taught said he should revere his father and care for the needs of his family. But he couldn't bring them back to Yōmei Machi: he wasn't wealthy enough to support them, he wouldn't be able to justify the shift to the governor of this province, and it would draw attention to something everyone was supposed to pretend never happened.

Finally he said, "I am glad that we have. Even if I can't stay here, I… I will send part of my stipend to you."

Masa shook his head firmly. "I refused payment when Sir Keijun took you with him. I don't want it now."

"But–"

"You saved me, and my daughter, and our village," Masa said. "You have done enough."

A ruined village, and Sekken was the one who saved Chie. It

didn't feel like enough. A son was supposed to be obedient to his father, though, and so Ryōtora bowed his head.

Then inspiration came. To Chie, he said, "You were the one who found the amulet."

She ducked her chin again. "I didn't realize it would cause problems."

"I'm not angry," he hurried to reassure her. "Only… I proved to have the gift of speaking to the kami. You don't, I think – you would have known by now – but if there *is* some kind of spiritual merit in our family line, then you should be the keeper of the new shrine." That title sometimes carried a small stipend. He would see to it that she received one.

"Me?" Chie said, startled into looking up. "I've danced for the ceremonies before, but… I'm not a priestess."

"I can teach you," Ryōtora said.

Masa touched Chie's hand and nodded at her. "All right," she said, shyly. Then she added, "Elder Brother."

"Chie." Her father's voice was reproving. "You must not call him that."

"I know," Chie said. "I won't do it again. But I wanted to, just this once."

It brought a pang deep inside, but not a bad one. "Little Sister," Ryōtora said. "We'll begin your lessons tomorrow."

"You're both badly weakened," Moriuji said, examining Ryōtora again that night. "As if you suffered a wasting disease, compressed into a few moments – one that affected your spirits as well as your bodies. You may find you have difficulty focusing, or maintaining your composure."

That last comment was a polite acknowledgment of the fact

that Ryōtora felt on the verge of tears. He didn't know what to do with the fact that he was alive, or that he'd found his birth kin, or that Sekken still hadn't woken up. All the strain of the battle and the days leading up to it had vanished, and without that weight pressing him down, he felt as if he might fly apart. "Lord Asako," he said, fighting to keep his voice level. "Will he… recover?"

"I believe he will wake," Moriuji said. "Recovery for both of you will take some time, though, and probably a great deal of assistance. Physical and spiritual alike. We have plenty of supplies; eat as much as you can. Once you're able to travel, I'm going to recommend to Lady Agasha that you be taken to Ryōdō Temple. It's where I trained; the physicians there are very skilled. They can help restore what you've lost."

What I've lost. A suspicion began to stir in the depths of Ryōtora's mind… but until Sekken awoke, he couldn't confirm anything.

The next morning, the Phoenix was still unconscious. Moriuji had to help Ryōtora bathe, scrubbing away the accumulated filth of too many days without washing; then one of the Mirumoto bushi who'd accompanied the detachment from Heibeisu helped him walk to the restored hot spring. Hatsuyo had promised to look into better solutions in the longer term than an imprisoned hiderigami; they didn't want the ward failing again if the yōkai escaped. For now, though, Seibo Mura had a functioning spring again, and the thought of immersing himself in its soothing waters produced a desire in Ryōtora's heart that was very nearly a physical ache.

Desire is a sin, he thought ruefully. But he was no ascetic monk, denying himself all comforts. And the kami would like having their efforts rewarded with company.

"I can walk back on my own," he told his escort. "You don't have to stay here."

"It's no trouble," the bushi said. Ryōtora waved him off, with an increasing lack of subtlety, until the man went. It might mean having to take the journey back in stages, but it would be worth it to have some time alone, with his fears and his guilt and his relief.

In hindsight, it might have been better to let the Mirumoto stay, because Ryōtora fell asleep. Only luck kept his head from slipping into the water. He jerked upright when a familiar voice said, "It would be an ignominious end for a hero if you drowned in the bath."

"*Sekken,*" Ryōtora breathed.

If the Phoenix had been his usual lively, elegant self, Ryōtora would have been sure it was a dream. But Sekken, crouched a little distance from the edge of the spring, was still short-haired and thin-faced, and he looked like the only thing holding him upright was the inugami at his side.

He was still the most beautiful sight of Ryōtora's life.

Sekken scratched behind the dog's ears. "I woke up to find this fellow sleeping next to me. Do you remember what I told you, about tsukimono-suji being a thing passed down in families?" Ryōtora nodded reflexively; his mind and tongue were bereft of words. "Apparently I'm a witch now. May I join you?"

The dampness of his cropped hair said he'd already washed. Ryōtora still couldn't speak, but Sekken took his silence for permission; he began, with the kind of slow, careful movements Ryōtora knew all too well, to remove his clothing. Ryōtora closed his eyes again, hoping it would look more like exhaustion than embarrassment. He hadn't felt this self-conscious about bathing with another man since the early days of his attraction to Hokumei.

You may find you have difficulty focusing, or maintaining your composure. He should climb out of the spring before he said something he'd regret. Or before Sekken asked questions he couldn't answer. But his limbs had all the strength of overcooked noodles, and he had too many questions of his own.

A gentle splashing heralded Sekken's arrival in the water. "I've already reported to Lady Agasha. I told her – and you should know, too – I, ah, wasn't supposed to be here. My travel papers only authorized me to go to Quiet Stone Monastery. Under the circumstances, she said the Dragon would probably forgive my transgression."

"You saved me."

Ryōtora opened his eyes to find Sekken scrubbing one hand through the damp spikes of his hair, looking awkward. "I… Ah. There ought to be some graceful way to say this, but I can't think of it. I told Lady Agasha it was Kaimin-nushi's doing… which isn't a lie? Because I couldn't have done it without her. I'll tell her the rest of the truth if you want me to. Lady Agasha, I mean. I just figured you ought to hear it first."

"What did you *do*?"

Sekken's face was red, and Ryōtora didn't think it was only from the heat of the water. "You… gave everything away. Until you had nothing left. So I gave you half of what I had."

Half of *him*. Not a wasting disease: they were both weak because each of them had half a man's strength.

Half of Sekken's strength.

The pricking in his eyes could not be permitted to fall as tears. "You shouldn't have done that," Ryōtora whispered.

"Why?" Sekken asked. "Because your parents were peasants?"

It drove all the air from him, even though he'd known it must be coming, ever since he saw Chie's all-too-recognizable features.

Sekken said, "You write your name in an odd fashion. Not 'son of the tiger,' like I assumed, but 'son of the northeast.' An old character, that one, and usually pronounced *ushitora* instead of just *tora*. I think of Seibo Mura as being to the west, but for you, it's northeastern Dragon lands. I didn't figure it out, though, until I saw Chie – your younger, female mirror."

At least Ryōtora could pretend the wetness on his face was water or sweat.

"I know it's a bit awkward," Sekken said, "but you're not the first shugenja to be found among peasants and adopted into a samurai family."

More truths he shouldn't tell. But he'd already trusted Sekken with everything else – and he still couldn't stand the thought of being dishonest with this man.

"I wasn't a shugenja at the time," Ryōtora said quietly. "I couldn't even speak yet. Isao Keijun adopted me, and only later found out I had that gift."

Puzzlement etched a thin line between Sekken's brows. "Why–"

"Because we don't have enough children." Ryōtora trailed one hand through the water, watching the ripples rather than looking at Sekken. "Samurai as well as peasants. But we have to keep our numbers up, and so… it's what the Isao do. Travel through rural areas and examine the children for 'spiritual merit.' Those with enough are adopted."

Heresy, according to the Celestial Order. And also necessary.

Silence fell. Ryōtora was braced for the response, part of him wishing he'd let the Mirumoto stay, that he'd been escorted back to the village rather than falling asleep in the water, that he'd left before Sekken came – but the rest of him was glad to have spoken. Even if Sekken condemned him and the Dragon, he was more at peace having spoken than if he'd kept it secret.

"Now it makes sense," Sekken murmured.

That brought Ryōtora's gaze up. "What do you mean?"

The Phoenix gestured at him, water dripping from his long-fingered hand. "You. Why you're so honorable, and why you flinch when I point that out. I thought someone in your past had convinced you that you were somehow inferior – but it was you yourself that did it."

"Because it's true," Ryōtora said, flat and weary. "If I'd been meant to be a samurai, I would have been born to that station."

Sekken dismissed that with an unconcerned shrug. "That's one road to it. But Kaimin-nushi wasn't a samurai, was she? The way she spoke about the followers of the Kami, it doesn't sound like she was one of them. And who was Agasha? A woman who stepped up to serve Togashi-no-Kami, and was rewarded for her service with a family line. In those days there *were* no samurai. Only people who served."

A wry grin tilted his mouth up at the corner. "At the risk of sounding pedantic, that's where the word comes from. It was originally *saburai,* from the archaic verb *saburau,* 'to serve.' You are unquestionably a *saburai.* And all the more admirable, I think, for having stepped up to meet that challenge."

The knot that had lived for so long in Ryōtora's heart eased another notch. First Masa, then Sekken: balms laid on the wound he'd carried ever since his adoptive father told him the truth. A wound torn even wider when Hokumei learned that truth – and spurned him.

"So don't tell me I shouldn't have saved you," Sekken said, more vehemently. "All I did was share what I had. Because you're a good man, and the Dragon Clan needs such people. The whole Empire does."

"But you…" He had to try again to get the words out. "When you thought there was a witch here, and you might be related to them. You hid it from me because you didn't want to admit you might have a connection like that."

Sekken swept one hand through the water, watching the ripples. His voice lowered. "I don't claim my reasoning was *good.* I was worried about the wrong things, and I hurt you. I'm sorry." He ran that hand through his hair again. "And I'm sorry for upsetting you now. I shouldn't do things like that."

Ryōtora wiped his cheeks and managed a smile. "No, it's all right. I only – thank you. For saving my life, and for standing with me against the Night Parade. And… for saying what you have. Hearing someone like you say such things…"

"Someone like me?"

He sounded honestly confused. Ryōtora said, "I'm from a vassal family, and from peasant stock before that. You're an Asako, and your family has position, influence, wealth – I'm sorry. I didn't mean for that to offend you."

"I'm not offended," Sekken said, but his expression said otherwise. They were both less controlled than they should be; no courtier should have let so much through. "It's only…"

Ryōtora almost prompted Sekken when he paused, but managed to keep the words back. If the other man didn't want to speak of something, it would be rude to push him.

Pushing wasn't needed. Flicking his fingers in the water to send droplets flying, Sekken muttered, "I like it when you look at me with admiration. But I don't want you admiring me because of who my *family* is. My whole life, I've been the useless one – and worse, I've been pleased by it. Not until I came here did anybody treat me like what I did might be valuable. Like *I* might be valuable."

"You are!" It came out an embarrassing yelp.

The look Sekken turned on him was heart-stoppingly vulnerable. "Then if my good opinion matters to you, know that you will always have it. My good opinion… and more."

His hand brushed Ryōtora's wrist, beneath the surface of the water. Somehow, without Ryōtora noticing, they'd gone from being on opposite sides of the spring to almost next to each other.

His breath caught. "Lord Asako–"

"You called me 'Sekken' before." The other man's smile was gentle. "Are we really that formal now?"

Ryōtora whispered, "We have duties."

"Which we're doing an admirable job with. I'm not married. Are you? No? Then neither of us will be disgracing our spouse by carrying on some outside affair." Sekken was only a breath away now. "And the healer warned me I might not have my usual self-control for a while."

His lips were soft against Ryōtora's, and warm with the heat of the spring. For the first heartbeat, Ryōtora sat rigid, waiting for his mind to offer some argument for why he should pull away. All it offered, feebly, was that Desire was a sin, and one shouldn't give into it.

But he wasn't an ascetic monk.

The water splashed as Ryōtora's hands came up, sliding across Sekken's shoulder to pull him closer, threading into his damp hair.

The sweet ache of their kiss filled him like light, banishing the shadows of past pain.

By the time they parted, he was light-headed. Words came with difficulty. "I, uh. I should get out of the water, before I shrivel up entirely."

"That would be a very great shame," Sekken agreed. It took both their efforts to climb out of the spring, with the inugami offering itself as a convenient handle. By the time they made it out, both of them were panting for breath.

When he could speak again, Sekken said, "I've found a good duty for myself. This place is close to the border, and the Phoenix will take a very strong interest in keeping the Night Parade suppressed. Family influence is a useful thing: I'm going to have myself put in charge of brokering an agreement to have us provide support to this village. And then administering it, of course. With frequent inspections."

"That will mean a lot of time on the road," Ryōtora said, eyeing his towel and wondering if he'd be able to walk to it, or if he'd have to crawl. "And staying in Ogano's house."

Sekken snorted. "The half of it that's still standing? No, the first thing we'll do – all right; the second thing, after restoring the shrine – is have a separate house built for samurai visitors. We can still share a room, though. I promise, I don't sprawl."

"You do, a little," Ryōtora said, then smiled. "But I don't mind."

A GLOSSARY OF 100* DEMONS

* In truth, there are sixty-seven listed here. I am significantly indebted to Matthew Meyer for his series of books on yōkai: *The Night Parade of One Hundred Demons, The Hour of Meeting Evil Spirits,* and *The Book of the Hakutaku,* as well as Zack Davisson's *Kaibyo: The Supernatural Cats of Japan.* For brevity's sake I've given only a few details on each creature; in many cases there are variant stories that may have different details, and many of these creatures have different names.

– *MB*

akaname – A goblinoid that lives in dirty homes and baths.

amanozako – A female demon with dangling ears, tusks, and a long nose like a tengu.

ame onna – A rain woman who seeks to steal newborn children, especially girls.

ao nyōbō – A yōkai who appears to be an ancient and tattered court noblewoman, her clothing and appearance now ruinous.

azuki babā – A hag who appears at twilight, counting beans as she washes them in the river. If she catches a human, she often eats his flesh.

bakeneko – Cat yōkai who, like many animal yōkai, are shapeshifters. Their tails can start fires.

basan – Birds with brilliant plumage who eat ashes and charcoal. Usually they are shy, and vanish into thin air when they realize they've been seen.

buruburu – An invisible creature that causes fear.

furu-ōgi – A fan spirit, possibly born from a fan that awakens through long use.

hahakigami – A broom spirit, possibly born from a broom that awakens through long use.

hari onago – A girl with hooks in her prehensile hair, which she uses to attack her victims.

hiderigami – A grotesque female yōkai with only one leg, arm, and eye, who causes profound drought.

hihi – A violent, monkey-like creature whose blood grants the drinker power to see invisible spirits. It also makes an excellent red dye.

hyōsube – Greasy, hairy humanoids related to kappa, found in warmer and more humid climates.

ikiryō – A living ghost, i.e. the spirit of a person projected out of their body, usually due to great emotional distress.

inugami – A dog spirit, sometimes bound to a witch or their family as a servant.

itachi – A weasel yōkai. Generally they are tricksters, but less dangerous than their kama itachi cousins.

itsumade – A human-faced bird with a snake-like body. Its name means "until when?", and it appears where suffering has not been alleviated.

ittan momen – An animated length of cloth that tries to strangle people.

jami – One of many types of mountain spirit that can cause disease.

jubokko – Vampiric trees created by the shedding of blood in a war or massacre. They stab their prey with their branches and drain their blood, then let the bones fall at their roots.

kama itachi – Weasel yōkai with blades in place of their feet. Trios form a whirlwind and attack people, often without being seen.

kamikiri – An insectoid creature that cuts off people's hair.

kappa – A reptilian, aquatic humanoid with a cup-shaped depression on its head that is filled with water. If a kappa bows, the water spills out, causing the kappa to lose its power and possibly die.

kasha – The most evil of the cat yōkai, kasha sometimes snatch corpses during funerals.

katawaguruma – A flaming ox-cart wheel ridden by a naked, screaming woman. Like wa nyūdō, they drag their victims to the underworld to be judged, and also spread terrible curses.

kawauso – An otter yōkai, whose tricks are usually more

playful than dangerous. They like to seduce young men, then run away when he tries to follow through.

kerakera onna – A huge, middle-aged woman in a brothel kimono and overdone makeup. Her laughter can haunt a man who visits prostitutes.

keukegen – A walking mass of hair that lives under the floorboards. They bring disease and bad luck.

kitsune – Fox yōkai who sometimes possess people.

kodama – Spirits of trees that can appear as spirit lights or as tiny, humanoid figures.

kuchisake onna – A mutilated woman with her mouth cut open from ear to ear, who asks her victims if she is still beautiful. Sometimes she can be diverted by throwing money or hard candy at her.

marushime neko – An older form of the maneki neko (sometimes called an "inviting cat" or "lucky cat").

mikoshi nyūdō – One of many "priest"-type yōkai. This one can grow to immense height; looking up at one as it grows causes a person to fall over, making them vulnerable to the yōkai's attack.

minobi – One of many types of spirit light, this one burns straw raincoats.

mokumokuren – Ghostly eyes that appear in the holes torn into an old paper screen.

nekomata – Relatives of bakeneko, these cat yōkai have two tails. They are more malicious than bakeneko, and not only start fires but puppet human corpses.

nobusuma – A bat yōkai sometimes created from a bat that lives to a great age. They drink blood and blow out lanterns.

nopperabō – Faceless yōkai, usually encountered on empty roads.

nozuchi – Mallet-shaped, snake-like creatures that attack animals and humans and can cause terrible fevers.

nue – A strange chimera formed from a monkey's head, a tanuki's body, a tiger's limbs, and a snake's tail. It is an omen of terrible disaster.

nukekubi – A variant of the rokurokubi, this woman can detach her head completely to suck the blood from her victims or bite them to death.

nure onago – A wet, disheveled girl, sometimes covered in leaves and debris, who often haunts anyone who encounters her.

nure onna – An aquatic serpent with a woman's head and sometimes upper body and arms, who disguises herself as a distressed woman carrying a baby to lure her prey in.

obariyon – A hairy child who leaps upon the back of a passing human, growing heavier with each step they take, and chewing on their head. If the victim can stagger all the way home, the obariyon is replaced by a sack of money.

okiku mushi – A yōkai born from the murder of a woman named Okiku, whose bound body was thrown into a well. Okiku mushi resemble caterpillars with the torso of a bound woman.

okuri inu – A black dog who follows travelers and will attack them if they fall.

ōmukade – A centipede of truly monstrous size, capable of killing even dragons. Their only known vulnerability is human spit.

raiju – A creature that embodies lightning. It can shoot through a person's body and kill them.

rokurokubu – A woman who can extend her neck to impossible lengths to attack small animals or lick up lamp oil.

sagari – A severed horse head that drops down from a tree without warning. It can cause fever.

sarugami – A violent monkey spirit, prone to attacking children and kidnapping young women.

shōgorō – A gong spirit, possibly born from a gong that awakens through long use.

suiko – Malicious cousins of kappa who drink blood and can possess people.

tanuki – Trickster animal yōkai sometimes called "raccoon dogs." Statues of them are recognizable for their enormous testicles.

tengu – Crow-like humanoids who may be unpleasant tricksters or wise teachers.

tenome – An old man with eyes in the palms of his hands instead of his head.

tsuchigumo – One of many types of monstrous spider that attacks and kills people.

tsurube otoshi – Enormous disembodied heads that fall onto the unwary.

ubume – The ghost of a woman who died in childbirth, often seen carrying her baby or a stillborn fetus.

ushi oni – An aquatic ox creature that comes in many hybrid forms, including part-spider. It breathes poison and brings disease.

utsuki warashi – A child yōkai who lives in the dirt under the floorboards and creates mysterious noises and thumps, or leaves dirty footprints throughout the house.

wa nyūdō – A flaming ox-cart wheel with a man's head in the center. Like katawaguruma, they torment their victims and attempt to drag them into the underworld to be judged.

yamajijii – An old man with one leg and only one visible eye (the other is too small to be seen). His shout can splinter trees and move rocks.

yatagarasu – A three-legged crow that lives in the sun.

yosuzume – Night sparrows that appear in a flock, and can only be heard by a single individual. They sometimes herald the approach of an okuri inu.

yuki onna – The snow woman, with unearthly beauty and a touch that can freeze her victims solid.

ACKNOWLEDGMENTS

A book like this requires a pretty substantial amount of research. I owe particular thanks to Matthew Meyer of yokai.com, not only for his three excellent books on yōkai, but for kindly answering some queries by email. The same goes for John K Nelson, author of *A Year in the Life of a Shinto Shrine,* who helped me thread the needle of how an enshrinement ritual might go in the altered context of Rokugani religion, and the kind souls of the "Shinto: Way of Kami and People" Discord. As usual, any errors here are mine, not theirs. Finally, and approximately eighteen years after the fact, I'd like to thank the people responsible for the Hida Minzokumura, whose open-air museum provided me with a sense of what a Rokugani mountain village might look like.

ABOUT THE AUTHOR

MARIE BRENNAN is a former anthropologist and folklorist who shamelessly pillages her academic fields for material. She recently misapplied her professors' hard work to *Turning Darkness Into Light,* a sequel to the Hugo Award-nominated series, The Memoirs of Lady Trent. As half of MA Carrick, she is also the author of *The Mask of Mirrors,* first in the Rook and Rose trilogy.

swantower.com
twitter.com/swan_tower